STEPHANIE
DENNE

FRACTURED FATE

5

BLACKTHORN
SAGA

Published in Canada by Amethyst Corvid Press, Ontario, Canada.

Fractured Fate
First Edition.
ISBN: 978-1-7381014-4-3
Stephanie Denne.

See more books by Stephanie Denne at https://stephaniedenneauthor.com
Editing by Kelly Schaub

Cover Design by Stephanie Denne

Dedication

While a romance, I want to dedicate this book to two very special people who passed away during the making of this book.

Russell Payne

September 21, 1958 – January 26, 2024

My father, who believed in me and supported my dreams no matter what. Who guided me as best he could as I grew into the woman I am today. I owe so much to him, and I hope that I can continue to make him proud.

Doris Payne

September 26, 1937 – March 26, 2024

My grandmother, who supported me through the years and never gave up on me. She was as close to a mother as I could have ever wanted growing up. Her unwavering love and understanding throughout my life is something I will always cherish.

Content Notice

This book contains content that may be unsuitable for certain readers. Please read responsibly.

Themes and content featured in this book:

Graphic violence, graphic death, graphic sex, blood drinking (consensual), coarse language, stalking, discussion of previously deceased parent(s), body dysmorphia, discussion of past sexual harassment, depression, PTSD

Kinks explored: Light bondage, rough sex, praise, backdoor play, exhibitionism, sensory deprivation, dirty talk, dominance/control, edging, good girl, biting/marking (hands/bruising grip/nails), breeding kink, light spanking

Extra bit: Subdrop

A Message from the Author

This story features a character who struggles with diagnosed depression, and another character with undiagnosed PTSD. Please read responsibly for your mental health if this is something you would be uncomfortable with.

Charlotte navigates the world with the ability to mask well. Some days are worse than others. Her depression mostly manifests itself in anger, insecurity, and how she controls her environment through planning and keeping everything around her in a neat and tidy manner. But some days, it is a dark cloud that threatens to send her to her bed until everything is okay again.

Depression affects everyone differently.

No one experiences these struggles the same way. If you suffer from depression—clinical or not—her experiences do not invalidate yours. Just because you don't walk through life the way this character does, or might not be triggered by things like change, does not make your experience any less valid. Your struggle, triumphs, and story are your own.

Like in previous books, I hope by reading a character that perhaps shares some of your experiences, or faces struggles of her own, you can relate and possibly find peace in that.

For those who do not face these types of struggles, hopefully this will help you better understand anyone you may know that navigates life the way Charlotte does, and that you are able to take something away from that. If anything, it gives you the understanding that when someone says they are depressed, it doesn't always look the same. Never dismiss their struggle because it doesn't look the way you think it should.

A final note on PTSD:
Many believe this condition is exclusive to veterans, but it is not.

PTSD is a trauma disorder that affects millions. Anyone who has experienced trauma at some point in their lives can suffer from this condition. Our responses to traumatic events can be life-altering and debilitating. The same things that trigger one person may not trigger another.

PTSD is treatable. Healing from trauma is difficult, but it is possible. Through seeking help from available resources, it is possible to live a full and healthy life after a traumatic event.

Aiden's experience with PTSD, like Charlotte's with depression, is his own. His experience is unique to him, and in no way encompasses the entire gamut of ways PTSD can manifest itself.

Take care of yourself, and remember, if you find the subject matter too difficult, allow yourself a moment to breathe.

If you need to stop reading, do so.
Your mental health is important, always.

Happy reading!
– Stephanie

The past will always have its claws in the present.

Playlist

Find the playlist on Spotify by scanning the QR code:

https://sptfy.com/R45i~s

Songs

Starset – Telescope
Faith Marie – Antidote
Alice Kristiansen – Lost My Mind
MS MR – Hurricane
Sam Tinnesz, Zayde Wolf – Man or a Monster
Sleep Token – The Love You Want
Tragedy Machine – Into A Dream
Matthew Mayfield – The Wolf in Your Darkest Room
Nathan Wagner – Innocence
SVRCINA – Astronomical
SVRCINA – Sweeter Place
Evans Blue – This Time It's Different
Evans Blue – Buried Alive

Beth Crowley – End of the World
A Perfect Circle – Pet
Aesthetic Perfection – Under Your Skin
Aesthetic Perfection – The Ones
Nathan Wagner – Lonely
Beth Crowley – The Dark
Beth Crowley – Dangerous Hope
EarlyRise – Narcissistic Cannibal
Bad Omens – The Worst in Me
Roses & Revolutions – The Pines
Night Argent – Kamikaze
Karliene – Become the Beast
Secession Studios – Our Reckoning

Spicy Instrumental Music:
Denispimp – Molly
Denispimp – Immersion

Haven:
Mobiius – Hunger
Mobiius – Deadeyes
Aesthetic Perfection – Spit it Out
Smash Stereo – Modus Operandi

Blackthorn Academy Campus

It's easy to lose your way at the mysterious Blackthorn Academy. But with a little luck, and this handy map, I'm sure you'll do just fine… maybe.

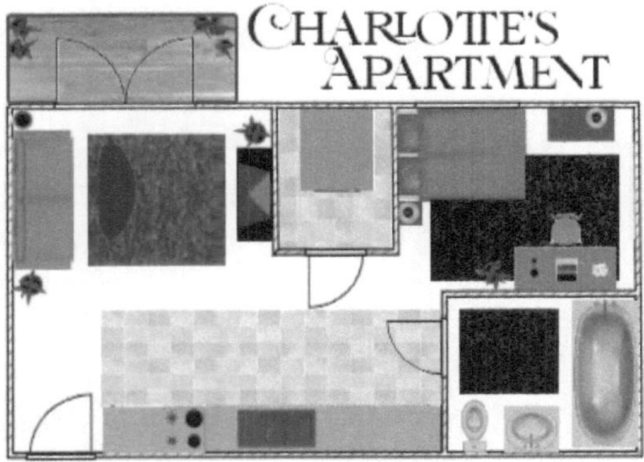

A small representation of the layout of Charlotte's apartment in Athens.

1

Paranoia

Charlotte's heart sank as she stared at the textbook in front of her, overwhelmed by the sinking feeling she'd made a grave mistake by moving four hours away from home to Athens for college.

She stretched her back, shifting on the hard seat of the chair at her classmate's small dining room table. If she didn't want to serve tables or work a cash register for the rest of her life, she needed to be here. That understanding did nothing to settle the yearning for her family and friends back in Rosebrook Valley.

Monique drew Charlotte's attention away from the book. "When I took the financial statement you prepared to Mr. Kay to get his input, he told me the list of total expenditures was wrong."

Charlotte frowned. "Wrong? What's wrong with it?"

Monique pointed to a column listing several high-cost trips Mr. Kay and his wife had taken to various well-known vacation spots around the country. "The vacation time."

"And?"

"He said they didn't take any vacation time this year."

Charlotte blinked a few times. She wasn't mistaken in her research. For confirmation, she glanced toward their other project partner, Rachel, but she was in the kitchen staring out the window at the rain.

Monique sighed, lifting another form to inspect it. "That man never leaves his computer."

She wasn't wrong. Based on the logs he provided them, if he wasn't working, he kept busy playing the stock market. But his bright red nose and arms were a dead giveaway that at least the trip four weeks ago to Puerto Plata was accurate. No one would be that much of a lobster hanging out in the Georgia sun—even someone as pallid as him. The sunburn he sported made his skin appear tight and painful. The blistered spots dotting his red and shiny skin made Charlotte suspect sun poisoning.

"He's lying," she said with confidence. The receipts from the beginning of May refuted his claims.

Rachel dropped the curtain and stepped around the bar separating the kitchen from the dining room. "He probably is. I mean, look at him, he looks like a tomato."

"Oh, I know." Monique waved a hand. "His wife was bragging about the VIP accommodations at the resort they stayed at when I met with her last week to pick up the paperwork." Muttering, she added, "Lucky bitch."

Rachel groaned and dropped her shoulders. "I wish I could take a vacation. It's June! We're supposed to be at the beach, not crunching numbers."

Charlotte pressed her fingers into her eyes, trying to ease the ache behind them from an impending headache. The stress of the situation was taking its toll on her, manifesting itself as a throbbing pain in her temples.

The front door of the apartment opened. "Who wants coffee?"

She looked up from the paperwork at the lighthearted query. Noah, their fourth study partner, stood in the doorway holding a tray of drinks, the hood of his navy-blue sweatshirt partly hiding his face.

"Noah! You're an angel!" Rachel rushed over and took the tray of drinks from his hands.

"Caffeine addiction isn't healthy, you know," Noah said, stepping into the apartment and shutting the door as Rachel snarked about him buying them anyway. He pushed the damp hood from his head and shook out his chin-length, curly brown hair. Dropping into the chair next to Charlotte, he set a bag in front of her. "Got you an apple fritter."

She looked into the bag and then back at Noah.

"I know you hate coffee." He gave her a half smile. "Everything okay?"

Her stomach chose that moment to growl. She'd forgotten to eat lunch again.

She huffed, ignoring how her cheeks heated. "Yeah. Mr. Kay is just being difficult. How are we supposed to finish this project if we can't get him to cooperate? Mr. Hernandez's paperwork is already squared away, and Monique finished the spreadsheets for the PowerPoint presentation already, but with Mr. Kay contesting whether the data is factual, I don't know what to do."

Rachel took a seat next to Monique on Noah's other side. "He's so full of it," she said, before sipping on her coffee. She hummed with contentment. "God, that's the good stuff."

Noah turned his attention back to Charlotte. "What's going on?"

"The vacations his wife confirmed, he's denying," Monique said.

"It's easily ten grand in the last twelve months. We can't overlook it."

The bright scent of citrus, lavender, and sage of Noah's cologne wafted up when he leaned in to study the paperwork. Charlotte glanced over at him, taking in his sharp profile. His nose wrinkled, his dark brown brows lowering over narrowed blue eyes.

"Put it in anyway." Noah slapped his hand on the table as if to say, "problem solved." He leaned back in his seat, crossing his arms over his chest. "It's just a project. He's not going to see our presentation, and these reports don't go to the IRS. It's on him if he doesn't claim everything when he files his taxes next year."

She considered his words. While true, once they got their degrees and moved into the world where companies hired them to do their accounting, they might run into these situations. They needed to know how to handle it. This was the kind of thing that landed people in jail. She tore a piece off the fritter and stuffed it into her mouth, once again wondering if she made a mistake in her choice of major.

Almost halfway into the summer extended session at the University of Georgia, she felt at her wits' end. It didn't help that homesickness lay heavy on her heart.

She couldn't imagine how bad it would be if she had to take all the non-major courses before delving into her accounting program. At least by taking general education classes through the Dual Enrollment program her counselor recommended during her junior and senior years in high school, she was on track to enter her junior year in the fall instead of starting as a freshman.

Other than school trips, she hadn't left Rosebrook Valley much without her mothers. She thought moving only four hours away wouldn't be so bad. That she could gain some independence at nineteen. But she didn't expect the aching loneliness.

She wiped her fingers on the napkin and pushed the paperwork over to Monique. "Noah's right. It's not on us if he commits fraud or whatever. We're not actually working for him. We got the numbers. Professor Landers only needs that." She yawned.

Rachel set down her coffee. "What else is left?"

"I need to put the spreadsheets together for Mr. Kay's business, and then you can work your graphic magic for the PowerPoint, and we'll be good to go," Monique said, tucking the papers into her backpack.

"So we don't need to meet anymore?"

Rachel threw a balled-up piece of paper at Noah. "You're not getting away from me that easily, handsome. We still have to get together to study for our next test."

Noah tilted his head, his brown curls falling over his eyes. "We do?"

"You weren't there last week, but Professor Landers said the tests after the midterm project is over has group sections based on the previous things we've done together."

Noah glanced at Charlotte. "Looks like we'll be seeing more of each other."

She shrugged. "Looks like it."

She glanced at Rachel, who frowned and quickly looked away. Rachel's crush on Noah was obvious, but he appeared either oblivious to her feelings or unwilling to upset her. At twenty-six, and working on her second degree, Rachel was older than all of them. Charlotte couldn't help but wonder if the age gap was the reason for his disinterest; Noah was nineteen, same as her.

Some people were into an older woman and younger man, but from her experience, it was the other way around. She shuddered at the memory of all the older men propositioning her when she worked at the diner through high school and for the following year.

A dream job, it was not.

Rachel stood and tossed her empty cup in the trash. "We should get together and have dinner to celebrate wrapping up this nightmare project."

Noah looked up at her. "We're not finished, though."

"I know." Rachel toyed with the ends of her straight black bob. "but we'll be finished by the weekend. Why not then?"

"Where do you wanna go?"

She shrugged. "I'm up for anything."

"I'm gonna need loads of alcohol after this is over," Monique quipped. "Why don't we go to a bar instead?"

"We could go somewhere like Applebee's. There's a bar there, and we can eat as well. I don't drink," Rachel said.

"You don't?"

"No."

"Well, that settles that," Noah said. "You like Applebee's?" He looked at Charlotte.

"I've been a few times. It's alright." She liked their chicken wonton taco appetizer.

Monique looked at her phone and stood. "Let's talk more about this tomorrow. I've gotta get going. Jayden's here to pick me up. Do you need a ride to your apartment? It's been raining." She looked at Charlotte.

"No, I'm good. The bus stop isn't far."

"Will you be in class tomorrow?" Monique shifted her attention to Noah, putting her backpack over her shoulder.

"Yeah." He stood and picked up a large box sitting on the floor beside the table that held all their research materials that Monique had brought to their meeting. "I can't miss any more days. I've had to take too many personal days."

After they left, Charlotte packed up her things while Rachel cleaned the table. She wanted to ask about Noah, but Rachel got to it first with a smile.

"So, you and Noah?"

Charlotte tucked her red curls behind her ears. "He's nice, but there's nothing there, no."

She figured it best not to pretend she didn't understand exactly what Rachel meant. The looks her friend gave them whenever Noah showed any kind gesture toward her spoke volumes. Rachel wasn't nasty about it; the looks were curious. With Rachel's obvious crush, it didn't take a rocket scientist to deduce there might be lingering jealousy in those looks—even if the interactions she observed were entirely friendly in nature.

Rachel leaned her elbows on the kitchen counter, clasping her hands in front of her. "He know that?"

"What do you mean?"

"Does he know you're not interested?"

Charlotte lifted her chin. "I didn't say I wasn't interested. I meant there's nothing between us. He's not said anything to me, and I haven't to him."

Rachel wrinkled her nose. "Well, he's interested."

Charlotte sighed.

She wasn't *not* interested in Noah, but she wasn't thinking about a relationship either. Her main goal was to figure out what she wanted to do with her life. If she returned to Rosebrook Valley, she wouldn't see Noah anymore, anyway. Whether he felt anything for her was irrelevant. She wasn't interested in short-term hookups. "It doesn't matter. I might change my major, and he won't even see me after summer session ends. That's only like a month and a half away. Not much can happen in that short of time."

Rachel stood upright, her mood shifting, her face holding concern. "Change your major? Why? Is everything okay?"

That sounded more like the Rachel she had gotten to know over the last few weeks in class. Up to now, the girl didn't hold ill will toward her, but maybe Rachel's feelings for Noah would change that.

"Well, I'm not passionate about accounting, if I'm honest. I really want to help my moms out with their businesses, so I chose accounting, thinking it would help when I finished, but it's soooo boring." She sat back in her chair and huffed. "There's other business-related stuff I could study, but I don't even know if I want to stay in Athens. I miss home."

Rachel sat down next to her. "It'll suck if you go, but you gotta do what makes you happy. If this shit isn't making you happy, then don't do it. This kind of career is not for people who don't like it. Numbers can be really boring, even for me, and I like this stuff. Besides, if you change majors, then I get Noah all to myself."

Charlotte widened her eyes.

Rachel laughed. "I'm kidding—sort of. I like him, but not enough to be a bitch about it. Besides, sometimes he seems weird."

Charlotte laughed and shook her head, stood, and then picked up her bag. If she wanted to make the bus, she didn't have time to question what Rachel meant about Noah being weird. It wasn't like her to gossip about good people anyway. "I'm at least going to finish this semester either way. I'm not going to leave the group high and dry." She put her backpack on her back. "I better get going. The last bus will be by soon."

Rachel waved a hand at her. "No worries. We can talk more later if you want. I can help you figure out a major that appeals to you and will help out your parents."

When she stepped out onto the sidewalk in front of Rachel's apartment, Charlotte blew out a breath, thankful the rain had finally stopped. She still needed to walk to the bus stop, and with the humidity and the rain, her curls would turn into a frizzy mess.

Peeking at her phone for the time, she shook her head. She only had five minutes before the bus passed through. Glancing around, she frowned at the shadowed areas of the yard across the street from the complex. The streetlamps casting a soft light on the sidewalk made it difficult to see anything with the lights off inside the home. Still, she couldn't shake the feeling something, or someone, waited in the darkness.

Turning away, and ignoring the weird feeling, she headed toward downtown with Rachel's words spinning around in her mind. Why should she stick with a career that wouldn't make her happy? Even if it would help her achieve her goal of helping her parents, she hated the idea of doing something she didn't enjoy for the rest of her life.

She groaned, impatience growing while she waited for the light to change so she could cross the street. Normally, the wait wouldn't bother her. The bus stop wasn't far, about a block away from Rachel's apartment, but it was catty-corner across a major intersection on Hickory, forcing her to use two crosswalks in a row to get there, waiting for traffic and the light change both times. With her sour mood from the regret over her major choice, she wanted to get home as soon as possible. Even with the long wait for the lights, this stop beat the closer bus stop near the North Oconee River, which was way too dark. She didn't like walking close to so many trees in the middle of the night.

In the distance, noises drifted up from campus; but overall, the nighttime air remained quiet around the deserted crosswalk.

After the light changed, she crossed. She'd heard footsteps on the pavement behind her as the signal changed, so as she paused on the other side to push the button for the walk signal, she glanced back the way she came.

Standing several feet from the place she had stood before, a man—or at least what she assumed was a man, based on his build and height—stood with a hood over his lowered head, hands tucked into the front pockets of his hoodie. She couldn't see his face, even though he stood beneath a streetlight. Lights from the dorm apartment windows on the side of the street she stood on didn't reach the other side, and with only a grass lot behind him, no other light helped her see the man clearly.

She turned back to the street in front of her and exhaled hard, her cheeks puffing out. *Ignore it. He's not following you.*

The small figure on the crosswalk sign illuminated, indicating it was safe for her to cross. She fought every urge she had not to sprint across the road to the other side.

Whether driven by survival instincts or sheer foolishness, a voice inside her cautioned that running would only make her appear vulnerable—more vulnerable than she already appeared being a smaller woman walking the streets of Athens near midnight.

She could have let Noah walk with her. But she'd done this walk several times without incident and didn't consider the need for extra precautions with how close the bus stop was. She could see it from here. Walking around this late near campus wasn't abnormal for coeds.

Footsteps sounded behind her as she continued up the hill to the bus stop only a couple of streetlights down from the crosswalk. The hair lifted on the back of her neck. She didn't want to stop, but if she didn't, she would miss the last bus. She peered up the street and breathed easier seeing the familiar headlights of the approaching bus.

Stopping beneath the green sign, the bus hissed as the driver put on the brakes and opened the doors. Charlotte braved a glance back in the direction of the man.

Nothing.

Had he turned down Hickory Street? Did he turn back and go into the dorm apartments? She scanned her surroundings as the bus approached and came to a stop, but no one else stood on the streets.

Maybe her new medication had the unwelcome side effect of paranoia. She needed to Google that later. Getting jumpy over a pedestrian on the street, just because—

"You gettin' on, hon?"

She spun to look up at the older woman sitting in the driver's seat. "Yeah, sorry." Climbing the steps onto the bus, she showed her UGA student ID card and took a seat near the front. She didn't feel comfortable being alone, and with no one else on the bus, the driver would have to do for company.

Leaning on the window, she looked out at the street as the bus drove in the opposite direction of her apartment; it would eventually circle back and head toward her street.

As the bus chugged through the intersection, she saw the hooded man leaning on a lamppost watching the bus until the dorm apartment building hid it from view.

Okay. Maybe not paranoid.

She pulled out her cell phone to distract herself, opening her texts to find three missed messages. One from her mom regarding the full moon on the twenty-third of June—the Flower Moon, she called it. Normally, the peculiar messages wouldn't be concerning, but her mom had been harping on how something big loomed, and that by the summer solstice her life would be forever changed. The words had her on edge with the recent strangeness.

She checked her phone calendar. June tenth.

Midterms fell on the same day as the solstice, but the professor scheduled the presentation earlier in the week. It made her wonder what, if anything, was going to happen next Friday.

When she was younger, her friends often thought her mom's eccentric words and beliefs were related to her Native American heritage, but they were wrong. Stereotyping her mom that way felt offensive. She never forgot where she came from, but most of her insight came from elsewhere. Charlotte had felt something mystical about her growing up, but now the idea seemed silly.

She glanced back down the street through the window. Even knowing she was far from the man, she still couldn't shake that feeling of being followed.

Turning her attention back to the phone screen, she swiped away her mom's message and opened the one from her ma. The message brought a smile to her face. Her ma had found the owners of the Pittie Charlotte rescued before her big move to Athens.

If someone brought a stray to her ma's veterinary clinic, they would take them to the local shelter instead of keeping them on board, but there was something special about the big-eyed pupper she couldn't refuse, so she begged her ma to keep him. They posted flyers everywhere, hoping to locate the owner. He acted friendly, making it obvious the dog had owners and wasn't a random stray, but he lacked a microchip and tags.

According to the text, the owner's five-year-old opened the back gate, and that's how the dog—Oliver—escaped. They didn't keep a collar on Oliver at home to avoid a choking hazard, but with the scare of losing the furbaby, they purchased the chipping service from her ma's clinic.

After sending a quick reply, she swiped away the message and opened the final unread text.

Aiden:

This game isn't as fun with randoms.

Smiling, she tucked her phone away, not wanting to wake him with a response if he was asleep. Her ma kept her phone on silent, so she wouldn't see the reply until morning.

Another reason leaving Rosebrook Valley weighed on her… Aiden Easton.

In the last year, they started getting to know one another through a series of strange circumstances.

Her best friend, Blaire, received a scholarship to join Blackthorn Academy, the mysterious and ultra-exclusive university in Rosebrook Valley. She wasn't jealous Blaire got in and could stay in the area, because she had needed to escape a dangerous situation. Blaire's stepbrother was a monster.

Charlotte leaned her head back on the seat and sighed. If only she could be so lucky to be offered a scholarship at random like that. She missed her best friend and wished she could visit and spend the night together like they so often used to.

That wouldn't happen though. She didn't know if it was an elitist thing or what, but she never entertained the weird rumors circulating the town about the Blackthorn Academy, even before getting to know some of the students in Blaire's new friend circle.

Small town gossip in the South often swayed in the direction of religion; the misunderstood were marked as sinners or evil. A tale as old as time, religion thriving by feeding on the fears of the unknown.

It wasn't a secret that a majority of the older denizens of Rosebrook Valley believed the school a front for a cult, and the students followers of Lucifer.

She laughed to herself.

Idiots, the lot of 'em.

Remaining isolated behind elaborate gates, not allowing outsiders in, and not involving themselves in social events in the region didn't help Blackthorn's reputation.

The middle and high school branch locations operated the same.

She recalled one couple complaining to her ma while their dog received a checkup. Not only had they not been able to enroll their child in Blackthorn Primary, but they offered no extracurricular programs outside of school for her little boy. "Not even a peewee football team," the wife had complained.

All of the Blackthorn schools lacked sports teams. Which was basically sacrilege in the South.

Charlotte had met all of Blaire's new friends from the academy, soon becoming fast friends with the manic pixie Riley, Aiden's younger sister, who now worked for her mom as an apprentice at the clothing boutique. While she was a year or so younger than Charlotte, Riley was finishing her sophomore year too, working toward a fashion design degree. It surprised her to learn Riley skipped a grade in middle school.

Aiden had reached out when Blaire got kidnapped by some weird guy who became obsessed with her, and ever since, he had kept in close contact. Charlotte welcomed the connection.

Blaire and Riley believed something was happening between them, but there was nothing. Not that she would be completely against it. Aiden was a sweet guy, and gorgeous, too.

They just shared similar interests. It turned out he loved video games as much as she did, and it was nice to have a friend to game with online; Blaire wasn't into it. But they had little time to play together online anymore since she joined UGA, so their communication had dwindled.

She struggled to convince herself staying in Athens was a good idea.

Approaching her apartment, she cringed. A bundle of pink roses lay in front of her door.

Quickening her steps, she reached her door and unlocked it. She picked up the wrapped bundle and rushed inside, not bothering to see if anyone lingered in the hall. After the man on the street earlier, and now the roses, she needed the safety of her studio apartment.

Closing the door behind her and locking it, she carried the bouquet into the kitchen. She placed the roses on the long granite counter. A small white note card tucked into the flowers taunted her. Instead, she turned to glance around the apartment for anything out of the ordinary.

A tiny closet only big enough to house a stacked washer and dryer behind a door divided the living area from the bedroom area. Against the left wall of the laundry room, a small entertainment center faced the living area. On the right side of the laundry room, her headboard butted the wall beside a window with small fairy lights draped over it. A small night table with a lamp draped in a sheer celestial print scarf to dim the light fit next to the bed. The remaining space at the foot of her bed held a tall chest of drawers. A closet with mirrored doors took up most of the wall on the far side of the bed.

On the opposite wall from the dresser, her computer, several candles, and tiny plants decorated a small desk with two framed star charts representing the night sky when she was born, and the other, the night sky the night she was adopted. A bathroom on the other side of the wall behind her desk afforded the only privacy in the small apartment. The door to the bathroom stood to the right of the kitchen area.

Nothing looked out of place, but sweeping her apartment for any disturbance had become a habit for her over the few weeks since the rose deliveries started. Even if it were only a secret admirer, it still made her paranoid. Guys who liked her in the past didn't come to her house or have gifts delivered, so this situation was completely new to her, and she didn't like the feelings it elicited.

She crossed the living room to sit on the small gray loveseat under a line of framed art prints of the various zodiac signs represented by fairies. The loveseat sat perpendicular to the sliding glass doors, facing the entertainment center. Kicking off her flats, she grabbed the remote from the coffee table and turned on the television, turning the volume down low. She wasn't interested in what was on the screen, only the background noise it provided.

She pulled out her phone and leaned against the throw pillows in the corner of the loveseat to scroll through TikTok, distracting herself from the unpleasantness on the counter, but eventually, even songs made from cat noises couldn't stave off her curiosity.

For almost a month, everything remained consistent. Pink roses were left in front of her door with no clue as to the sender. Never had there been a card included, and it got under her skin that the status quo changed.

Throwing her phone on the cushion, she stood and stomped over to the kitchen, pulling the note card from the bouquet. Flipping open the flap, her blood ran cold at the typed note.

You looked lovely this morning. Purple suits you.

She looked down at the lavender short-sleeved blouse she wore with a pair of dark jeggings. Anyone could have seen her in her outfit that morning. She went out for breakfast, stopped by her advisor's office, and attended classes. The University of Georgia wasn't a small school. On average, total enrollment was over forty thousand. Fewer students attended in the summer—around sixteen thousand—but that left tons of options. Whoever kept leaving roses for her didn't have to be in her program of study.

Then there was whoever kept following her.

For longer than the roses started showing up at her door, she had the feeling of someone following her, but hadn't been certain. Until tonight. She hadn't seen anyone before now, so she questioned if being so far from home was to blame for her paranoia.

Rosebrook Valley was a town you could walk around in without question at any time. Athens had the same kind of casual atmosphere where students walked the streets at night without worry, but the population was larger, and the shops, bars, and restaurants weren't condensed to a small outdoor outlet mall. The larger area took time to get used to.

Still, she had questioned her sanity whenever she suspected someone followed her, and now she tried to rationalize the unwanted attention as side effects to her antidepressants. Anything to not accept the sickening reality.

A crash in the bathroom made her yelp and drop the card. She rushed back over to the front door and grabbed the baseball bat she kept there for protection.

She had laughed when her neighbor gave it to her when she mentioned she lived alone. He told her his daughter who was the same age lived alone on the other side of the country. He insisted his daughter do the same thing. Charlotte didn't know how fathers behaved, never having one in her life, but he didn't seem creepy, so she humored him.

"Thank you, Trevor. I'll never doubt your intentions again," she muttered as she approached the bathroom door with the bat held high.

The door stood cracked open, and the interior light was on. Did she leave it on that morning? She couldn't remember.

Hooking her bare foot around the door, she pulled the door open and lifted the bat, ready to pummel whoever stood on the other side.

Nothing.

Stepping deeper into the bathroom, she passed the small counter where a small mirror hung on the wall above the sink and stood in front of the toilet. She poked the shower curtain with the bat, and when she didn't connect with anything hard, she pulled the curtain open. Her shampoo lay in the bathtub, having fallen from the shelf. Lowering the bat, she shook her head. Her nerves couldn't keep up.

She turned out the light, shut the door, and returned the bat to the front door before returning to the loveseat. She picked up her phone.

Almost one in the morning.

Aiden would be asleep, but her nerves were wrecked. Her mothers would only make it worse when they freaked out themselves.

With a sigh, she opened her contacts and pressed the button to call Aiden.

One ring… two… three… four… maybe she should hang up—

"Hello?" Aiden's deep voice, gravelly from sleep, filtered through the phone.

She shivered at the sound so close to her ear. She had never heard his voice like that before.

"Hi, Aiden."

Shuffling sounded through the receiver, and Aiden cleared his throat. "Charlotte? Everything alright? It's one in the morning."

"Yeah, I'm sorry to wake you."

"No, you're fine. I was actually having a bad dream, so I'm glad you called. What's going on?"

"Bad dream?" she asked, deflecting from the question, grabbing a pitcher, and filling it with water.

"Yeah, it's nothing." He groaned. "You sound out of breath."

"I just got home." She crossed her kitchen into the living room and started watering the plants on her entertainment center in decorative planters accented in moons, suns, stars, and zodiac symbols.

"Where were you so late? Isn't it a school night?"

"I was at Rachel's apartment with the others for our group project."

She didn't even have it in her to make a joke about him parenting her like he did his other friends.

"Rachel… the girl who used to live down the hall from you?"

"Yep." She returned the pitcher to the kitchen and crossed to the living room again to sit on the loveseat. "She lives a few minutes from here at another apartment building. Her lease was up a few weeks after I got here, so she moved." She pulled her legs up, tucking them beneath her. "Speaking of moving…" She took a deep breath and blew it out, preparing herself for her next words. "I'm thinking about coming back to the valley for the rest of the summer and pick things up again in the fall."

"What? Why?"

Other than someone following me around and flower deliveries?

The first bouquet she received came the same week she started at UGA. She came to Athens at the beginning of April to get settled in, but classes didn't begin until May fourteenth. Until her first week of classes, she only felt like someone had followed her from time to time—which she tried to reason away. Now she knew for sure; it wasn't paranoia.

She couldn't tell Aiden, though. He'd think she was crazy for suspecting someone of stalking her. She hated even labeling it as stalking. Who was to say this wasn't the first time and all the previous instances were genuine paranoia? Overthinking it made her head hurt.

"I'm not sure if accounting is for me. I think a major change might be in my future. This stuff is a nightmare."

Not a lie, but not the entire story. Giving part of the truth made her feel less guilty about what she didn't tell him.

"That's fair. At least you know now and not a couple years into your degree."

"I just don't want to disappoint my moms."

Her adoptive parents did a lot for her. They weren't her biological parents. She didn't even know who her father was, but her biological mother died not long after giving birth. Her mothers didn't have to adopt her from Ireland when she was an infant, but they did.

Being not only a same-sex married couple, female business owners, and one of them being Native American, things didn't always go smoothly for them. Charlotte saw racism and bigotry growing up directed at them whenever they traveled, or when they had to do business out of town, but the people of Rosebrook Valley embraced them and their businesses. They were accepted and treated well in their home community. Another reason she hated leaving for college.

Taking in an orphaned baby from another country spoke highly of their hearts and character. She could never do enough to repay them for that. Hopefully, getting a degree that benefited their dream businesses would be a start. The career path kept her close to home and took care of her family. A win-win in her book.

"I doubt you could ever disappoint them. They love you a lot. You don't have to become an accountant to make them happy."

"I know that much, but I want to do something to help."

"Well, if you decide to come back, are you getting rid of your apartment? If you need me, I can come up there and help you pack and bring things back down here. Or are you leaving everything until you decide?"

"I'll keep the apartment for now. I'm not even sure I can come back to Rosebrook now that I'm locked into classes."

Even if she dropped her accounting major, she didn't want to leave her group hanging on their own with the projects and the upcoming tests. She also didn't like leaving things unfinished and wasting potential credits she could earn to finish out the summer semester and potentially transfer into another business-related program.

All she knew was she couldn't continue with something that didn't make her happy. She needed to speak with her advisor and see what options were available to her and go from there.

She yawned and rubbed her eyes.

"Sleepy?"

It surprised her that the answer was yes after everything she felt earlier.

"I think so. I have to be up in five hours." She wiggled, nestling down in the corner of the loveseat against a plush throw pillow. "I don't wanna go to bed though," she half-whined.

"Why's that?"

"Your voice is relaxing." Did she really say that out loud? She winced at the silence on the other line. Maybe she was too tired to be on the phone.

"Your voice is nice too," he said, voice dropping an octave, and the frequency went straight to her lady bits. *That's new.* Their casual flirting never hit like *that* before. That voice. It had to be the sleepy, or sleep-deprived, voice. "Definitely preferable to nightmares." He chuckled.

She bit the pad of her thumb. Oh, that lazy, deep chuckle sounded dangerous too.

When she didn't respond, trying to get a hold of herself and ignore the way his voice sent her lower half into crisis with how long it'd been since she'd allowed her body any attention from the opposite sex, Aiden spoke, his voice clearer and free of the seductiveness from before. She wondered if he wasn't even aware of how he sounded and only she was affected. Probably.

"Why don't you call me tomorrow and we'll talk more about it?" After a brief pause, he added, "I mean, if you want to. We can talk more about the apartment and stuff. Or whatever else you want."

When they talked, Aiden sometimes seemed nervous and uncertain about if she wanted to talk to him. She found it strange. She enjoyed his company. He was her friend's brother and had become a great friend to her. Why wouldn't she want to be around him? Right now, she wanted to be more than around him.

She rubbed her face, warning lights flashing behind her eyes. *Stop that line of thinking* right now.

Taking a calming breath, she spoke soft and calm, and not like her libido was demanding recognition. It didn't have to be him or anyone else, her libido could sit the hell down and chill for five minutes while she finished a phone call. "I have classes in the morning, but I will text you after lunch. I want to talk to my advisor to at least scope out my options."

"Good idea." He yawned. "Get some sleep. If you need me, you can call again. Don't worry about waking me up."

She wondered if he knew something happened beyond the school situation, or was he simply being the caring guy he acted like with everyone?

"Thanks, Aiden. Goodnight."

"Goodnight, Charlotte. Sweet dreams."

2

Haunted

The force of his knees smacking the marble floor sent a jolt through Aiden's body. The pain from the tight grip on his hair couldn't compare to the pain ricocheting in his chest at the sight of his best friend's Korrena mate restrained against the wall. Pain from the knowledge he couldn't protect her.

The cold barrel of the gun dug into the flesh beneath his jawline while the rogue taunted him, telling him how stupid his decision to save Blaire was. The rogue reeked of cheap alcohol and stale cigarettes; sharp fangs glinted beneath the lights of the chandeliers overhead.

Aiden didn't dare turn to face the man, fearing if he made a sudden move, the gun would go off and splatter his brains across the walls of the ballroom.

"We're takin' the little human, no doubt about that, mate. But you coulda made this so much easier. Coulda saved yourself. Avoided being the hero." The rogue at his side spat the last word, as if being a hero offended him.

Aiden wasn't trying to be a hero. Lukas couldn't get to Blaire. The clan was too busy fighting the other rogues to realize the danger Blaire was in. Seth was too busy trying to protect Riley.

He was the only chance Blaire had of making it.

He had to try.

He jerked against the rogue's hold, but the gun pressed deeper into his skin. From the corner of his eye, he could see the shaky finger poised over the trigger. One wrong move and it would be over.

He was much larger than the rogue. If there wasn't a gun to his jaw, the man wouldn't stand a chance against him. But they both knew whoever had the gun held all the power in this situation.

"Seth," Riley cried. "Let me go. Let me go now!"

Aiden looked up to see his little sister squirming and kicking at Seth. Dominic helped to reinforce the restraint on her petite body. Aiden had no doubt she had tapped into her preternatural strength if both guys had difficulty restraining her.

"My brother needs me!"

Her broken plea tore his heart in half.

"Know what we're gonna do with our little human before the doc starts filleting that pretty flesh?" the man who held Aiden sneered, licking his lips noisily. He didn't seem to like Aiden's attention divided from him. "Gonna show her how real Vasirian men can please her. Not some schoolboys or Korrena lovey dovey crock of shit. I bet she tastes like peaches." He spoke louder, "What do you think, Jude? Peaches? What's her blood taste like, mate?"

Aiden's teeth felt like they would grind to nubs with how hard he clenched his jaw while the rogue babbled on and on with his friend who restrained Blaire with his preternatural abilities. The cold metal pressing against the delicate flesh of Aiden's neck remained an ever-present reminder he couldn't attack the man for his words.

"—before we rid the world of this parasite."

Aiden didn't catch the beginning of the man's statement before he lumbered to his feet, the tight grip on Aiden's hair flexing with the move.

The gun disappeared from his neck, only to be positioned at his temple.

His eyes met Blaire's.

It killed him to know he would never see her again. She wasn't his fated pair, but he felt a connection to her from the moment she joined Blackthorn Academy. She was important to his life. Something more existed between them than the prophecy detailing how she would save their kind.

He loved her.

Not in the way one would cherish a lover. No. He loved her in the way one would cherish a piece of their own soul. Now, he would never know why.

As tears ran down her face, he held her gaze. "I'm so sorry," he said.

Shifting his blurry gaze to his friends Seth and Lukas, he swallowed the lump lodged in his throat and blinked. Tears tracked down his cheeks as he spoke with a rasp. "Take care of Riley."

His gaze moved to his little sister.

Never again would he argue with her about her shopping addiction. Never again would he be able to reassure her and soothe her heart when the world became too much. He had to pass that job on to Seth now. He prayed to whoever would listen that Seth and Riley would work out their mess so she wouldn't be alone.

Smokey blue eyes swam and glittered in the amber light of the ballroom as mascara streaked over pale cheeks. He would miss her face.

"I love you."

The crack against Aiden's head following his declaration made him jolt upright in bed, sweat running in rivulets down his face.

He touched his temple with a trembling hand. The skin felt intact.

He turned on the lamp on his bedside table and peered down at his glistening fingertips. No blood, only sweat.

The events leading up to his death tormented him. The despair in his sister's eyes and the helplessness he felt knowing he couldn't protect her. Couldn't protect Blaire.

They relied on him, and he failed them.

In the end, Blaire had to save him.

His dreams either went the way of the events leading to his death, or the strange middle space afterward that made little sense to him. His mind conjured up memories he wasn't sure had happened.

Knowing he would never go back to sleep, he stumbled out of bed and into the bathroom.

Standing in front of the mirror, he took in the red flush to his cheeks. Sweat ran down his bare chest, and his tendons shifted as he flexed his fingers into fists and out again.

He was alive.

In the here and now, he lived.

He was safe.

Heaving a sigh, he turned on the tap and splashed cold water over his heated skin, scrubbing his face. He grabbed the hand towel from his counter and dried off, rubbing over his arms and chest to rid himself of the sweat. He wasn't in the mood to shower, so this would have to do.

Tossing the towel in the hamper and turning off the light, he went back into the dimly lit bedroom. He glanced at the window. Sunlight filtered through the tiny gap in the closed curtain. Morning already. It hadn't seemed long since he got off the phone with Charlotte.

He entered his closet and got dressed for the day. He couldn't stay in his room. Not with the fresh memories of what happened in Europe haunting his mind.

Leaving his room, he adjusted the black and burgundy plaid tie at his neck. Any other day, he wouldn't mind it, but not even ten minutes into wearing it, he felt choked. Giving up on proper dress, he loosened the knot and let the tie hang loose around his neck.

After grabbing a blood packet and a raisin bagel from the canteen, he headed for his classroom.

Settling at a desk in the far back of the room, he demolished the bagel in a few quick bites and sipped his blood packet while scrolling his phone. With summer break approaching, he didn't have any actual classes now that he finished his exams. The only reason to come to class was for makeup exams, revisions, and preparation for fall. Anyone who lingered in class otherwise came for the social aspect.

For him, the lure of a different environment away from the bed where his nightmares gripped him made it worth putting on the uniform and attending class. He couldn't always attach himself to his friends and expect to use them as a security blanket.

"Hey, Aiden."

He looked up from his phone to the girl who sat sideways in the chair in front of his desk. He couldn't remember her name. Amber? Alicia? Something with an A.

She came around a lot. Had since they were young, but he couldn't remember her name. She didn't make a habit of talking to him for him to get to know her, but he saw her frequently.

She tucked her short, brassy hair behind her ear and smiled when he made eye contact. "You didn't have to do makeup exams?"

He looked at the bagel wrapper on his desk and took another sip from his blood packet before he said, "No. I passed." He thought his desk with no paperwork on it would make that obvious. As much as he tried to be nice to everyone, he wasn't in the greatest mood after his dream, so he hoped his short answer didn't come off as rude.

She giggled. "Of course you did. You're so smart."

His brow hitched.

"Anyway," she said, crossing her legs and turning in her chair a little. She deliberately hiked her skirt higher on her thigh when she did. The movement wasn't as subtle as she probably hoped for. "I was wanting to try this new Mexican restaurant that opened in Savannah this weekend, and I was hoping you would come with."

A frown etched his forehead. Why wouldn't she go with her friends?

"I mean, if you don't want to do that, we could do something else. We could watch a movie in the plaza." She smiled, sinking her teeth in her lower lip in an enticing way.

Barking up the wrong tree, he thought as realization dawned that she wasn't trying for a friendly conversation.

"Or… in your room?"

"I'm flattered," he said, choosing his words carefully to avoid upsetting her. "But now isn't the best time for me. I'm not really looking for anything."

It was the truth. With the nightmares and everything he'd been through in the last year, he didn't think entertaining someone new to see if he might feel a spark of interest was a good idea. Besides, a certain redhead had taken residence in his mind, and he wasn't sure he wanted her to move out yet.

"Oh, well…" She stood, tugged her plaid skirt down to a normal length, and cleared her throat. "If you, uh, change your mind…" She waved her hand, face flushing.

"Alex!"

They both looked up as a girl with jet black hair in a high ponytail called out.

Alexandra. He remembered now.

"Yeah, I gotta go."

He watched her turn and approach her friend, disappearing out of the classroom. He hoped he hadn't upset her, but he couldn't give her what she wanted.

His phone buzzed, and he pulled it from the pocket of his slacks.

Riley:

Mama wants us to come over for dinner.

He hadn't been to see his mother since she gave him hell after he got back from Europe in April. When she heard everything that happened to him during the battle in the ballroom when rogues attacked the Blackthorn Clan, she was a hysterical mess. If the others hadn't been there, he wouldn't have put it past her to lock him in his childhood bedroom and never let him leave.

She was probably worried sick. He didn't go over a few weeks without seeing her, and here it was June.

Aiden:

She want us to bring anything?

Riley:

Just the others.

Aiden:

Others?

Riley:

Seth, Blaire, and Lukas. Duh.

He almost asked about the others, but he realized their mother didn't know Dominic well, and unless Riley had introduced her, he didn't think she knew Layla at all.

Aiden:

Gotcha. You tell them?

Riley:

Yep. We're gonna head over now so we can swim a while before dinner. You wanna come?

He wasn't doing anything sitting around. At least a swim with his friends in his parents' pool would take his mind off his disturbed sleep.

Aiden:

Gotta stop and grab my trunks and change out of my uniform, but I'll meet you at the gate in 15.

Riley:

Hurry up.

He refrained from texting back. If he said anything, his little sister would spam him with messages, and he would never get anything done.

A smile crossed his face. He was thankful for her distraction now more than ever.

3

Discontent

Entering the classroom at the end of the hallway, Charlotte rubbed at her tired eyes. She must have looked a mess having not applied makeup when her alarm failed to wake her. With minimal time to spare, she threw a few cosmetics into her purse to apply after her first class, grabbed a banana and her morning dose of medication, and barely made it to the bus stop.

"You look hungover," Rachel said, holding out a bottle of water as Charlotte trudged up the steps beside the stadium style seating overlooking the teaching area. "Where did you go after you left last night?"

"Good morning to you too." She took the offered water, collapsing into her chair next to Rachel behind the long, curved desk on the third platform designed to sit six students on either side of the wide stairs. She opened the water and took a long drink. "Thanks."

"Seriously. What happened? You look wiped." Rachel pulled another bottle from her bag and set it on the desk.

"I stayed up a while last night. I couldn't sleep."

"Why not?" Noah asked as he lowered himself into the seat on her other side. "Are you sick?" He pressed the back of his hand to her forehead.

"No. I'm fine. Nothing major." She offered a reassuring smile before pulling her supplies from her bag and placing them in front of her, trying not to dwell on the physical contact. Her conversation with Rachel the night before last heightened her awareness of Noah's frequent touches. He barely made physical contact with their other friends. She wasn't sure how she felt about that.

Noah eyed her for a long moment and turned his attention to pulling out his own supplies.

Thankful to be out from under scrutiny, she sniffed and faced the front of the class. She didn't feel comfortable sharing with people she hadn't known long about the recent events occurring in her life.

Her phone buzzed on the desk. Checking the screen, she smiled.

"What's up, Buttercup?"

She looked over at Rachel. "What? Nothing." She tucked her phone into her bag and put it between her feet on the floor; she'd reply to Aiden later.

"You sure look happy all of a sudden."

She shrugged.

"Come on, spill. Is the sender the reason you didn't sleep?" Rachel gasped, raising her voice and grabbing Charlotte's arm. "Oh my god, did you spend the night with someone?" She covered her mouth with her hands and winced when a couple of guys on the platform below them looked back.

Charlotte's face flamed. "No. I mean, we were talking on the phone, but I didn't spend the night with him."

"Okay, I need details. Who is he? What program is he in?"

"Just a friend. And he's from back home. He doesn't go here."

Rachel deflated. "Oh." Pursing her lips, she twisted in her seat. "Do you have a picture?"

"I do…"

Tilting her head, Rachel stared.

Charlotte sighed. "Hang on." Pulling out her phone, she opened her photo gallery, scrolling to a photo of Aiden and his little sister Riley sitting together on the floor of her mom's clothing boutique in the back room.

"Lord have mercy."

"What?"

"Tell me he's single. That isn't his girlfriend, is it?"

Charlotte laughed. "As far as I know, he's single. That's his sister."

"You gotta introduce us. He's huge! Look how tiny she is next to him!"

"To be fair, Riley is tiny compared to most people. She's the same height as me, though, but we're different in our frame. I weigh more than her." She glanced down at herself. Compared to Riley, Charlotte felt chunky. She wasn't fat by a long shot, but "curvy" would be an apt descriptor. Despite having a flat stomach and diminutive frame, she had an hourglass figure highlighted by a larger-than-she-desired bust. The attention she often got because of her breast size made her uncomfortable. And finding shirts that fit right annoyed her.

At six-two, with a physique that made it obvious he not only had a workout routine but also lifted weights, Aiden made her feel petite.

"So? Can you imagine being carried around by him? I'm sure he'd have no problem picking you up and manhandling you." Rachel gave an exaggerated shudder. "Ooo wee, I wouldn't mind him tossing me around like a rag doll."

Charlotte giggled. "You're ridiculous. Aiden isn't a caveman."

"Shame."

Noah snorted, and Charlotte turned to look at him.

"Don't start," Rachel warned. "You wouldn't understand the complexities of my obsession."

"Your obsession with tall men? Sure I do. You told me all about it when you were chasing after that one dude who transferred out last month in our gen ed class."

Rachel looked at Charlotte. "Oh man, you should have seen him. He made even Noah look short."

"He was *six-seven*; he'd make anyone look short. I'm a respectable six-one, I'll have you know."

"Oh, I know." Rachel gave Noah a not-so-subtle once over.

He rolled his eyes. "Obsessed. Point proven."

"Short women need love too."

"How tall are you, exactly?"

Rachel sat up and straightened her shoulders. "Five-six-ish."

Noah inclined his head and gave her a droll look. "Without heels."

She blushed. "Five-two."

Charlotte pulled out her phone and began scrolling through the article she bookmarked earlier about potential degree options she could transfer to with her current credits, tuning out Noah and Rachel as they continued with their back and forth about height. She wasn't one to care about if her boyfriend stood taller than her or not. It always worked out that way for her in the end, anyway.

"You're thinking of leaving the program?" Noah asked minutes later, grabbing her attention.

"Huh?"

"Rachel just said you're thinking of dropping."

She fisted both hands on the top of the tabletop. "Maybe." She hadn't told Rachel not to mention it, but she wished she had. "That or transferring to a new program instead. Accounting isn't doing it for me, but I want to help my parents."

"Fashion design?"

Both Noah and Rachel knew what her parents did for work. They both met them when they came to visit her two months in.

She shook her head. "I can sew to repair something, but I'm not creative."

"So veterinary studies, then?"

"Oh, lord no." Her lips twisted into a frown. "I couldn't handle it."

"Why not?"

She deflated, recalling the one time she assisted her ma with a euthanasia. She couldn't perform the procedure, only bring the supplies, but seeing the sadness in the poor cat owner's face, and then seeing her ma's teary eyes after the owner left the clinic carrying an empty carrier, was not something she ever wanted to witness again.

She didn't know how her ma did it.

No one would know it to look at her ma while she performed the procedure, but every loss affected her. Her ma had developed a relationship with many owners and their pets over the years, so the loss felt like her own. She loved the animals like family.

Charlotte would break down in front of the owners and make it harder for them if she were in that position. They needed someone to be strong for them.

Her ma took over the practice when the old owner retired last summer; the dream she had been working toward for years finally came to fruition. She loved animals and wanted to run her own clinic, where she could make the calls and help families who couldn't afford care. It meant the clinic wasn't as well-to-do as some of the larger practices in surrounding towns, but her ma felt the loss of money was worth it to keep families together. Charlotte agreed.

"I love animals, but I'm not cut out for that sort of thing," Charlotte finally answered, keeping it simple.

"Fair enough." Noah leaned back in his seat and brought his thumb to his mouth, chewing the side of his nail. "So you're going to stay at UGA, at least?"

"I don't know. I kinda miss home."

"That's because you haven't done a lot up here to get used to the place. Why don't we go out? I can show you a few of the bars with the best music. Oh! And the theater, where they have the best live shows."

Rachel tugged on Charlotte's arm, grabbing her attention. "Oh yeah, the last time I went to the theater, this reggae band performed and there were live painters on the edges of the stage doing these huge paintings throughout the show. It was amazing." She tilted her head. "Though I can't promise you won't get a contact high while there. The shows are filled with smoke."

"Smoke? How do they get away with it?" She never touched pot herself, so the idea of getting high by being around others smoking it put her off of the idea. Being in a crowded venue filled with strong-scented smoke and loud music sounded like one of the circles of Hell.

She enjoyed a night out, and even the random concert, but something about the way Rachel spoke painted a visual that turned her off. Past alcohol, she didn't partake in any other substance, and had no intentions of it. She didn't fault anyone who did, it just never appealed to her personally.

"I have no idea. I saw security while there, but no one stopped anything. I mean, it's dark, so I guess it's hard to find the guilty parties when the smoke is everywhere and not localized to a group. I don't smoke, but being around it doesn't bother me."

Charlotte frowned.

"You smoke?" Noah asked.

She turned to him. "No. I don't like that sort of stuff." If she had extra money to splurge on any addiction, it would be video games. Her drug of choice to escape reality rivaled the cost of a marijuana habit if she chose not to restrain herself.

"Yeah, me either. But there are other shows besides that. Not all artsy shows are fueled by weed."

Murals and music filled the entire town, making it obvious Athens was known for the arts. What little Charlotte did venture out, she always found herself fascinated by the bright and colorful art pieces decorating the town. She especially loved the fibreglass bulldog statues ornamented in vibrant colors standing guard throughout Athens from the "We Let the Dawgs Out" public art exhibit.

Making more of an effort to connect with her surroundings might make it easier to stay, but she already cemented it in her head that this wasn't her place. She couldn't ignore the tug in her heart calling her back to Rosebrook Valley.

"So you wanna go out sometime?" Noah asked.

"I'm in," Rachel said, leaning to look at him. At his frown, she raised both brows. "Oh. Did you mean a date?" She looked at Charlotte. "Whoops. My bad." She sat back in her seat, a small flush staining her cheeks.

Charlotte's eyes rounded, and she looked at Noah, who also had pink tinting his cheeks.

"Well. So much for subtlety." He cleared his throat. "How about it?"

"I don't think I'm ready to date right now, but…" She tried to think of how to word her trepidation without hurting Noah's feelings. It wasn't that she didn't want to date *him*, but she wasn't in the right place to date *anyone*. She needed to be okay with herself before she could be what someone else needed.

"Hey." Noah reached out and tugged on one of her curls. When she looked up at him, he released it, and it bounced back into place. "It doesn't have to be a date. I wasn't meaning a date. I mean, I'm not opposed to it, mind you." He shrugged one shoulder. "But if it's not for you, then it's whatever. I just wanna show you around."

"I'll think about it."

As the professor called for everyone's attention to review information for the day, she sank back into her seat. She didn't know Noah well but didn't think going somewhere alone with him would be so bad. That's what people her age did. Dates or not.

Hookups on dating apps were a thing too. Most of those people hadn't seen each other for more than a couple hours before they were sharing a bed. Definitely not her cup of tea. She wasn't opposed to sex, but the only guy she'd been with was her ex-boyfriend. Random hookups didn't appeal to her. She needed an emotional connection first before crawling into bed with someone.

She glanced at Noah out of the corner of her eye. He furrowed his brows, concentrating on the paper in front of him, following along with something the professor said.

Maybe it would help her feel better to get out with new people. But she wondered why Noah seemed resistant to the idea of Rachel going with them. Did he realize she liked him?

The rest of the class went by in a blur of note taking and quiet, making it impossible for Noah to further question her about her plans for transferring or dropping out, but as class came to a close, Charlotte predicted Rachel would have something to say about the date subject.

It came as she packed her things away.

As soon as Noah headed down the stairs, Rachel rounded on her and grinned. "I told you he's interested."

Charlotte groaned. "Well, you heard me tell him I'm not up for dating right now."

"Never say never."

"Why aren't you mad?"

"Huh? Why would I be mad?"

She set the empty water bottle on the table to throw in the recycling bin on her way out. "Because you like him?" She exhaled a soft laugh.

"Oh. Well, yeah, but I'm not going to be pissy if you two hook up. There's plenty of options in this town."

"You really don't care?"

"When the summer session is over, this place is going to be packed with all kinds of fresh meat. If you want Noah, go for him. Won't bother me none."

Charlotte's nose wrinkled in distaste at the terminology. "You're impossible."

"Just telling it like it is." Rachel stood and leaned on the edge of the desk. "Though I'll warn you." She glanced down the steps to where Noah lingered near the door, talking to the TA.

"Warn me?"

"Yeah," she said, looking back at Charlotte. "We joke around and talk a lot, but there's a reason I haven't taken an honest crack at him."

Charlotte rose from her seat and looked at Rachel, a chill going down her spine at the sudden serious look on the other girl's face. Something seemed off.

Rachel leaned in, talking in a hushed tone. "See, Noah's a new transfer. He missed the first batch of classes from fall to winter. Most of the students taking the extended summer courses are going for extra credits to speed up their degrees, but he's having to make up for lost time."

"So? That's kinda what I'm doing. I came in late, but I'm doing it to get it over with faster."

"Yeah, but you're different."

Charlotte's brows lowered, and her nose scrunched. "Different?"

"Yeah. You talk to people and participate."

"Noah does too." She didn't get where Rachel was going with this line of thinking.

"Yeah, no. He doesn't. At least, he doesn't when you're not around." She glanced over her shoulder again. Noah stood in the empty doorway looking up at them. She lowered her voice further. "He's only sociable and easy-going when you're around. At first, I thought he was shy and had taken a liking to you, but I see the way he touches you, and I don't know… he kinda gives me the creeps now."

Charlotte didn't know what to make of that. Rachel liked Noah. She flirted with him. Was she saying this to scare her off so she could have him to herself?

"The creeps," Charlotte deadpanned. "Yet you flirt with him and like him. I don't get that."

Rachel's lips flattened, and she drew a deep breath through her nose. Exhaling, she said, "I dunno. I guess I'm trying to give him the benefit of the doubt. I'm attracted to him, and the personality he shows when you're around or we're in group meetings is appealing to me. That's what I like. But sometimes he gives me the heebie-jeebies."

Charlotte considered that. Maybe Noah didn't feel comfortable around people he didn't know or hadn't talked to much. Maybe that's why he opened up in their group, and by default, he would be open around her because she was in the group with him. They also could relate to one another, both being new transfers. Rachel was probably overthinking it, but Charlotte wasn't sure.

She didn't know Rachel all that well. The only reason they became familiar at all was because they briefly shared a hallway and took the same classes. It wasn't easy to know Rachel's thought process when their conversations never carried much depth. Not that she didn't think Rachel capable of it. It wasn't her fault.

It came down to keeping people at a distance. Not wanting to get too close when things started getting strange. Charlotte was afraid to set down roots in an area that wasn't her home, another reason she hadn't explored Athens.

Another reason to avoid dating the locals too.

"I'll keep that in mind," she said after giving it some thought. She couldn't dismiss Rachel's words any more than she could accept them without prejudice—she could only go on her own impression and experience with the guy. She looked down at where Noah had stood earlier, but he was already gone. "But I don't think he's a bad guy."

"Just be careful if you decide to go off with him on your own. You can call me if you need to."

She nodded, following Rachel down the stairs. She needed to meet with her advisor, and then she could go back to her apartment and talk to Aiden. He should be out of classes by then.

The meeting with her advisor went as expected. Now armed with a list of programs that the credits from her current classes—if she finished them—could seamlessly transition to, she had a better foundation to decide her future. She still lamented not choosing a school closer to home or doing a remote online degree program, but she had more options if she stayed here than she realized.

When she mentioned she thought her only options were accounting or something in marketing, her advisor seemed surprised. She spent the next hour describing the different programs available that would enable Charlotte to work with both her mothers' businesses, like marketing and E-commerce.

The knowledge should have elated her, and it did for about five minutes, but after leaving her advisor's office she could barely manage to rouse anything more than a sigh of relief that she had options. She hated days like this, when the lows were particularly low and sucked the hope and joy out of everything.

Still, with the strange events lately, and the return of the depression she had struggled with since puberty, taking a break before moving into a new program seemed like the smartest choice. Thankfully, her advisor agreed and let her know her credits wouldn't expire if she took a temporary leave. She also informed Charlotte that if she wanted to keep her grants, she couldn't drop out completely, but the temporary leave was acceptable.

Charlotte didn't mention the things occurring around her, or her mental state, only that she considered returning home before transferring.

The line at Barberitos in the Tate Student Center was longer than expected, but the smell of marinated steak appealed the most when she passed by the eateries available to students. A burrito would be worth the wait. It was the first thing in days she wanted to eat. Any other time, she made herself eat so her medicine didn't make her sick. Her appetite disappeared a month ago, and it felt more like a chore than anything to eat some days.

Her phone chimed. Pulling it from her back pocket, she smiled.

Aiden:

Riley is dragging me and Seth out shopping and to dinner later... send help.

Giggling, she tapped out a reply before stepping up to place her order.

Charlotte:
I thought you liked hanging out with Seth.
Aiden:
I do, but I wanted to stay in the dorm. Tired.

She took a measured inhalation through her mouth, releasing a slow exhalation through her nose. It was her fault he felt too tired to go out with his sister and her boyfriend Seth. She shouldn't have called Aiden last night. Pressing her lips in a tight line, she tapped at the screen.

Charlotte:
I'm sorry.
Aiden:
For?
Charlotte:
Keeping you up last night?
Aiden:
Nah. I told you. Had a bad dream anyway. I wasn't gonna sleep much after that. Besides, I'm mostly tired from swimming all day yesterday.

She found it hard to believe. Had she not called him the night before last, and then kept him up on a video call last night, the dreams he had both nights may have faded away and he would have enjoyed a peaceful sleep. Looking down at the burrito in her hand, she frowned. The spark of appetite she felt earlier was gone.

She stepped out of the flow of foot traffic and leaned against the wall, closing her eyes to take a break from the chaos around her. Her mood had been deteriorating throughout the day.

"Charlotte?"

Opening her eyes, she peered up at Noah. His brows crumpled as he studied her.

"What are you doing hanging on the wall?"

She pushed down the emotions bubbling under the surface and forced a smile, sliding her mask back into place.

The day was wearing on her. The brief high from her meeting with the advisor faded quicker than she expected.

"Just needed a breather. It's so busy in here today." She lifted her burrito, scanning the crowded tables. "I don't even think I want to try to find a seat. Maybe I'll take this home and have lunch there."

"No more classes?"

"Nope. I just saw my advisor." She perked up. "Did you know there's like a bunch of different programs I can take that would help my moms?"

"No shit?"

She nodded. "I think once we're done with all our group stuff, and I can close out these classes, I'll put in the major change request."

"Know what you're gonna do?"

"Not a clue." Her laugh was stilted and a half scoff. That problem was for future Charlotte to face. Back in Rosebrook Valley. Back where she could breathe again without it hurting.

Lifting his fast-food bag, he gave her a lopsided grin. "Wanna eat together? We can go outside."

She should eat. "Why not? Maybe we'll get lucky and find a table on the way out."

She managed to eat a little over half of her burrito before her stomach tightened and called it quits. Noah had been more than happy to finish it for her, so her waning appetite didn't seem suspicious.

He walked her to the bus stop, which made her feel safer, but she still couldn't shake the feeling of eyes on her the whole way.

He didn't seem to notice anything out of the ordinary, and she wasn't about to bring attention to it. She didn't want him to think she was delusional and paranoid. The one time she mentioned she thought someone was following them, when Rachel convinced her to go to a late-night show at a local bar, Rachel brushed it off instead of taking the situation seriously. She decided keeping it to herself in the future was the best option. To be fair, Rachel had been drunk, but it still made Charlotte hesitant to bring up the subject again.

If someone was indeed following her, they didn't seem dangerous. Aside from following her to the bus stop last night, whoever they were didn't bother to bridge the gap between them.

It would be foolish to ignore the situation, but she didn't have to get everyone around her in a twist over it.

If they even believed her to start with.

4

First Contact

By the time she reached her apartment, she didn't even feel fear at the roses lying in front of her door. Didn't even question why there was a second delivery in the same week.

Irritation prickled her skin, trying to worm its way inside her body like an uninvited guest. What was it about today that made it harder to keep her emotions in check?

She picked up the bundle and moved into her apartment, locking the door behind her. Setting the bouquet on the kitchen counter, she opened her bag and pulled out her phone and put it on the counter.

She groaned.

In the bottom of her backpack lay a squished banana and her tiny pill organizer. The little white pill mocked her forgetfulness through the see-through lid. That explained a lot.

"Medicine doesn't work if you don't take it, Charlotte," she chastised herself, now understanding why her mood had soured as the day progressed. Her previous dose from last night wore off as the day pressed on.

She'd not only forgotten her medicine but didn't even eat her breakfast. Her medicine burned through her system fast, so missing even a single dose left her feeling off-kilter and moody. Maybe her doctor could switch her to the extended-release dose. Those worked for her when she took medicine in her early teens.

Would it be too late to take her pill?

She sucked in her cheek, pursing her lips. If she didn't, she'd feel like crap for the rest of the day.

She swallowed the pill with a glass of water and stared at the roses on the counter. No note this time.

She wanted to throw them away, but when her frustration at having a secret admirer got the better of her last week, and she took the bag to the community trash, she received a fresh bouquet on her doorstep and a note taped to her door telling her how it wasn't nice to throw away gifts. It freaked her out enough that she decided from then on to keep the roses until they died.

There wasn't a threat on the note, but for some reason, she felt threatened by it.

She had contemplated going to the police, but without an actual threat, and no proof anyone was following her, she didn't have much to give them. Though this week escalated things with the note and actually seeing someone following her. Maybe it was time to seek help.

Whoever kept sending roses only sent a bouquet when she threw out the dead ones once a week. It still made little sense how they knew. No one could watch her twenty-four-seven. Did they have access to the security cameras at the apartments?

She shook her head.

It wasn't a possibility she wanted to entertain. She didn't want to think about what could be. If she went down that hole, she would be worse off than she already felt.

She was so lost in her thoughts that her cell phone ringing on the counter startled her, and she almost dropped the water glass. Sitting the empty glass on the counter, she grabbed her phone and swiped the screen without looking at it, hoping to catch the call before the ringing stopped.

"Hello?"

Silence greeted her.

She looked at the screen: "unknown caller." She lifted the phone to her ear again.

"Who is this?" She pressed the phone to her ear tightly, listening to the sound of breathing on the other end. "This isn't funny."

"Did you like the roses?"

The deep timbre coming through the phone caught her off-guard, and she stepped back in surprise, bumping into the counter. She reached back with her empty hand to grip the edge to steady herself.

A dark chuckle filtered through the receiver. "No? Would another color suit your tastes better?"

She tried to get her breathing under control so the man on the other end of the call didn't hear how panicked she felt.

"You know," he drawled, "I chose pink to suit that lovely blush your cheeks get that make your freckles stand out. I so love those sweet little freckles, Cherry."

She cringed. She hated that nickname.

Too often, handsy men at the diner she used to work at would call her Cherry and make lewd jokes about her "pie" being on the menu. Or worse, how they would love to "pop her cherry" as if she were a young virgin girl. For one, she wasn't. For two, she was underage when it started. All those men saw were large breasts, and they turned into animals.

Was this creep one of her old customers from Rosebrook Valley?

Her old boss, Ricky, encouraged the behavior by making the waitresses wear tight mini dresses as uniforms. He did nothing whenever his employees complained about the harassment. The memory angered her.

"That's not my name," she forced through clenched teeth. Her hair wasn't even cherry-red anymore. It had faded back to its natural ginger shade. She found the upkeep of the unnatural red too much to handle.

"Mm, but I think it suits you."

She said nothing to that. What could she say? Thank you? Curse at him and tell him to stop calling her? *Yeah, that's exactly what you should do.*

Gritting her teeth, she summoned up the irritable feeling from before and said, "I don't care what you think suits me. Don't call me anymore. Stop sending me roses. I'm not interested. Goodbye."

The growl that filtered through the phone sounded tinny and distorted, but it was enough to make her pause with her finger hovering over the end call button.

Did he seriously just growl at me?

Surely, she heard wrong. Maybe his pet dog was too close to the phone. Though it didn't sound like any animal she'd heard before.

"Now, now, Sweet Cherry." He paused, and she knew he was waiting to see if she would bite back at the stupid addition he made to the nickname.

He could wait forever.

It frustrated her she couldn't place his voice to anyone familiar, but she spoke little on the phone except with those back home, so it made sense. People sometimes sounded different on the phone.

The only locals she spoke with on the phone were UGA faculty members and Rachel—and that was mostly about school.

When she still said nothing to his stupid nickname, he said, "You should be grateful for receiving such a lovely gift. I even take such great care to ensure a steady supply to decorate your kitchen counter."

She jerked, spinning to look at the vase on her kitchen counter filled with bright pink roses with the newly wrapped bundle resting beside it. How did he know where she kept them? She rushed from the kitchen into the living room and closed the blinds on her sliding glass doors that led to the balcony. The balcony was visible from the kitchen, so maybe someone else could see it too from farther away.

"I didn't plan on sending roses today after sending a bouquet two days ago, but I saw you were having a bad day."

That brought her up short. She stood in the center of her living room, brows pulled low. "What are you talking about?" She didn't want to give this guy her time; she worked hard to hide her internal mess.

It seemed he agreed, because he said, "You can smile and act for the rest of them, but not for me. I see you. I know you."

This needed to stop. She wanted to hang up, but after the note left when she threw away the dead flowers, she could only imagine his response if she disrespected him by hanging up the phone.

"You don't know me."

He chuckled. "Oh, but I do. I know you want to go home. I know you're not happy here." That wasn't a secret. She'd shared that with others already. It made her angry he insisted he knew her. "I also know the things you hide from others."

"Oh, real cryptic." She rolled her eyes. "You're starting to sound like a try-hard." In fact, his hubris made her relax. He sounded like a joke. She walked to the loveseat, kicked off her shoes, and sat.

"I wonder what Blaire would think if she knew you resented her."

Come again?

Charlotte didn't resent Blaire. She was the sister she never got the chance to have. Sure, she felt jealousy because she wanted things to be different for herself, but she would never hold contempt for her best friend.

After Blaire quit working at the diner and joined Blackthorn Academy, she didn't keep in touch despite being right there in town. Every time Charlotte left work, she would look up and see the beautiful academy at the top of the hill overlooking the town, and every time she wondered why her friend didn't call her, or even visit.

Charlotte couldn't visit Blaire either. Only those who worked for the academy and the students were allowed beyond the tall, black gates separating Blackthorn Academy from the rest of the town.

At her silence, he said, "I know you resent her for getting into Blackthorn Academy and leaving you, forcing you to leave town for college."

She sat upright and stared straight ahead, her eyebrows meeting.

"Not such a try-hard now, am I?"

She clenched her jaw, forcing herself not to make a snappy comeback.

She looked at the pill bottle on her kitchen counter. The depression she thought she had finally recovered from in her early teens set in again shortly after Blaire left for Blackthorn Academy, but she'd tried to ignore it for the most part over the last year. She had wanted to handle it without pills.

The jerk on the phone wasn't helping her cope at all.

"Are you there, Cherry?"

The taunt in his tone practically gave away the satisfied grin he wore—even if she had no idea what he looked like.

Her hand fisted on the cushion at her side. No matter how much she reflected on home and the things that happened before she left, she couldn't avoid the here and now. Her hand tightened on the phone.

"I'm here."

"I told you. I know you."

"You're wrong."

"Is that so?"

He had no idea what he was talking about.

When she found out about the crazed student that kidnapped Blaire, keeping her away from everyone for a couple of months, followed by all the testing the school required her to complete after the ordeal, Charlotte rationalized the separation as not her friend ghosting her but unfortunate circumstances. Blaire reconnected with her more often after that until Charlotte left for Athens.

"That's so. I'm happy for her."

"But you want the same thing. You feel alone. Isolated. Like an outcast."

"Stop it," she whispered, barely able to muster up a rebuttal. He spoke the truth.

The separation from her family made the depression she struggled with threaten to drown her. Then the flower deliveries started. Coupled with the uncomfortable feeling of being followed, the depression gnawed at her, and it all became too much, causing her to need medication again like when she was younger. She quit back then because of the unpleasant side effects, but so far, they hadn't plagued her this time.

"There's no need to worry, Cherry. You don't have to be alone anymore. I'm here for you."

Isolated and scared was a combination she didn't handle well.

Even with talking to Aiden and her parents often, she still felt alone. Deep down, she felt like an outsider.

Not her parents' biological daughter. Not good enough to become one of Blackthorn's elite. And she couldn't shake the feeling her new friends kept things from her. Another blow that let her know she didn't fit in with those that attended Blackthorn Academy. She wasn't enough. The only outlet she had was…

Her breathing stalled as she jerked her gaze toward her bedroom.

She jumped from the loveseat and ran toward her nightstand. Pulling open the drawer, she exhaled a heavy sigh of relief when she saw the little leather-bound book in the drawer. *Still there.*

"Something wrong?"

"No." She crawled over her bed to the window and pulled her curtain closed.

"Don't lie to me, Sweet Cherry."

She ground her teeth, getting to her feet.

Depression didn't make her a doormat who would tuck tail and play a cat and mouse game. She always strived not to let people run over or bully her. A voice over the phone would *not* get to her. She needed to keep reminding herself of that. A lot.

"Do you understand?"

"Yes," she bit out, unable to keep the trembling anger out of her voice.

Knowing this psychopath had entered her apartment and read her private thoughts gave her mixed emotions. Indignation that someone had the audacity to invade her privacy. Fear that someone could get into her apartment without her knowing.

What else had he messed with? Had he taken anything?

She looked around her room for anything out of place or missing, but she didn't know for sure. With the group project and her mood lately, she could easily lose something and not realize it for a long time.

Breathing in and counting to ten in her head, she exhaled and asked, "Why did you call me?"

"I don't know."

That surprised her.

"Something about your expression today in the food court burrowed into my heart. I needed to speak to you. I'm sorry it's taken me this long to make the connection beyond flowers."

She suppressed the urge to tell him he could wait another ten years for all she cared.

Feeling violated and angry, she wanted to end the call.

"I will make more of an effort. For now, I need to go." He sighed when she didn't speak. He didn't deserve her words. "Very well. We may or may not speak soon." He paused, then spoke with a light tone. "Oh, and Cherry?"

"What?" It was difficult to keep the contempt out of her voice.

His voice lowered, and the threat in his tone came through loud and clear. "Leaving Athens changes nothing."

5

Different Worlds

The long weekend finally arrived, and Charlotte welcomed it with open arms. Her classmates had noticed how on edge she acted after her phone conversation with her new unwanted friend, so after her professors canceled tomorrow's classes due to a busted water main, she delighted in the opportunity to decompress inside the safety of her apartment away from scrutiny.

The air conditioning ran at full blast, fogging the windows with condensation from the high humidity outside. Summer wasn't even officially here yet, and the air felt stifling.

She moved about the kitchen, trying to decide what to have for dinner. Cooking wasn't an attractive option with the heat, plus she didn't think the air conditioner could compete with the stove given how hard it already worked to cool her small studio apartment.

The wilted pink roses in the vase on her kitchen counter sat as a testament to how well the air conditioning worked. She made a mental note to contact the building manager about maintenance on her unit on Monday. Nothing they would do about it on a Thursday night, and it was harder to get them to come in on a Friday than convincing a toddler to eat vegetables.

Takeout would be easier, but she didn't have the money. At least, not money she would spare on takeout.

Treating herself to a movie with Rachel and Noah on Wednesday as a compromise to get more acquainted with Athens had met the quota she set for frivolous expenses for the week.

Her parents weren't rich, but they did well. Well enough that they sent her pocket money to live on to sustain her outside of what grants provided for living and school expenses. She wanted to make sure it lasted for the month, so she limited herself in areas where she had alternatives. Like cooking over takeout.

Opening the refrigerator, she looked for items to make a sandwich, but there wasn't much in there. Milk, a few condiments, yogurt… She was due for a grocery run for the essentials soon.

She huffed in frustration. She needed to cook. If she didn't, her medicine would make her sick. She refused to skip dinner for that reason alone.

Eyeing the jasmine rice and container of diced chicken leftover from two days ago, she decided on fried rice. She grabbed the eggs, a carrot, and the leftover essentials.

After cleaning the kitchen, she moved over to sit on her loveseat with a steaming bowl of chicken fried rice. She bundled her long curly hair on top of her head, securing it with a clip, and turned on the TV, navigating to Netflix. She didn't want to watch a movie, but if she started a series, she would binge it and not sleep. Not that she got much sleep in recent nights anyway between the janky air conditioning and every little bump in the night startling her awake when she normally slept like the dead.

She frowned while browsing through her options. *What's with all the stalkery shows?* Not what she needed right now.

Settling on a series based on a Stephen King novella, she tucked into her rice bowl and propped her bare feet on the coffee table.

She was three episodes in when her phone buzzed on the cushion beside her, rattling her empty bowl. Picking it up, she smiled and hit the button to answer the FaceTime call.

Aiden's wide green eyes greeted her. "Are you naked?"

She laughed at his strangled voice and pulled the spaghetti strap of her tank top over her shoulder that had slipped down. "No. I'm wearing pajamas." She shifted the camera down. She wore a baby blue tank top with cotton shorts in the same color, with white stripes and a cute white ribbon tying the waist. "It's hot here, but not enough to go naked." She would never answer the phone naked. She squinted. "Are *you* naked?"

A warm chuckle filtered through the tiny speaker, and he shook his head. "Nah. I'm wearing joggers." He panned the phone down like she had; he had a lot more skin on display than she did. She didn't see much because he moved to sit back on his bed, putting his back to the wall with his legs outstretched in front of him, ankles crossed. The camera moved back to his face. "Just got out of the shower."

Now that he mentioned it, she noticed his dark hair appeared shinier and messier than usual, likely still damp.

"What are you doing this weekend?"

Pausing the TV, she stood and took the empty bowl into the kitchen and placed it in the sink, holding the phone in front of her. "Probably staying in the apartment. I need to put a work order in to get the air checked, but it's still cooler than outside." She panned her phone to the sliding glass doors on the other side of her living room. "See the moisture on the windows?" She struggled to see her potted plants on her balcony through the condensation.

"It's hot here too, but at least the dorms are temperature controlled. Riley wants to go back to Tybee Island once summer break starts."

She groaned. "I would kill for a trip to the beach again."

"Well, if you decide to come home, you know you can join us."

She pushed off the counter and walked toward her room. "Yeah, I know." Though she wasn't sure she would come. She didn't contribute to the food or drink budget the last time they went, and she felt like a freeloader for it. She picked up the paper with class options off her desk. "I talked to my advisor, and she gave me a list of options available for transferring programs, but I'd have to finish out this course load to keep my grants if I wanted to do that."

"So you're staying?"

"Well, some of them can be done online, but I have to finish out this last presentation with my group first."

She had struggled with the decision for days, going back and forth with the pros and cons of leaving versus staying. Every time she thought she had her answer, she changed her mind. She knew in the end it wouldn't help her situation if she allowed someone to run her off if she had any intention of returning. The whole situation would wait for her return.

She sighed. "I think it's better if I stick around."

It stood to reason that whoever kept sending her roses, following her for as long as they had, and now calling her, wouldn't stop if she took a break. Like the man said, leaving Athens would change nothing.

The recent direct contact made her consider getting the police involved, but she wasn't sure they would do much over a phone call and flower deliveries. It's not like she could prove someone was following her—she only saw someone one night.

"If that's what you wanna do," Aiden said, pulling her back from her thoughts. "Don't push yourself. Sara told me how you haven't been away from home much." His black brows lowered. "You sure you're alright? I mean, the last couple times we talked…" His face pinched as if he were searching for the words. "You look tired. Are you sure things aren't too much?"

If you only knew.

"I don't mean to upset you or anything, but I think I've gotten to know you well enough to at least see the difference in how you were before you left here and now. You seem stressed out lately, and we don't even play games anymore." He reached up and scratched his face where black stubble ghosted across his skin. He usually remained clean shaven, but the light dusting of stubble peppering his sharp jawline suited him. "For a bit there, I wondered if you were getting sick of me or something." He laughed, but concern filled his sheepish expression, and his laugh lacked his usual humor.

"Oh no, not at all." She let out a heavy exhale. "This project has been rough on me, but we just wrapped up the major stuff, so all that's left is presenting it." She sat on the edge of her bed. "I miss playing games. I haven't even had time to play by myself."

Charlotte grew up playing different types of games, but her favorite was indie horror. When Blaire told her that Aiden was a huge gaming nerd, she felt so giddy. They bonded over their mutual love of video games, and she missed the times they played together.

Gaming was common among the guys she knew but making friends with them proved difficult. Whenever she joined a public lobby and spoke in voice chat, the mood shifted, and the jokes and comments escalated from misogynistic to sexual in the blink of an eye. If she had a dollar for every time someone said girls don't play "real games" or requested an OnlyFans link… They didn't even know what she looked like.

"What if I came up this weekend? I could bring my laptop. I wanna show you this co-op horror game."

"What's it called?"

"Lethal Company."

"I heard about that one. I watched some YouTube videos of people playing it. It looks fun."

"Then why don't I come up?"

Charlotte looked at her bed and then around the room. There wasn't a place for him to sleep. Had he forgotten? He helped move her in.

As if reading her mind, he said, "I could come up for the day Saturday or Sunday and leave that night. It's only a few hours away."

His shoulder lifted in a casual shrug like it wasn't a big deal, but she hated the idea of him driving four hours to only stay for a little while and then drive back. Hanging out with her wasn't worth all that, and she said as much.

"Look, I'd rather spend the day running away from monsters with you than shopping with my sister." He smiled when she laughed in response. "Seriously. If I don't get out of here, I'm going to go mad. It's too hot to stay outside long. Lukas is up Blaire's ass, and ever since Seth and Riley got together and he changed dorms—"

"He moved out? Why? Did you two have a fight?"

Aiden pulled air through his teeth, grimacing. "Not exactly. I wasn't supposed to mention that last part." He exhaled. "He's sharing a dorm room with Riley."

Charlotte's face screwed up in confusion. "Come again? Administration is okay with that?"

"Things are different here at Blackthorn," he said then fell silent.

She fell back onto her bed with a loud huff. Once again, they iced her out of knowing anything. She closed her eyes.

“What’s the matter?”

“Nothing.” She opened her eyes. As much as she tried, she couldn’t mask the flat sound to her tone.

“Look,” he said, a tightness in his voice. “the admins here don’t care about students sharing dorm rooms. Their gender doesn’t matter.” He rubbed a hand over his face and then lifted his head to meet her eyes. “Things aren’t exactly conventional around here.”

She studied him. He looked tense with his drawn brow and the constant rubbing at the side of his neck. She cut him a break.

“It would be nice if more schools were so lax.”

His hand dropped. “What?”

“You know, the loose rules about roommates.”

Lines formed between his brows as they pulled together. “You have someone you want to room with?”

“Well, no. Besides, I have an apartment. I can let whoever I want live with me. Though I only have the one bed, and the entire place is basically open concept besides the bathroom, which, you know. It wouldn’t work.”

Aiden’s shoulders lowered, and his expression softened.

“Anyway, what were you saying about him and Riley getting together?”

She hoped Aiden wasn’t against it. Riley’d had a thing for Seth since they were kids but didn’t know Seth felt the same. Even with how little Charlotte knew of them when they met, it was obvious they wanted one another. It would break Riley’s heart if her big brother opposed.

“Not at all. It’s about time those two got their heads straight.” He chuckled. “I just meant that now that he’s gone and I’m in this room by myself like I used to be the last school year, I’m bored out of my mind. I'm kind of the fifth wheel."

"What about Layla?"

"She and I aren't really close. Plus, she isn't always around. She's more Blaire and Riley's friend anyhow." He shook his head.

Her phone alerted her to another call.

Unknown.

"Nope." She pressed the button to end the interrupting call.

"Nope?"

"Wrong number."

She wasn't about to tell Aiden about the man who called her. She didn't even know if he was the caller, but she doubted telemarketers called at nine at night.

The phone alerted her again, and she groaned, ending the interfering call.

"What's going on?"

"They're just calling back. No big deal."

"Maybe it's important."

"Doubt it. God, it's hot."

Again, her phone interrupted their FaceTime call.

"Oh my god, hang on." She sprang up and accepted the call, snapping, "What?"

The familiar deep voice from before *tsked* and said, "Is that any way to answer a call?"

"What do you want?"

Humidity made her top stick to her skin. She hated it and it made her irritable. Irritable enough she didn't register the danger on the other line—or at least didn't care.

"I want you to answer me when I call you." The man's voice rumbled through the phone, angry and harsh. He didn't appreciate her tone. *Too bad.*

"And I want you to never call me again." She pressed the end call button to reconnect to Aiden. "Sorry about that," she said, flopping back on the bed again. She rubbed her eye with the heel of her hand.

"Everything good?"

"Huh?" She waved a hand. "Oh, yeah, it was nothing."

"You look frustrated."

"I'm just hot and uncomfortable. I can't do much else other than walk around naked or live in a cold shower."

When he chuckled, she grumbled and sat up, and her clip popped off her hair. She put the phone against the pillow so she could fix it. If the humidity didn't ease up soon, it wouldn't be long before she resembled a shorter-haired version of Merida from *Brave*. She couldn't imagine having hair down to her hips.

Maybe it was time for a haircut.

Over the last year, she let it grow out until the curls reached her bra line. It was the longest it's ever been. The added weight from the length kept her hair from becoming a super poofy riot of curls—but in high humidity, frizz was unavoidable.

A loud crash on the other side of the apartment made her startle and look away from the phone still propped against her pillow.

"What's wrong?"

She looked back at the screen. "Did you hear that?"

"I didn't hear anything. What's going on?"

"I think something fell. Hang on."

She climbed off the bed and moved to her nightstand, opening the drawer.

Her ma gave her a small container of pepper spray disguised as perfume before they left her at the apartment when she moved in. *"Just in case,"* her ma said. Charlotte laughed it off then, like so many other warnings. Like the ones from her neighbor about living alone.

Clutching the pepper spray, she moved out of the nook where her bed sat into the area that divided the living space from her bedroom. Standing in front of the laundry room door, she didn't see anything amiss, but she didn't have the full view of her living room.

Rattling, like someone was trying to open her sliding glass doors, broke the silence.

She tightened her grip on the pepper spray and drew in a lungful of air, calling out to whoever waited around the corner. "I've got pepper spray and I know how to use it!" Her voice cracked, betraying her.

The false bravado died with her last words, laying her fear bare for anyone to hear. "Keep it together," she muttered to herself, hoping that if anyone *was* listening, they wouldn't hear her weak attempt at a pep talk.

As she crept into the living room, the sight that greeted her made her legs weak and her knees buckle. She braced her hand on the wall for support. Two things registered in quick succession…

One, on her coffee table lay a single pink rose. And two, the glass doors to her balcony were open.

She rushed across the room to the door, hoping no one was waiting on the balcony for her. Slamming the door and locking it, she peered down at the terrace through the condensation. A flower pot she had on the railing lay smashed on the floor—the reason for the crash she heard.

Drawing the curtains closed, she rushed back toward her bedroom, ignoring the rose. It would seem her new "friend" didn't appreciate being ignored.

How did he get in so fast—or at all? Had he been waiting on the balcony and called her from there? Had she forgotten to lock the balcony door after watering her plants earlier? Had he come through the front door, and she missed it while in the shower? It was a lot easier to climb down from a balcony than it was to climb up to it.

The questions whirled around inside her mind, and she didn't have an answer to any of them. She only knew for sure that someone came into her apartment uninvited. Someone invaded her personal space.

"—lotte? Hey, Charlotte. What's going on? Are you okay?"

She jerked and pivoted toward the pillow. She'd forgotten she still had Aiden on FaceTime, and she didn't know how long he'd been trying to get her attention while she sat on the edge of her bed having an internal freak out.

"Charlotte?"

"Shit—I mean, shoot." She struggled to hide the tremor in her fingers as she turned on the bed and picked up her phone. She tossed the pepper spray back in the drawer before moving back into the living room.

"What are you doing?"

"Just hang on."

She set the phone on the coffee table, leaving Aiden facing the ceiling, and pushed it across the floor. Next, she went to the side of the loveseat and pushed it toward the sliding glass doors, turning it to block the length of the glass. If someone wanted in, they could climb over the couch if they wanted, but she wouldn't make it easy for them. This setup would alert her to the noise they would make breaking in, giving her enough time to get out the front door.

She scratched her head, fluffing her hair into a mess as she caught her breath. "Maybe it's time to talk to the police." She closed her eyes with a heavy sigh that puffed her cheeks out.

"Charlotte!"

Her eyes flew open. *Crap.* She'd forgotten Aiden again. Snatching up the phone, she held it up in front of her, brushing her curls off her sweaty face. "Hi. Yes. I'm here," she breathed, forcing a smile. "Sorry about that."

"What in the hell is happening over there? You're starting to freak me out. What about the police?"

"Nothing. I'm fine. Everything's fine."

"So, what's going on? Why do you keep leaving the phone? You're out of breath." The concern on his face made her chest tighten. His brows drew together. "Is your couch in front of the balcony?"

She looked over her shoulder. "Uh, yeah?"

"Okay. You've gotta tell me what's going on." He knocked his head against the wall behind him. "I'm worried about you," he added in a softer tone.

She closed her eyes. "Please don't worry. You know I'm not used to being away from home. The heat's getting to me. It's really nothing."

"And the police?"

"I didn't say anything about the police," she fired off fast, averting her gaze. "Listen, I'm tired." She looked back at the screen. "I think I'm just gonna take another cold shower and turn in. Call me tomorrow?"

The corners of his mouth turned down. "Yeah, sure. Whatever you want." He took a deep breath and released it. "Try to get some rest. We'll talk tomorrow." He smiled, but it didn't meet his eyes. "Goodnight."

"Goodnight, Aiden."

She didn't miss how his smile dropped, and his jaw clenched right before he disconnected the call. He didn't believe her, but he refrained from calling her out on lying.

What could she say to him?

If she told him someone broke into her home, he would drive all the way to Athens to help her in the middle of the night. Aiden was a protector by nature. She knew that. From the moment they met, he seemed on a mission to save someone. He was the first to approach her about Blaire's whereabouts and was the first to suspect the TA's involvement in the kidnapping.

From what she heard from Blaire before that happened, Aiden had helped her boyfriend, Lukas, when they first got together. It seemed Lukas had issues with commitment, and Aiden helped him with those issues. Riley said Aiden also helped both her and Seth but didn't elaborate on it.

Blaire had laughed at Charlotte when she referred to Aiden as an "alpha knight," but that's what he acted like. He embodied strength and protectiveness. He was the chosen leader of their group of friends. They all called him the big brother of the group, but that sounded weird to Charlotte. She never called him that.

She didn't want Aiden as a brother.

Her face screwed up at the thought. She couldn't picture it.

They flirted a little before she left for Athens, but it was all in good fun. Nothing came of it. She doubted he ever felt anything for her. She couldn't feel anything for him.

They came from two different worlds.

His world held money and status, if the rumors of Blackthorn Academy families were to be believed. Her world held a public university, grants, possible future loans, and mental illness.

Other than the crazy TA who wasn't at the academy anymore, she doubted he had to deal with weirdos like the one who broke into her home in his gated world. The security had to be top-notch.

Laughing to herself, she went to the kitchen to get a glass of water.

She at least knew the money part of his world was accurate. Riley's shopping addiction rivaled her gaming addiction. Only one of them could actually support the habit, and it wasn't her.

After taking her medicine, she moved into her bedroom, now armed with a chef's knife from the knife block on her counter. It was still early, and she didn't want to take another shower, even though she felt sweaty and gross. It wouldn't matter when toweling off would only make her sweat again.

She sat on the edge of her bed, placing the knife on the nightstand within arm's reach of where she slept.

Going to bed early wouldn't kill her. She needed to get up early anyway to go file a report at the police station. *So much for a long weekend.*

She couldn't continue living this way.

She needed total darkness to sleep; but tonight, every light in her apartment remained on. Until the police caught whoever broke into her apartment, it would stay that way.

6

On Her Own

Charlotte's stomach twisted with anxiety as she stood in the silent parking lot staring up at the gabled roof of the Department of Police Services building. The entrance to the open-air passageway loomed, casting dark shadows across the glass wall at the front of the police station.

Taking a slow, steady breath, she stepped forward from the asphalt to the concrete sidewalk, only to startle at laughter erupting behind her.

Her palm met the large square pillar beside her as she watched two officers walk past her, deep in lighthearted conversation.

"Get it together," she mumbled to herself.

Lowering her hand, she squeezed her fists tight and nodded.

She could do this.

The police existed to protect people like her in these situations.

Steeling her nerves, she walked toward the front doors with her head held high. She pulled open the doors, passed through a second set of doors, and then stepped inside the air-conditioned building before the apprehension swimming around in her stomach began crawling its way up her throat.

The short-lived strength she felt coming into the building evaporated, replaced with uncertainty. She tasted bile, and it took tremendous effort to not vomit into the nearest trashcan.

Was this a mistake?

What evidence did she have? Some flowers? A phone call? A broken flower pot? She feared and expected to be laughed out of the station.

Sighing, she shook her head.

This wasn't who she was. Timid. Uncertain. Riddled with guilt. She didn't deserve this, no matter how much her brain tried to tell her she did. Tried to tell her it was a punishment for abandoning her family. She missed who she was.

"Can I help you?"

She wrung her hands in front of her, picking at her fingernail as she looked up at a woman sitting behind the desk at a computer.

The woman's sculpted eyebrows pulled together when Charlotte didn't step forward or speak. She placed a steadying hand on the counter that separated them.

"Is everything alright?" The woman glanced behind her before returning her attention to Charlotte. "Do you need help?"

Drawing in air through her nose, Charlotte stepped forward to the counter and met the woman's umber eyes. "I need to report someone," she mumbled.

"You're gonna have to speak up, sugar." The woman tapped her finger on the headset Charlotte missed before because the woman's long box braids matched the color of the headset. "Can't hear you well."

Charlotte cleared her throat, speaking louder. "I need to make a report."

"What kind of report?" The woman slid her chair forward.

Glancing around to make sure no one could overhear, she leaned forward. "I think someone's stalking me?" She didn't mean for it to sound like a question. Stalking felt like the only word she had to describe the events happening to her.

The woman's lips flattened like she questioned the claim.

Charlotte looked back toward the door. He could be watching her right now.

Licking her lips, she put both hands on the counter and looked at the woman, desperate for her to listen—to believe her. "I mean, I'm getting phone calls, and I think someone broke into my apartment."

The woman's mouth relaxed as her features shifted to a neutral expression. "What's your name?"

"Charlotte. Charlotte Walsh."

The woman looked at her computer, typed something on the keyboard, then turned her attention back to Charlotte. "Can you take a seat over there?" She stood, pointing to a row of chairs along the wall. "I'll have an officer come speak with you."

"Yes, ma'am."

She moved to the seats along the wall, her stomach still tight and aching. Lowering herself in the seat, she stared down at the sandals on her feet. The chipped lilac polish on her pinky toe reminded her she wasn't okay. She never neglected her nails.

"Miss Walsh?"

She looked up to find a young female officer in uniform who couldn't be much older than she was watching her with a strange expression on her face. "Charlotte?"

"Yes, that's me."

"I'm deputy Madeline Burgess. If you'll come with me."

Blowing out a puff of air, Charlotte stood. *No turning back now.*

The deputy led her through the busy station to a maze of hallways in the back. Several doors lined the final corridor, but the deputy took her straight to the farthest one at the end of the hall with a placard on the front.

Before she had the chance to read the engraved writing, the officer pushed open the door and motioned for her to step inside.

A middle-aged man with a light blond crew cut sat behind a long desk, studying his computer screen, brow puckered in deep concentration.

"Lieutenant Meyer?"

The lieutenant looked up from the screen, his pale blue eyes assessing Charlotte as she stepped into the room.

"Come in. Have a seat." He extended his hand, motioning toward the pair of armchairs with gray upholstery in front of his desk.

Taking the seat on the right, Charlotte put both her hands on her thighs, sitting ramrod straight.

The deputy who led her into the room moved around the desk to stand on the left side of the lieutenant with her feet shoulder-width apart, her thumbs hooked on her nylon duty belt.

"So what can I do for you, Miss Walsh?" He sat back, interlacing his fingers across his stomach. "Simone tells me you think you have a… stalker problem?" His fuzzy eyebrow arched in question. The slightest hint of amusement flickered in his eyes before he schooled his expression, but she still caught it.

"Simone?"

"The lovely lady at the front desk."

"Oh." She clenched her fists on her jean-clad thighs. This already didn't look good. She hadn't sounded certain or sure of her claims from the moment she opened her mouth at the front desk. It didn't surprise her they didn't seem to take her seriously so far. "Well, yes, I think that's what you would call this."

"This?"

"Yes, sir."

"So tell me about it. What makes you believe 'this' is a stalker?"

Charlotte nodded, clearing her throat.

She proceeded to detail how, for the last two months since moving to Athens for college, she suspected someone following her and now saw them. How every week for the last month she received pink roses delivered to her front door from an anonymous stranger. The recent phone call where he gave her—in her opinion—a threat regarding leaving Athens. She was sure the lieutenant would think it a threat if someone told him leaving town wouldn't change things. How she thought the man broke into her apartment and read her journal, giving him insight into her life.

The deputy hummed her disapproval. "You're reporting someone reading your diary?"

Had she heard nothing else?

"Well, yes, but so much more than that. Just last night, he—*someone*—broke into my apartment while I was home and left a rose on my coffee table."

The lieutenant sat up in his chair. "You caught him in your home?"

"I didn't *see* him, per se…" Before Lieutenant Meyer had the opportunity to dismiss her, she rushed to add, "But I heard a crash, and there was a broken flowerpot on my balcony. That's when I found the rose."

"And you're sure this rose wasn't from your vase?" The deputy asked. "You said you kept the roses in your kitchen. Why would you keep roses from someone you believed meant you harm?"

She looked up at the deputy. The officer seemed to doubt her more than the lieutenant did.

"I'm absolutely sure. I put them in the vase and don't touch them until they die." She looked back at the lieutenant. "The last time I threw them out before they died, I found a note on my door telling me it wasn't nice to throw gifts away."

"And did you keep this note, or the one you mentioned about your shirt?"

Charlotte pursed her lips. "I… No. I didn't think about keeping them." Her eyes shifted down. How could she have been so stupid? Of course, evidence would help her not seem crazy. She couldn't even provide a phone number because the calls came from *Unknown*.

"That's unfortunate," the lieutenant said, sitting back. "But it doesn't mean there aren't other avenues we can take."

The hope that sparked in her chest almost took her breath away. Did he believe her?

"Is there anyone you believe would do this? An ex-boyfriend? Friend who you're having a disagreement with?"

"No, not really."

"Think real hard, Miss Walsh. There isn't a boyfriend who wasn't happy with the breakup?"

She shuffled her feet, bumping her toes together. "Sir, I've only had one boyfriend, and that was in high school when I was seventeen. I haven't dated anyone since I was a senior in high school, two years ago."

The deputy tilted her head. "Two years isn't necessarily a long time for someone with a grudge."

"Yes, ma'am, I understand. But Shawn and I didn't break up because of bad blood. He was moving to Arizona for college. We decided it was better to make a clean break. It was mutual, and we'd known each other as friends before that."

The lieutenant nodded, seemingly satisfied by her response. "Any friends or enemies that would wish to play a prank on you?"

"None that I can think of..." She shook her head. "I'm sure no one like that is doing this. It started when I moved here. I left all my friends back in Rosebrook Valley."

"No one who you've had issues with since your arrival?"

"Other than whoever is doing this, no."

The deputy crossed her arms. "No one-night-stands gone wrong?"

This woman...

Everything Deputy Burgess said sounded like an accusation.

"I'm not like that. I don't sleep around."

The deputy squinted. "Really," she deadpanned.

"Really," Charlotte snapped with more bite than she intended. What happened to protect and serve? She wasn't the criminal. She was the victim here.

The lieutenant cleared his throat, and the deputy turned her attention to him. He shook his head and looked at Charlotte again.

"With no leads on possible suspects to check into, at this point, we can only look for physical evidence." He leaned to the side of his chair, propping his cheek against his index and middle finger. "We can request the CCTV footage from your building, see if we can catch the delivery person on camera, and follow up with the flower shop to get a name there. We'll also follow up with your building manager to see if there are any cameras with views of your balcony." He sat up and jotted a few notes on a legal pad on the desk in front of him. "I'll have a couple of officers come to your apartment, dust for fingerprints on your balcony—you haven't been out there and cleaned up the flowerpot, have you?"

Her curls brushed her cheeks as she shook her head hurriedly.

"No, sir. I haven't felt comfortable moving the loveseat from in front of my sliding glass doors."

"Good, good. Hopefully, we can find something useful there on the door, or perhaps the broken pot." Setting his pen down, the lieutenant sat back in his plush desk chair, his elbows on each arm. He steepled his fingers. "I can't promise you anything, but you've taken the proper first step by coming in today. We'll file this and get on checking into these avenues. In the meantime, if anything changes, I want you to contact us."

"Yes, sir."

It wasn't much, but it was more than she could do for herself.

He turned to his computer and began typing. "I'll contact the business manager today and get that footage. I can send officers now to dust for fingerprints and look for other physical evidence if you have the time." He glanced over at her.

"I have a meeting with my group members for a school project, but that isn't until after eight tonight."

"This shouldn't take that long." He looked at his watch. "It's only ten-thirty. It shouldn't take all day."

"Okay." She shifted in her seat, trying not to make eye contact with the deputy, who eyed her with a sour expression. "I can meet them over there once the next bus comes through."

"That won't be necessary. I'll have them escort you home. Considering the scope of things, it wouldn't hurt. I'd like you to avoid sticking to your usual routes. Whoever this person is likely knows of your schedule and routine. In similar cases, the predictability of your day-to-day life can be the draw for these types of people."

She frowned. This reminded her of all the things she read online when she researched how to deal with a suspected stalker.

Make sure you don't wear clothes that are too appealing. Never wear a ponytail at night. Carry your keys when going to your car. Don't stay out after dark alone. Stay in a group. Never walk to your car at night alone.

Now, don't have any kind of routine or structure in your life or you're inviting unwanted attention. Do better. Know better. Act better. Society always held women responsible, regardless of their actions.

She understood where a predictable schedule might make it easier for someone to keep tabs on her, but it wasn't her fault someone didn't know how to behave like a decent human being. Still, she could do better.

"Right then. Deputy Burgess will escort you back to the front. If you'll just wait there, I'll have two officers join you shortly after I debrief them on the situation." He sat back in his chair. "We'll do everything we can, Miss Walsh, but like I said before, I can't promise you anything."

She pressed her lips together and gave a tight nod, standing. "I appreciate anything you can do."

Deputy Burgess rounded the desk, motioning with her hand for Charlotte to go through the door. "Just a moment."

Once Charlotte entered the hall, she turned back to find the door pulled to but left cracked open. The deputy's argumentative voice caught her attention. She stepped closer.

"—honestly believe that, do you?"

"Maddie, it's not a matter whether or not I believe it. We take every report that comes through this office seriously."

"It's a waste of resources. She has nothing to go on." The deputy snorted. "Flower deliveries scaring her? Come on, Frank."

"I'll admit, weekly flower deliveries are strange at best—makes me lean toward secret admirer. It's not too far-fetched in a college town to have an admirer, but if someone has broken into her home and is making threatening phone calls…"

"It was windy last night. Flower pots on railings fall. I had to clean the patio furniture off my back lawn this morning before coming into the office."

A thump on the desk was followed by the lieutenant's exasperated voice. "I know we've had this situation happen more times than I care to count—it's a college town, but we can't ignore it. If that little girl goes out there and something happens…"

"With all due respect, Frank, how many of these cases are college girls with egos the size of the Saluda wasting police resources?"

Charlotte wrinkled her nose in disgust. How could the deputy speak so callously about this kind of situation?

"Fair point, but I still can't ignore this." His voice hardened. "So you get out there, grab Hopper, go to that apartment, and do your job."

"Sir."

She scrambled away from the door when she heard movement on the other side.

Deputy Burgess stepped out into the hallway, pulling the door shut. The fluorescent lighting reflected off her hazel eyes, making them appear to glow a beautiful citrine. When she turned from the harshness of the light, and her eyes met Charlotte's, they looked normal, but she failed to school her expression fast enough. Charlotte caught the sneer on the deputy's face before she forced a strained smile.

"Ready to go?"

Charlotte pressed her lips together and inclined her head. It wouldn't be smart to say anything to a woman who seemed to dislike her so much. Something about the way the deputy looked at her made a chill rush down her spine.

The deputy led her to the front of the station. "Wait here while I go get my partner." Without waiting for an answer, the woman turned on her heel and walked away.

Charlotte lowered herself onto the chair and clasped her hands between her knees, staring at the floor. The lieutenant seemed concerned enough to follow up on the report, but even she recognized the skepticism in his voice. The deputy sure didn't believe her.

If Rachel hadn't listened before when she mentioned she thought they were being followed, what made her believe the police would care?

7

The Shadows

Charlotte rubbed her tired eyes. She wasn't in the mood for a group meeting, but it was almost over. After the day she'd had, all she wanted was to crawl beneath her sheets and sleep the rest of the night away. The entire weekend if she could. Friday was supposed to be resting and hibernating in her apartment, but she'd forgotten about their group meeting after how long the police took at her apartment.

"Shouldn't take long" my ass.

As much as she wanted to be optimistic about the two deputies coming with her to her apartment, it turned out worse than she suspected. Not only did the lady deputy not believe her, but the other guy muttered comments along the same lines when they didn't find fingerprints or any other physical evidence.

When they left, they informed her they would stop and pick up the security footage, but if they uncovered no leads, there wasn't much they could do.

Noah sat in the chair next to her at Rachel's dining room table. "You know pizza is better with stuff on it, right?"

She looked up from her dissected pizza. "Huh?"

"Did you not like the toppings? Why didn't you speak up when we called in the order?"

"No, it's not that. I'm just thinking." She started layering the pepperonis back on top of the slice in front of her.

"What's up?"

"Just tired. I wanna go to bed."

The meeting ran longer than expected. The only reason for the meeting was to review the final presentation before Monday's class. Monique and Rachel wanted Charlotte and Noah to approve changes they'd made, but when Charlotte pointed out inconsistencies in the data, they spent another two hours sorting the numbers and another thirty minutes for Rachel to rework the PowerPoint. Then Monique sat on the couch and moved everything over to her laptop while they ate dinner.

The job didn't require four people, but Rachel insisted on dinner, and Charlotte didn't want the questions if she left early.

"Why don't you duck out early?" Noah smiled at her, fine lines appearing at the corners of his eyes. "We can finish this up. The hard part is done, and you caught something important."

"What's the matter?" Rachel asked, grabbing another slice of pizza from the open box on the table.

"Charlotte's tired."

Rachel shrugged. "It's eleven. Not surprised with how hot it's been. You get your AC fixed?"

Charlotte grumbled. "No. Maintenance isn't in until the start of the week, and it was functional enough until the weekend."

"My microwave is functional, but it can barely heat a bagel. There's functional and there's working half-assed."

"Yeah, well, nothing I can do about it until Monday."

"Why don't you crash here tonight?"

As nice as it sounded to be in an apartment with decent air conditioning, it wasn't smart to stay with anyone while someone crept around in the shadows of her life. She wouldn't put someone else in danger.

"It's fine. I didn't bring extra clothes, and I need to take care of some things back at the apartment."

"Suit yourself." Rachel shrugged. She left the table and flopped down on the couch next to Monique.

Monique looked up from her laptop. "Once I finish this, I'm getting out of here, too. I had a date with Jayden tonight, but since this went on so long, we had to reschedule." She twisted her lips to the side and gave a brief shake of her head. "Ah well. I'm sure there's something we can do tomorrow."

Noah turned back to Charlotte, nudging her thigh with his. "You gonna get out of here, then?"

"I guess so."

No one seemed bothered by the idea of her leaving early, so at least she wasn't disappointing anyone.

"Want me to walk you to the bus stop?"

"Oh no, I don't want to trouble you."

It wouldn't be a good idea. As much as having someone there to make her feel secure seemed nice, it would be like staying the night at Rachel's apartment—she would put them at risk. Still, the police told her to not do the same things she always did. It upset her stomach to go back-and-forth in her head about it.

He stood and picked up her backpack. "Come on, it's not any trouble. It's hot, you're tired. I don't want you to pass out and hurt yourself. At least let me walk you down to the street. If you fell down the stairs, I'd feel like shit."

The humidity index reached a record high today, but she never passed out before. Still, she didn't want to argue when he only wanted to help.

"Fine. To the street."

He would be able to see her get to the bus stop if she walked fast enough.

Noah's eyes squinted with the wide smile that overtook his face. "Awesome. Come on, let's go." He looked at Rachel and Monique. "I'm gonna walk her downstairs. I'll be back. Don't eat my pizza." He gave Rachel a pointed look.

She held up her hands. "I don't want your pizza."

The muggy night air made breathing uncomfortable, and Charlotte already felt her curls sticking to her neck as Noah led her down to street level.

Once they reached the sidewalk, he turned to her. "I was gonna ask you about going out to dinner tonight, but I didn't expect the project to need revising. I don't know why the hell those two changed things." He looked back toward Rachel's apartment. "It was fine as is."

"I thought so too, but they meant well." She shrugged. "Besides, the new additions will go a long way in improving the presentation. I mean, now that the data is right."

Noah turned to her. "Yeah, well, it's done now." He pulled his T-shirt away from his stomach and fluttered it a few times, fanning himself. "Damn, it's hot out here. You sure you're good to wait for the bus?"

"Yeah. I mean, aren't you gonna do the same?"

"Nah. My roommate is picking me up in half an hour. We have some stuff to take care of before going home."

"At almost midnight?"

His shoulders lifted in a light shrug. "No rest for the wicked." His easy-going smile made her roll her eyes.

"How cliché."

"I'll have you know, we know how to show out when we want to. Super wicked. The baddest."

She scoff-laughed, her hand pushing his arm. "You're so weird."

The laughter died in her throat when he wrapped his fingers around her wrist and pulled her in, stepping closer until they were almost touching. She looked up at him, her mouth parting to ask him what he was doing, but he cut her off by reaching up and running his fingers over her cheek with gentle strokes. She hoped he didn't hear her swallow; it sounded so loud to her ears.

Before she could process the move, his head lowered, tilting as he closed the distance between them. When his lips touched hers, her body went rigid.

He lifted his head, a frown marring his brows. "Charlotte?"

When his grip on her wrist fell away, she stepped back. Clearing her throat and shaking her head, a shaky laugh slipped past her lips.

"Hey..." Noah stepped forward.

She put both hands up, resting them on his ribs, and looked up at him. "I'm sorry. I don't think—"

"Hey, no." He stepped back, allowing her hands to fall, and scratched the dark scruff on his jawline. "It was stupid of me to assume you were interested like that."

"It's not that. I just don't know what my plans are." She scratched at her palm in front of her, looking down at her feet. "I need to focus on my schooling. Until I get any of that sorted, I can't even think about this"—she motioned between them—"kind of thing."

She looked up, expecting disappointment, maybe anger. Not the gentle understanding she saw in the way his eyes crinkled with his smile.

"Look, I like you, Charlotte. But I get it." He reached out and lifted her arm, his hand trailing down until he clasped her hand in his. "This doesn't have to be anything more than what it's been. Your schooling is more important. I'm not going anywhere, okay?" His hand squeezed hers. "And if you decide to never see where it can go between us? No worries. I'll still be your friend. It doesn't have to be anything."

In her experience, boys didn't act this way. Men didn't either. Entire forums existed on the internet that put men on blast for acting entitled to a woman's time and vice versa. People seldom responded well to the friend zone.

She looked down at their joined hands. "How are you okay with that?"

"Why wouldn't I be?"

Her lips twisted to the side. "Just the way it usually goes."

Maybe her experience made her jaded. Former classmates from high school often got angry when she dismissed their advances. They accused her of leading them on when she hadn't. She never wanted to hurt anyone. She only wanted friends.

"Yeah, my roommate's little brother got into hot water for not taking no for an answer last year."

Her eyes rounded. "He didn't…"

"Oh, shit, no. No. He didn't, like, assault the girl or anything. Jesus." He cleared his throat. "My roommate Jonathan told me his brother spent months harping on it and spamming the poor girl through texts after she told him she wasn't interested. She wanted to be friends, but he wouldn't let up trying to get her to agree to more. Eventually she ghosted him, and her dad paid his parents a visit when he saw her phone."

"That's… something else."

Noah chuckled. "Yeah, but Jonathan's been working on him. He's only thirteen, so he can still learn. The girl forgave him when he apologized, but she still wanted nothing to do with him. I don't blame her. I saw some of the texts." He whistled low. "Her dad basically forbids them from communicating at all now. Anyway, I'm not so hard up for sex that I can't be friends with a woman."

"I would hope not." She picked her backpack up from the sidewalk, where Noah set it before kissing her.

"Listen, just forget that happened. I promise it's not a big deal."

Somehow, that disappointed her. While she didn't have time to invest in a relationship, to have him water down what happened as insignificant felt bad. Made her feel cheap, like sharing a kiss with her meant nothing.

It's college, Charlotte. You're nineteen. This is how it works.

She never liked the "pep talks" her mind gave her. College life or not, she wanted something meaningful, if she had anything at all. That Noah could blow off what happened showed her he wasn't right for her. Sure, he showed respect, but he didn't have to downplay it. *Full of yourself, much?*

No. Plenty of girls wanted relationships with substance and depth. Probably the same amount of girls who would rather have a quick hookup to scratch the itch. There was nothing wrong with either; she just fell into the former category.

"What's wrong?"

She looked up at him. "Nothing. Why?"

"You look mad. Did I do something?"

"Nope. Just tired." And a little off-kilter from the kiss. "I think I'm gonna get going before I miss the bus."

Noah tucked his hands in his jean pockets. "If you get to feeling sick later, text me. You can come over to our place or we can take you back to Rachel's."

"Sure."

"I'm serious. Promise you'll let me know?"

"Yes, *Dad*."

He snorted. "I never thought I'd hear you call me daddy."

"Oh, gross. I will never—no."

"Did you just kink shame me?"

She balked, spluttering at his serious expression. "No, I—"

He threw his head back, laughing loudly.

"Oh, you ass." She shoved him and he stumbled, putting his hands on his knees as he continued to laugh until she couldn't help but join him.

"That's more like it. I'm glad to see you perk up a little. Go on and get going. I'll have my phone on me if you need me."

Pulling her cell phone out of the front pocket of her backpack, she held it up in acknowledgment. Hitching her backpack on her back again, she turned, heading toward the bus stop, hoping to get there before Noah went inside. She didn't want to ask him to wait to avoid unnecessary questions, but she wouldn't miss the opportunity to have someone watching whom she knew.

She hummed to herself as she approached the intersection near the bus stop. Before she crossed the intersection, a low distressed sound caught her attention. She turned and saw a small cat limping and yowling as if in pain.

Stuffing the phone in her back pocket, she detoured in the cat's direction, following the illuminated sidewalk to where the cat circled a light post.

When she got close, she said in a soothing voice, "Hey sweetie, are you okay?"

The cat hissed and darted into the alley beside the apartment building she passed.

She put her hands on her hips and frowned. "Not that injured if you can run away like that."

Turning toward the intersection, she began the trek back the way she came. Before she even made it a few feet, the hairs on the back of her neck rose like a sixth sense alerting her to danger. The same feeling that always came when she knew someone was following her.

Her sandals' steady rhythm faltered on the sidewalk. She could see the intersection but had moved far away in her pursuit of the cat.

Not now...

She kept her eyes focused ahead of her, trying not to give any outward appearance of awareness to whoever followed her.

In hopes of throwing them off her trail, she crossed the street and turned down a small side alley that would circle back around above the bus stop.

She breathed out in relief when she saw a couple ahead making out against the wall. No one would attack her with witnesses around. Right?

Keeping her eyes averted, she approached, preparing to pass the couple without impeding their privacy, but the clear sound of pain instead of pleasure made her stop short.

Her eyes had adjusted to the darkness of the alley lit by the dim glow of street lamps from the main road, so she could make out the figures against the wall.

A man with a shock of red hair had his head tucked close to the neck of his partner. They weren't kissing. The other guy's head rested against the bricks, his face visible and contorted into a grimace.

A wet, popping sound reached her ears as the young man against the wall cried out. The sound turned her stomach. Those weren't cries of pleasure. His partner was hurting him. How?

Cold tendrils of fear unfurled in her belly when her eyes connected with the man in pain. His lips moved, but she didn't hear.

Again, he tried, and a broken plea reached her ears. "R-run... go..." He squeezed his eyes tightly as he gnashed his teeth and groaned in discomfort.

At his words, the red haired man hunched over him lifted and turned his head to look at her.

She choked on the scream lodged in her throat.

Eyes glowing blue like a glacial cave stared back at her in the dim light. Blood dripped from his lips and chin. Blood belonging to the young man who remained motionless against the brick wall, supported only by the hood on his jacket, and the grip of the other man.

When the man's lips peeled back in a sneer, she saw the sharpest canines she'd ever seen. Longer than the rest of his teeth, they grazed his lower lip. They, too, were coated in blood.

When a low rumble echoed in the alley, she started. The growl coming from the man was enough to shake her from her silent, but stunned, perusal of his features and make her turn and run in the opposite direction, darting down another alley to throw the red haired man off her trail.

What in the hell had she witnessed?

That wasn't a trick of the lighting. There wasn't any blue lighting around. His eyes glowed.

And the blood.

So much blood coated his face.

The other man had to be dead by now. His last words had been a plea for her safety, not his own.

Tears filled her eyes, blurring her vision as she stumbled on the sidewalk, her foot slipping on the edge of her sandal in her frantic attempt to get back to a busy street and the bus stop before it was too late.

It was the weekend in a college town. The main streets were always filled with bar hoppers. She only needed to reach them or the bus stop.

Dragging her arm across her eyes, she wiped the tears away. She couldn't mourn the young man right now. She needed to ensure she didn't meet the same fate.

What fate would that be?

What *was* that?

Long, sharp fangs flashed through her mind.

It couldn't be real.

Vampires weren't real.

How else could she explain what she witnessed?

She rounded another corner and heard the hydraulics of a bus. She wanted to sob in relief.

She didn't dare look back. Someone was trailing her. If not her shadow, then the nightmare that lurked in the real shadows.

As she turned the last corner, the bus approached the stop, not slowing because no one was waiting.

"Stop!"

She picked up her pace as she ran down the sidewalk, waving her arm in a frantic effort to get the driver's attention. A group of girls in the back saw her and a couple of them stood. They called out to the driver.

When the bus slowed and came to a stop, her knees almost buckled, but she wasn't safe yet. The doors opened and she climbed aboard, panting and pulling her student ID from her pocket, holding it out with a trembling hand.

"Almost missed me, hon."

She gave a weak smile and made her way to the middle of the bus, looking over her shoulder at the girls toward the back dressed for a night on the town. She lifted a hand in thanks before turning back and putting her head against the window, not giving them the chance to engage her in conversation.

If she tried to talk to someone right now, she would become a hysterical mess.

Holding her cell phone in front of her, she looked at the screen.

Last night she told Aiden she would stick it out, but tonight not only tipped her over the edge—it picked her up and tossed her over it.

She needed to sit down with her mothers and discuss her career path. If she didn't return to Athens, she didn't have to face the man who tormented her day and night. The man who told her leaving changed nothing. Of course nothing changed if she returned. But if she didn't? Everything would go back to normal in her world.

She didn't even want to think about what she witnessed in the alley.

Vampires? Real?

She peered out the window as the bus stopped at a red light, certain she would see glowing blue eyes staring back at her. The relief nothing was waiting there loosened the vice in her chest.

People believed stranger things existed in the world. Was it so far out of the realm of possibility? Not if the things she grew up learning and studying with her mothers held any weight.

Her mothers always expressed a fascination with the strange and eclectic, and she followed in their footsteps.

At an early age, she developed an interest in the occult and the existence of unexplainable beings in the world. The internet had a plethora of information for her to soak in.

While her ma seemed more drawn to Western horoscopes, crystals, and the like, her mom gravitated to things like moon phases, celestial bodies, and other ancient beliefs.

She shook her head.

She put little stock into most of it but found the subjects interesting. She especially enjoyed the New Age, celestial, and witchy aesthetics. Over time, she became a fan of the unknown, darker, and unexplained side of life.

Now, coming face to face with a being in direct alignment with the things that fascinated her, she was uncertain and confused. The idea of the existence of vampires sounded amazing, but the reality horrified her. Beings designed to kill. Indiscriminately taking a human life in a dark alleyway.

No amount of study could have prepared her for the reality.

The young guy—*victim*—was someone's son, might have been a brother or even a young father.

She swallowed hard. She couldn't tell her parents what she saw.

The monster she observed looked nothing like the romanticized creatures the internet and media made them out to be.

Even if they could be like humans, they were all killers. Not just a few bad seeds like humans. Vampires needed to kill to live. There was no possibility of redemption there.

If what she saw was real.

Surely it had to be a fever dream brought on by the heat. Her real body was in her bed having a nightmare. She needed to wake up and get water to cool off.

She pinched herself in an attempt to force herself awake but sighed when nothing changed around her. She didn't wake up in a cold sweat. No, she remained on a bus where streetlights filtered orange light through the windows as the bus made its way through her college town.

Delusional? No.

Medication side effects? Maybe.

Overactive imagination because of my interests? Not out of the realm of possibility.

Heatstroke? Highly likely.

Her mind whirled with possible reasons to explain what she saw, ignoring the obvious need to accept reality.

She squeezed her eyes shut, hoping to block out the mental image of the look of pain on the young guy's face from the alley.

Why didn't he ask for help?

Not that she could have done much, but usually someone cried for help when attacked, not thought of the other person's safety.

She would have called out for help.

Her mind kept trying to rationalize what happened and find a logical explanation.

One thing she knew for certain: if she found herself face to face with one again, she wouldn't stop and stare. She wouldn't hesitate to run.

It was one thing to read about it, but discovering the truth was a whole different ballgame.

In the shadows, far more sinister things lurked than creepy stalkers. Vampires existed, and tonight, they snuffed out an innocent life without restraint.

8

Sleeplessness

The heavy double doors separating the throne room from the rest of Blackthorn Manor splintered. The shrill alarm that followed threatened to make Aiden's eardrums bleed. His preternatural healing would repair the damage, but the sudden shock made his head reel.

Chaos erupted around him.

Dozens of rogue Vasirian charged down the long hallways, weapons in hand. Somehow, rogues had breached the security of the manor and were headed straight for them.

King Adrian rose to his feet, the vein at his temple standing out in a clear sign of his rage at the intrusion into their sanctum.

"Clear the area!" he shouted. "Take the side doors and head toward the staff quarters. Libby, show them where to go. Quickly!" He pivoted when a tall woman dressed like the servants of the manor approached him. "Where is my security detail?" The unmasked ferocity in his bellow made her spine straighten.

Libby turned to the Blackthorn Academy group. "Hurry! Quickly!"

As they followed her at a run toward a side door, Lukas covered Blaire's ears to protect her human eardrums. If the alarm had shocked his system, Aiden couldn't imagine how difficult it was for her to endure. Headmistress Velastra, Seth, and Riley followed as the shouting grew louder.

Aiden glanced back. A couple of rogues were converging on them. If he didn't do something, they wouldn't all make it through the door before the rogues stopped them.

His eyes met his little sister Riley's. He couldn't let anything happen to her.

"Get her out of here," he snapped, his gaze connecting with Seth's.

He pushed Riley into Seth's arms and pulled the door closed as her screams of protest filtered through the door.

"What? No! Don't you leave him!"

Swallowing down the emotion bubbling up in his throat, he turned from the door to face the incoming attack. He hoped this wasn't the last time he would see his family.

His eyes flew open, and he took in huge swallows of air, trying to resurface from the miasma that held his mind captive.

Sitting up and pushing the covers away from him, he drew his knees up and propped his elbows on them. He held his face with trembling hands. Sweat ran in rivulets down his temples from his damp hair.

After taking a moment to compose himself, he turned on the lamp on his bedside table. Light flooded the room, and he took a breath when the familiar sights of his dorm came into focus.

Closing his eyes, he took a calming breath, reflecting on the latest nightmare.

If it hadn't been for Dominic's help, he wouldn't have made it out of the throne room to reunite with the others.

Fighting the rogues came easy; he had the strength to match

theirs, if not more than some. The problem came when they fought dirty and several attacked at once. He would have taken a blow to the back of his head if Dominic had not stopped the rogue sneaking up behind him brandishing a pipe.

Even then, it didn't stop him from dying.

Shoving away the covers pooled over the lower half of his legs, he climbed out of bed and moved to his computer, resigned to another night of minimal sleep.

He slumped in his desk chair, booted up his computer, and threw on a set of headphones.

Online gaming, perfect for insomnia.

Opening Discord, he checked to see if any of the people he sometimes played with were online. His brows rose when he saw Charlotte's online status. He looked at the time. Three in the morning. What was she doing up at this hour? Even on a Friday, he seldom saw her online this late.

He took his headphones off and got up, snatched a white T-shirt off the foot of his bed, and tugged it over his head. He lowered himself into his chair again and put on his headphones, clicking the button to connect to a video call.

It took so long to connect he thought maybe she was asleep, and her status hadn't changed to away.

When her web camera flickered on, he smiled. "Hey," he said, sitting back in his chair. "What are you doing up at this hour?"

His smile faltered and fell flat at the sight of the pale girl on the other side of the screen. Other than her red, irritated-looking nose, her fair skin that always held a natural blush looked ashen. Her startling malachite eyes glistened like she had been crying.

"Charlotte? What's wrong?"

Her laugh sounded strained and forced as she swung her head

from side to side. "Nothing's wrong. What do you mean? Why're you up so late?"

Lying again.

The last time they spoke, Charlotte seemed off and denied having any problems, but she didn't have a good poker face.

"You look like you've seen a ghost. You're not watching horror movies again this late, are you?"

"One time," she said with a huff, rubbing her face. "That was one time, and I said I'd never watch them alone again."

Around the time they returned from Europe, he talked to Charlotte at midnight, interrupting a horror movie marathon. After he let her go, she called him back an hour later, freaking out. She was used to watching scary movies while living with her mothers, not alone.

"Then what's going on? You look scared to death."

She looked to the side and mumbled, "Long night."

"Wanna talk about it?"

"Nope." She sighed. "No, sorry. It's been a long night. I forgot I had a meeting with my group to hash out the last stuff for our presentation next week, and after I left..."

When she remained silent a moment too long, he prompted, "After you left?"

She looked back at the screen. "I think the stress and heat are getting to me."

"How so?"

"Ma always said I have an overactive imagination like Mom." She gave a mirthless laugh. "I think she's right."

For a long time, it confused him how Charlotte called her mothers different variations of their title. She didn't call them by their names; instead, she called her mother Sara, "Mom," and her mother Elizabeth,

"Ma." He was sure it prevented confusion in their household, but it took him a while to wrap his head around it.

"Why do you think that?"

"Saw a couple together in an alley, but thought the guy was hurting his partner. Thought…" She waved a hand. "It's stupid. Maybe a side effect of my new medicine."

"New medicine?" He didn't know she took medicine.

"Well, not so new anymore. Been on it for a little bit, but I wasn't on it down there."

He wouldn't ask her what she took medicine for. It was her private business. But he couldn't help but feel concern for her. What ailed her to the point she needed medication regularly?

A loud noise came through his headphones, and Charlotte jumped on the screen, staring to the right with wide eyes. From the shake in the picture, she was trembling.

"What was that?"

She lowered her head, shaking it, once again laughing without humor. "Probably drunk undergrads stumbling home from a party. Heard them laughing after they hit my door. Probably fell into it, actually. Wouldn't be the first time."

Something was no doubt going on if things like drunken college kids in her hall made her jumpy. He needed to go see her.

"Enough about that." Her head canted to the side, a tendril of hair falling from the bundle on top of her head. "Why are *you* up so late?"

"Bad dream."

"Again?"

"Yeah, again."

"Aiden." The way she blew a quick breath after saying his name in exasperation puffed her cheeks out. "This has been how long now? The nightmares, I mean."

His shoulders lifted.

He knew the answer, but if he told her, it would lead to questions. Questions he couldn't answer for her. Still, she worked it out herself—he could see it in how she considered him with a look of concentration. She then asked him what he wished she wouldn't.

"Did something happen in Europe?"

"What? Why?"

"You've had these nightmares since you got back."

His knee jiggled up and down and he tapped his finger on the desk, glad she couldn't see below his chest. "Coincidence, I'm sure." He hated lying to her. Lying went against his nature, but it became necessary to protect both himself and her.

"What do you dream about?"

Charlotte asked him once before what his nightmare entailed when he made the mistake of mentioning it was always the same, but at the time, she had a visitor show up and had to cut the call short. He doubted someone would visit at three in the morning, but he could hope.

"It's not always clear." Not a lie. "I'm sure it'll go away." A big fat lie.

Until he went to the psychology department and spoke with a professional like both Blaire and Riley suggested, he doubted this would ease. Even then, he wasn't sure how talking about what happened would change what his subconscious put him through nightly.

He couldn't remember the last time he experienced a proper sleep.

Charlotte stretched, her back arching and pushing her chest out, exposing a large swath of smooth, pale skin when her tank top rode up to her ribs.

Fuck me.

More and more, he found himself attracted to her. The first time he saw her dressed in the too-tight, too-short, red mini-dress her old boss made his employees wear at the diner, it shocked him how much he found her attractive. Especially when not long before, he had convinced himself he felt something for Blaire.

Discovering that the feeling was connected to their ancestors and the magic of their bond made a lot of the deep feelings of love he developed for Blaire make sense.

Charlotte couldn't be the same, could she? He doubted it. How could he have the dying will of more than one person inside of him? No. This felt genuine. This felt like a different kind of pull.

"One sec," she said, taking off her headphones. She stood and moved across the room, giving him an unobstructed view of her bare legs. The tiny shorts she slept in made her legs appear longer; though she was all of five-four, her proportions were perfect.

When she stepped out of frame, he leaned back and sighed.

He wasn't a priest. He could appreciate the beauty of a woman. Not in the way Seth used to by sleeping around, but he wasn't immune to the opposite sex. Like appreciating a painting, he could objectively see where a woman held appeal or didn't.

He wasn't one for casual sex, though. Didn't get flustered over being around a pretty girl. He'd had a girlfriend he lost his virginity to in high school, and he could count the number of girls he slept with on one hand. Only three carried the girlfriend moniker.

To say he was picky was an understatement. It wasn't that he had a physical type; he required an emotional connection to pursue anything. The only person he slept with who wasn't a girlfriend reinforced that sentiment when, after sleeping with her, he felt hollow and more than a little embarrassed. The sex had been terrible, and he struggled to stay aroused. He didn't even finish. After that, he didn't try with her again—he didn't see the point when he didn't enjoy it. It felt more like work than connection. Eventually, they broke up.

His friend Mera said he sounded demisexual, but he didn't know what that meant. After researching it, it made sense. He never thought to label it, though. He was simply himself. But it fit enough to consider it.

He had made a move on Blaire only after they developed a close friendship.

It took a connection with someone before his body responded, so it alarmed him the day he met Charlotte and his cock stood up and took notice when all she did was speak to him. That had never happened before.

Charlotte flopped down onto her chair and put her headphones on her head. "Sorry about that," she said, snapping him out of his thoughts. She held up a tumbler and shook it. The ice rattled inside the metal container, sounding tinny through the small mic on her headset. "Wanted to get some tea. It's too hot. I wish this heat wave would pass, but it's supposed to be here another week or two."

Georgia hadn't experienced a heat wave this severe in two years. A drought hit the area and didn't let up until the months leading up to Blaire joining Blackthorn Academy, when it rained and stormed as if Mother Nature were making up for lost time.

"I wish this place had a swimming pool." She paused, a cute frown tilting her lips. "Though I'm not sure I'd use it right now if it did."

"Why's that?"

She groaned and rested her head against her chair, exposing her bare throat where a few damp tendrils stuck to her neck. "Probably shouldn't have said that."

"You're gonna have to tell me what's up."

Although her color had returned to normal and her voice sounded less strained, she continued to keep him locked out. It got under his skin.

"I told you—"

"You've told me nothing."

"Because that's—"

"Not all there is."

"Ugh. Seriously?" She leveled him with a look he suspected was supposed to be intimidating, but it made her cuter. Like an angry kitten.

"Talk to me, Charlotte. I swear I won't judge you, whatever it is."

She visibly wilted.

When she put her elbows on the desk and buried her face in her hands, he assumed she wasn't going to say anything. He worried he'd crossed a line and pushed her too far until she met his eyes through the screen.

"I think someone has been following me."

He sat up straighter. "What? What are you talking about?"

Her tongue darted out to wet her lips, before she drew in a long inhale and released it in a laugh. "I thought I was crazy. Thought I was being paranoid about a new town and being away from my moms. But so much has happened that proves it isn't all in my head."

"Like?"

He unclenched the fist resting on the desktop. He needed to remain calm, but every protective instinct he had flared inside and told him to drive to Athens immediately.

"It's a lot. I don't want to get into it right now. It'll just upset me, and I'm really tired."

While he wanted to push, he had to respect her wishes. Clearly, she looked tired. Faint shadows lay beneath her eyes, something she probably covered with makeup during the day. A clear sign the situation made her lose sleep—not specifically her school woes.

"What would you like to do?" he asked, instead of pressing her for more information. He could get that later when he paid her a visit, because nothing would keep him from dropping in now that he knew her discomfort and stress went beyond normal college life.

"Sit under an air conditioner and play video games naked for maximum cooling."

He snorted, pushing aside the mental image of all her pale skin on display. "Why can't you?"

"Well, the air conditioning sucks."

"We could play video games, at least." He refused to address the naked part.

"Naked?" She screwed her eyes up. She would be the one to address it then.

He turned it on her, trying to direct his thoughts to more comedic grounds. "Trying to get me naked?" Her situation and how she looked because of the heat tested his resolve as he pivoted between frustration and arousal.

She spluttered, "What? N-no!" When he smirked, glad she'd taken the bait to lighten the mood, she mumbled, "You are such a dick."

He shrugged. "You're the one trying to see it."

Her eyes rounded in alarm, and he burst into laughter.

"Wow… just… wait." She smacked her desk and pointed at him through the screen. "I'll have you know I've practically seen you naked anyway!"

It was his turn to flounder and trip over his words. "What? When?" He would remember that. He remembered nothing like that.

She drew up and covered her mouth with one hand. With a quick shake of her head, she muttered, "Never mind."

"What was that?"

"Never mind."

"You're gonna sit there and tell me you saw me naked and then not elaborate?"

She dipped her head, leaving him staring at a mess of beautiful, fiery copper curls, and said, "Tybee Island." After a beat of silence, she lifted her head. "Did you hear me?"

"Yes, but I'm trying to think of when and how you saw me naked. I don't think I ever got that drunk." Not to mention his body would burn through the effects of alcohol fast enough that unless he shotgunned drinks all night, he would remain tipsy at best.

"The truth or dare game. When you streaked around the house."

"Oh." *Ohhh.* "You watched?" He couldn't stop the smug grin that crossed his face. He wouldn't admit it out loud, but a part of him liked the idea she wanted to watch him, even if it surprised him.

He shifted in his seat; it seemed more parts than only his brain liked the idea of it.

"I didn't see anything."

His head tilted. "You said you saw me naked."

"Well." Her face flamed as bright as her hair. "I saw you without your shirt, and I didn't look away fast enough, so I saw some of your butt."

"So no dick. Now I understand why you're trying to see it."

"What?" she shrieked.

He couldn't hold it together. He tried. Getting a rise out of her was becoming addictive.

"That's it. Get it all out." She stuck her tongue out at him, but then dropped her eyes. "At least I'm good for something."

The laughter died a swift death in his throat. "What?"

She waved him off. "Nothing. It's stupid. I'm just being dumb."

"You're not dumb. Why would you say that about yourself?" He sat back and crossed his arms. "You're good for a lot of things. I wasn't laughing at you. I found the situation funny."

"Sorry," she mumbled.

"Hey. Come on." He wasn't sure what made her feel stupid; she was anything but, as evidenced by her easy entry to UGA. "You're smart. I don't like you talking bad about yourself."

"I'm sorry. There's a lot been going on lately that makes me feel like I've made a lot of stupid choices."

"If it helps, think of it this way… To get into a state university and have a head level enough to realize what you want out of life instead of going with the flow and sticking with a program you hate takes more than many people our age can manage."

She lifted one shoulder. "I guess."

"No. Seriously. Say it with me. 'I'm smart.'"

"You're ridiculous."

"And you're stalling."

"I'm smart," she muttered.

"What's that?"

She tucked her chin and smiled. "I'm smart."

"That's better."

Seeing her smile after the way she looked when they started the video call lifted a tremendous weight from his chest.

"I think I'm finally sleepy," she said, rubbing her eyes.

He hoped talking to him would help ease her stress. He wouldn't fool himself into thinking he relaxed her enough to rest, but he could provide a distraction from the day-to-day monotony.

"Sleep. I should probably try again myself."

She rubbed her shoulder, and a look of concern crossed her face. "You can call my cell if you have another dream."

"I'll keep that in mind. Goodnight, Charlotte."

"Night, Aiden."

The video call disconnected, and he slumped in his chair.

Someone had her frightened. That much he knew for sure. She hadn't admitted to being afraid, but her mannerisms screamed the truth for her.

It was time to pay Athens a visit.

9

Rogue Movement

The cacophony of voices in the cafeteria did little to help the pressure behind Aiden's eyes as he moved into the crowded space. It wouldn't be long before the headache passed, but it still didn't mean the wait wasn't uncomfortable.

Another night of little sleep. Another night where fragments of an event he couldn't quite remember haunted him. At least Charlotte eased some of the discomfort, even if her revelation made him itch to drive up there.

Needing to avoid the noise or suffer a never-ending loop of a reoccurring headache, he fired off a text to his friend Lukas, who sat in the back corner at their usual table with their other friends. He couldn't stay.

Shoving his phone into his pocket, he turned and moved toward the canteen on the other side of the hall. He didn't feel like anything too filling, so he opted to grab a bottle of electrolytes and a protein bar for later. Anything more than the drink right now might make him throw up.

Why couldn't he shake the headache? It never lasted this long before. Something felt off.

Taking the stairs at the back of the building at a fast clip, he made it to the bottom floor in no time. The sunlight on the ground floor filtered through the stained glass in shades of red and black on the high-standing walls, painting the marble floor in shades of crimson. He welcomed the darker lighting from the color of the windows; the pressure on his eyes eased with each passing minute.

The cafeteria on the top floor of Blackthorn Academy didn't follow the old-style Renaissance and Gothic architecture that the bottom floors of the main building, the library, and the interior of the staff and administration buildings displayed. The academy restored the exterior of the centuries-old buildings on campus but kept as close to the refined architecture the region was known for, leaving the stained glass and stonework intact. The aesthetic had become a calling card in the public eye representing Blackthorn Academy with not only the university branch bearing the appearance, but also the branch locations for elementary through high-school-aged students in neighboring towns.

While they kept the interior of the administration and staff building true to the original style from when the school was founded hundreds of years ago, the school renovated the dorms and the upper floor of the main building to bring it to contemporary standards to fulfil the needs and wants of university students of this century.

The front of the main building from top to bottom displayed arched windows and stonework covered in hanging ivy, but on the top floor at the back of the building overlooking the forest behind the academy, floor to ceiling windows all around the modern cafeteria allowed students to take in the Georgia sky and the lush greenery below.

While the bright cafeteria was nice to eat and socialize in on any other day, it felt like torture today. He needed to get away.

Walking down the hall through the shafts of diluted sunlight, beneath the warm amber glow of elaborate chandeliers hanging overhead every few feet, he made his way toward the front of the building where a set of large, heavy wooden doors stood between him and the bright courtyard on the other side.

"Hold up!"

At the sound of Seth's voice, Aiden looked up toward the stairs that ran parallel to the hallway he exited into the main foyer. Seth hurried down the wide staircase, followed by Riley and his other friends, Lukas, Blaire, and Mera.

"What's going on?" Seth asked when he reached the bottom.

"What do you mean?"

"I saw the text you sent Lukas."

"Oh." Aiden sighed. "I couldn't tell you, man. I keep having a reoccurring headache and it lasts a lot longer than it should." He opened the bottle of sports drink and took a gulp. "I can't really stomach a lot of food either."

"What about blood?"

"Nope."

Riley stepped around Seth and propped her hands on her hips. "That's dangerous. When's the last time you had a packet?"

Aiden craned his neck from side to side, trying to recall. "Last night, after I got off the computer with Charlotte. Got one from the canteen."

"That alone could be why you have a headache," Riley said, sounding a lot like their mother.

"Possible early signs of *sanguis manie*," Mera added, her expression neutral as she gave him a slow assessment with her eyes. She always unnerved him when she put on her medical hat.

"What the hell?" Riley snapped. "*Sanguis manie*, Aiden? Really?"

"Maybe." He didn't think so, but he didn't want to risk it. He also didn't want to upset his little sister. Especially when he often lectured her about the same thing. She too often forgot to eat or drink blood, and *sanguis manie* meant certain death if sustained for a long period.

No one, no matter how strong their willpower, could avoid blood mania.

"I'll be right back." Riley ran down the hallway Aiden exited, the buckles on the sides of her knee-high boots jangling with every stomp of her platforms.

"You know you're gonna have to drink it now, right?" Lukas said leaning on the banister, a small grin bowing his lips.

Blaire peered up at him. "What do you mean?"

"Pretty sure she went to the canteen or cafeteria to get him a blood packet."

"Riley is relentless," Seth said. "I don't think she'll give up until he does."

Blaire looked down the hall and hummed. She turned to Aiden. "Do you need to go to the health department?"

"Nah. I mean, if this keeps up, I will."

She looked at Mera. "Does he need to go to the health department?"

"Why didn't you ask her to start with if you weren't going to take my word for it?" he asked with a chuckle.

His rapid healing should have kicked in and rid him of the headache sooner. Not only had healing been slow to take hold, it didn't last long before his headache came roaring back. The logical conclusion sounded like the start of blood mania, as his sister suspected; but he didn't feel any other symptoms, and he could go longer than this without blood. He'd done it before.

"If he doesn't improve, yes," Mera said, crossing her arms. "If it gets worse, absolutely."

"I need to sit down somewhere quiet."

"Text Riley and tell her to meet us in the hedge maze's center courtyard," Lukas said, looking at Blaire. He turned to Aiden. "Can you handle the sun?"

"Not really. It was one of the reasons I avoided the cafeteria. This heat wave is brutal."

Blaire looked up from her phone at Aiden, tucking her long blonde hair behind her ear. "What about your dorm room? We can hang out there."

"Works for me. I don't have anything else going on today. I thought about borrowing Mom's car to drive up and see Charlotte tomorrow, so I wasn't going to do much today."

"Charlotte?" Blaire tapped her phone, presumably texting Riley where to meet them. "Why?"

"I'm a little worried about her," he said as he started toward the doors that led outside, the others following. "Ever since she settled up in Athens, and we returned from Europe, she's seemed more and more stressed." He wouldn't tell them what she confided in him about. He didn't know if she'd want them to know.

As soon as the heavy double doors swung open into the courtyard, he regretted not finding a quiet spot in the library to hide in. The bright sunlight was oppressive, the humidity stifling. The sound of students laughing and talking as they walked around the expansive cobblestone courtyard sounded like his eardrums were being raked over a cheese grater. Even the sounds of bubbling water from the massive tiered fountain in the center court in front of the main building made his eye twitch.

"Come on, we need to get you back inside. You look pale," Lukas said, stepping around Aiden and descending the wide stairs, the chain on his hip swinging and clinking in a way Aiden hadn't paid attention to before in all the years Lukas had worn one.

With the headache bringing the surrounding sounds into sharp focus, Aiden wanted to rip the chain from his best friend's belt and toss it to the ground.

Once they reached the dorm building and took the stairs to his room, he finally relaxed. His room had the curtains pulled shut, blocking out the hot sun, and the air conditioning kept it chilly. A slice of paradise.

He set his things on his desk before collapsing on his bed against the wall and throwing an arm over his eyes. A weight settled next to him on the edge of his bed.

"If the blood doesn't work, I'm calling a nurse," Seth said from beside him.

"I'm sure I'll be fine."

In the pause, Aiden imagined Seth turning his sharp, steel-hued gaze to Mera when she said, "He's more than capable of assessing his own symptoms. Not everything requires medical intervention."

Seth groused. "But what if this has to do with you being shot?"

Aiden didn't want to think about it. Every night he had to think about it. Wake up with memories that didn't feel like his own. How could he remember something he wasn't alive for?

"I didn't even think of that," Blaire said from far away. He suspected she was sitting on the bed on the other side of the room that used to belong to Seth before he moved out. "I thought with your healing, and everything that happened, there would be no lasting effects."

"None of us have ever come back from the dead," Lukas said.

"Not like this."

"What do you mean by 'like this'?"

Lukas must have been lost for words, because after a long pause, Mera took a scant breath and said, "Like you humans, we can come back from clinical death, but once we reach legal death, we can't heal through that."

"I thought death was death," Seth said.

Aiden lowered his arm now that his eyes had adjusted to the room's dimness.

Mera gave a brief shake of her head. She sat at the foot of the far bed near Blaire and Lukas with her legs crossed. Her foot swung back and forth, the metal ends of the shoelaces on her combat boots tapping lightly with the motion. "Clinical death happens when the heart stops, and legal death is when the brain stops."

He hadn't heard of that before but knew for certain he went beyond clinical death when a rogue put a bullet into his skull. Shuddering at the memory, he refocused on Mera, who continued to explain things to Blaire.

"—top of that, there are some injuries too severe for our healing to react to fast enough before we either bleed out or something equally severe."

Seth shifted on the bed. "Remember what Kai said?"

The corners of Blaire's lips turned down as she studied Seth. "About?"

"When you first joined the academy and asked about our kind, you asked questions about vampire myths and legends."

"Oh yeah," Blaire said, a hint of embarrassment in her tone.

"Yeah. Decapitation, wood through the heart, and even fire would kill anyone, not just our kind."

"I know that now."

Seth nodded. “We have a higher survival rate because our healing allows things that can slowly kill you to heal before they have the chance to take us.” He leaned forward, clasping his hands in front of him with his elbows resting on his spread knees. “And while it’s rare to survive a gunshot wound, our healing is no match for what Aiden went through. I’m just wondering if there isn’t some lasting effect associated with his dying and resurrection.”

“I’ve tried to research it,” Mera said. “But I’ve found no records. I can’t talk about it with the leaders of the department without raising unnecessary questions and bringing more scrutiny on Blaire.”

None of them had the answers. Aiden doubted the medical staff at the academy would know either. None of them were prepared to face the new reality they found themselves in.

They could only rely on facts.

A rogue shot him. He died. Ancient magic housed inside Blaire brought him back to life.

Beyond those facts, everything remained speculation.

If he experienced detrimental aftereffects, did it mean he would die sooner than he was meant to? He wasn’t immortal, but if he took care of himself, he had hundreds of years left. His chest seized, and he rubbed roughly at his sternum. Panic had been a constant companion since their return from Europe.

“Speaking of Kai, where is he?”

Mera looked over at Blaire. “Meeting with a professor about next year. I need to return to California for a brief internship, which acts as part of my accelerated learning, but since we can’t be separated, he will have to work out a virtual learning program. If approved, we leave this summer and won’t return for a year—at minimum.”

He remembered Kai telling him and Lukas something about missing a year of school, but he didn’t realize it would be so soon.

When Professor Velastra took over as headmistress a few months ago, she implemented a change to the structure of classes—much to everyone's relief. Blackthorn Academy students now received a longer summer break from mid-June through end of July, instead of only one month in July. It was only two additional weeks, but next summer it would be a full two months. She hadn't been able to adjust the exam schedules this year in time to grant anything more. The new change allowed students to catch up if they fell behind so they didn't fail, and it gave a proper break to those who needed it.

The door to his dorm room swung open and Riley rushed in, carrying a blood packet. She pushed Seth out of the way, forcing him to the foot of the bed while she dropped down beside Aiden.

"Here. Drink," she ordered, holding out the packet.

When he looked up at her pale blue eyes, the slightest shimmer reflected the light from his desk lamp. Red rimmed her lashes. She was worried about him.

Choosing not to argue, he sat up and took the packet. Even if it made him sick, he'd feed to rid his sister of her pain.

He never again wanted to see the look of anguish he saw when he told her he loved her right before being shot in the head. The image remained etched in his retinas. He couldn't erase the look of horror on her face from his mind; couldn't stop hearing her cries. It played on repeat in his dreams nightly.

The thick liquid soothed the hunger he'd felt all day, but he feared the nausea that usually accompanied his headache. He didn't want to vomit.

"I don't like this," Riley said.

"I'll be fine."

"Seth thinks it might be from when he got shot."

Riley whipped her head around to look at Blaire. "How? You

healed him."

"But what if it didn't get everything? I don't know how this magic stuff works. I don't even remember what happened."

From the way they told him it went down, Blaire's entire eyes glowed gold, and he and she were both enveloped in gold and red magic. That when he took the first breath, coming back to life, she collapsed. She had her own out-of-body experience, it seemed—or her body acted on autopilot.

"So what can we do? How can we check?"

Seth clasped Riley's hand in his. "He said he'll go to the nurse if it doesn't improve."

"All we can really do is wait to see if the blood helps," Mera added, her eyes on Riley.

"My headache is easing," he said, hoping to reassure Riley. "I think the low lighting and finally putting something of substance besides sports drinks in my body is helping."

The blood *had* helped. Only halfway through the packet, he felt stronger and less floaty. No headache, no nausea. Emboldened, he sucked down the rest.

"Don't freak me out like that again," Riley said, smacking him on the chest.

"So, what about visiting Charlotte?"

Riley turned toward Blaire. "What about Charlotte?"

"He mentioned visiting her while you were gone."

"Yeah," he said, tossing the empty packet into the trashcan beside his bed. "I dunno what it is, but something seems off. Maybe the stress of starting college, but she seems down. Figured she could use a distraction."

"A distraction? Meaning you?" Riley cocked her head to the side. "I saw those texts you sent her."

"What texts?" Seth smirked.

"Aiden's been flirting with Charlotte." A saccharine smile spread across Riley's face. "And she's been flirting right back."

"We haven't I mean, not much. We're friends. Just playing around."

Blaire tapped her fingertips on Lukas's thigh as she studied Aiden. "I thought y'all couldn't date humans." She looked up at Lukas. "Except in our case, I mean."

"We can. There're no laws prohibiting relationships between our kind and yours, but it's frowned upon and not recommended," Lukas said, brushing a strand of Blaire's hair from her face with his fingers, tucking it behind her ear.

"Why?"

"Because in the end, we can't form a lasting relationship if they are going to die while we live hundreds of years. Questions will pop up. Not to mention the whole blood thing."

He'd heard it all before. He and Lukas already discussed the possible fallout if Charlotte found out about who he was when Lukas asked if he was interested in her before. They discussed how it might shake her relationship with Blaire. How the Blackthorn Clan might order her memory wiped.

He hadn't told Lukas he felt something for Charlotte because he still had to sort through his feelings himself. He liked the girl, and she was fun to be around, but there couldn't be anything long lasting. If he found his Korrena mate, or she discovered what he was, anything they built between them would have been pointless.

He also didn't want to put her in danger.

He wouldn't hurt her, but if she discovered his secret, or someone at the academy got wind of his involvement with a human, they might hurt her.

He cracked his neck. "I'm not getting into anything with her."

The day at the diner when he first spoke to her, when Blaire first introduced them, wasn't the first time he'd seen her. Before they discovered how her old boss had conspired with Blaire's stepbrother against her, he and his friends often visited the diner where she worked, but because of her status as a human, he never spoke with her.

When he finally got the opportunity to meet her, he had the strangest feeling he knew her. Something felt familiar and nostalgic. The others reasoned it was from their previous visits, but he wasn't so sure. Even her scent seemed familiar.

A sweet combination of pineapples, vanilla, and warm, buttery brown sugar, reminding him of homemade pineapple upside down cake.

Great. *Now* he was hungry.

"I swear, it's just friendship," he said, ignoring how his stomach rumbled. "I thought about going up there and playing some video games to take her mind off things."

Seth asked, "What's wrong with her?"

"She's been telling Blaire and me she hates her major," Riley said.

"Same here," Aiden said, shifting to sit against the wall, giving Seth and Riley more room. He felt better, but he didn't want to risk another sudden headache by moving around too much. If it came back, he would visit the nurses. It wasn't normal.

Blaire asked, "When are you going?"

He looked at her. "Thought about early tomorrow, since I'm not feeling it today. Come back in the evening. Think I should?"

"It can't hurt. Want me to come too? I miss her already."

In truth, he wanted to go on his own.

While he wasn't lying about only friendship existing between them, part of him didn't balk at the idea of something more, even if short-lived. He wanted a lasting relationship. He wanted his Korrena—his other half. But it didn't mean he couldn't have a meaningful relationship in the meantime. Both his friends and little sister had found their pair, so now he felt like the odd man out.

"About that..." He rubbed the back of his neck, a nervous habit he disliked about himself.

"He wants her all to himself," Riley said with a sharp nod. She added in singsong, "Someone has a crush."

He chuckled at her taunt. "It's not like that."

"Hey, we're not judging," Seth said, pulling Riley into his lap. She sat sideways, leaning against him, and he wrapped his arm around her waist. "I don't see the big deal if you do. Personally, I think the clan should allow her to know. She's been involved in our lives but kept in the dark since Blaire joined the academy."

"I didn't know you felt that way," Blaire said, looking up from typing on her phone. "I wish she could know. It would make things easier. I miss her."

"Yeah, well, I saw the way she acted at Tybee Island when we went," Seth said. "Whenever something slipped, or we stopped talking about things when she came into the room, I could see it on her face. She seemed unhappy."

Leave it to Seth to notice things before the rest of them. The quiet observers always did.

"What?" Riley twisted to look up at his face. "Why would she be unhappy?"

"Wouldn't you be if your best friend suddenly became part of a clique that you weren't really a part of?"

"She *is* part of our group!"

Seth arched an eyebrow at Riley's outburst. "Baby, think about it. We have to keep her at arm's length. No matter how much we try to include her, there's always gonna be a wall."

"I don't like that." Riley's shoulders slumped. She stared at her lap, picking at the sparkly black polish on her nails.

"Me either," he said, tightening his arm around Riley's waist. "I know she means a lot to you and Blaire, which is why I think it's stupid for her to not know."

"She's human," Mera said at the same time Blaire said, "But it's against the rules."

"And there lies the problem. With her getting closer to everyone in the group, I think reevaluating the rules or making exceptions should happen, but I doubt they'll give a shit. She's one human and we're a bunch of students."

Mera's lips pressed into a tight line, the only sign she felt anything about the situation. Maybe she agreed with the rules. Maybe not. She wasn't as familiar with Charlotte as the others, but she didn't have a problem with Blaire, so Aiden doubted her expression was anything less than a support for change.

Lukas sucked his teeth. "Blaire isn't just any student, though."

Maybe the Blackthorn Clan might extend an exception to someone meant to save their kind from certain destruction. One little human not descended from the magical bloodline only Blaire belonged to couldn't upset the balance that much, right?

"Yeah, well, as much as I agree, I doubt anything will change," Aiden said with a sigh, moving to stand when someone knocked on his door.

"I got it," Lukas said. He strode to the door and opened it. "How'd you know where we were?"

"Blaire told me," Dominic said, holding up his phone.

In the short time after Dominic joined the academy as the eyes on the ground for King Adrian Blackthorn, he found a comfortable place with their small group.

Aiden glanced over at his little sister, cuddled in Seth's arms.

It surprised him how much Seth accepted Dominic, considering the circumstances of his arrival.

Dominic had wanted to date Riley; he'd asked her to become compatible pairs, since neither had yet found their Korrena. Aiden found it disrespectful to both Seth and Riley when he discovered Dominic knew of Riley's feelings for Seth and still pursued her.

Once he discovered Riley's effort to distance herself and move on with her life, it all made more sense. She remained clueless to Seth's feelings for her, despite numerous attempts to make her aware of them.

He also didn't fault Dominic; once Riley said she couldn't commit to him, he accepted the rejection with grace and expressed genuine happiness for them when he learned Riley and Seth were Korrena pairs.

Dominic entered the room and squinted. "Why's it so dark in here?"

"Aiden has a headache," Riley said.

"Not anymore, but I did. You can turn the overhead light on."

Collective groans sounded when Dominic flipped the switch, several of them shielding their eyes as they adjusted to the brighter room.

Dominic glanced around at everyone with a sober expression.

Aiden sat up straighter. "What's wrong?"

Dominic moved over to the desk and pulled out a chair, then straddled the chair back, facing the room.

Blaire tucked her phone away. "Dom?"

"I just got off the phone with my cousins."

"Which one?" Riley asked.

He looked at her. "*Cousins.* It was a conference call with the entire clan and a couple members from the extended court." He placed his hands on the back of the chair and leaned forward, his eyebrow piercing glinting as it caught the light. "I said it wouldn't be long before we had rogue issues over on this side of the world, and don't you know it, it's on our doorstep."

"What?" Blaire swung her gaze from Dominic to Lukas and back again. "What does that mean?"

"The clan has received many reports of rogue movement along the Eastern seaboard. It's foolish to think they weren't around, as I said long ago, but the problem is their movements have become more organized, and it's no longer petty gang crimes."

Aiden's brow pinched. "What are they doing?"

"Shipments of weapons in high volume and Folinarin have trickled into the country for the last month at an alarming rate."

Mera's finely sculpted brows rose. "Folinarin? The suppression drug?"

Dominic nodded.

They had told Mera and Kai all about their experiences with the new drug while in Europe hoping Mera knew about it, but she didn't. There wasn't a lot known beyond the drug's ability to suppress preternatural abilities, making Vasirian nothing more than humans while the effects lasted.

Humans that still required blood to survive.

"What? But why?" Lukas looked at Dominic with lowered brows and frustration clouding his eyes. "What's the point of all that?"

Dominic rolled his neck from side to side, as if steeling himself. "Gabriel thinks they're preparing for war."

Riley looked at him with big eyes, twisting in Seth's lap. "War?"

Dominic inclined his head.

Aiden looked from his sister to Dominic. “War with who?”

Chocolate brown eyes shifted to Blaire, and Dominic’s grip tightened on the chair. “With anyone who supports her awakening.”

When they learned about the existence of rogues while in Europe, it didn’t surprise Aiden. Most species had outliers who didn’t adhere to the social structure and accepted hierarchy. Different animals drove out those who disrupted the balance. Humans had gangs and other criminals. Prisons were full of those who went against the system and lost. His kind had Cresbel Asylum—a place rumored to be several stories high and spread across a lot of acreage. They didn’t even have photos in their textbooks of the asylum. The rule of thumb was that no one wanted to go; and if they knew what it looked like, they likely weren’t leaving.

“I don’t understand how the rogues can be so against Blaire becoming a Vasirian,” Riley said, nose wrinkling like she smelled something foul. “Our kind needs that to happen to survive.”

“Know how we guessed some didn’t believe it or didn’t hear that piece of information?”

“Uh huh.”

Dominic dropped his hands in his lap. “Well, Tobias and a few other members of the extended council captured and interrogated some rogues when they seized one shipment. Turns out they are aware of the prophecy, but the rhetoric spreading through the underground is that it’s false. That the Oracle is becoming too old to have clear sight.”

“I’ll be damned,” Seth muttered.

Lukas’s brows tightened as they pulled together. “So these idiots are going to risk the future of our kin on the off-chance the Oracle is, what? Senile?”

“They’re desperate. They don’t want Blaire to return the bloodline to what it used to be. Strong. With magic. Allowing those of us without Korrena mates"—Dominic looked at Aiden—"to perhaps find them with humans who would be born with magical blood or have dormant blood now. As long as Blaire remains human, those with latent blood will remain dormant. No future magical children will exist."

Lukas raked a hand through his long hair and rested his head against the wall. "What the fuck? They won't believe the restoration will save us but believe the rest of it?"

"You can't cherry-pick what you believe and don't believe. It either is or isn't," Seth said.

Aiden crossed his arms over his chest. "If they don't think she'll save us, then she won't return our bloodline back as it was, either. How do they even believe any of the Blood War information and that there ever was magic if they don't believe the Oracle knows what she's saying?"

"Again, cherry-picking."

Dominic let out a long, drawn-out sigh. "The semantics of it aren't what's important. It's that they are moving and becoming more organized than ever before. Both Adrian and I believe it won't be long before they make a move this direction." His eyes connected with Blaire's. "Before they come for you."

10

POSTURING

Charlotte hadn't gotten around to grocery shopping with the way the last couple of days had gone. Her refrigerator held the bare necessities, but nothing she wanted to cobble together for lunch.

Instead, she decided on the campus eatery. The temptation of air conditioning was strong, although people around her would lure her into spending money she didn't want to spare.

She couldn't stand sitting another minute alone in her apartment, waiting.

Waiting for the boogeyman to come and steal her away. Though she still questioned if she had witnessed a vampire or was suffering heatstroke.

She also waited for her "friend" to make a reappearance.

Since the night he broke in and left a rose in her apartment with her there, he hadn't tried to make contact. She wondered if he knew she had gone to the police and it scared him off. Somehow, she doubted it.

The pink roses on her kitchen counter were almost dead, the heat speeding up their decay. If the roses were from someone she knew and had an interest in, she'd tell them to stop sending them—at least until she could get a regulated temperature in her apartment. It wasn't fair to bring life into her home knowing it wouldn't reach its usual life cycle. She already felt guilty about the abundance of plants in her apartment facing the humidity. Her mom tried to tell her humidity wouldn't hurt them—something about greenhouses—but she still questioned it. Her roses wilted in the humid apartment, after all.

Maybe it seemed silly to think about that sort of thing, but plants were living things too. Maybe they couldn't feel like humans, but they still lived and died.

As she followed the path toward the Tate Center, she adjusted the sunglasses that had slipped down her nose. She swiped away the light sheen of sweat.

Humidity made sitting outside near impossible—even the shade under the trees shielding students from the sun did little to protect them from the oppressive humidity. The lack of an advisory surprised her, although she hadn't checked, so there could still be one.

Before she reached the large glass doors leading inside, her cell phone chirped in her pocket. She pulled it out, swiped to unlock it, and peered down at the screen.

Aiden:

You home?

Charlotte:

Nope. Grabbing lunch.

Aiden:

Where?

Her forehead wrinkled, and her eyes darted around behind her shades. Instinct told her he wasn't far away. How she knew, she wasn't sure. Still, it pleased her he had come all the way to Athens to see her. It may have been presumptuous of her to assume that, but what other explanation could there be? He did mention coming, even if she objected to the idea.

Charlotte:
In front of the Tate Building.
Aiden:
I have no idea where that is.

Well, that confirmed her suspicions of his whereabouts.

Charlotte:
Where are you?

When several minutes passed without response, she started to call him, but another message popped up.

Aiden:
Someone told me where it is. Hang on.

Hang on? How long did he want her to wait? The campus was huge. He could be anywhere.

She moved away from the main entrance, seeking shade from the bright sun beneath a tree while she waited for his call or text.

"Did you get his number?"

"No way. I couldn't ask him that."

"He was gorgeous. I would have asked for it."

"Did you see his eyes?"

"His eyelashes are better than mine."

She rolled her eyes as she listened to the feminine voices approaching from behind. How nice it would be to giggle and gossip about college boys instead of looking over her shoulder for threats. She envied them.

The two girls passed her tree and then paused on the walkway, glancing behind them.

"Oh shit, he's coming this way!" The one on the right giggled.

"Shhh! He probably can hear you," the other chastised, swatting at her friend. "Of course he's coming this way. He asked for the Tate Building."

The one on the left covered her mouth, and they took off at a brisk pace. Charlotte suspected they didn't want to be caught gossiping.

Moments later, Aiden passed her, striding toward the Tate Building's main entrance with purpose.

She couldn't stop the smile that spread across her face as she watched him look all around himself searching for her. It made her feel good.

"Aiden!"

He turned as she strode toward him, but her steps faltered at the scowl on his face. He shoved his phone in his pocket and came toward her.

Without a word, he reached out and pulled her close, wrapping his arms around her, pinning her arms to her side, pressing her face into his broad chest. "I'm glad you're alright."

She laughed. "What are you talking about?"

He smelled like ice cream and cologne. The combination settled her nerves better than her medication ever could. She didn't even know she needed it until his arms banded around her.

This was new.

When he let her go, she stepped back and looked up at him, pushing her sunglasses on top of her head.

"You seemed really afraid the last time we talked, and I didn't hear from you at all yesterday. With you mentioning someone following you…" He scratched the side of his neck and looked around. "And we're out for our summer break as of Friday, so it wasn't a big deal to borrow Mom's car because she won't have classes to teach tomorrow…" He blew out a harsh breath. "I just wanted to see you were okay with my own eyes. Maybe I overreacted. Sorry."

"Why? You're fine. You've just never hugged me before, that's all."

"I haven't?"

She rolled her eyes and pulled her shades down to hide the blush spreading heat over her cheeks. "Nope."

"Does it bother you?"

"Your sister does it every time I see her." *You're not attracted to his sister, though.* "Why would it bother me?"

He tucked his hands in his jean pockets. "Alright." His lips tilted into a half smile. "I'll keep that in mind."

She dropped her gaze down to her sandals, tucking her curls behind her ear.

"So what's for lunch?"

Her head snapped up. "Oh. Um. I dunno. I didn't even plan to go out today and waste money, but I haven't gone grocery shopping, and what's at the apartment sucks."

"Why don't I take you—"

"Hey, Charlotte."

Aiden looked over her head as she turned around.

"Oh hey, Noah. What are you doing…" Her words died as she took in Noah's appearance. His lip had a severe split, and extensive swelling and bruising trailed from his right eye down to his jaw and across his cheekbone. “Oh my god, what happened?”

Noah chuckled and then winced when his smile pulled his split lip. “Got my ass handed to me.”

“Obviously. But how? Who?”

Inhaling through his nose, Noah shook his head. “It’s not important. Got ahead of myself. Won’t happen again.” His eyes flicked up from her face to Aiden before dismissing him. “What are you doing out here?”

She didn’t like how he avoided her question, but she wouldn’t push it.

“Going to grab lunch in the Tate Building, but Aiden showed up.” She motioned over her shoulder to where Aiden had taken a step closer to her back.

“Aiden? The guy you mentioned in class?”

Aiden arched a black brow at Charlotte, and his lips tipped up in a teasing grin. “You talking about me?”

“No! I mean, yes, but it wasn’t anything bad. Rachel did most of the talking.”

“Color me curious,” he said, chuckling.

“Well, I’m starving,” Noah said, interrupting them. “Wanna get something together?”

“Um.” She turned and looked between him and Aiden. “What do you wanna do? You drove all this way.”

The way Aiden stood staring at Noah with narrowed eyes made her shift from foot to foot in discomfort. Noah had the same sour look on his face. Their dislike for each other was clear, but she couldn’t understand why.

“Uh, guys?”

Aiden looked down at her, his harsh expression clearing. He

smiled. “I thought I’d get us set up to play back at your apartment. If you want to grab a bite and then meet me there? Or I can come back and pick you up?”

“Apartment?” Noah asked.

Aiden’s eyes moved up to Noah and his face went stony. “Yes, apartment. I’m here to play video games with Charlotte for the day.”

“Ah, yeah? I didn’t know you were into gaming.” Noah looked from Aiden to her as a haughty smile spread across Aiden’s face.

She shrugged. “Oh, yeah. It’s fun.” She had never shared with Noah her love of video games. She didn’t know why, but she didn’t tell many people outside those down in Rosebrook whom she considered close friends. Like Aiden, Riley, and Blaire.

The crackling atmosphere as the two guys stared at each other over her head made her tense and uncomfortable. She didn’t know what their problem was, but she’d never seen Aiden like this before. Agitated was the only word to describe his body language and the tense set of his shoulders. His forehead kept lining when he couldn’t keep his expression neutral. What made him so upset?

If she didn’t separate them, Noah might end up with another black eye.

Noah looked like he might throw a punch himself.

She’d never seen either of them like this before.

Thinking fast, she dug her apartment keys out of her purse and handed them to Aiden. “Here. Take these and get set up. I’ll grab a quick bite with Noah and be there soon. Want me to get you anything?”

He took the keys and looked down at her with that swoon-worthy smile he used when he gave someone his full attention. “I’m good. I’ll take you out for groceries later, since I have the car. A lot easier than taking the bus with it.”

"You don't have to."

"I want to."

"Okay," she said with a nod. Her face warmed again at his words.

He cared so much for people and took care of them. It made her feel warm and fuzzy, even knowing it wasn't preferential treatment. Aiden was altogether a kindhearted guy.

"Don't be long," he said, before turning and striding away from them, gripping her keys in his hand tightly.

"You sure he isn't your boyfriend?"

She turned to Noah. "What?"

"You said in class he was single, but he acted like a jealous boyfriend just now."

She giggled. "No way. You're imagining things."

Noah's dark brow arched. "Really? He didn't seem to like me talking to you very much."

She posted her fists on her hips and cocked her head. "You didn't seem to like him either."

He shrugged. "I'm indifferent. I don't know him."

"Well, you were looking at him the same way he looked at you."

"Huh. Didn't know that."

She decided pushing the subject wouldn't do much good. If he didn't realize the way he acted, then she may have misunderstood. It wasn't like either of the guys would see each other again.

"Come on, let's get a burrito," he said, motioning toward the Tate Building.

As he led her toward the main entrance, he kept looking behind them with a strange expression on his face.

11

Confession

The door to Charlotte's apartment flew open. Startled, Aiden jumped up from the loveseat, ready to fight whoever rushed into her home unannounced.

Slamming the door, Charlotte locked the deadbolt and doorknob with jerky movements. She checked and double-checked the locks, slamming her hands on the door and dropping her head forward between her shoulders. Her ragged breathing was loud in the quiet room.

He took a tentative step toward her. "Charlotte?"

Her shoulders tensed before easing, as if she hadn't recognized him at first. Turning and pressing her back to the door, she looked at him across the room.

He hadn't moved, afraid to frighten her more than she already looked.

Her purse fell from her shoulder when she pushed off the door and ran to him, crashing into his body. He wrapped his arms around her shaking form and stared down at the top of her head, surprised by the sudden physical contact.

He'd hugged her earlier, overwhelmed by the worry he felt after she revealed someone had been following her. He hadn't been able to stop himself.

"What happened? Did that guy do something to you?"

Taking a deep inhale, she stepped out of his embrace. Losing her body heat bothered him, but he didn't have time to question the realization.

Sparkling green eyes looked up at him. "No. Noah's fine." She looked back at the door and then around Aiden at the sliding glass door. Moving around him, she climbed onto the loveseat to check the lock on the sliding glass door. She slumped, exhaling as she pressed her forehead to the back of the loveseat.

"Charlotte."

Her head snapped up, and she spun on the loveseat. "I think someone followed me home."

"What?" He looked back at the door. "Hang on." He turned. He didn't know what he would do when he found the piece of trash who thought it was okay to follow a woman around, but he had a few ideas.

When the sharp sting of nails pinched his arm, he looked down. She held his forearm in a death grip, looking up at him with wide, pleading eyes.

"Don't go. I'm sure they're gone now."

He looked at the door and back again.

She added in a soft whisper that he almost missed, "Please stay."

A faint tremor wracked her hands as she held onto him tightly. Abandoning her in this state was out of the question for him. He could practically taste her fear saturating the air.

With a nod, he decided changing the subject and shifting her focus away from the scary encounter might be the best course of action. “Something came for you while you were at lunch.” He glanced at the kitchen. “I signed for it. I hope that’s alright.”

She finally released her grip on his arm and stood, already calmer now that he agreed to stay. “A package? I wonder if it’s from my moms.”

“Nah. It was from a flower shop.” He paused, watching the color drain from her face. “Uh… The delivery guy said normally he leaves them at your door, but since I was here, he had me sign.” His stomach tensed as he took in the look on her face.

“Where is it?” Her voice sounded hoarse. She swallowed, and after clearing her throat, she spoke clearer. “Where are the roses?”

He didn’t specify roses.

“On the kitchen counter next to your other vase of similar ones.”

She pushed around him and raced to the kitchen, staring down at the bouquet of roses lying on the counter next to the vase of wilted ones.

He had wondered why she kept half-dead roses in a vase when he arrived earlier, but now he questioned the identical bouquet, and why she seemed almost frightened by it.

“What’s going on?”

She turned her face up to the ceiling, closing her eyes and muttering something under her breath. When she opened her eyes and looked down again, she unceremoniously scooped the dying roses from the vase and tossed them in her garbage bin. She emptied the vase, and then filled it with fresh water, mixing in the packet of powder that came with the roses.

Plant food? He assumed it was plant food.

She pulled a pair of scissors from the drawer. Unraveling the wrapping around the new roses, she clipped each of the stems at an angle.

Since she wasn't answering him, he tried something else. "Why are you cutting them?"

"Makes them live longer."

"How so?"

"Well, it prevents blockages. Cutting at an angle makes more surface area for water to be absorbed." At his bewildered expression, she picked up a rose she hadn't cut and dropped it into the vase, then another that had been cut. "See how the uncut one sits flush on the bottom and the other one doesn't?"

"Uh huh…"

"If it's against the glass, the stem doesn't soak up much water. The angle," she said, motioning to the cut rose in the water, "has the entire cut area exposed to water. If I left the rose in there like this, it would have the best chance of survival versus the other. Something Ma taught me." She plucked out the uncut rose, snipped the end, and dropped it back in the water.

He never gave consideration to flowers and their longevity before. His mother liked to have flowers in their family home, but he never messed with them. Though, he did know a lot about outdoor flowers from listening to her gardening shows while he did homework when he lived at home.

Still, he knew Charlotte was deflecting from something. No one looked that horrified by a flower delivery for no reason and then stuck them in a vase to display.

When she finished cutting the stems and arranging the roses, she disposed of the waste in the garbage. She turned around and looked up at him with an exasperated sigh. "What?"

He stood in front of her, arms crossed, feet spread. Riley liked to call it his intimidation stance, but he thought little of it. He simply wasn't backing down. "Tell me why you reacted like that."

"Like what?" She adjusted the vase and took a washcloth, wiping the counter to clean up the remaining debris from her flower arranging.

"Like instead of a flower delivery, someone delivered a bomb."

She looked over her shoulder, her mouth parting slightly. "A bomb?"

He shrugged. "Something that spooked you, I dunno."

"Yeah, well, it's fine." She rinsed the washcloth and wrung it out, draping it over the side of the sink to dry. "I don't know what you want me to say."

"How about what's really going on?"

"It won't make a difference," she said, her shoulders lowering with her exhalation.

He didn't like the idea of pushing her and making the genuine uneasiness she carried worse, but he needed to know. How could he fix it if he didn't know?

"It will. If anything, you'll feel better if you talk about it." He glanced toward the living room. "I'm piecing together things, but I'd rather hear it from you."

"What do you mean?"

"For starters, the loveseat blocking the only other door into the apartment." He lifted his chin toward the loveseat. "You said someone's following you. How long has that been going on?"

She wrapped her arms around her middle and stepped into the living room. "I don't know when it started. Not long after I started at UGA."

"What?"

"Someone's been following—"

"No, I heard you." His fingers twitched at his side as his agitation grew. "I'm just trying to figure out why in the hell didn't you tell someone before now. What were you thinking?" He'd never spoken to her like this. Never felt irritated with her. Judging by the incredulous look on her face, she did *not* like it.

In reality, he felt mostly irritated with the situation, but the lines blurred when he considered she didn't tell someone and left herself in danger.

"Seriously?" She crossed her arms and glared at him. "It's not my fault. I wasn't thinking. I wasn't even sure it was for real until the jerk started sending roses."

He opened his mouth to speak, but her glare made him snap it shut.

"And for your information, when he broke into my apartment when I was on the call with you, I went to the police the next day."

Good. At least she didn't ignore the seriousness of the situation and sought help. He felt a pang of remorse for getting upset with her, considering the effort she made to confess that her discomfort about staying here went beyond her major.

He blew out a long breath, recentering himself, and schooled his voice. "What did they say?"

Her shoulder hitched, and his eyes zeroed in on the redness on the bare skin along the thick straps of her tank top. He wondered if she got sunburn waiting for him when he texted.

"They took the report. Came and did a sweep of my apartment that lasted forever and said to keep in touch if anything else happened. Said they'd contact me if they discovered anything from the security footage. Nothing turned up when they looked into the flower delivery service."

"Nothing?" His brows rose in surprise.

"Nothing," she said flatly. "I called the lieutenant assigned to my case this morning to follow up, and he told me the flower shop security system had been on the fritz lately, and every two days they wipe the tapes to reuse."

He leaned against the kitchen counter and crossed his arms. "What about records of who made the orders?"

"That's the weirdest thing." She shook her head, putting her hands on her hips and pacing in front of him. "They have zero paperwork on anyone requesting anything delivered to this address." She spun and pointed at him. "And before you ask, I asked about reoccurring pink rose deliveries, because surely someone would remember large bouquets of pink roses every week for weeks, right?" When he nodded, she said, "Well, the lieutenant had the same idea. When he asked about it, no one working there had any clue what he was talking about." She threw up her hands. "No one! Not even the manager! How screwed is that?"

The news raised every red flag in the back of Aiden's mind. The only time he knew of human businesses lacking a paper trail, coupled with no memories of events that undoubtedly happened, Vasirian were involved. Did one of his kin use compulsion to cover their tracks—or at least cover the stalker's tracks? It made little sense. Why would a Vasirian invest themselves in a random human to that degree? Maybe he was overthinking it, but usually his instincts didn't lead him astray.

He would need to be vigilant and keep an eye on her. She already had one Vasirian sniffing around her; she didn't need another. In truth, she didn't need any, but he disliked the idea of distancing himself from her.

Even if he couldn't reveal things to her, she meant something to Blaire and had worked her way into his and his friends' lives to where it felt *wrong* to not have her there. He wished he could include her more, but it would put her in danger, and they would lose her entirely when the Blackthorn Clan erased her memory for knowing of their existence.

She stomped over to the refrigerator and flung open the freezer door, sticking her head inside. "If this idiot doesn't drive me off, the broken air conditioning will." Her voice sounded muffled in the freezer.

He chuckled, watching her.

"What sucks even more?" She pulled her head out of the freezer and slammed the door shut. "I can't even get a protective order against the person because I have no idea who it is!" She slumped against the wall beside the refrigerator. "I don't know what to do."

He pushed off the counter and strode toward her. She craned her head back to look up at him. She was so small—so vulnerable. The closer they became to one another, the more he saw glimpses of the fiery disposition she kept pushed down. He saw it surface from time to time with Blaire. It seemed she needed to be comfortable with someone before she allowed herself to be open. He wondered what made her filter herself.

"Why not come home? I mean, back to Rosebrook Valley. I know you said you wanted to stick it out, but…"

"But what?" She straightened, moving off the wall, almost brushing her chest against his ribs. He stepped back to give her space.

"But this is bigger than uncertainty about your major."

She moved away from where they stood in front of the refrigerator to the door. Picking up the purse she dropped in her panic, she placed it on the counter. "I can't."

"Why not? Your moms would understand—especially if you tell them about all this."

Her head swung to stare at him, eyes widened in alarm. "Hard no. They can't know about any of this."

"Again, why?"

He didn't understand what her reservations were about leaving Athens, and even more so, what made her hesitant to share this with her parents when she went to the police already. Did she not want to leave because of that guy he met earlier, Noah? The idea set his teeth on edge, but he had no claim to her.

"I don't want to worry them." She stepped in front of the kitchen sink and began sorting the dishes drying in a plastic drainer. "I can handle this." She opened a cabinet overhead. "I'm an adult." She placed a clean glass in a neat line with several others on the shelf. "I can't run to Mom and Ma every time something goes wrong." She closed the cabinet. "They have enough on their plate without me adding to it when I'm the one who insisted on attending UGA."

She recited her reasons like rehearsed bullet points; he wondered if she reminded herself of these things often. It didn't have to be so black and white.

Unable to watch her spiral, he stepped up behind her and clamped his hands on her shoulders, startling her. Had she forgotten he was even there?

"It's okay. It's not important now," he murmured, lowering his head next to hers, trying to sound soothing to help ease the tension in her muscles under his hands. He didn't understand what was going on, but he didn't enjoy seeing her distressed. "Let's go pick up some groceries so you don't have to deal with that later, and then play some video games. Gaming was the plan, remember?"

Dropping the cloth in her hand, she nodded. "I think I'd like that," she said in a neutral voice, unlike her usual self.

The grocery shopping didn't take long. She had all the little extras already, like condiments and spices. They primarily stocked up on things like meat, produce, dairy, and snacks, grabbing a little extra for their game night.

He couldn't imagine how she brought everything home herself—on the bus, no less. He suspected she didn't get as much when she went alone, and she confirmed this when she told him she frequented the grocery store more than once a week.

Once they packed everything away, they finished setting up for their evening of fun, only stopping to have an early dinner of chicken pineapple wraps Charlotte toasted on the portable indoor grill that fit on her kitchen counter.

The time flew as they lost themselves to the chaos of fending off monsters and collecting all the rewards in the different games they played.

Only when he got up and went to the bathroom did he notice the night sky through the crack in the curtains pulled closed over the sliding glass doors in her living room.

Pulling his phone from his jeans, he frowned at the display. He hadn't meant to still be in town this late.

"What's wrong?" she asked, glancing up at him from where she sat cross-legged on the floor in front of her TV with a controller in her hand. They had started gaming on their computers but switched to consoles around dinner time.

"It's ten o'clock."

"Already?" She grabbed her phone from where it lay face down on the floor. She hadn't touched it all night. "Crap. Aiden, that's too late for you to drive home."

"Not really. I'll probably get there around two in the morning."

"That's too late, especially passing Atlanta. You can stay here."

"I can't—"

"You *can*. You're gonna be so tired."

As if summoned by her words, he yawned and she raised a brow at him as if to say "See, told you so." He groaned.

He had hardly slept, and the situation was deteriorating. He'd hate to fall asleep behind the wheel. Even if the likelihood of him being okay because of his rapid healing, he didn't want to ruin his mom's car.

She had told him to keep the car for a couple of days anyway since she didn't have classes to teach, and she wanted to do some deep cleaning of the house and wouldn't need to go anywhere.

"Fine. Sure. I'll take the couch."

"What?" She looked at the loveseat against the sliding glass doors and back at him. "Tell me you're joking."

"No? What's wrong?"

"What are you, like six three? Four?"

"Six two."

"Well, it feels like more since I only come up to your shoulders."

He wasn't as tall as Lukas and Kai, but he understood. Charlotte was as short as his little sister, and Riley always had something to say about his height.

"What about it?"

"It's a loveseat, Aiden. It's not a full-size couch. It's like the perfect length for me to lie down on, not you."

"I can make it work."

"And I would feel uncomfortable knowing I had a full bed to myself while you were subjected to that."

He scratched his jaw. "So should I go then?"

She set the controller down and stood. "No. You should take the bed and I'll take the loveseat."

"I'm not putting you out of your bed."

"No, you're accepting my gracious offer of a more comfortable place to sleep," she said matter-of-factly, as if that solved everything.

"I'm not letting you sleep on the loveseat in your own home."

Her hands went to her hips. "And I'm not letting you sleep on it, either."

They stared one another down and for the life of him, he couldn't understand what the big deal was. It's not like he hadn't slept on a couch before. He was trying to be a gentleman by not letting her sleep on living room furniture in her own place.

Seeing that he wouldn't get anywhere with the firm resolve written all over her face, he sighed. *This has to be a redhead thing, or maybe a short girl thing, since Riley is just as stubborn.*

"I'll sleep in the bed under one condition."

"Name it," she fired back, a triumphant look on her face.

"You sleep in the bed too."

Her arched brows raised as her mouth gaped. Maybe he shouldn't have proposed that solution, but he didn't want to put her out.

"You want us both to… to…" She rolled her hand in front of her as if encouraging him to finish the sentence she couldn't complete herself.

"Sleep together, yes."

"Right." Her laugh was breathy as she dropped her hand and turned away from him. "It's a logical solution," she said, her voice pitched higher.

"If you're not comfortable—"

She turned back to face him and waved a hand, trying to seem indifferent, but her body seemed wound tighter than a coil. "No, I'm fine. Fine. Really. I've just never slept in the same bed as a guy before. Kinda caught me off-guard there."

"Never?"

"Nope."

"Well, we could put pillows between us if it makes you feel better."

Her gaze shifted to the floor, and she shook her head from side to side. "No, it's not that big of a deal. We're adults. We can share a bed without being weird about it. We're friends, right?"

"Right."

He hated the sliver of disappointment at her words. Of course they were friends. They couldn't be more than friends without him hurting her in the future, when he couldn't give her more than a fling.

"Right. So, you don't have extra clothes, do you?"

"No, but I can always wear this again tomorrow."

"Gross. No. It's way too hot, and after driving up here and being in this hot apartment, I'm sure you're sweaty." She motioned to the closed door on the wall that divided the space between her bedroom and the living room. "I can wash your stuff for tomorrow."

"What will I sleep in?"

Her lips twisted, and then her face flushed pink. "Um. Well." Her face flamed brighter. "You know what? Never mind. I can wash them tomorrow before you go. I can't do them while you shower, anyway. Yet another thing I need to discuss with maintenance tomorrow. Hot water dies too fast if I run a load while showering."

"What were you going to say?"

"Huh?"

"Before the stuff about the hot water."

"It's nothing. We have a solution."

"Still wanna know what you were going to say." He crossed his arms and tilted his head, studying her blush again. Her flustered expression increased his curiosity.

"Wasgonnaaskifyou'reaboxerorbriefguy," she rambled off so fast he didn't make it out clearly.

"Do what now?"

She huffed in exasperation. "I was *going* to ask if you were a boxer or brief guy. Happy?"

"Yes. And to answer you, it depends on the day and if I'm wearing my uniform, jeans, shorts… Sometimes boxers, sometimes boxer briefs, never briefs." He shrugged like it wasn't a big deal as he watched her freckles stand out against the growing blush on her pale skin. He tried to keep amusement from his voice and said in a casual tone, "Why did you want to know?"

"Figured if it wasn't… revealing… you could sleep in it. Like boxers are similar to shorts. Oh my god, just let it go."

He snorted a laugh. He couldn't help it. Her shyness felt refreshing and cute, and the way she tried to hide it emphasized the tough kitten act he felt from her before.

"I can't believe you're laughing at me."

"I'm not laughing at you. I'm laughing with—no, yeah, I guess I am laughing at you." He laughed again. "I'm sorry, but you remind me of a kitten. All adorable but temperamental."

"Kitten?" She stared at him. "I am nothing like a kitten."

"Whatever you say." He rolled his lips in and got himself under control while she moved around him to straighten up the kitchen from their dinner. "To answer, I've got boxers on today."

She looked over her shoulder at him and he didn't miss when her gaze flicked down to his jeans and back. The move aimed to be subtle. If he'd blinked, he'd have missed it—but he caught it.

She resumed towel drying the plates they used, returning them to the cabinet. "If you want to shower and sleep in them, it's fine. It's just shorts. I'll shower when you finish. It'll give me the chance to clean up and get the room ready. I need to get up early tomorrow to visit the office about the air and water."

The shower did little to cool him off once he stepped out and dried off. The air conditioning was on. He felt it in the bedroom when he moved in there to sit on the side of her bed while she took her shower.

When he came out, she was in the living room and didn't even look up at him. She said to leave his clothes at the laundry door, and she'd start it before coming to bed. He hoped he didn't make her uncomfortable by wearing only his underwear, but she was the one who suggested it.

The bathroom door clicked when he settled on the bed. The sounds of the shower filtered through the walls of the apartment.

He smelled like her now. At least partially. Not having his own bath products left him using hers, which didn't match the pineapple upside down cake scent she wore throughout the day. Possibly a perfume. Her body wash and shampoo smelled like coconut and vanilla. At least it complimented the perfume and didn't blend to a stomach-turning concoction some women wore.

He lay back on the bed and shut his eyes, listening to the sound of the water.

They'd had fun tonight, but the reality of what she faced with her unwanted admirer still weighed heavily on his mind. If she had a genuine stalker, he needed to convince her to return home, but he didn't know how. She had limited opportunities to continue her education down there at a physical school. He didn't know enough about her career path to know if she could do it online, but he assumed she'd considered that option already.

The water turned off, and he listened to her moving around in the bathroom before coming out and moving to the kitchen, running the tap, and then moving to the laundry.

He couldn't see her, and didn't know what all she was doing, but knew she was headed his way when the laundry door shut.

When he heard a sharp intake of air, he opened his eyes to find her standing a couple of feet away from the side of the bed, staring at his bare chest. He didn't make a sound to let her know he was awake, not wanting to embarrass her as her bright malachite eyes did a slow perusal of his bare chest to his abs.

He knew he had a nice physique. He wasn't cocky about it. He simply worked hard to achieve it because it made him feel good about himself. Lifted weights in his dorm. Ran around the perimeter of the campus frequently. Went to a local gym occasionally if time permitted, which in the last year, it hadn't.

When her eyes traveled from his stomach and down to his boxers, he needed to give her a sign he was awake before another part of him did the job for him. Her dilated pupils and change in breathing let him know she wasn't unaffected by his appearance, and that knowledge made his cock twitch. He needed to do something before they both ended up embarrassed.

He shifted, groaning, and reached up to run a hand over his face as if waking up. As if he'd fallen asleep while waiting.

She flinched, and he slowly sat up.

"Finished?"

Her face appeared redder than earlier, and she cleared her throat, toying with the hem of her sleep shorts. The same little striped pair she wore on FaceTime one night, only in white and lime green instead of baby blue. The green matching spaghetti strap tank top did little to hide her response to seeing him half naked. He turned his gaze away before she caught him staring at her breasts. He'd overheard her complaining to Riley about men doing that.

"Yeah, the clothes are in the dryer." She looked at the nightstand.

"Dryer? Didn't you need to wash them?" He leaned forward and rested his elbows on his knees.

"I threw them in when I jumped in the shower. I had a shower this morning and washed my hair and all, so I only needed to wash the day off my body. The hot water would last for that." She shrugged. "I didn't want to wait up to move the clothes between the washer and dryer, and the cycle isn't long. Oh, and it shouldn't get too hot. I'm running the air-dry cycle. I think that puts out less heat? I dunno for sure."

"Fair enough. What side do you want?"

She twisted her toes on the area rug that took up most of the bedroom floor as she shrugged. "I can take the far side next to the window, since you're already on this one."

He stood as she stepped forward, which brought them almost flush with one another. She looked up at him, and he wondered if she could hear how hard his heart hammered at the proximity. Something about her got him twisted inside—it had been that way for months, becoming worse the more they got to know one another. And standing so close together with so little clothing threatened his normal composure.

He cleared his throat and stepped to the side, allowing her to pull back the covers and climb into bed, scooting to the far side.

She turned away from him, which was fortunate because they were teetering on a perilous edge, and he didn't want to jeopardize their friendship with a relationship that couldn't be serious.

He climbed back into bed and settled under the covers, reaching out to turn the lamp off and plunging the room into total darkness. She didn't even leave the stove light on to illuminate the space to get to the bathroom. It made the space cooler, but he wondered if it made her uncomfortable to sleep in blackness when someone knew where she lived.

"Goodnight, Charlotte."

"Night, Aiden," she mumbled, sounding half-asleep already.

He was in hell.

Aiden didn't even believe in hell, but if it existed, this was it. It was the only way to describe his predicament.

At some point in the night, Charlotte had kicked the covers off and buried him in them—which had him sweating and sticking to the sheets. Not how he wanted to wake up from yet another nightmare.

But that wasn't even the worst part.

She apparently became possessed in her sleep. Currently, he had five tiny toes with pastel purple nail polish in his face. She lay turned with her head at the foot of the bed, one arm on the bed above her head, the other hanging off the end. Her legs were spread eagle, with one across his chest placing her foot in his face, while the other foot rested on her pillow.

He attempted to shift away, but she kicked her foot out, jamming her toes into his nose. He had to bite the inside of his lip and grit his teeth to keep from yelling out and waking her.

He lifted his hand and gently gripped her foot to avoid another incident, moving it from his face so he could slide out of bed. Placing her foot on his pillow, he stretched, making his back pop.

Her thrashing in her sleep had pulled aside the curtain on the bedroom window, allowing ambient moonlight to illuminate the bed.

The apartment felt cooler than it did earlier when they were awake. With the lights off, and the lack of activity, the air conditioning didn't have to work as hard to cool the space. Still, being buried under an entire comforter and the matching sheets next to another heat-generating person had his skin soaked. Sweat ran down his spine.

He crept on silent feet to the bathroom so as not to wake her and closed the door behind him before turning on the light, squinting as he adjusted to the sudden brightness.

After relieving himself of his full bladder, he moved to the sink. Splashing water on his face, he peered into the mirror, checking his nose for blood. The girl had one hell of a kick. He wondered if she played soccer back in high school.

Shaking the thoughts, he dried his face and took in his surroundings.

She kept her bathroom neat and tidy. The counter space didn't compare to what the larger ensuite bathrooms Blackthorn Academy gave their students. The space accommodated only a sparkly toothbrush holder, a wide-tooth comb, a few hair ties, and a small black bag adorned with silver stars and moons, which he assumed contained cosmetics. A purple hairdryer hooked over the towel rack had a strange round attachment on the end like a trumpet with teeth. He wondered what she used it for.

He folded the towel he used for his face and put it over the larger towel on the rack to keep her space neat. The black towels matched both the cosmetic bag and the shower curtain, which had the same silver celestial design. Even the toilet seat cover and floor mat were black.

When he helped her move in months ago, he noticed her penchant for celestial decorations. Even her comforter followed the same stylistic choice in black with white moons, planets, and constellations.

The entire apartment held her personal touch, and he hated that someone had violated her space even a little.

Tomorrow, he needed to revisit the conversation about returning home. It wasn't like she couldn't get a place in Rosebrook Valley and give it her personal touch. Hopefully tomorrow she would be in better spirits to have that conversation.

Either way, if he wasn't returning home straight away, he needed to find a local clinic with Vasirian on staff. He hadn't had blood since before the drive up to Athens yesterday morning. He'd never gone twenty-four hours without blood, and it would push his limits to wait, but she needed him.

He rubbed his tired eyes. He needed a decent night's sleep. It wasn't even her fault. If he hadn't had the nightmare, he wouldn't have stirred at all, even with her thrashing.

Turning off the light, he returned to bed.

Charlotte had moved from her position and now was at risk of rolling off his side of the bed.

Scooping her up bridal style, he put a knee on the bed and leaned down to place her gently on her side of the bed, brushing a few curls from her face as he released her.

He stood, looking down at her sleeping form.

She looked beautiful lying beneath the moonlight, her fair skin on display in her dainty sleepwear. He didn't think she wore it because of him, but more to stave off the heat.

His eyes trailed down across her hip and over the expanse of her legs, giving her his appreciative perusal like she'd given him earlier.

If he were more poetic, he could articulate how lovely she looked in that moment, but the best his sleep-deprived brain could conjure was how her skin looked smooth and decadent—like the filling of a Cadbury Creme Egg.

He immediately cringed at the thought. *Not creepy and inaccurate at all.* His stomach growled, and he rolled his eyes.

Riley had given him a Cadbury Egg from her candy stash before he made the drive north, and now his stomach hijacked his fatigued mind. Great.

Charlotte's skin was smooth, yes, but it looked nothing like yellowy goo.

Pushing aside the ridiculous thoughts, he fixed the twisted bedding and climbed beneath, gaze drifting around the moonlit bedroom.

As soon as his head hit the pillow, she shifted and threw her arm across his chest, hitching her leg over his hip.

At least she wasn't kicking him in the face anymore.

He looped his arm around her shoulder, soaking in the comfort it gave him to have someone by his side. Someone he enjoyed being around. Maybe it would help him sleep better. If not, at least he wasn't alone while he stared at a blank ceiling until morning.

Anything beat being trapped in a cycle of fear, knowing every time he fell asleep, he would die all over again.

12

Hostage

The sound of running water made Charlotte groan. She wasn't ready to get out of bed, but the sound made her bladder perk up and demand attention.

She rolled over and buried her face in the plush pillow next to her, breathing in the delicious smell of citrus and vanilla mixed with a hint of coconut like her body wash.

It came back to her in fragments as the soothing scent of creamy orange permeated her senses.

Someone had followed her home.

The roses.

Aiden.

Aiden staying the night.

Aiden sharing a bed with her.

She bolted upright and looked around the empty, quiet room. She wondered why she thought she heard water. What had she been dreaming about?

Sunlight streamed through the window onto her bed, and she moved to her knees, inching toward the window to close out the offensive brightness before collapsing back on the bed.

He left.

Of course he left.

The only reason he stayed was because it was too late to drive. Now that morning had come, there was no reason for him to stay.

She chastised herself for the pang of disappointment that gave her.

Her stomach cramped, telling her to get out of bed. It wasn't her cycle—that had come and gone last week. She was free from Shark Week for another month. No, if she didn't get out of bed, she'd need to wash the sheets for an entirely different reason.

She rolled over to grab her phone, noticing a piece of paper tucked beneath it with neat handwriting.

Couldn't sleep. I'll see you soon.

She wondered how long it would be before she could see Aiden again in person and not on FaceTime or video chat online.

Checking the time on her phone, she sighed. Almost noon. Management never stayed in the building past noon. They went to lunch and took off, leaving only the phone service open to submit requests. She'd have to do that after she emptied her bladder.

Dragging herself out of bed, she stretched and relished the popping sounds her spine made.

It had been a while since she had a decent sleep. She didn't think she would with Aiden in the bed, but not once did she wake to noises like usual, worrying that her own personal boogeyman had come to visit.

Her phone chirped in her hand, and she looked down at the notification. Monique had sent a text to the group chat.

Monique:

Bad news. Professor Landers has food poisoning and has rescheduled all presentations until Friday.

Rachel:

Hell yeah. I was on my way to campus, now I can go shopping. See you bitches Friday.

Noah:

K

She exhaled a relieved breath. She'd forgotten all about the presentation today, with Aiden dropping by. At least she didn't have to go to campus at all today.

She tapped out a hasty reply as her bladder urged her fingers to type faster.

Only when she headed toward the bathroom did she realize she wasn't alone. The sounds of someone moving around in the bathroom filtered through her wall. It couldn't be Aiden; he left already. That only left one other possibility...

She rushed to the nightstand and jerked the drawer open, grabbing the chef's knife she now kept on top of her journal. She knew keeping it there would come in handy.

Picking up her cell phone, she dialed emergency services. The sound in the bathroom stopped; he was waiting to ambush her. The bathroom had no other exit.

She wished Aiden hadn't left.

"Athens-Clarke County—"

"Someone's in my apartment," she whispered with an edge

of distress, cutting off the male dispatcher. She crept toward the bathroom.

"Who's in your apartment?"

"I don't know."

"Can you see them?"

"No, they're hiding in my bathroom." She tried to keep the panic out of her voice while she tightened her grip on the knife's handle.

"What's your name?"

"Charlotte Walsh."

"Okay, Charlotte. I'm going to get officers to you as soon as possible."

"Okay," she whispered, inching toward the wall separating her bedroom from the bathroom.

"What is your address?"

She rattled off the address to her apartment and moved against the wall to see if she could hear anything.

"Charlotte? Are you still with me?"

"Yes," she whispered.

"Do you know if he's armed?"

"No. I don't know. I can't see him. I have a knife, though."

"Are you able to leave the apartment?"

"Yes. Uh. I-I don't know." She looked at the front door. Her voice quavered, her eyes stinging, as she said, "He'll hear me." She didn't like how fear held her hostage more than the man in her home.

"Can you get to your neighbors?"

"Yes."

"I want you to put the knife down, quietly exit your apartment. Go to your nearest neighbors until officers arrive."

Taking a long inhale through her nose, she nodded. She was fine. It would be fine. "Okay."

"Can you call me back when you get there?"

"I'm on my cell. I can take it with me."

"Okay. Good."

When she pushed away from the wall and crept across the smooth tiles of the kitchen floor toward the front door, the bathroom door swung open and she screamed, spinning around and holding the knife up in front of her.

Aiden stood in the empty doorway with wide eyes, hand still gripping the knob.

"Oh my god," she said, choking on the sob she held back the entire phone call. "What is *wrong* with you?"

She still held the knife in front of her, but with how hard she trembled, it wouldn't have intimidated anyone.

"—Charlotte? Charlotte! Are you okay?"

She started at the voice, forgetting she had the dispatcher on the line.

"Yeah, yeah. I'm okay," she said, breathless. She needed to push her heart back into her chest where it tried to burst through her chest cavity; but otherwise, sure, she felt *fine*.

"What is happening?"

"My idiot friend was in the bathroom. I *thought* he went home this morning." Her eyes narrowed, giving a shell-shocked Aiden a pointed look.

"Are you sure?"

"Yes, I'm sure. I'm looking at him right now." She deflated a little, feeling stupid for calling. "I'm so sorry. I don't need help." She felt terrible wasting resources and wondered if she'd get in trouble for wasting their time.

"Not necessary. It's better to be safe than sorry."

A heavy knock sounded at the door, and she spun with a yelp, dropping the knife.

"Athens-Clarke County Police," said a muffled male voice from the hall.

"The police are here," Charlotte said to the dispatcher, and Aiden's brows rose. "That was fast."

"Open the door. Even with a false alarm, if they are already there, let them know you're alright. They'll just check that everything is okay and be on their way." The man on the line sounded calm and reassuring, so she hoped it meant she wouldn't be in trouble. "I'm going to hang up now. Take care of yourself, Charlotte."

She nodded, even though the dispatcher couldn't see her, and went to the door, pulling it open after disconnecting the call. Two officers waited on the other side, peering over her head.

"I'm so sorry you had to come out. It's a false alarm."

The taller man of the two raised a brow.

"Sorry. My friend was in the bathroom." She motioned to Aiden. "I thought he went home this morning, and..."

She glanced down, registering the tiny sleep shorts and tight tank top. She wrapped her arms around herself, shielding their view of her chest. With her in skimpy pajamas to combat the heat, and her words, they would naturally conclude her friend was here for more lascivious activities. It made her self-conscious.

The tall man tilted his head to look around her, motioning to the floor. "And the knife?"

"I had it in my hand. I told the dispatcher. For protection."

The shorter of the two squinted his hazel eyes and spoke with a thick Southern drawl. "What's it doin' on the floor?"

"I dropped it. The knock scared me."

"Huh. Mind if we come inside and take a look around? Protocol an' all."

"Sure," she said, stepping back and allowing them to step inside. "You got here so fast."

The shorter officer nodded. "We were parked on the next street over taking our lunch."

"I'm sorry I interrupted."

"Nonsense. Can't be too careful."

Both men clocked Aiden right away; he remained near the bathroom door.

He wore the casual medium-wash jeans and white T-shirt from yesterday. The taller officer straightened and puffed up upon seeing Aiden, and she resisted the urge to laugh at how comical it looked. The officer had to be twice Aiden's age and stood eye-to-eye, but Aiden held a clear physical advantage. The way his tight T-shirt stretched across his broad chest and shoulders made it obvious.

They had nothing to worry about. Aiden was harmless, and his size didn't make him dangerous. She didn't even know if he could fight.

"And you are?" the taller officer who had squared up upon seeing Aiden asked.

"Aiden Easton, sir. The friend."

The officer made a soft sound of derision at the respectful honorific. She wondered if it made him feel old.

Some of the middle-aged patrons at the diner responded the same when she called them ma'am or sir. Her fourth-grade teacher had always said, "Classy Southern ladies show respect, no matter the situation." Honorifics showed respect. Charlotte learned early on that it was wiser to err on the side of caution than risk ruffling a few feathers—especially when tips were involved.

The officers moved into the apartment, checking behind the laundry door, and in the bathroom once Aiden stepped away. They also checked in the area where her bed remained an unmade mess. Once satisfied, they returned to her.

"It was good of you to call in when you didn't know who was here," the shorter officer said, giving Aiden a side glance, returning his gaze to her. His eyes were kind as he smiled down at her. "Never think you're troublin' us. You got nothin' to be sorry for. You can never be too sure nowadays."

"Yes, sir. Thank you for coming out. Again, I'm sorry."

"If you need any further assistance, just give us a call," the taller officer said, letting himself out.

"Y'all have a good day now." The shorter officer smiled again before following his partner out.

She shut the door behind them and exhaled, slumping against the door.

"What in the—"

"Hold that thought," she said, pushing off the door and throwing up a hand to stop whatever Aiden had been about to say. She rushed across the room toward the bathroom. "How I didn't pee on myself through all that is beyond me." She slammed the door behind her.

Once she finished emptying her bladder, she went to the sink to wash her hands, groaning at the sight that greeted her in the mirror.

Her cheeks were flushed, and her curly hair appeared wild and untamed. She looked like she'd stuck her finger in a light socket.

Digging around under the sink, she pulled out a spray bottle of water and her leave-in conditioner. She wasn't going to shower again, but she could tame the rat's nest on her head before she faced Aiden again.

Correction.

Before she murdered him.

Once satisfied, she swept her hair over her shoulder and marched out of the bathroom like a soldier heading to war.

"I can't believe the police showed up."

She arched a brow. "No? Because *of course* they're gonna show up if I'm calling for help because I think someone is breaking into my home." She propped her hands on her hips and gave him a withering look. At least he had the good sense to look somewhat guilty. "I thought you were gone," she said with a sigh.

"Why?"

She stomped over to the nightstand and snatched up the note, thrusting it forward. His brows pinched as he took it from her hand.

"I said I'd see you soon."

"Yeah, soon. Not when I wake up soon. Soon can mean anything. You didn't quantify the length of time and now I look like a crazy person to the police when I've already made myself look like an idiot reporting a stalker I have absolutely no proof of."

Her explanation sounded unhinged even to herself. He wasn't to be faulted for writing "soon" instead of x-amount of time, but she still felt the uncomfortable and real fear that came with someone invading her space, even if it didn't happen. The feelings remained.

She pushed around him, and he barely budged. *Stupid mountain of a man.*

Her feet slapping on the kitchen tile sounded louder with her frustrated gait, but for some reason, she couldn't let go of her irritation. She felt something—something besides emptiness and hopelessness—for once, and she latched onto it, no matter how unhealthy it might be.

Snatching up the knife, she jumped when his warm hand touched her bare shoulder.

Before she could turn in surprise, he ran his large hand down her arm to the hand holding the knife, coaxing it from her grasp before she could do something stupid like stab him on accident. She ignored the goose bumps his touch brought.

"I'm sorry," he whispered entirely too close to the side of her head as he stood inches from her back with his head lowered. "I wasn't clear. I went out to get some breakfast." Cuffing her left bicep, he turned her with the hand not holding the knife to face the kitchen counter where a paper bag sat. "I brought you a biscuit."

She sagged against him, the fight leaving her body at his calm and measured cadence.

He took a long inhale through his nose before lifting his head from next to her ear and stepping away to give her space. She missed his comforting presence immediately.

"Eat something. It might help calm you down. I really am sorry. I didn't mean to scare you."

"I'm fine," she said, more confident than she felt. She walked over to the refrigerator and pulled out the carton of orange juice they bought yesterday, pouring a small glass to go with her breakfast. "Want some?"

"I'm good."

She opened the cabinet above the sink and grabbed her medicine. Shaking out a pill into her hand, she popped it in her mouth and chased it with the juice before moving on to pulling the still warm biscuit from the bag.

"Are you okay?"

She turned at the concern in Aiden's voice. Swallowing the bite she'd taken, she said, "Yeah, why?" She held up the sausage, egg, and cheese biscuit. "This is good, by the way."

"You're not sick, are you?" He stood a few feet from her, his eyes focused behind her. Her eyes followed his line of sight to the pill bottle. She cringed.

"Not in the way you think," she muttered, averting her gaze.

He approached and propped his hip against the counter, crossing his arms. "You don't have to tell me. I was only curious."

The last bite of the biscuit felt like sandpaper going down her throat.

She wasn't ashamed of needing medicine.

Liar.

Okay, she felt somewhat embarrassed for needing medicine because her brain hated her for not handling change as easily as others—among other things. The shame wasn't in what others would think, but more so that she felt defective. People took medicine for a myriad of reasons, both for physical limitations and mental, but she didn't want something to be wrong with her.

"You're thinking really hard there," Aiden said, a lazy smile hooking the corner of his mouth when she turned her attention to him.

"It's for depression," she said. Her mouth parted in response to how at ease with him she felt saying the words. His smile disarmed her. She was getting too comfortable with him. *That can't happen*, she reminded herself. She didn't fit in his high-class world. She stuffed the empty biscuit paper in the bag.

"Depression?" His eyes narrowed and the muscles in his jaw tightened.

Why did he seem angry? She did nothing wrong. It wasn't her fault the chemicals in her brain acted out.

Before she could do anything like snap at him for being mad at her for something she couldn't control, he surprised her by grabbing her by both arms and turning her toward him.

His eyes softened when she looked up at him. "Is it because of the asshole following you around?"

"No," she whispered.

"Then why? I don't understand."

"I'm struggling." She pulled against his hold, and he released her without hesitation. Her arms circled her stomach. "I thought I could handle this, but with the added problem of *him*, I feel like I'm drowning." Her shoulders lifted; her eyes locked on the glass of juice like it was the most fascinating thing ever. "I took antidepressants when I was a young teen, when the transition into high school was hard on me. Then I met Blaire, and it got easier until I didn't need them. It was a little hard when she transferred into Magnolia Heights her senior year, but I still saw her at the diner, and we still hung out, so it helped."

She cringed. *Codependent, much?*

When a long silence stretched after her words, she chanced a glance up at his face.

The understanding on his face surprised her. She couldn't explain how she knew he understood, but something in the softness of his eyes and relaxed set of his mouth eased her discomfort. He wasn't judging her.

"It was hard for me when my brothers and sisters all moved away," he started, shifting to lean against the counter again, giving her space she wasn't sure she wanted now. "I was thirteen when Brandon moved to Seoul to become an international chef at twenty-three. Heather's the oldest, and as soon as she found her Kor—her partner," he said, pausing to clear his throat, "and got married, she left home. I think I was around three? Something like that."

"Wow. How old is she?"

"Thirty-five."

"So she left home as a teen?" At his nod, she shook her head. "I couldn't imagine leaving home for marriage at this age. College is one thing, but marriage?" She laughed. Marriage sounded nice, but she wasn't thinking about things like permanent commitments to anyone. She still had to sort out her own life.

"When you know, you know," he said simply. "But yeah, Brandon leaving was hard on me. Mom says I had trouble with Heather leaving, but I don't remember that young. I think if Riley wasn't around, I'd likely struggle with depression too. Especially with Dad living in New York."

"Wait. Your parents aren't together?"

"They are. Dad's job requires him to be there."

"Why doesn't your mom move north?"

"She teaches at the high school branch for Blackthorn. She loves her job, and Dad didn't want to take her away from that. Plus, Riley and I were in elementary school when Dad got the job and she didn't want to leave us."

"Why didn't she transfer y'all?"

He shifted, hooking his hands over the edge of the counter behind him. "Our family has all attended Blackthorn Academy's school system for generations. Kind of a family legacy thing. It was important to the family that we continue that tradition."

Huh.

Charlotte wondered if it embarrassed him that his family followed traditions like that because he looked incredibly uncomfortable. Southern families often held onto old traditions and obligations to preserve their family legacies in terms of school, work, and marriages in order to maintain connections with other legacy families and preserve their wealth. Her family had nothing like that, but she understood the concept.

Taking the hint that he didn't want to delve deeper, she said, "It must have been rough losing your siblings like that. Especially going so far away. Did Heather stay in Rosebrook?"

"Nah. She moved to New York too. She works for a pharmaceutical company in the city."

She turned to the counter and gathered up the trash from her late breakfast and opened the cabinet beneath the sink, tossing it in the garbage can. She made a mental note to take the trash to the chute later before it got too full.

Relating to his situation proved challenging, but at the same time, remarkably easy.

She didn't want to diminish his loss of family or insult him by comparing her situation to his, but losing Blaire to Blackthorn Academy felt like losing a sibling. In reality, she had no siblings. Part of her wanted to associate the fact that she didn't even know her father with the absence of Aiden's, but again, it didn't seem right.

Maybe it hurt more to have something and lose it than to never know it? She'd never know the answer to that question.

Turning to him after rinsing her glass and putting her medicine away, she huffed. "I need to change, then leave a message with management about the air and water."

He cursed. "I forgot you needed to be up early to go down there. I would have woken you up. I'm sorry."

"It's fine. After the start to the day I've had, I can suffer another night of heat. I'll be glad when this heatwave passes."

After gathering her clothes for the day, she disappeared into the bathroom. Trying not to take too long, she shucked off her pajamas and slipped on the high-waisted white shorts and off-the-shoulder, short-sleeved, purple peasant blouse, tugging down the bottom so it didn't show off her stomach with its shorter, fitted bodice.

Once satisfied with her appearance, she left the bathroom and dropped her sweaty pajamas in the laundry basket.

When she entered the living room, she stopped short. Aiden sat unmoving, staring at her with lowered lids and a blank expression.

"Everything okay?"

His eyes trailed over her like a gentle caress, taking in her appearance from her blouse to her legs, making her want to squirm. He shook his head. "Yeah. You look nice," he said.

Her brows twitched, her lips thinned, and her fingers flexed as she resisted the urge to tug on the hem of her shorts. Did he think she looked dumb? The outfit was new. Something she allowed herself as a treat—and because the coloring felt appropriate for the heat. But with the way Aiden gave such a flat response, she couldn't help but feel self-conscious.

Her eyes met his, and something in his expression shuttered. She'd missed something.

This was ridiculous.

"Do I look *that* bad?"

His mouth parted in shock at her sharp tone. Canting his head, he squinted in confusion. "Do what?"

"You're looking at me funny."

"I'm not."

"And you said I look nice."

"You *do*."

She curled her toes into the area rug beneath her feet. So saying nice wasn't all that bad, but the delivery left a lot to be desired.

"Still sounded funny, just like the look."

A wry grin spread across his face. Her cheeks puffed with her indignation, making him break into a full-on laugh. She hated it. To be fair, it was a nice laugh, but she hated it on principle.

"Don't laugh at me."

"Okay, Kitten."

His laughter roared back to the surface as she gaped at him.

"I'm not a damn kitten." Her hands went to her hips. "I just bought this outfit. You don't ever say anything about how I look. And you were just… staring. I assumed that meant I looked bad."

"Aw, jeez." He leaned back and ran a hand over his face.

Her gaze latched onto his bicep flexing in his tight T-shirt.

She didn't know how often he exercised, but anyone could see how well Aiden took care of himself. Aside from his large arms, wide set shoulders, and chest stretching his T-shirt, he had a narrow waist and thick thighs—which she remembered from the way he looked spread out napping on her bed last night in only a pair of snug-fitting boxers, looking like a buffet for one.

All signs he worked out and ate right.

Her face heated when she recalled how his naked backside flexed when he dropped his shorts during their beach trip to perform a dare in the drinking game she had taken part in with Blaire, him, and their friends. *Oh, he definitely works out.* She hadn't meant to look, but it took her longer to look away when she did.

Even now, she tried not to stare too much, but it would be rude to ignore a work of art.

Aiden Easton defined beauty in more ways than one. His midnight hair appeared artfully messed with long locks both over his forehead and pushed back. Long lashes most women would kill for framed his intense forest green eyes. They almost touched his cheeks when he closed his eyes, drawing attention to high cheekbones that led down to a sharp, squared jawline.

Someone called in favors when he was conceived, because not only did he have gorgeous looks, but he held the heart of a saint.

It was another reason she questioned his reaction to her outfit. She never thought him to be mean.

"Are you even listening to me?"

"Huh?" She blinked, his voice breaking through the haze around her mind. It's like he carried his own Charlotte-attracting gravity, and she was helpless to it whenever she focused too hard on him. Had she seriously moved closer to the loveseat? She straightened and took a step back.

"I *said* I was sorry if you thought I didn't like it. I said it was nice because it really suits you." His tongue barely grazed his lip in an unconscious gesture he surely didn't know came across as panty-melting to women around him. "You're beautiful. Don't know why you'd think otherwise."

She didn't mean she was ugly, but she wasn't about to brush off the compliment. Even if he was her friend, she wasn't immune to him. If things were different—if her status were different—maybe she'd try her hand at flirting back, but she needed to resist those urges now that they were spending more time in front of each other, either in person or video. Texting before heading off for her big college adventure was one thing, letting it go farther was another can of worms entirely.

Clearing her throat, she forced down the uncomfortable lump lodged there. "I'm going to send an email to the office now."

"Alright."

She fidgeted, not sure what to say to him. Was he going home soon? What made him stay longer now that it wasn't night?

As if reading her thoughts, he said, "I was thinking I could spend today hanging out, since you've had some weird things going on. What with the flower delivery and this morning. Which I know was my fault"—he held up a hand to stop her before she could blame him for scaring the pee out of her—"but it still bothered you. I can head back at sunset."

"That'd be nice."

She turned without another word and went to her computer. She felt off-balance from not only misunderstanding his reaction to a stupid outfit, but also how her hindbrain hijacked the more capable faculties of her mind. Like it had last night with Aiden lying almost naked in her bed.

Once she had fired off the email, she sat back and sighed, wondering what her mothers were up to.

Aiden chose that moment to appear next to her desk, his bulky shoulder leaning on the wall as he fixed her with a look, his arms crossed over his chest.

"Why don't you tell your moms about this guy?"

Her brows tightened. "Could you quit that?"

"Quit what?"

Her hand waved about in the air. "The mind-trick Jedi thingy."

He snorted. "Okay, I'll bite. What's the 'mind-trick Jedi thingy'?"

"You keep reading my mind."

His head recoiled in surprise. "I don't have that ability."

"I'm pretty sure no one really does. I'm just being stupid. But you have an uncanny knack for saying things relating to my thoughts."

"Huh. Well, one, you need to stop with the stupid talk. It's kinda pissing me off." He moved in front of her and spun her chair. "Two, you're thinking about telling them?"

She decided addressing the topic of how she talked down to herself on occasion wasn't the best hill to die on, so she focused on his second point.

"Not telling them, but I was thinking about them."

"Ah. So telling them. Thoughts?"

She slumped back in her chair and closed her eyes. "I want to show them I can make it on my own—be independent, you know? Even if I plan to come back to Rosebrook Valley to help with the business, I need them to know I can take care of myself," she said, never opening her eyes for fear of what she'd find waiting in his.

If her mothers knew that the moment she left Rosebrook Valley she had attracted a stalker, they would bring her home and never let her leave. They worried like that. They were awesome. She rubbed at the stupid ache in her chest.

Her eyes opened when the air shifted against her legs as Aiden crouched in front of her. He reached up and rested his hands over the top of hers on the arms of the chair.

"It isn't your fault some weirdo took a shine to you. Your mothers wouldn't see that as your lack of ability to look out for yourself." He squeezed her hands. "You went to the police. You've kept up with your classes. Leaving a dangerous situation when the stakes get to be too much is a sign of maturity."

Well, when you put it like that…

She shifted in the chair, her eyes moving to the planter filled with succulents on her desk with phases of the moon circling its surface.

The stakes had become way beyond stalker levels. She didn't know if what she saw in that alley was real or not, but if it was… Would the man—vampire—let her exist with his secret? Did he follow her home or know where she lived? A tendril of fear slithered down her spine. She didn't want to bring the undead back to her mothers and put them in danger. But who could she turn to with that who wouldn't immediately lock her in an institution somewhere?

She doubted even Aiden, with his kind heart and understanding eyes, would take her seriously if she told him what she'd seen.

13

Violation

The rest of the day passed by peacefully. Charlotte managed to forget about the chaos of her life by exploring the town with Aiden. Primarily indoors because the humidity made her clothes want to stick to her skin, and she didn't want to chance that in white shorts, even though she wore a thong to avoid any see-through mishaps.

Like all good things, the peace wasn't meant to last.

Sunset approached, and Aiden prepared for the drive back to Rosebrook Valley. However, before he needed to depart, they made a quick stop at a café to grab a meal to take home for one last dinner together.

Pushing the door open after unlocking it, she froze.

"Gonna let me in?" Aiden chuckled. He must have noticed her tense posture, because he hardened his voice. "Let me through."

His tone compelled her to obey, so she gravitated closer to the wall beside the door. If she didn't use the wall, she wouldn't be able to stand. Her knees weakened at the sight before her.

Her apartment looked like a tornado ran through it. A picky tornado, but a tornado, nonetheless.

Picky, because not everything appeared destroyed.

A few throw pillows from her loveseat appeared cut into by a sharp object, but the loveseat itself remained intact.

Textbooks and school papers lay scattered across the living room floor, buried in dirt from the house plants that were now toppled over and torn from their planters.

Framed photos of her with friends and family lay smashed on the floor.

Someone had shattered the vase she kept roses in on the tile of her kitchen floor, scattering pink rose petals everywhere. Nothing else seemed to be disturbed in the kitchen.

Aiden stormed into the apartment, doing a sweep of the place. To see if whoever broke in was still there or not, she assumed. Her fear prevented her from pleading with him to stay back in case someone was there and would hurt him. Her voice didn't seem to want to work.

"Call the police," he shouted from her bedroom.

Her hands trembled as she set the bag of food down next to her feet, not moving from where she remained plastered against the wall. Pulling out her phone, she dialed the familiar emergency number again. The irony wasn't lost on her that she had a real break-in to call for help about. It was like the universe needed to balance out the false alarm from this morning.

"Athens-Clarke County—"

"There's been a break-in at my apartment." She cut off the dispatcher the same as earlier, immensely grateful it was a different person this time, a woman.

"A break-in?"

"Yes. My apartment is a mess."

"What's your address?"

She gave the address and paused. "Um. I called this morning because I thought someone broke in, but this time I'm serious."

The line was silent for a moment before the female dispatcher asked, "You called this morning?"

"Yes, my friend was here, but I didn't *know* it was them in the bathroom." She waved a hand before smacking it down on the side of her thigh. "I just woke up and heard them in there and thought someone broke in because someone has been stalking me. I've been to the police station. There's a report. But this time it's for real. My apartment is a mess and—"

"Ma'am." The woman's stern voice grabbed Charlotte's attention, cutting into her panic-induced rambling.

"Yes?"

Softer, the dispatcher asked, "What's your name?"

"Charlotte."

"Okay, Charlotte. I'm gonna need you to take a deep breath for me, okay?"

"Okay." She inhaled deep in her nose and exhaled it from her mouth.

The dispatcher asked for her address. Charlotte recited it by rote.

"Good. I have officers in route. Now, can you tell me if anyone is there?"

"Just my friend." She looked up as Aiden walked across toward her, his boots crunching over the broken glass on the kitchen floor until he came to a stop in front of her. "He checked to make sure no one else was here."

If Aiden hadn't been here, she would have fallen apart.

"Okay. Is there anything missing that you can tell?"

"I haven't—there's..." Her eyes moved up to Aiden's, and she blanched. *If that son of a donkey...* Somehow, she found the strength in her legs to move forward and head for her bedroom.

Straight for her nightstand.

The drawer sat open, and her journal lay there with all the pages shredded. She didn't even care if Aiden saw her battery-operated boyfriend tucked beneath the journal as he stepped up behind her in silent support.

This final violation of her personal space shifted something inside her, and she wasn't sure how she would get over it.

The journal was big. Three-hundred full index pages, bound with a thick leather flap that buckled on the front. Burned into the leather on the center of the front cover was a celestial sun and crescent moon; her name in script was burned into the bottom corner. Her ma had given it to her as a graduation gift, and it meant the world to her.

To make it last longer, she sectioned off the pages with a ruler and only added important things, as well as a weekly summary, rather than writing nightly.

Her ma told her they could always remove the pages for safe keeping and have new ones bound inside, but she wanted to avoid too much wear and tear on the inner spine.

Now someone had ruined it, and she would either have to add new pages or let it go. It felt tainted now, and that hurt.

She resisted the urge to touch the shredded paper, knowing that touching evidence wasn't smart.

"Nothing seems missing," she finally said in a flat voice.

She turned then, scanning the room, pushing aside the discomfort she felt over her journal.

Her drawers were open; panties and bras spilling out of the top. She wondered if he'd stolen any. It seemed like a stalker-esque thing to do, right? What remained appeared torn and slashed.

"Officers should be there shortly. Do you need me to stay on the line with you until they arrive?"

With no one waiting to ambush her in her home, she didn't see any reason to keep the woman occupied when she could be helping others. Besides, what more could she do than what she already had?

"I'll be fine."

"If you need anything, call me back. My name is Denise. You can ask for me."

"Thank you," Charlotte responded, already forgetting the name as she dropped to sit on the edge of her bed, pressing the button to end the call.

Aiden took the seat next to her and wrapped his arm around her shoulder, pulling her against his larger frame.

She pivoted her body toward him and wrapped her arms around his torso, burying her face against him, and cried.

"I'm so sorry this is happening," he whispered against the top of her head. His large hand moving to rest on the back of her head while his other arm banded around her back and pulled her tightly against him. "I think it's time to come back to Rosebrook. You can't stay here."

She sniffed and pulled out of his embrace, swiping at her cheeks. "I can't do that. You don't understand."

"I don't, no. I don't understand why you want to stay here and continue to put yourself in danger."

"*Aiden,*" she pleaded, her voice breaking as fresh tears slipped down her cheeks. "He told me leaving changed nothing. I think… I don't know if he meant that if I came back he'd be waiting, or if…" Taking a measured breath to steady herself, she asked, "What if he follows me back? I can't put my family at risk." She didn't include the lingering fear of what she saw in the alley to her excuse.

Her spine straightened at the thought. She looked around at the mess in her apartment. What if *they* did this?

It didn't seem like the logical option, considering the personal nature of the destruction. Her eyes shifted to the destroyed journal. The stalker knew about the journal already.

No. That creature didn't do this, but he might also follow her home.

Leaving meant danger for her family from more than one direction. She couldn't do it no matter how scared she felt.

Aiden sighed as he took in her expression. "You're serious about staying."

"I am."

"Then so am I."

"You're what?"

"I'm staying with you."

She blinked once. Twice. Three times. Did he suggest moving in with her? Surely not.

"What are you talking about?"

His thumb brushed a lingering tear from her cheek. "Until this gets sorted out, and the police catch this guy, I'm going to stay here." He paused and seemed to consider his words. "If you'll let me, that is." His face held that sheepish look, paired with the nervous quality of his tone again.

"I don't have anywhere for you to stay." She looked around. "I can't expect you to drop your life for this—for *me*."

"I'm not. I'm bored out of my mind with everyone hooking up. Whenever Dom and Layla—"

"Dom?"

"Ah, you haven't met him. His name is actually Dominic. He's a transfer. We met him in Europe on our school trip. Nice guy. He does stuff with us, so maybe you'll get to meet him when you're down next." He shifted his eyes away. He didn't look too thrilled with the idea. *Weird.* "Anyway, whenever they aren't with us, I feel like a seventh wheel to all the couples." He leaned back on his hands on the bed. "I mean, we have fun. But I do not take pleasure in watching my sister stuff her tongue down someone's throat."

She giggled. It felt good to laugh, even though the world was collapsing around her. His smile in response to her laugh made her stomach flutter.

"We're out for the summer now. I've got the rest of this month and next. If they haven't sorted this by then, we'll figure it out when the time comes."

"What about your things?"

"I can buy clothes and things I need. I've got my laptop, which is the only thing I'd miss."

She rolled her eyes and smiled.

Instead of driving eight hours total to get his things for two months, he would buy completely new things. He had seemed nothing like his sister Riley until then. She had a shopping addiction and didn't blink twice at spending money on new things when she already had so much already. Charlotte didn't think badly of Riley for it, but she didn't understand the lifestyle. Not that she didn't love shopping. Splurging on the occasional treat or new outfit made her happy—splurging on a game made her giddy—but she would take the inconvenience of the drive before spending her grocery money. Of course they didn't have to make a choice.

And there came the reminder of where she didn't fit in their world. She didn't even understand it.

A rapid series of hard knocks sounded on her door, jerking her from the spiral she had started down.

"Athens-Clarke County, open up!"

She slid a nervous glance at Aiden, and he stood, hand touching her shoulder to steady her.

"I'll let them in."

While Aiden let the officers in, she took a moment to compose herself.

As heavy footsteps approached, she looked up at the shorter officer from this morning.

"Afternoon, ma'am. Didn't think we'd be seein' you again today," he said in greeting, an easy-going smile on his face.

Her smile was as forced as her laugh. "No offense, but I hoped to never need to."

"None taken. No one wants to deal with this situation." He cleared his throat. "So your boyfriend here tells me y'all came home to find it like this?"

Her eyes widened, and she darted a glance to Aiden, who looked just as surprised by the officer's assumption.

"He's not—"

"She has a report in with the police about a stalker already," Aiden said, and she gave him a confused look. He wasn't going to correct the officer? He wanted them to think they were a couple? Something about the way his eyes looked when he looked at her prompted her to go along with it. "We believe the same guy did this."

"That so?" the second officer said in a low, smooth voice.

He was taller than Aiden and built like a truck. Likely one of those CrossFit bros. He could crush her like a bug if he wanted, with the way his muscles looked ready to burst out of his uniform.

But that wasn't the scary thing about him.

It was his tawny eyes. They reminded her of the eyes of a big wild cat, almost glowing in the sunlight coming through her window like animal eyes when light reflected off them in the night. Predator eyes. Eyes trained on her, narrowing by the minute.

She shifted, apprehension making her skin feel tight. The urge to get up and run away from the room was overwhelming.

"Brooks," a voice she recognized as the taller officer from that morning called from her living room. "Got something."

The intimidating officer—Brooks—broke the stare-down and turned to go see what the other man had to say.

She teetered on the verge of collapsing when the intense pressure on her chest released. *What the hell was that about?*

Aiden was by her side in an instant, his expression thunderous.

He sat next to her and grabbed her hand. His grip held tight—almost too tight, but she welcomed the bite of pain. It grounded her after that weird experience.

The shorter officer squinted in the direction the bodybuilder in uniform went. "Don't mind him. He was supposed to be off shift now. Decided to tag along." He shrugged and muttered under his breath, but not quietly enough, "Don't know why if he didn't wanna be here."

"What's this about?"

They all looked as the tall officer—though not as tall as Brooks, so now she needed to read his badge to get his real name—stepped into the room. Douglas. Officer Douglas.

She noticed the business card in his hand, but she didn't know what he wanted to know. There were a few business cards in her kitchen drawer.

He held the card up and read, "You looked lovely this morning. Purple suits you."

Her breath caught in her throat, and all eyes turned on her. Brooks joining them in the small space to add to the scrutiny.

"I-I received roses. I've *been* receiving roses." She looked at the short officer—Evans. "It's also in the police report I filed." She licked her dry lips. "This guy has been sending me roses for weeks, and that's the first time he put a card in the bouquet. I dropped it. Didn't know where it ended up."

Officer Douglas motioned behind him. "Found it sticking out from under the edge of your fridge."

"This guy," Brooks started, his cold features giving nothing away. "What's his name?"

"I don't know."

"Then how do you know it's a guy?"

"Because he called me," she said, not able to hide the irritation in her voice. She didn't like Officer Brooks. He made her extremely uncomfortable.

He made a humming sound that sounded more like a growl than she cared for, and Aiden's grip tightened on her hand in response.

"If you check with the station, you'll find all the information about this," Aiden said. "He's escalating."

Brooks narrowed his eyes at Aiden, observing. "He is, is he? You seem to know a lot about the situation." The two of them seemed to have some sort of standoff before Aiden broke eye contact.

"Brooks," Officer Evans chastised. "He's her boyfriend. Course he's gonna know about it."

Brooks scoffed. "Boyfriend?"

Did he not think they could be a couple? *Rude much?*

"Yes, boyfriend," Aiden said, giving the officer a pointed look she didn't understand.

"Interesting."

Her mouth gaped as Officer Grouchy-Pants walked away. *Weirdo.*

The two remaining officers watched Brooks leave before returning their attention to the room.

Trying to divert attention from the whole boyfriend thing, she said, "Nothing is missing, and the things destroyed—aside from plants and throw pillows—are all personal. Photos, my journal, my underwear… It doesn't seem like a normal break-in. It's not, right?"

"It certainly isn't commonplace. Seems personal," Douglas said.

"We're gonna have a team come in and take some prints and look for anything of interest," Evans said, hooking his thumbs into his belt. "Think y'all could go someplace until we're done?"

"Sure." She looked at Aiden. "We can do a little shopping. I need some new things now that…" Her voice trailed off, and she motioned to the drawer spilling out her most intimate clothing, torn and useless.

Aiden released her hand and slipped his arm around her waist, pulling her tight to his side in an intimate gesture she felt positive was for the officer's sake. "I also need to get some things. I plan to stay with her for a while until this gets figured out."

"That's a smart idea," Officer Douglas said with a nod. "If we can't find anything to connect this to someone, there isn't a lot we can do except add it to your existing report."

"But rest assured," Evans interjected. "When we do find this person, these reports will go a long way to solidifying a case against them. Evidence is important in cases like this."

Douglas inclined his head in agreement. "For now, keeping your boyfriend with you—or possibly staying at his place—is a good solution until the investigation is complete."

"I won't be leaving her side."

"Good man," Evans said with a pleasant smile. "We're gonna get on outta here. We'll have investigators drop by shortly. Don't touch anything." He looked around and his expression dimmed. "Afterward, you're free to clean up how you see fit. Damn shame this happened to you."

14

Attraction

Charlotte pushed the door closed as the last of what she assumed was a forensics team left her home carrying trash bags filled with her broken possessions.

They stayed longer than she expected; but what she hadn't expected was how two of the women offered to help her clean the mess.

Did she look that pathetic?

It took effort not to break down when she and Aiden returned from their shopping trip and early dinner to find people combing through the mess in her apartment.

It was hard to pretend everything was okay when it wasn't.

Warmth met her back, and she sank into the feeling as two muscular arms enclosed her at her shoulders.

The support Aiden gave her through all this helped more than she believed he realized. In less than two days' time, he made her laugh and smile in ways that made her forget what kept happening to her.

"Are you okay?" he asked, turning her in his arms, not separating them.

“As good as I can be.”

She propped her chin on his body to look up at him; he didn’t give her an inch to do much else. Her arms dangled at her sides. She didn’t want to loop them around his body. Well, she *did*, but she shouldn’t. Her emotions were frazzled, and allowing herself to get too comfortable with Aiden when they always kept a platonic distance might not end so well.

She already told herself he was out of her league. She didn’t need to complicate things by reading too much into his protective nature. He was protective of everyone.

She wasn’t special. He was simply a good man.

She broke eye contact and pressed her forehead against his chest.

Aiden sighed. “It’s okay to not be fine, you know.”

Was it really? It didn’t feel like it.

If she were back home with her mothers, maybe she would fall apart, but this was a new chapter in her life. The Independent and Strong Charlotte chapter. The shadows would not give her a reprieve to fall apart.

Aiden continued, like he knew what she was thinking. “I’m not leaving until this is sorted.”

She appreciated the reiteration; she kept expecting him to change his mind at any moment and say her drama was too much.

“I’ll protect you,” he whispered against the top of her head as he lowered his to press his nose into her curls. She heard his slow inhale, like he was breathing her in—smelling her. Maybe he liked her shampoo.

“You don’t have to,” she said, lifting her head to look up at him again. “Stay, I mean.” His grip on her tightened. “This isn’t your problem, and I could already tell the cops made you uncomfortable.”

At least one of them, that is. It seemed so weird how they both sized one another up. Did the officer think Aiden was a bad guy? Surely not.

"I know I don't have to stay. I *want* to stay." He smiled down at her. "And the cops were fine," he added, but his smile fell as he said the words. Big fat lie.

"Officer Brooks acted like he had a stick up the rock he calls a butt," she said to lighten the mood.

Aiden snorted a laugh and raised a brow. "Rock?"

"He had muscles on muscles."

"You like that sort of thing?"

Her cringe made him laugh. "I like muscles, but *that* is overkill."

"Fair."

She started to pull away from his hug that had gone on far too long. "You, on the other hand…" She paused when his grip on her tightened. Her eyes moved up to his.

"What about me?"

His eyes were doing the same lowered lid, stern expression he did when she put on her new outfit.

"Um. What?" She forgot what they were talking about.

"Me on the other hand?"

"Oh. uh. You have the right amount of muscle," she said, her face burning.

It wasn't like someone couldn't tell he looked muscular, but she saw an up close and personal view when he lay on her bed, eyes closed in rest. Never again would she get such an unobstructed, lingering view like that. Not that she *needed* to see it again, but she wouldn't deny the man looked gorgeous.

She also wouldn't deny that the image might star in some of her fantasies to use when she spent time with her B.O.B. in the future. *If* she did. With Aiden staying here for the foreseeable future, she doubted she would get much alone time.

"Charlotte?"

"Hm?"

"I asked you a question. You're just sort of… staring at me."

Oh, crap. "Um. Can you repeat that?" The man and his muscles were a distraction. She wiggled out of his grip. Space. Yes, space would help.

"I asked if you were looking at me. My muscles," he added with a chuckle.

"Don't be cocky." Her fists went to her hips. "You know you look nice."

"Nice?"

"Yes, nice."

Before he could say anything else, a knock behind them at the door startled them both.

Aiden moved her to the side and around him in a protective gesture before looking through the peephole she had never looked through. She wasn't tall enough.

The growl that came from Aiden's throat made her jump.

"What? What's wrong?" As much as she tried, she couldn't keep the fear from her voice.

Fear wasn't an emotion she experienced often, but since leaving Rosebrook Valley, it followed her around like a reaper, tearing at her soul a little piece at a time. Maybe one day it would destroy her completely.

He glanced over his shoulder, and his features softened. "It's Noah," he said, voice tight.

"Noah?" What was he doing here? How'd he know where she lived? In the weeks since they met, they did all their project work at Rachel's place.

Aiden stepped away from the door and moved over to the wall, leaning against it. His arms crossed over his chest as he watched her open the door with undisguised frustration.

She wondered what his problem was. He acted the same way when he met Noah yesterday.

Pausing with her hand on the doorknob, she looked back at Aiden again. "Be nice."

His expression went blank, and he squinted at her. "What?"

"Don't know what the deal is, but you two acted like someone stuffed a porcupine in your boxers when you met."

"A porcupine?" he deadpanned.

"A porcupine."

Before he could respond, she pulled the door open. She could still hear his snickering in the background as she faced Noah.

"Hey, Noah. How'd you know where I live?"

His hand brushed his curls back from his face, and he gave her a broad smile. His face looked better. The bruising didn't appear as prominent around his eye; less swollen. His lip still appeared split and scabbed, though. Probably because he kept smiling and opening the wound. He always smiled.

Still, it looked a lot better than she would have looked so soon after a fight.

"Rachel. She told me you moved to the same hall she lived on before. Gave me the address."

That sounded weird. Was it common for people up here? Give out private information like that? She sure wouldn't. Rachel had told her to be careful with Noah, and yet she gave him her address. Or had she given Noah her address herself? They didn't know each other in April when she moved in and Rachel moved out of the building.

"Is that a problem?" he asked, his smile dropping to be replaced with uncertainty.

"No, it's fine. Um. Come on in." She stepped back. "Want something to drink?"

"No, I'm good. I'm only here for a minute," he said, stepping into the apartment, his eyes scanning the space. Fortunately, he had never seen her apartment before. Without the framed photos, plants, throw pillows, and some of her knick-knacks lying around, he might ask questions. She didn't want to drag him into her mess. "I wanted to ask..." His words died off in his throat as he caught sight of Aiden standing against the wall like a silent sentinel. Noah spun to face her.

He looked between the two of them before raising a brow at her as if to ask a silent question.

They met yesterday. Aiden was supposed to come hang out at her place for the day. He was still here today. In the same clothes from yesterday.

Her head dropped back between her shoulders as she looked up at the ceiling for guidance. She knew the question without having to ask. It wasn't hard to put two and two together and know Aiden stayed the night. Noah knew he was from out of town.

Ignoring the question in his eyes—if he wanted to know, he could be a big boy and ask—she asked, "So what brings you to my place?" He could have called if he just wanted to ask her something.

Shaking his head, Noah said, "It's about the project."

"The project. What about it?" He'd responded to the group text, so he knew they didn't have to do anything with it until Friday.

"I wanted to see if you had an extra copy of the script Rachel gave us for the presentation. I lost mine, and if I asked her for a new copy, I'd never hear the end of it."

He wasn't wrong. Rachel was the least responsible of their group, so if Noah slipped up, she would never let him live it down. If they had to make the presentation today, he'd have had to face Rachel's wrath.

"Yeah, I can email you a copy to print." She slipped off the sandals she still wore from when they were out and crossed the floor toward the bedroom area where her computer was. She thanked her lucky stars whoever broke in didn't destroy that. "Why didn't you just text?"

She stopped before she reached her desk and looked back when he said nothing.

Aiden and Noah now stood in front of each other, speaking too low for her to hear. Aiden shook his head and narrowed his eyes at something Noah said. Noah threw his hands up and turned, jerking back at seeing her staring at them.

"Sent that email?"

"No," she said, drawing out the word. "I asked you a question. What are y'all arguing about?" Her arms crossed beneath her chest. "Better yet, does anyone wanna tell me why y'all seem to hate each other? You just met."

Noah held his arms out to his side. "No argument." He stepped forward, smiling. "I don't hate him. I don't even know him."

Maybe she was reading too much into things. The paranoia that accompanied someone stalking her made her wary of every situation and interaction.

Aiden kept his eyes on Noah, but he didn't refute his statement. Which further backed her suspicion that paranoia fueled her reaction to the two of them together.

It probably was little more than Aiden being protective.

She needed to get the email sent to Noah and send him on his way.

The air felt too tense for her liking with both guys in her home. Besides, she and Aiden needed to unpack their shopping bags, discuss sleeping arrangements, her class schedule, and any other important things he might need to know for his stay with her.

Noah approached, putting a hand on her shoulder and leading her away from Aiden. "I wanted to ask you something. It's why I didn't text you about the paper," he said when they were at the edge of the kitchen tile.

"What's up?"

"I wanted to see if you'd go out to dinner with me tonight." His head tilted as he looked down at her. "Just us. No Rachel or the others."

"I thought you understood."

"No, I do. I'm not rushing you." He looked up as Aiden approached. "I just wanted to spend some time with you alone."

Aiden stopped, looking between them, before entering the bathroom and shutting the door harder than he probably intended. She flinched at the sound.

Noah met her gaze again. "Maybe if you get to know me better, you might find yourself open to the idea of more. If not, we enjoyed the time as friends. No expectations."

It seemed a little pushy for him to ask her out, knowing she wasn't open to dating anyone while sorting her life out. He didn't even know how much she needed to sort. Maybe that was the entire problem. He only saw her apprehension about her major and remaining in Athens as the hangup. The reality was much more complicated.

She crossed her arms and stepped around him to go to her computer. He followed, glancing over at the unmade bed behind her. She'd had more men in her room in the last twelve hours than her whole life. At least her underwear wasn't hanging on display like when the officers were here.

She focused on emailing as she responded. "I can't tonight."

"Tomorrow then?"

"Probably not." Her lips flattened, and she took a steadying breath as she pressed send on the email, turning to him. "Look, you're a nice guy. I like you, I do. Just… not like that."

"It's him, isn't it?" He rested a hand on her desk, leaning a little to the side. The stiffness in his posture gave away his thoughts on the matter, even if he appeared to try for a casual demeanor.

"Who? Aiden?" She shook her head. "It's more than that. I've told you."

"You're right. I apologize." He straightened. "I really like you, and I'm sorry if I came on too strong."

"Friends?"

"Of course," he said, but he failed to mask the disappointment in his voice. "If you've sent that, I'm gonna get out of here. See you in class tomorrow?"

"Yep." She stood and led him to the front door.

He turned to her, and his signature smile was back on his face as if nothing had happened. "I'll see you tomorrow." Turning before she could say anything, he disappeared down the hall.

She closed the door with a yawn. Even without classes, the day had exhausted her. The police at her home twice. A suspected break-in, and then an actual break-in. Pissy officers—or at least one in particular. Now friends who didn't seem to know when to say when.

The bathroom door opened, and Aiden stepped out, meeting her eyes with frustration marring his handsome face.

"So, a date, huh?"

Her expression pinched. "What? No?"

"Sounded like it to me," he said in a conversational tone, but there was a lingering bite to the sound she didn't understand.

"He asked." She crossed the kitchen to her room, where she had placed the shopping bags with his clothes and her new underwear. "I turned him down," she said as she passed him.

Aiden leaned against the corner of the wall where it ended and created an entrance to the space she used as a bedroom. "So, he *is* interested in you?"

"I don't know. I guess."

"How do you not know? He asked you out. Trust me, he's interested."

She shrugged, folding the delicate pieces she bought, her body blocking his view of them. "I mean, he's made it clear, so I guess I know now. But I didn't before recently." She carried the folded underwear across the room and began putting them away. "I've never really been able to tell when someone is interested unless they are being vulgar at the diner or flat out tell me. I didn't realize it for sure until he kissed me, even when Rachel thought he asked me on a date before." She shut the drawer and turned to find a very irritated-looking Aiden staring at her. "What's wrong?"

"He kissed you? When?" The deep timbre of his voice as he spoke the last word through gritted teeth made her shiver.

"Friday after our group meeting."

"You mean the same night you looked scared out of your mind when we talked on Discord?" He straightened and looked ready to turn and head for her door—presumably to chase after Noah.

"Whoa, wait. Wait a minute." She moved over to stand in front of him. "He didn't upset me."

Aiden ran his hand over the length of his hair and scratched the crown of his head. "Then you were okay with the kiss?"

"No." She grabbed his forearm when he tensed. "I mean, I didn't care for him kissing me. I let him know I wasn't looking for anything. He respected that."

Some of the tension drained from Aiden's body at those words.

"Then why's he asking you out now?"

"I guess trying his luck? I don't get it much either." She turned and walked over to the closet, opening it and pushing her clothes to the side. "You can hang your new clothes in here. What are you gonna do about your mom's car?" She pulled down several hangers and brought them over to her computer chair, sitting them on it before moving to her bed to sit down next to the bags of his clothing.

"I called her while you were in the lingerie store," he said, rubbing a hand over the side of his neck and glancing to the side. "She told me to keep it while I'm here. She'll use the other car."

She moved the bags out of the way as he moved to take a seat next to her. "You told her about all this?"

"No. That's your business. I told her I was staying with a friend for the summer."

"And she didn't question it?"

That made no sense. From what Riley told her, Annie Easton helicopter parented with the best of them. Maybe she didn't do that with her sons, or either Riley being the youngest made her mother act differently.

"Oh, she questioned it, alright. But it's fine. She gave me the green light in the end." He sighed. "I can't believe you can't tell," he mumbled.

"Can't tell what?"

"If someone is into you."

She laughed. "It's not a foreign concept. Do you know every single person who is attracted to you?"

"Well, no." He at least looked somewhat chagrined by the realization. "But when we were at the beach, you kept up with that stupid drinking game just fine."

When they went to Tybee Island during spring break, they

indulged in some silly high school games. During Never Have I Ever, she got tipsy, and she guessed Aiden was paying attention.

"Just because I have experience, doesn't mean I knew the guy was interested before I was in a relationship with him." She shrugged. "Like I said, I didn't even know Noah was interested until recently. Usually, Blaire was the one to point out if a guy was genuinely flirting with me and not being a lecherous creep."

Aiden leaned forward and rested his forearms on his thighs, clasping his hands. After a moment of silence, he asked, "What about me?"

Her brows bunched. "What about you?"

He glanced over his shoulder at her. "Can you tell what I think of you?" His voice had dropped, and her heart beat faster in response.

Toying with the hem of her white shorts for something to do, she said, "Well, until you asked that question, I thought I did."

"What did you think before?"

"That we were friends."

"We are," he said, sitting upright.

She relaxed at his statement. Aiden didn't need to know that she felt attracted to him more than a friendly appreciation. She knew to stay in her own league.

"Why did the question make you think otherwise?"

"Huh?"

"You said before I asked the question you thought you knew."

"Oh." So much for letting her guard down. "The way you sounded, it almost seemed like you thought more of me." She downplayed the embarrassment with a laugh. "See, this is why I can't tell if someone likes me." Her face burned, so she looked away, suddenly fascinated with the shoes in the bottom of her closet. The heat in her apartment did nothing to help.

"And if I do?"

Her shoulders inched up to her neck, and she froze. *He did not just say that.* Was she having another heatstroke? *You can't blame a heatstroke anytime something unbelievable happens*, she chastised herself.

She jumped when his hand slid over hers and tugged her to turn toward him.

Once he had her attention, he said, "I mean, I'm not going to lie and say I'm not attracted to you." Before her heart could keel over, he added, "But to act on that right now when you're going through what you are is an asshole move." He tilted his head to look deep into her eyes. "I've been attracted to you for a while, actually."

His large hand moved to cup the side of her face, and she couldn't stop the soft, barely audible, desperate sound that came out. Brushing his thumb across her cheek, he leaned in as if drawn to the sound.

He was going to kiss her.

Her eyes fluttered closed and she could smell her minty toothpaste on his breath fanning across her lips. He must have brushed his teeth when he went to the bathroom earlier after their dinner when Noah was here.

A weird vibrating noise came from Aiden, and she pulled back, looking down at his lap.

"I muted it earlier when the police were here," he said. "I can call back."

"No, it might be important. Go ahead."

The moment was gone anyway. Really, it was a good thing. Kissing Aiden would be a very bad thing. Even if it would feel so good in the moment.

His eyes showed how reluctant he was to get up, but his phone started vibrating again. He pulled it out of his pocket and groaned at the name on the screen.

"What is it, Riley?" he said, answering the call as he stood and walked to the kitchen. "Yes, I'm staying at Charlotte's for a bit." A pause. "No, you can't come too. There's no room." A longer pause. "Seth with you? Give him the phone." After a minute, Aiden sighed. "Hey, man. Listen, I'm dealing with some stuff up here and I won't be back for a bit. Yeah, everything is fine, but I'm gonna need you to keep Riley occupied. I'll reach out again soon." After a brief silence, he said, "Thanks man, I'll see you later."

She watched him while he stood in the kitchen for a moment, taking several deep breaths, clenching and unclenching his fists. Call it sixth sense, but she didn't think his frustration was with Riley. It felt like something else.

He turned and walked toward her again. "Sorry about that. Mom told Riley. I'm sure you know how that went."

She giggled. Riley was a handful. Hearing the one-sided phone conversation told Charlotte all she needed to know about what his little sister had likely demanded of him.

Smoothing her hands over her thighs, her gaze snagged on a shoebox on her nightstand she hadn't seen before.

"That's odd."

"What?"

She slid over to the corner of the nightstand and lifted the black box that had a dark red X painted on the top and set it in her lap. "Think the forensics team left it behind?"

"I don't think they'd keep supplies in a shoebox," he said, crossing his arms.

With a sinking feeling in her gut, she lifted the lid from the box and choked on the gasp that bubbled up her throat but never escaped.

Inside the black shoebox lay a dead bird and a single pink rose.

15

RULES

Useless. The urge to say the word out loud to the officers handling Charlotte's case burned at the back of Aiden's throat the entire time he sat across from the lieutenant at the police station.

The man was nice—oblivious to the various Vasirian working in the same place as him, but nice. The curious looks from his kind didn't escape Aiden's notice. The female deputy working alongside the lieutenant seemed especially surly regarding Charlotte's case. Her irritation, coupled with Officer Brooks' attitude, made him question if the Vasirian officers were protecting the stalker and covering up evidence.

What purpose would any of it serve?

Was it to protect their kind? Keep human authorities out of Vasirian matters? Did that mean the officers would report it to the Blackthorn Clan?

He doubted it.

Vasirian never went to humans to report crimes. They didn't involve themselves in human matters, and anytime there was a crime committed in their world, it went to the Blackthorn Clan, or the lower Orders in their respective areas of the world—if it went reported at all.

Aiden pushed the glass doors open, leaving the comfort of the air conditioning to face the balmy heat of the outdoors. Cicadas sang their shrill buzzing song, and the smell of fresh cut grass around the station added to the ambiance of summer.

Climbing into his car, he started the engine right away. Flipping the air to full blast, he relaxed back in the driver's seat trying to sort through everything that had taken place since he arrived in Athens.

Like with the break-in, the police did no more than document the shoebox with the dead bird and rose left behind in Charlotte's apartment. They said they would take fingerprints and photos. But like they told her, if they didn't find a lead to go on, there wasn't much they could do outside of record the information and hope the man would make a mistake.

He only hoped the mistake wouldn't cost Charlotte her life.

His knuckles blanched on the scalding steering wheel as the thought of something horrific happening to Charlotte crossed his mind. The fear he experienced at the real possibility of her demise made his stomach sour. His demons rose to the surface, reminding him of his own dance with death.

He wanted to help her, wanted to fix the situation so she could go to school and have the independent life she strived for. But a gut feeling deep inside told him something more held her to this college town than wanting to prove to her family she could make it on her own. Something deeper than her fears of a stalker.

He needed to figure out what. It was the only way to help her.

Putting the car into gear, he backed out of the parking space and left the police station. He needed to get back to Charlotte before the sun set. Leaving her alone after the break-in didn't feel right, but she'd had classes to attend.

He suspected her classes were over for the day, but he didn't want to risk interrupting her if they weren't by calling or texting her cell phone.

Instead, he made the twenty-minute trip across town to the blood donation clinic.

Sooner rather than later, he would need to figure out a stable solution to make sure his needs were met. He couldn't leave blood packets in her refrigerator, but he couldn't make a habit of leaving her place multiple times per day. Round trip, it took anywhere from thirty to forty minutes depending on traffic.

That left her vulnerable. It wasn't an option.

If she was in class, it would be easy to get what he needed, bring it back to feed, and dispose of the evidence in the trash chute after putting it in something so it wasn't obvious a blood bag was in the trash collection.

Until he found a fixed solution, he would have to make do with a morning feeding. He'd done it before, but it wasn't a viable long-term solution.

Not wanting to risk running into her with a blood packet, he finished it in the bathroom at the clinic before leaving.

He didn't fear not finding someone to accommodate his needs at the clinic. Across the world, wherever a blood and platelet donation center existed, at least one Vasirian was on staff to assist the needs of those not in the school system. One with the ability to compel humans into believing everything was legitimate and to do damage control when someone needed to feed on site like he did moments ago.

Arriving back at Charlotte's apartment as the sun began its descent over the horizon, turning the sky warm with shades of orange and pink, he parked in the neighboring parking lot.

He didn't know if the parking garage had assigned parking. He would need to ask Charlotte to use her reserved space before he ended up being towed.

Crossing the street, he came to an abrupt halt.

Noah was walking toward the front entrance, glancing around before grabbing the door handle. When his eyes met Aiden's, his brows lifted and he released the handle, changing direction toward the sidewalk.

"Why are you here?" Aiden didn't mean to sound gruff, but every time he ran into Noah, he felt agitated. The guy's mere presence set Aiden on edge.

"Whoa, now. I come in peace, big guy." Noah held both hands up in a placating gesture, and Aiden noticed the notebook in his left hand. "She left this in class today. Thought she might want it."

Aiden crossed his arms, his feet placed in line with his shoulders as he stared Noah down. He came all the way to Charlotte's apartment to deliver a notebook? Doubtful. Aiden didn't call him on it, though. He didn't have time to deal with one of Charlotte's admirers—even if his interest was suspicious.

"I'll give it to her," he said, holding his hand out.

"What? I can't even visit?" Noah's grin was lazy, taunting. "You're not even her boyfriend, and you're throwing your weight around like she's yours."

Aiden pressed his tongue against the inside of his cheek for a beat of silence before saying in a low tone, "She's not yours. You know the rules."

"Doesn't mean I can't have a little fun," Noah taunted.

Aiden's hand shot out so fast it startled them both, gripping Noah by the front of his shirt and jerking him forward until they were nose to nose. He could smell the coffee on Noah's breath. Charlotte would hate that. She hated coffee.

"Off Limits," he snarled, a deep rumble vibrating in his chest.

Noah's eyes narrowed at the sound.

"I mean it. Touch one hair on her head and I will end you."

Aiden stopped short of demanding he never speak to Charlotte again. Though he wanted to with every fiber of his being. They were classmates and needed to work together. Not to mention she seemed to like the guy, so it might hurt her if Noah ghosted her.

Noah shoved him back, and he stumbled a few steps before righting himself.

"You know you can't have her either. The rules apply to you too. You can't have anything more than a little fun or you'll expose us all."

Aiden knew that. Knew it, and hated it, with every fiber of his being. The more time passed around the red-haired girl, the more he wished there wasn't a divide between them. That species didn't matter.

The depressing reality made his anger settle, and he schooled his expression to keep Noah from seeing how the words affected him.

"She's my friend. There's nothing to worry about."

He wasn't lying. It didn't matter if his mind flirted with the idea of something meaningful beyond what a friendship provided. Like Noah said, if he tried, it would expose their secret. He wouldn't put that on Charlotte.

"Then there's nothing wrong with me being her friend, either."

"It better stay that way," he sneered.

"Don't worry. I know when I'm not wanted. I'm not so desperate to continue trying when she made it clear she wasn't interested."

The way Noah was grinning, the asshole only meant to provoke him. Noah had already decided not to pursue Charlotte and had goaded him into acting rash.

It made anger bubble back to the surface, but he wouldn't let it control him. Jealousy made him want to lay Noah out on the sidewalk, but Noah's taunts were a product of his own jealousy. Aiden had what he didn't. Even if neither of them could have what they wanted with Charlotte, they both could have her friendship.

He knew as well as Noah did who had the stronger bond.

When Noah left, Aiden pulled his cell phone from his pocket and swiped the screen, placing a call to Lukas. He needed someone to talk to about everything.

"Hey," Lukas said.

Nothing more, nothing less. Always the Chatty Kathy, as his mother once described him in jest. The thought made him smile.

"Hey, man. Got a minute?"

"Yeah. You back? I can come by the dorm."

"No. Riley didn't tell you?"

"I haven't seen her today, but she met Blaire for lunch in the courtyard, so maybe Blaire knows."

"I'm still in Athens. I'm gonna be here for a while. Maybe the rest of the summer."

A door shut on the other end and then Lukas's voice came through again. "Why?"

"I don't know what's going on, but some asshole has attached himself to Charlotte."

"Attached himself? What does that even mean?"

"A stalker, man. She has a stalker."

"The fuck?"

Aiden laughed and laid his head back, looking up at the darkening sky. "That's what I think. It's surreal. This guy has not only been following her around for months, but he's sending her roses. If that wasn't bad enough, he's broken into her home a few times." He took a deep inhale, the smell of begonias in nearby flowerbeds drifting on the faint breeze. "I was there for the last one. Well, not there in the apartment at the same time, but we came back to the place wrecked. He's escalating."

"Any idea who it is?"

"None. But if we were placing bets, I'd be tempted to put some money on one of her classmates who's taken an interest in her."

"You think the guy is doing it because he's into her?"

"No. I think he's doing it because he's like us."

"What's that supposed to mean?"

Aiden sighed. "He's a Vasirian."

After a long pause, Lukas said, "Just because he's a Vasirian doesn't mean he's a stalker. We're not stalkers." He added the last few words as if Aiden needed reminding.

"I know that. It's just convenient timing. He's hanging around her while she has a stalker. Going to a human college." His hand tightened on the notebook he held. "I don't trust him."

"I hate to say it, but you might be overthinking this one. Some Vasirian do break away from the Blackthorn school system. Rare, but they do."

Aiden hadn't considered it. His family was all Blackthorn Academy alumni, and both he and Riley would follow in their footsteps.

"I wish she could join us at the academy. Wish the rules were different and she could know things since she's already so involved in our lives. Then none of this would be an issue. Blaire would have her friend back, and..." He trailed off, not wanting to get too deep with his personal feelings, but Lukas didn't seem to have such reservations.

"And you'd get to have her by your side?"

Aiden dragged his hand over his face. He should have never mentioned his budding feelings for the girl months ago.

"I liked you better when you were a grouchy brat," he said, a lightness to his words.

In reality, he wouldn't change the transformation Lukas had gone through for the world.

Gone was the perpetual grump hiding from the world and using indifference as a shield. Replaced by someone caring, easygoing, and proactive in his relationships.

Aiden always knew Lukas cared and had it in him to be there if someone needed it, but his own insecurities and broken heart about his family made him hold the world at arm's length.

That was until Blaire came along and tore down his walls with a sledgehammer.

"Listen, I need to get off here. Charlotte's probably home. I don't want to leave her alone too long."

"She's home."

"How you know?"

"Blaire's on the phone with her now. I stepped outside to give them privacy and hear you better. After we get off, I'm gonna swing by Riley and Seth's room to pick up a game before coming back. Give them some time to talk."

"Alright."

"Keep in touch. I'd offer to come up, but you know I couldn't come without Blaire."

"Yeah, I know. I'll keep you posted."

He tucked his phone in his pocket.

As much as it would help to have his friend around for the support in finding the guy, Lukas couldn't separate from his Korrena long. Blaire couldn't come either. Charlotte's apartment couldn't hold all of them, anyway, making it unrealistic to expect them to waste the summer out of town with no guarantee of finding the guy. He also didn't want to put Blaire in danger. She wasn't like them. Putting another human in danger wasn't right.

Keeping them away and staying close to Charlotte afforded him the best opportunity to protect his friends.

16

Confidant

Watching the sun set over the horizon from her bedroom window, Charlotte leaned back against her pillows with her phone in hand. She needed to reach out to someone before the things eating away at her insides devoured her whole.

Having Aiden there felt nice, but she couldn't tell him everything. She didn't even know if he understood how frightening it felt to have someone invade her privacy and believe they were entitled to pieces of her life without her consent.

She knew someone who would understand. Someone who experienced the invasion of her privacy by someone who thought they owned her. The difference was this person knew the identity of her personal boogeyman. Her own stepbrother.

Opening her contacts, she scrolled to her best friend's name and hit call. The line rang twice before Blaire's voice came through.

"Hey, Charlotte!"

She smiled, her eyes misting. She missed her friend more than she realized. Her voice alone made her eyes burn.

"Hey there."

"What's up?"

A deep male spoke in the background, but she couldn't make out what he was saying.

"Am I interrupting?"

"Not at all. Lukas is on the phone with Aiden."

That made her pause. Aiden was supposed to be at the police station reporting the dead bird box she found in her bedroom. They had already touched the box, so they tampered with the evidence, but she hoped the police could find something from the interior. They left that alone.

He had insisted she stay home after she got out of classes earlier in the day while he made the report. He reasoned she had already experienced enough emotional turmoil, and he wanted to take care of it for her.

When she asked him why he didn't go this morning while she made her presentation with her group, he told her he wanted to stay at the apartment in case the guy tried to break in again. She didn't understand how he could be so brave. To take on an intruder without thought. If she didn't know any better, she would say it wasn't bravery but sheer stupidity.

"He's gone now. He took the phone outside. So, how have you been? Riley said something about Aiden staying with you. What's that all about?"

Straight to the point it is.

She propped her head against the wall above her headboard and closed her eyes. She needed to do this; needed to tell someone.

"I've got a stalker," she said in a casual tone, lighter than the heaviness she felt on her chest. When Blaire said nothing, Charlotte opened her eyes to look at the screen, squinting when she saw the call still appeared active. She put it back to her ear. "Blaire? You there?"

"Did you just say you've got a stalker?"

"Yep," she said with a casual air, trying to remain relaxed.

"What the hell, Charlotte?" She heard shuffling on the other side of the line. "What are you talking about? Who? Since when?"

"I'm talking about someone following me around, sending me weekly flower deliveries, breaking into my home. I don't know. Since moving up here."

"You sound way too calm about this."

"Trust me, I'm not."

It took great effort for her to rattle off the bullet point summary of the actions the man had taken against her in a calm, steady tone.

"Hang on," Blaire said.

Charlotte's phone started making noises signaling a FaceTime call. Serious conversations always called for video. At least that never changed between them. Part of her almost wished it had.

She braced her forearm on her knee and accepted the video request.

As soon as her friend's heart-shaped face filled the screen, tears filled Charlotte's eyes and spilled over her cheeks.

"Oh, Char…" Blaire sniffled, trying to hold it together for her. "Talk to me. Tell me what's happened."

She detailed everything. How she thought someone followed her, saw someone, the calls, the break-ins, and now the dead bird. By the end of the explanation where Blaire sat silent with a horrified expression on her face, Charlotte felt exhausted.

"Do your moms know?"

"Absolutely not, and you can't tell them. I can't make them worry more than they already are about me being up here."

"But Charlo—"

"No." She swiped her cheeks and sat up, crisscrossing her legs, and giving Blaire her most intimidating stare. "You say nothing."

"*Fine.* But what are you going to do about it?"

"I've made a couple police reports."

"Charlotte, you need to come home."

She grumbled. Now Blaire sounded like Aiden.

"Aiden's staying with me until they solve the case, so I'll be fine. Or at least that's what he said."

Blaire tucked her long hair behind her ear. "If he said it, he'll do it. You should know him well enough by now to know that."

She wasn't wrong. Charlotte had spent more time talking to Aiden than she had her own best friend since Blaire joined Blackthorn Academy last April. It seemed surreal.

"I still don't understand why you wouldn't come back home. I would have packed everything up and hopped the first bus south the first time I knew for sure."

She didn't doubt it. She knew the only reason Blaire didn't make a run for it when her stepfamily made it their mission to control every aspect of her life was because the Wilcox family had too much power. Her life was in danger if she left.

The thing Blaire didn't understand, though, leaving Athens put everyone Charlotte cared about at risk. Anyone she associated with might fall prey to the stalker. He'd never expressed what he wanted with her. She didn't know how far his delusions went. Who they might extend to.

Then there was the attack she witnessed in the alley.

It benefited everyone for her to remain put. Everyone except Aiden. She hated putting him in the crosshairs by being near her.

"I want my life to be normal. I want to make this work. The police will catch this guy soon, and if I up and leave, he might switch his sights on someone else. At least now I have someone with me. Who knows, maybe the guy will leave me alone if he sees me with Aiden."

Stalkers gravitated toward people who lived alone, right?

"Maybe," Blaire said, but the frown marring her face spoke of her lack of faith in the statement. "Weren't you considering quitting?"

"Let me guess… Riley?"

"No, you."

"Huh?"

"You've talked to me and Riley about it a few times in the past month."

Her hand at her side gripped the comforter beneath her. "I forgot," she mumbled.

This wasn't the first instance where she forgot something she'd done or said to someone. It seemed to get worse when things were unstable around her, but what could she do about it? The doctor already had her on medication. She didn't want to make another appointment with everything happening.

Even if the mandatory student health plan covered the service, she didn't want to waste a professional's time when she couldn't be open about what she experienced. She didn't want to trigger a false diagnosis.

She knew she had depression. The symptoms were the same as before. She recognized the problem, but if she went and expressed further concerns about her cognitive functions, they might misdiagnose her when she didn't reveal the whole story. She didn't relish the idea of what that might mean.

"Do you need me to come up there? It's summer break. I can stay with you." Blaire's eyes shifted up over the screen and her face fell.

"I forgot about that," she said. Her gaze shifted to the screen. Her expression looked pained with whatever thought crossed her mind. "I, uh… I actually can't. I can't leave."

Charlotte didn't ask her what would keep her from coming to stay with her. She didn't have room for Blaire anyway, and she wouldn't put her friend in that kind of danger. Aiden was here because of their agreement. She could stay only if she allowed him to stay with her. He was big, strong, and male. That would discourage her stalker—she hoped.

"That's alright. There's only one bed here, anyway, and the couch is too small to sleep on."

"What?" Blaire's eyes went as big as saucers. "Where's Aiden sleeping?"

"Oh, well…" Her face screwed up, teeth sinking into her lip with her guilty smile. "Here. In the bed. With me." She forgot Blaire had never seen her apartment. Still, she didn't want to lie to her friend, so it didn't matter.

The camera jerked about, and Blaire rose to her knees as she squealed, "What?"

Charlotte's face heated, likely turning the same shade as the lingering cherry lowlights in her hair from when she colored it last.

"I can't believe you're sleeping together!" Blaire looked up. "Yes! She's sleeping with him!"

A male voice spoke in the background. Lukas must have returned.

"We're not sleeping together like that. Don't be weird."

Blaire lowered herself down, the camera losing its shaky quality. "Oh."

"Don't sound disappointed, either." Charlotte rolled her eyes.

"I'm not!" Blaire laughed. "I don't know what I was thinking."

The door rattled, making her spine stiffen and her breath catch.

"Charlotte? What's wrong?"

"Someone's here," she whispered.

"What? Now? No." Blaire's voice sounded far away as fear tried to pull Charlotte under. "Someone's there with her. No, not Aiden."

Aiden.

"Crap. It might be Aiden," she said with a shaky breath, her senses coming back to her.

She had given him a key to come and go freely, but completely forgot about it. He should be back by now, so it made sense.

"Charlotte?"

The familiar masculine voice coming from the other side of the wall made her sink into the pillows and close her eyes. They needed to come up with a better way to let one another know when they were coming into the apartment. Maybe texting first. She didn't know if her heart could handle the unexpected scares.

"Is it?" Blaire said, her voice sounding panicked.

Pulling in a deep lungful of air, she opened her eyes to see both Lukas and Blaire staring at her with concern. "It's just Aiden."

"What's just me?"

"You're texting me before you come in next time. You about gave me a heart attack."

Aiden looked over his shoulder, back to where he came from, and then at her. "I scared you? Shit, I'm so sorry." He lowered himself to sit next to her against the pillows, his arm brushing hers. "I'll text you next time. I put your notebook on the kitchen counter. You left it in class. Noah dropped it off." He finally took notice of the phone. "Oh, hey. Why didn't you tell her it was me?"

"Hey," Blaire said. "I didn't know."

"No, I mean him."

Lukas shrugged. "I didn't know. We've been off the phone for a little while. Told you I was going to get a game."

Blaire waved a hand, dismissing their back and forth, making Charlotte giggle. "Charlotte was just telling me about her little… big problem."

"Yeah?" Aiden looked from the screen to Charlotte.

"Yeah." She looked at Lukas, noting his expression didn't hold an ounce of confusion. She looked at Aiden. "You told him?"

Both Lukas and Aiden's eyes widened in response to the question. *Bingo.*

"It's okay," she mumbled. "He's your best friend, and you're kinda living with me for now. Besides, I didn't really expect Blaire to keep it a secret."

"Hey, I can keep a secret. It's Riley you have to worry about."

"To be fair, she's gotten better about that," Lukas said.

"It's not that I didn't think you couldn't keep it to yourself," Charlotte said. "I just didn't expect you to keep something so serious from him. Lukas is my friend. I want him to know."

Lukas cleared his throat and lowered his eyes, his hand raking through his long hair as he sat back out of frame.

Blaire laughed. "He's shy."

"Hardly," Lukas said with a grunt.

"What? You're not happy she considers you her friend?"

"By the stars, woman," he muttered. "Yes. She's my friend." With a sigh, he added in a gruff tone, "I'm happy about it."

Charlotte's brows pinched. "Did you just say, 'by the stars'?"

Blaire's head whipped to look at the screen, her laughter fading. "What?"

"Stars? I've never heard that phrase before."

"I didn't hear that." Blaire looked at Lukas again, and he shrugged.

"I'm starving," Aiden said, drawing Charlotte's attention. "You want to do takeout?"

"I can't really splurge after the grocery shopping we did." She frowned. "I can cook."

"Well, it would be my treat, but I won't turn down a home-cooked meal." His smile made her stomach swoop.

"We'll let you guys go. We're heading down to the cafeteria for dinner, too." Blaire's cheerful expression fell. "Please call me if anything happens, Char. I love you. I want you to be safe. If it's too bad, promise me you'll come home."

Charlotte's throat felt tight as she swallowed. "Yeah, I promise."

17

Rejection

The verdict when Charlotte visited the rental office after finishing her presentation, and classes let out for the day, made her question the legality of allowing residents to suffer in the sweltering heat for extended periods of time.

After going all week without a word from management, she realized she needed to show her face before another weekend of discomfort. Emails and phone calls going to voicemail got her nowhere.

"Air conditioning is a luxury, Miss. Walsh," they'd told her. Told her they were waiting on a replacement system for the entire building that would take another month to get online between the delivery and installation. Some poor excuse about service worker schedules, followed by informing her she could buy a window unit.

At least they fixed the water issue by mid-week. That level of quick repair fit more with how they handled things around the complex.

The building wasn't a dump. The entire place was chic. Rooftop pool. Exercise room. Even a coffee shop below the apartments. The rent wasn't cheap, but her student grants and loans helped with that.

With the high-end environment, she questioned why the air conditioning wasn't a big deal to them. Of course, no matter how well maintained a place was, they still fell victim to the whims of being forced into the schedule of someone else. She understood, so she took the information and left without complaint, though she hated making Aiden suffer through the heat.

Her apartment felt like a sauna some days. She didn't feel comfortable opening the window or the sliding glass door for fear of her stalker getting inside. She still kept the loveseat against the glass doors.

Her head rested against the elevator wall as the metal box climbed to her floor.

As much as she loathed to admit it, it was one of those days where she wanted to disappear. One of those everything is overwhelming days, and if she could not wake up—if only for the next twenty-four hours—that would be great. She didn't want to kill herself or die; it wasn't *that* serious, probably in part thanks to the medicine.

No, she simply felt bombarded from all sides and stopping sounded like a great idea.

It made her angry with herself that the thought even crossed her mind. Here she had her parents working hard back home to send her money to live on beyond the grants, school friends who wanted to take her out and give her a reason to want to stay, and a man currently sitting in her apartment giving up his summer break to ensure her safety. He'd already lost the week to her nonsense.

And what did she give back?

She kept secrets from her parents and wanted to change her major from something that would help them and show her thanks for their support. Continued to dodge going out with her friends for the safety of her apartment and the bubble she created with Aiden. And to top it all off, she kept finding herself lusting after her friend who had come to help her.

Maybe the last point wasn't as bad. He didn't appear immune to her either, but he kept a respectable distance. Even the touches and hugs in the early days of his arrival when everything hit the fan had ceased.

Because it was only to soothe you as a friend should, idiot.

Her thumb and forefinger pressed into her eyes. Oh, how she wanted to go to sleep and try again tomorrow. The solstice had arrived, and so far, she couldn't see where her life was any different. Had her mom missed the mark for once?

One positive thing she could speak of was her secret admirer—or whatever he was—seemed to have taken a backseat to her life all week after the break-in on Monday. He hadn't replaced the roses that were destroyed in the break-in.

Maybe Aiden's presence really worked.

The elevator dinged, arriving at her floor. She stepped into her hall and made it to her door before she smoothed her hands over the front of her navy-blue sundress. It fell to her mid-thigh, with a sweetheart neckline that tied between her breasts, and puffy short sleeves. She paired it with a pair of white, cork-board platform sandals that looped around her ankles several times and tied in a bow at the back.

She looked cute—or at least she thought she did. Aiden was still asleep when she left that morning, so she didn't know what he'd say about it. But the look wasn't for him.

She wanted to make an effort today to counter the dark cloud hanging over her head and the poisonous thoughts taunting her. If her life was meant to change today, she wanted to look her best.

She even had one of her favorite jewelry sets on. Silver crescent moon earrings and a silver necklace with a matching crescent moon pendant encircling a mother-of-pearl disc. A shorter, dainty chain rested below her clavicle, with a tiny sapphire to match her dress. She owned several with tiny colored gemstones.

Running her hands once more over the soft, fluttery fabric to push out nervous tension, she used her keys to unlock the door.

"Aiden?" she called out when she didn't see him right away.

When she didn't hear anything, she crossed the kitchen toward her bedroom, eager to take her shoes off and tuck them away in her closet. Stepping around the corner next to her computer desk, she squeaked when she caught sight of Aiden standing with his back to her in nothing but a fluffy white towel.

Water droplets dripped from wet, midnight black hair and trailed down his back over a gorgeous tattoo of a large raven flying over his shoulder blade. Feathers fluttered in a trail across his spine to the other shoulder blade.

Her eyes traveled down from the tattoo, tracing the rigid muscles of his back to a set of dimples right above the towel. As if the guy needed to be any more attractive, he was blessed with the dimples of Apollo.

She shook her head and lifted her gaze from his lower back, catching him staring at her in the mirrored doors of her closet.

"Sorry," she mumbled. "I called your name." She rubbed her lips together, feeling the slide of her lip gloss. "You didn't respond," she added lamely. *Of course he didn't respond. He knows that.*

Her eyes dropped to his chest in the mirror, and his pecs flexed in reflex. She assumed it was reflex.

It was rude to stare, but she couldn't stop, and he wasn't stopping her. Why wasn't he stopping her?

Trailing her gaze down his torso in a slow descent over chiseled abs and a deep V, she sucked in a sharp breath when her gaze reached his towel.

Tenting his towel in an obscene manner, his cock pointed right at the mirror.

His eyes followed where she looked when he heard her intake of breath and he pivoted his hips away from the mirror, cursing to himself. "It's not what it looks like."

She spun around to face the kitchen to give him a modicum of privacy. What she should have done to start with. "It's," she started, but her voice sounded pitchy, so she cleared her throat. "It's normal. If you just got out of the shower, I mean. Hot water does that, right?"

She could have sworn she heard something about hot water making men's penises thicker. Did the heat give them erections? She didn't know, but she wasn't about to Google it right then.

It wasn't like she made a habit out of seeing men fresh out of the shower—or in the shower under hot water. And certainly not Aiden in the shower. *Ugh, don't think about him in the shower now!* Even with her ex in high school, she never saw him like that. The couple of times they went all the way weren't in the best situations to follow up with a shower.

She rationalized it with the phenomenon of morning wood. Guys woke up with erections, why couldn't hot showers trigger the same? They taught them as kids in sexual education classes that rogue erections weren't uncommon in males.

Aiden made a grunting sound that she wasn't sure meant an acknowledgment of truth or a denial of her assumption. It didn't matter either way.

"I'll leave you to get dressed in peace."

"You look… nice today," he said as she stepped away.

What a weird thing to say, all things considered. Though it made her feel more confident in her choice of attire.

A few minutes later, Aiden came around the corner into her living room in a new pair of medium-wash jeans and a black V-neck T-shirt that stretched snug over his biceps, shoulders, and chest. It fell loose from the ribs where his torso tapered in to his waist and came to rest above his pockets. His wet hair looked longer, smoothed back as he ran the fingers of both hands through it to finger comb the hair into place.

"Hey," he said, dropping his arms at his side. His chuckle sounded uncomfortable.

"Hi?" She unlaced the ribbon around her ankles and slid the sandals from her feet, groaning in relief as she wiggled her toes. Beautiful shoes, hell on the feet. "Sorry for walking in on you. I really didn't know you were here."

A faint hint of pink on his sharp cheekbones at her words didn't escape her notice.

"Nah, it's fine. You've seen me in either boxers or shorts at bed time. Not like you haven't seen everything, anyway."

"Not the tattoo," she said, tactfully choosing not to address the fact she'd never seen his cock before. Well, she didn't see it then either, only the estimated size based on how far out the towel looked in the mirror. She didn't even see the thickness or shape. *Stop thinking about his dick.*

"Huh? You've never seen it?"

"No, you sleep on your back, and I looked away before I saw it at Tybee Island."

He walked over on bare feet to sit next to her on the loveseat. She turned to face him, drawing her knees up onto the cushion.

"I would have figured you'd have seen it when we got ready for bed or something."

At night, she was either already in bed or trying not to look at him until they were both beneath the safety of the covers. In the mornings, she either got up and left before him, or he was up before her and dressed before she got out of bed. More often than not, if she didn't have classes, he got up and left for about an hour.

She had no idea where he went, but he always came back with a ton of energy compared to how he seemed to drag at night if they were up late.

She suspected it had to do with his nightmares. Although she hadn't witnessed any, he told her he sometimes woke up with them. She knew that already from their video calls and late-night chats before he ever came to visit.

"Do you want to see it?" His brows drew in. "I mean, a closeup. I don't mind." He chuckled. "I remember you like tattoos," he said, explaining why he offered likely in response to the confusion she knew was written on her face.

"Well, yeah. If you don't mind."

"It's on my back. It's not like it's on my ass."

She couldn't stop the giggle his sassy comeback elicited.

He grinned. Reaching behind his head, he pulled his shirt off with both hands and turned to face the wall, putting his back to her.

"How long have you had this?" she asked, leaning in to study the intricate lines of the raven's wings. Goose bumps prickled where her breath brushed his skin. "It's beautiful."

"Got it on my eighteenth birthday, so… it's June now, right?"

"Mmhmm. The twenty-first."

"So, almost two and a half years ago."

Reaching out, she absentmindedly brushed her fingertips across the bird's head, over the impressive wingspan, and into the chaos of fluttering loose feathers. Again, his skin responded to her by chasing her fingers with goose bumps.

"The ink's held up well," she said, lowering her hand, her fingers brushing over his shoulder blade, lingering a little longer before slipping away from his ribs where no ink existed.

She closed her eyes, steadying herself while he kept his back to her in silence. Leaning back into her corner of the loveseat again, she said, "Aiden?"

"Hmm?"

"You okay?"

He pulled the shirt back over his head and turned, drawing one leg up on the cushion to face her. "Yeah, I'm good."

She looked up at him, taking in the way his damp hair fell disheveled over his forehead and into his eyes. He normally kept his hair pushed back, showing off the cropped sides, but with removing his shirt, it looked in disarray. She could now see how long he kept it.

He said nothing as she studied him, almost as if he was allowing her to do it. It made her feel better to think he was letting her look rather than the likely reality that she was ogling him like a creep.

A heavy knock on the door made them both jump, breaking eye contact.

"I'll get it." Aiden stood from the loveseat and crossed to the front door. Looking out the peephole he said, "What the… No one's there." Unlocking the door, he pulled it open, and she watched as his shoulders and back went taut with tension.

"What is it?" She lowered her legs to the floor, standing.

Picking up whatever was on the floor that held his attention, he turned. He clutched a fresh bouquet of pink roses in his hand. Saying nothing, he marched over to the trash can and dumped them inside.

"Wait! What are you doing?" She raced across the floor to the bin and retrieved the bouquet, looking at him like he had lost his mind. "Why did you throw them out?"

"Why are you keeping them?"

Her head tilted back. She hadn't told him.

Tightening her hold on the bouquet, she said, "The last time I threw them out, I received a note on my door about it. It was the first time he contacted me in any way outside of the flower delivery. I didn't want it to happen again."

"Well, that ship has sailed now." He leaned back against the kitchen counter, folding his arms over his chest.

"Still. I don't want to bring extra attention than I already do." She walked over to the counter. She had an old vase she could use since her other shattered during the break-in.

"Nothing happened Tuesday," Aiden said, watching her with a tense set to his mouth.

He was angry she was keeping the roses, but what else could she do? Unless he proposed a better solution, she saw it as the appropriate response to avoid additional problems.

She bent to pull out the old vase and crossed to the sink to add water. "What are you talking about?"

"I tossed the ones that came Tuesday morning while you were in class, and nothing has happened."

She spun on him; the water sloshing in the vase. "You did what?" Her voice was loud, indignant. How could he do that? The realization her stalker had sent a replacement bouquet soured her stomach.

"Keeping these gifts on display is not only a constant reminder of the creep, but also feeds into his delusions. If this is about what the majority of stalker cases are about, you're feeding into his fantasies."

She placed the vase on the counter. "What fantasies? What do you think this is about?" It was something she questioned every day.

She had done nothing to grab anyone's attention. The flowers seemed like something from a secret admirer, so at first, she thought the person liked her and handled it poorly—not that she would give them the time of day, because handling it poorly or not, you don't follow someone around. But with the addition of breaking into her home, the creepy calls, the dead bird… She didn't know anymore. She had hurt no one or made anyone angry since her arrival to warrant the negative attention.

"He's a sick man who wants you," Aiden said in a flat tone.

She gave a rapid shake of her head in disbelief. "I thought he might like me, but not, like, want me."

She poured the plant food into the water and stirred it with the stem of one rose. Grabbing the scissors, she got to work on the mechanical task of preparing the roses for longevity. It became second nature; she'd done it so many times.

"Do you honestly believe that?" He pivoted to face her. "Someone who goes this far doesn't just *like* you. They are *obsessed*. Obsessed and twisted. Blaire's TA was obsessed with her and look what happened."

Her shoulders rose to her ears at the reminder of her best friend's abduction. That dark time had been the first time she really spoke to Aiden one on one. They all thought Blaire left Blackthorn Academy without telling anyone. That she broke up with Lukas and ghosted him. It wasn't her way. Blaire didn't act like that. Aiden thought Charlotte might have information, so he sought her out.

She hadn't even been told Blaire had been gone for a month already. It was a stark reminder of how she no longer fit in her best friend's world. Her new friends didn't even think to tell her. Now they were her friends too, but the memory still stung.

Putting the rose she cut into the water, she turned to him. "Didn't y'all say she disappeared without any sign?" At his nod, she continued,

"And did she receive strange gifts or threatening calls? Did the guy break into her dorm room?"

Aiden's forehead lined as his face contorted into a look of frustration. "No, but it doesn't always have to happen the same way. Vincent was around us daily. He got to see her up close and personal. Talk to her. This guy doesn't have that as far as we know. Until we know his identity, we can assume that. He seems to keep his distance, from what you told me. If he doesn't have easy access to you, it could explain the way he's acting."

She turned and put the rest of the flowers into the vase, and then dumped the trash.

She hadn't considered it that way before. Of course she knew the man was obsessed—twisted too if she considered the dead bird, but obsessed with wanting her instead of obsessed with tormenting someone? That theory settled like a lead weight in her belly.

Her eyes tracked down to the feminine outfit she wore. Legs on display, cleavage she couldn't really hide unless she wore a T-shirt or full coverage blouse. Even the designers made her dainty shoes to enhance her feminine appeal. She wanted to look cute, but the startling reality was she had attracted a monster.

She had ignored the warnings found online. Maybe if she had dressed in jeans and T-shirts instead of cooler outfits that were pretty and trying too hard, she never would have been a target.

"Charlotte?"

She glanced over at Aiden, realizing she'd fallen silent at his revelation. "Yeah?"

"What are you thinking?"

Her hands gripped the edge of the counter, her fingertips whitening around the navy-blue nail polish she wore to match her dress. "I think I need to change."

"Change?"

"Clothes." When he said nothing, she turned to him. "What?"

"I don't think I'm following."

"Look at me," she said, throwing her arms out to each side of her hips, hands palm up, facing him. "It's not like I'm trying to be subtle and reserved. I'm not dressed like a hoe or whatever, but I'm certainly not giving the 'stay away from me' impression."

Aiden's eyes narrowed, and he stepped forward, backing her against the counter, putting his hands on the counter's edge on each side of her. He brought his face down to eye level.

"No," he said once he had her where he wanted her. Caged in and unable to move away from him.

The one-word command made her eyes round with surprise.

"No," he repeated softer. "You don't get to do that. You don't get to blame yourself for this. You did nothing wrong. This is all on him." He pointed an accusing finger off to the side before returning his hand to the counter. "You're not dressed like a… hoe. And even if you were, you still aren't inviting anything. Is that what you wanted by putting this dress on today?"

Her head moved from side to side.

"What did you want, then?"

"I wanted to look pretty," she whispered.

His eyes slowly pulled away from hers, moving over her face to her throat as he eased away from her to stand upright. His gaze slid over her necklaces and down across her cleavage, traveling south over the dress she wore.

"You didn't succeed." His voice was husky and dark. It made her want to squirm. "Not even close."

Her arms rose to wrap around herself as insecurity swamped her, but he didn't let her put up her shield. He grabbed her biceps and stepped into her, bringing their bodies flush. She sucked in a sharp breath.

"You misunderstand." His slow words and low tone had her heart hammering in her chest, ready to take flight. "Pretty isn't the word I would use to describe you in this little dress." He slid his hands down to cup her elbows, stepping back to add a few inches of space between them.

She knew her gulp was audible. "Then what?" She hated how her voice sounded meek. Hated how she sounded fragile.

"Tempting."

The one word made every nerve ending in her body fire at once. She rubbed her thighs together as subtly as possible. She could feel her pulse in places she shouldn't. Not in response to him.

Her body tensed when his forehead dropped to her shoulder. His breath tickled on her chest, coming heavier than before. She bit the inside of her lip hard in an effort not to make a sound, drawing blood.

"You look beautiful," he said through gritted teeth. "Never change out of fear. I promised I would protect you, and I meant it. Don't change who you are. Don't let him break you."

His words penetrated the haze of desire hanging over her mind. Words he forced out, with how strained and raspy they came.

Lifting his head, he looked into her eyes.

Her lips parted, and his eyes latched onto them instead, making her breath hitch.

"Too tempting," he mumbled, his hand coming up to cup her cheek, thumb sliding back and forth over her skin as she leaned into the touch.

Lowering his head, his lips brushed over hers. A gentle graze, giving her the opportunity to stop him if she wanted, but quickly morphing into something deeper.

His tongue trailed over her bottom lip, and she whimpered, which gave him the access to slide inside and meet her tongue in a slow caress.

A deep rumble sounded in his chest as his arms moved to band around her, pulling her close to his body as the kiss went from slow and languid to consuming fire in an instant.

One of his hands moved up to cradle the back of her head, while the other slid down her back over her dress and around her hip, gripping so tightly she suspected there would be a lingering bruise. She wasn't opposed.

He jerked her lower half forward against his, and she wasn't sure if what she felt against her belly was arousal through his jeans or not. It sure felt like it. Hard, thick, long. Yeah, he wanted her, and she didn't know what to do with herself.

Her hands found themselves tangled in his damp hair, tugging on the length as she struggled for gulps of air between kisses.

If only she were a little taller.

If only he would pick her up.

No, not for you, she chastised herself.

The last time she wanted a man was in high school, and that had been a boy. A fumbling, unsure boy who was overeager and lacked finesse.

Nothing compared to the dominant man pressed against her, claiming her mouth like he owned it.

When a growl vibrated against her lips, she gasped. The sound felt hotwired straight to her clit, and she squeezed her thighs against the sensation. She'd never heard a man sound like that.

"Fuck, fuck, fuck," he cursed against her lips. "I can't." He tore his mouth away from her and fled to the bathroom with a look of horror on his face. A stain of red painted his lower lip.

She brought her hand up to her mouth and touched it. Her fingers came away glistening with blood. She bit the inside of her lip harder than she realized earlier.

Her body sagged against the counter as she panted heavily, trying to sort through the mental gymnastics that was what happened between them.

She felt sexual frustration around him but had no idea it could be going both ways.

What she didn't understand was why he ran away like his ass was on fire.

The rejection stung.

18

Surrender

He messed up.

Messed up on a stomach-churning, soul-crushing level.

Aiden gripped the bathroom sink as he stared at his face. Stared at the crimson staining his lips.

Blood.

Charlotte's blood.

It tasted like ambrosia on his tongue, tempting him to go back for more.

His tongue moved over his lower lip, drawing in the last remnants of the evidence of their kiss. He shuddered.

With limited feedings, he didn't feel as in control as before. Blood from a live source hit in a way much different from a blood bag.

He'd never taken straight from the source.

His grip tightened.

I didn't bite her.

The surety of that statement rang through him. Why did she have blood in her mouth?

Concern twisted his gut tighter, and he looked at the door.

He couldn't hear her on the other side, but she was there. He left her in confusion. Left her aroused.

He saw it in her dilated pupils and in her flushed cheeks and chest. Gorgeous and tempting, the pink staining the tops of her pale breasts peeking out of the top of her dress beckoned him. The blood that stirred beneath the surface called to him like a siren's song.

His gaze flicked to himself in the mirror, resisting the temptation to leave the bathroom and go to her. To take care of the state he left her in.

Messy hair greeted him, a product of her soft hands raking through it. He could still feel the tugging sensation at the roots.

It had to be the blood.

That was the only explanation for how he lost control of himself.

You hadn't tasted her blood when you chose to kiss her. Told her she was a temptation.

He groaned and squeezed his eyes shut.

He'd done so good. Resisted her in moments of torture. Lying in bed with her body near his. When she touched his bare skin.

All it took was her insecurity to draw out his natural need to protect and reassure, paired with the way she looked at him fresh out of the shower—like a dessert begging to be tasted—and he couldn't control himself.

He always held onto his control. Never once had he felt out of control.

Charlotte tested his control.

It wasn't so bad until they started sleeping in the same bed, and his feeding schedule altered.

Maybe it wasn't her that tested his control. His need for more blood made him less in control; and his natural attraction for her, that grew the more they got to know one another, heightened with that need.

He really shouldn't touch her the way he had. Tasting her blood in the kiss would explain why it went so far.

It wouldn't happen again.

For her sake, it wouldn't happen again.

Pushing open the bathroom door after composing himself, he found Charlotte standing in the middle of the kitchen, as pale as the white card she held in her hand.

His hackles rose at once.

Striding toward her, he took the card from her trembling fingers. He wrapped his arm around her shoulders, pulling her into his chest while he lifted the card to read over her head.

I know what you saw.
And nothing is going to save you from the truth. Not even your live-in boyfriend. He can't keep you from me.

You can't run anymore, Cherry.

Play house while you can.
I'm coming for you soon.

Aiden's chest vibrated with the inhuman growl he was suppressing. He didn't need her to hear it. He hoped she mistook the vibration as a shudder of anger, because he felt a lot of that emotion.

With his senses on alert from the taste of her blood, his body primed for more than it received, and now a direct threat to the girl in his arms, he didn't know where to steer the overwhelming feelings bubbling inside.

"I won't let him touch you," he whispered, his lips brushing her curls. He knew she couldn't feel it—he didn't want her to—but it made him feel better.

She tilted her head to look up at him. "Should we call the police?"

In any other case he would say yes, but nothing would come of it. The lieutenant had told them both that unless any solid leads presented themselves, all they could do was document it.

"No. But I'll take it down to the station while you're in classes tomorrow so they can file it with the rest of the evidence."

Her arms looped around his waist, and her small hands bunched in the back of his shirt. The gentle embrace calmed him.

"Thank you."

"For what?"

"For dealing with it. You don't have to, but you're doing it, anyway." She looked down. "It means a lot."

His eyes moved to the note card again. "What did you see?"

"Hmm?" She looked up at his face.

"It says, 'I know what you saw.' What did you see?"

Charlotte pulled away from his hold, and he let her. "It's nothing," she said, walking across the room to pick up her sandals.

He held up the card. "It has to mean something if it's on this. This guy wouldn't just put anything on here. It has to mean something to you."

Her steps quickened as she crossed the living room, passing him in the kitchen, before disappearing into the bedroom.

He followed her. "What aren't you telling me?"

Opening the closet, she set her sandals alongside the row of shoes on the floor. "You'll think I'm crazy."

He gave her a look he hoped conveyed how unimpressed he felt that she'd think he could ever see her that way.

"I'm serious, Aiden. I don't know why he's mentioning it. I'm not even sure it was real. I'm still convinced I had heatstroke. That kinda thing just doesn't happen." Her laugh was flighty and nervous, making him anxious. She wasn't acting like herself.

"So let me be the judge of whether it sounds 'crazy' or not."

She slumped down on the edge of the bed, clasping her hands together between her knees, drawing his attention to the smooth, pale skin of her thighs where her dress rode higher with the way she sat down so abruptly.

"So you know the stories about vampires? Dracula? Twilight? The whole Transylvania thing?"

"Uh huh," he said, dragging the word out.

He knew all about the myths in the media. Some of the stories were eerily similar to what happened when Vasirian experienced *sanguis manie*. Enough to where his friend Kai speculated that someone saw it, and that's where the legends of vampires came from.

"I thought I saw one."

His brows pulled together. "What?"

She looked up at him. "A vampire. I thought someone was following me, so I tried to cut across an alley to get to the bus stop faster. I saw a couple together and coulda swore they were making out, but then I saw the guy's face. He was in pain." She rolled her lips in and shook her head before making eye contact again.

His gut tightened, a sense of foreboding setting in.

"He told me to run despite the pain he was in. Even though the other man was hurting him." She lowered her gaze to the floor. "When I saw those glowing blue eyes and fangs… All the blood… I did just that. I ran and left that man there to die." She sniffed. "I'm terrible. I could have—"

"What? What could you do in a dark alley?" He crouched in front of her. "If someone is attacking another person, you don't try to be a hero. Not when that person is larger than you."

He assumed the Vasirian was bigger than her. It didn't matter. If she had witnessed a Vasirian attacking a human, she would have been in danger. Only rogues attacked humans. It was against their laws to harm humans. He had no doubts what she saw was a Vasirian. The glowing eyes and fangs were enough to convince him. He knew of no other being like his kind.

"I know, but he seemed so worried about me and not himself."

He rose to sit beside her on the bed, and she turned her body toward his as soon as he reached for her. He stretched his left leg out, leaning on the headboard with his right leg still on the floor to give her space between his thighs to settle close to him. She drew her legs up, curling them beneath her as she nestled against his chest.

"You think I'm crazy, don't you?" she whispered.

He stroked her shoulder and arm while resting his other hand on the dip of her waist. "Not even a little."

He wouldn't tell her what she saw wasn't real. He wouldn't gaslight her like that, but he wouldn't confirm it either. Even coming up with a plausible excuse didn't sit right with him. He didn't want to lie to her. She didn't seem inclined to ask what he believed, and he hoped it remained that way.

It unsettled him that not only had she witnessed a rogue attack, but that her stalker knew about it. Maybe the rogue was her stalker. That opened up an entirely different set of problems if it wasn't a one-off situation.

He squeezed her arm, and she wiggled deeper into his embrace.

As it stood, if the Blackthorn Clan learned the truth, they would wipe her memories. He tried to avoid this fate by not getting deeply involved with her, because if she discovered his secret, that was exactly what would happen. If they wiped her memories and she forgot about him, not only would he lose her, but she would be more vulnerable to her stalker without him around to protect her.

He couldn't even go to Headmistress Velastra for advice, because she would have to follow protocol.

No one knew the long-term effects a memory wipe had on humans; the procedure wasn't performed often. He needed to protect Charlotte from that. Needed to protect her from everything. And the only way to do that was to keep her secret.

He listened as her breathing settled and grew deeper as sleep claimed her. The sound had grown familiar after the many nights of her lying next to him.

He wouldn't compromise this.

"I think it's time I return to Rosebrook," she said, grabbing his attention. "I'm for real this time."

He looked up from the plate of honey Dijon chicken, green beans, and rice to find her nodding with a determined look on her face.

After the impromptu nap on his chest, she woke and insisted on making him dinner for listening to her "silly ramblings," as she put it. He had a feeling she was still trying to convince herself what she saw was a product of the heat, or something else—something except the reality. It pained him to let her accept that, but if she believed it wasn't real, maybe he could keep others in the dark about it.

She continued, unprompted, as she cut into her chicken. "I mean, after the break-in, the dead bird, and now an honest-to-goodness threat on that note, I can't stay here. I don't care if he thinks I'm giving in." She gave him a weak smile. "I'm stubborn, not stupid."

"Well, you know I'll stay with you until you're ready to go, and I'll take you back once the time comes."

Her smile brightened, and she nodded. "I know."

Dinner cleanup was a quiet affair.

After Charlotte told him about her desire to go home, she told him about how she was at a stage where the important parts for her class were completed to make it possible for her to transfer to another program without failing. He didn't realize how short summer classes were at her university, and she'd enrolled in the extended session. She still needed to square away things with her advisor, her landlord, and the financial aid department, but she wanted to leave within the week, if possible.

During the cleanup, he couldn't help but think about what it meant to take her back to Rosebrook Valley.

He wanted her away from the psycho who kept inserting himself into her life, but he had grown to cherish the time he spent with her here, alone. Returning to their hometown would end that. Even if they returned at the beginning of July, leaving another month of his summer break before she had to make any decisions about school, he couldn't stay with her like he did in this apartment. He would go back to Blackthorn Academy, and she would return to living with her parents.

The muscles in his chest seized at the thought, a fist gripping and squeezing at his heart. The idea of parting from her felt like someone had asked him to cut off a limb.

How had she worked her way so thoroughly under his skin?

Aiden sat on the edge of her bed with his forearms braced on his thighs, staring at the floor like it could give him the answers to explain his sudden need to not be separated from her.

He'd done his best to keep a physical distance between them to avoid tempting himself into pursuing the spark he'd felt between them since last fall.

Outside of hugging her, providing comfort when things were tense after his arrival, and outside of at night when she moved near him in her sleep, he stayed away.

Until today.

Until his need to take care of her won over and the enthralling taste of her lifeblood caressed his tongue and set his veins on fire.

His cock twitched in response to the memory, and his gums tingled above his canines.

Calm down.

The bathroom light switched off, casting the entire apartment into darkness except for the space where Charlotte's bed was located. A small lamp on the nightstand draped in a decorative sheer fabric cast the room in a soft light.

Intimate light.

It didn't help settle his desire for her.

She approached where he sat on the bed, but he didn't look up until small toes wearing navy blue polish came into view.

Gone was the flowy sundress, replaced by a thin white camisole in a strawberry print with lace trimming the hem and sweetheart neckline. Short sleep shorts in a matching style with lace trimming the bottom completed the outfit. The red bow at the waist waved in front of his hindbrain like a cape taunting a bull.

He reminded himself the pajamas weren't for him. She owned those before he ever spent the night with her.

He was sure if the air conditioning wasn't broken, she might wear something more modest around him at night. She seemed too concerned with someone mistaking her intentions not to.

This was a case of his fantasies getting the better of him. Fantasies of spreading her out on the bed and peeling off the dainty pajamas with his teeth and making her writhe beneath him until she forgot her own name.

"Aiden?"

"Huh?"

"You okay? You're kinda staring."

He shook his head a few times in quick succession to rid himself of the mental image he painted. "I'm good."

"Can I get in bed then?"

"Oh. Shit. Yeah."

She giggled as he stood and stepped aside for her to crawl beneath the covers.

He barely suppressed the groan that rose in his throat by biting his knuckles as he got a mouth-watering view of her shorts riding up, giving him an eyeful of the bottom of her backside. No panty lines. She was trying to kill him.

She flopped down and nestled into the pillow, looking up at him. "You coming to bed?"

He felt like an idiot. So caught up in lust that he forgot how to function.

This time he didn't answer her, choosing to climb beneath the covers himself. If he didn't, she'd end up with another eyeful of his manhood.

She turned to her side to face him. "Do you think my parents will be mad?"

"No. They'll be thankful you're safe."

"Yeah, but I don't know if I want to tell them about this."

"You don't have to, you know. I mean, you can just tell them the part about changing your major. It's not like it's a lie."

"Mm," she hummed in acknowledgment, snuggling further into the comfort of the bedding.

He turned off the lamp, plunging the room into darkness except for the moon spilling across the bed.

"I guess Mom was wrong for once."

"What do you mean?"

"It's the solstice." When he hesitated to say anything, not knowing how to respond, she continued, "Mom sent me a text earlier this month saying something was going to change my life today. Doesn't feel like anything changed. Unless deciding to go home is life changing?"

"It can be," he said, suppressing a yawn.

She made another humming sound and shifted, falling quiet.

His eyes slipped closed, and he settled. Tomorrow he would visit the clinic and tame the thirst that had burned his throat ever since he tasted her blood. Then he would visit the police station to file yet another report. He wasn't even sure it mattered at this point if she planned to leave. But if she returned to Athens, she would need this guy caught.

Riley was crying.

He needed to go to her. Needed to wake up from the beautiful space keeping him suspended in time.

His little sister needed him.

His eyes slipped closed, blocking out the beautiful aurora and stars in his peripheral as he floated through space and time.

It no longer surprised him. He knew exactly where he was.

The rogue had shot him, and he found himself trapped between life and death once again. Trapped in a beautiful purgatory all his own.

The crying grew louder.

He always assumed the cries he heard upon his death were those of his friends. Assumed the loudest wails were those of his baby sister. But the longer he floated, the more he questioned the sound.

He knew Riley's cries and Blaire's. He doubted King Adrian's sisters or any of the female members of the clan would mourn him with such sorrow. Lukas and Seth didn't sound feminine, and Aiden even knew what they sounded like when they cried.

Someone else was mourning him. Someone else sounded devastated and broken, heaving and sobbing at the loss of his life.

He wanted to tell her it was temporary.

Wanted her to know that in a few minutes Blaire would bring him back.

"Please don't cry," he said, but no sound traveled into the vacuum of cosmos balancing his soul precariously on a knife's edge.

If Blaire's magic didn't reach him, he would slip into nothingness. But he knew it would. Soon, warmth and life would fill him again, bringing him back to those he needed to look after. Needed to keep safe.

He floated longer than ever before, making it possible to hear the cries as clear as if the person were in front of him.

It wasn't his family.

Something tugged on his heart. An unfamiliar sensation that never happened in previous versions of this never-ending nightmare.

His soul knew her voice.

"If you don't come back, her heart will remain lost forever. Another bond lost to time."

The disembodied voice made his skin prickle. Another new thing. Never had he heard a voice. Only the wails of a female in mourning.

He always assumed them to be Riley's, but now he wondered if what he heard after being shot was someone else entirely.

The tugging on his chest grew and pain lanced through his body, soaking his nerves in a sea of fire.

It was her.

Whoever she was needed him. Called to the very fiber of his being.

The answer hit him with the force of a hurricane: his Korrena was calling to him. Mourning the loss of what would never be.

Aiden sucked in a gasping breath as he came to, heart pounding out a dissonant rhythm that couldn't be healthy.

Was his Korrena born already? Or was it a sign of what would be?

His mind rioted with scattered thoughts that made little sense. When everything happened, he didn't hear a voice. The cries weren't clear. It was his sleep-deprived mind adding things to the story that weren't true.

A soft, warm hand lay on the center of his chest. "Aiden? Are you alright?"

A sharp pang splintered his chest.

Without questioning his actions, he rolled over the top of Charlotte, planting his knees at the sides of her hips, bracing his hands on either side of her head.

Her beautiful eyes opened wide; the moonlight made them sparkle almost unnaturally. He knew better, though. She wasn't like him.

Another pain seized his chest.

He dropped his head, capturing her lips parted with shock, desperate to soothe the ache that burned within.

She didn't resist, didn't even try to pretend to be modest and uncertain. Something in him knew she craved him as much as he craved her, and no matter how hard he tried, he couldn't remember why he never acted on that need.

Her arms came around the back of his neck, pulling his body into hers as she met his passion with her own. He groaned into the kiss as her manicured nails raked the short hair at the back of his head.

When her teeth sank into his bottom lip, he growled in response. Her hips canted upward to press against his straining erection.

He supported his body weight on his forearm and elbow as he moved his left hand down to slide up her waist and ribs, pushing her camisole up until his thumb brushed the bottom of her breast.

Breaking from their heated kiss, he dragged open-mouthed kisses across her jaw and down her neck, scraping his teeth across her collarbone, making her squirm to try to get her pelvis closer to him.

His lips trailed over her sternum, and he rose, pushing the camisole up until it bunched above her breasts.

His mouth watered.

Her breasts were generous, far more than a handful. Heavy, balanced, the perfect teardrop shape. They taunted him with what he'd never thought he'd have. It felt like sheer torture to watch her in her tight tank tops at night. He tried ignoring the way her nipples would pebble beneath the fabric without her realizing it, but it added to the temptation.

She lay panting beneath him, her eyes wild and blown with need. He could hardly see the gemstone green that captivated him. He wondered if she realized she hadn't stopped squirming her hips the entire time his mouth lay siege to her.

Lowering himself, his ribs nestling between her thighs, he held her small body still as his mouth descended on her pale pink nipple.

His tongue ran across the tiny bud, flicking in a way that made her pant and reach into his hair. When she pressed harder, he bit her nipple, and a hitched cry escaped from her mouth. The flat of his tongue chased the sting to soothe the tender flesh.

His mouth moved from her nipple and across the expanse of her breast, kissing and sucking in random spots until she tugged at his hair.

"Harder," she demanded.

Who was he to deny her?

When he sucked the side of her breast into his mouth, he latched on with his blunt teeth at the same time, making her back arch off the bed as she yelled into the darkness of the room.

Lifting his head, he looked at the pretty pale skin lit by moonlight. An angry red and purple welt shaped like an eclipse painted her skin. There was no mistake what left that mark. No mistake he had marked her.

A piece of that pain piercing his chest fell away.

Sliding down her body, he showered her skin with kisses, licks, and lingering bites.

He'd never seen someone so fair before.

In the daytime, her skin held a soft pinkness beneath the surface; beautiful and delicate, like petals in a milk bath. But her skin under the moonlight reminded him of the fresh fallen snow he'd seen from his window one night on vacation in the mountains when he was younger.

Ethereal. Haunting.

She had him under her spell, and the more he lavished her body with attention, the deeper he sank into depths he didn't know if he could return from. Was the solstice meant to change his life instead? This felt life changing.

"I want you," he murmured as his lips ran across her navel. "Please let me have you."

He didn't recognize his own voice.

Never had he felt the desire to beg. But the desperation to lose himself inside of her tore at the core of his being, demanding satisfaction.

Her answering moan set his blood on fire.

His teeth sank into the soft flesh of her belly, not quite breaking the skin. She squealed, choking on a half-moan, half-sob.

"Please, *please*," she mewled. "More."

Rising to his knees, he unraveled the red bow at her waist. Unwrapping a gift made for him.

As he tugged down the tiny sleep shorts, his earlier suspicions were confirmed. Not a scrap of cloth underneath. He laid his head back between his shoulders with a groan. If he didn't calm down, he would embarrass himself.

He'd never felt this way before. Never felt such an intense burning need to be connected this way to anyone.

When he lay the soft cotton aside, he lowered his mouth to the delicate, soft flesh beneath her belly, kissing a line from one hip to the other. Her curves were a wet dream come to life. A petite waist with full, rounded hips begging for his fingers to mark them.

His chest rattled with the needy, untamed sound he made as he looked down on her, tugging off his own athletic shorts and boxer briefs. There wasn't a part of him that didn't like the idea of her wearing his marks on every single inch of her body.

"Aiden," she whimpered at the loss of his touch. The sound of her need for him made him dizzy.

His hands found their way to her skin immediately, the soft, pliable flesh yielding to his rough caress.

Charlotte seemed to like it when he wasn't gentle. Liked when his worshiping kisses turned into devouring bites. Her moans, and the soft sounds she made when he tightened his grip on her hips, dragging his hands down her thighs to squeeze, made his balls draw up tight.

He intended to taste her. To see if her arousal tasted like the potent sweet blend of pineapple, vanilla, and buttery brown sugar that permeated his sinuses with every heavy breath he took. But he couldn't.

If he didn't get inside of her now, he didn't know if he would survive.

"Please," he rasped, his engorged cock pressing against her thigh, leaking and marking her skin.

She hadn't finished nodding her consent before he was already gliding his shaft over the dampness of her slit, coating himself to make it easier on her when he slid inside.

He wasn't a small man, and that extended to every part of him.

Their mutual groans of need and delight echoed in the room as he slid into the heat of her body.

He paused halfway in, giving her time to adjust. Giving her time to stop him if she needed—if it was too much.

When her breathing evened out, he pressed in, filling her inch by inch until his thighs met the backs of hers. Seated deep inside her, he felt her muscles clench and flutter around him already. He didn't think she would last long. He knew he wouldn't.

He leaned forward, hands bracing himself on each side of her head, gripping the pillow tight as he withdrew from her slowly. As much as he didn't want to, he rocked into her at a languid pace, easing her adjustment to his size. She'd told him she wasn't a virgin, but he didn't know the last time she'd been with a man and didn't know what she was used to.

The thought of another man inside her made another side of him sit up and take notice. His hips snapped forward at the thought, and he hit deep inside her with more force than he intended.

Her scream was a mix of pleasure-pain, and his eyes widened in alarm, only to be replaced with surprise when she looked into his eyes, panting the word, "Again."

He rose over her. Grabbing hold of her hips, he dragged his cock out of her to the head before slamming back inside. Her answering mewls flipped the switch the rest of the way, and he began thrusting into her at a punishing pace.

Fingers dug into skin, both hers and his, and he prayed to the stars his forearms would bear the marks of her passion come tomorrow instead of healing.

"Aiden, Aiden, oh god *Aiden*," she cried out, her body wiggling and her head thrashing from side to side.

His body fell forward, elbows taking his weight as he gripped her left breast in a firm squeeze, pinching the nipple as his mouth lay claim to the side of her neck. The sound of her repeating his name like a prayer made him feral. She needed and wanted him.

He felt the familiar tingle in his gums but was too lost to the sensation of pleasure to care.

His teeth scraped the column of her throat as her climax slammed into her. Her walls fluttered around his shaft, strangling his cock in a death grip.

Charlotte's cries as her orgasm swept her away, and the nails biting into his shoulders as she held on for the ride, were his undoing.

His canines elongated and raked the skin of her throat. Her answering gasping moan made his brain short-circuit.

Blood trickled down her neck, and he lapped it up without hesitation, sucking her flesh to steal whatever the slight break in her skin would give him. His own release took him, and he filled her with a piece of himself.

They lay still, panting in the afterglow. Sweat trailed over his temples and his skin glistened as much as hers in the moonlight. Several minutes passed where she clung to him, and he stayed buried within her until the haze of lust lifted and the reality of what happened crashed in around him.

Not only had he made love to her—there was no way he could describe it as anything but that—but he'd done it without a condom. Filled her without caution.

Part of him preened at the fact. Roared with satisfaction at marking her in the most intimate way he could.

A sinking feeling settled in, pushing down his ego.

He'd broken her skin with his fangs. He resisted the urge to bite into her, but he still drew blood and drank it without concern.

Withdrawing from her body as the cold reality of his situation made his cock soften, he fell onto his back. She rolled toward him and looped her leg over his, laying her hand on his chest without a word.

It didn't feel strange at all that they didn't use many words.

Everything felt so natural. Like their bodies knew what the other needed with little coaching. Without the fumbling that came with a new sexual partner.

Surrendering to their desire felt right.

She reached out, and he laced his fingers with hers, laying them on his chest. It felt so good to lie in bed with her naked body in his arms. It felt right. And that terrified him.

What would she think if she knew he was just like the monster that had terrified her in the alley?

19

INSECURITY

Waking up in bed alone, sweating, with sticky thighs, was not how Charlotte envisioned her morning going. She felt like someone had dragged her body over a cheese grater. Parts of her she didn't know existed ached.

She rolled onto her stomach and shoved the covers off. Sunlight beat down on her naked body while she buried her face in a pillow that smelled of orange Creamsicle ice cream, replaying last night's events in her mind.

She slept with Aiden. Not only in the literal sense, but also in the spread-her-legs-and-beg-for-a-thorough-dicking sense.

Not that she begged with her words, but she clearly remembered her lower half trying to attach itself to his before their clothes ever came off.

At first, she only intended to check on him after he jolted awake from a nightmare. It was only one of two times she'd witnessed him wake up frightened. What she didn't intend, or expect, was for him to roll over on top of her and turn her into a needy mess with a single kiss.

What was it about kissing him that caused her to cease all rational thought?

He wasn't always gentle, either.

He handled her one minute like she was the most fragile piece of glass, deserving of complete care, the next using her like he wanted to devour her very being.

The experience left her feeling a little shaken.

She eased herself up from the bed and walked on unstable legs to the bathroom.

Her core ached, but in a good way.

Aiden wasn't little, in all the ways that counted—it was like she could still feel him inside her. The aching reminder of the hard and rough treatment of her vagina made her shiver. Was it too soon for a repeat?

No, Charlotte. One time is one too many.

Once she finished peeing, she walked back into her room, determined to get clothes and take a shower to wash away the dried cum on her legs.

The sight that greeted her in the mirrored closet door stole her breath.

A dark, angry hickey in shades of purple and red formed a ring on the side of her breast, marring her otherwise unblemished skin. Another further down her body beneath her navel and above her pubic bone had mottled yellow around it. It looked like a cluster of bites and places where he'd sucked her skin.

Her eyes trailed over her hips, noting the finger-shaped bruising that darkened where his fingertips would have buried themselves in her flesh. A delicious shudder passed through her as she felt his phantom touch when she traced her fingers over the markings.

She had never surrendered herself to someone so completely. Let someone mark her. When her ex-boyfriend had wanted to put a hickey on her, she told him if he ever wanted to kiss her again, he would think twice.

Her eyes moved up to her neck.

A large bruise was forming on the side that she would need to cover with makeup when she went to visit her advisor, and maybe once she returned home, if it still lingered. She didn't need her mothers asking questions.

She squinted and leaned in to examine the mark on her neck. *Is that dried blood?* There weren't any bite marks to show he broke the skin, but a hickey could break skin. She learned that from one of the other servers at the diner.

She slid open the closet and stepped inside, grabbing a pair of dark-wash denim shorts and a short-sleeved floral blouse with a peplum bodice. Stepping out to grab a pair of panties and bra from her drawers, she froze when Aiden came her way from the kitchen.

Her body temperature rose as his eyes did a slow descent, inspecting his handiwork. When his heated gaze reached her thighs, where the sticky evidence lay drying on her skin, his nostrils flared, and his eyes turned outright molten.

"I'm on the shot," she blurted.

His gaze flew up to hers, surprise coloring his features. All signs of a possible round two evaporated.

"I'm on birth control," she said, slowing her words. "You don't have to worry." Her hands tightened around the clothes she held. "And um. I'm clean," she added, looking away from him. "I haven't gotten tested, but I haven't had sex since high school. I got tested back then after my ex and I split up. So, yeah. Clean."

She hadn't slept with her ex without a condom. Aiden was the first to go bare, but she still made sure she hadn't caught anything. While she didn't think her ex would cheat, it didn't mean he hadn't caught it before her. He wasn't a virgin when he took her virginity.

The feel of fingers clasping her chin and turning her face caught her off guard.

Aiden looked down into her eyes. "How are you feeling?"

Of all the things she expected, concern for her *feelings* wasn't it. Maybe anger they hadn't used a condom. Awkwardness that she still had his cum on her legs. But concern about her well-being? He kept surprising her.

"I'm okay. Sore." When his lips flattened and turned down at the corners, she quickly added, "Good sore, I promise."

"I still don't like you hurt. I'm sorry I was rough." His fingers traced her jaw, running down the side of her neck over the bruising. "I should have taken my time."

Wait. He called worshiping her body and making her feel like the most cherished living being alive before he dickmatized her not taking his time? She wondered what taking his time looked like... *No. Stop that.*

She cleared her throat. "I should-I should go clean up. I have to meet my advisor today and tell her my decision. She has open office for consultations on Saturdays. It's the best day to get in."

Scurrying out of the room like he could see the doubts hanging over her like a black cloud, she locked herself in the bathroom and turned on the shower.

Last night made her feel things. Things she didn't want to feel. It made the emotions she pushed down to avoid admitting the truth rise to the surface and threaten to drown her.

She wanted to be with Aiden.

Swiping the tear from her cheek, she stepped into the shower.

Wanting something and being good enough to have it were two very different things; it was a gap she couldn't close.

The breeze made the sage green floral maxi dress flutter around her ankles and the wind chimes on the porch tinkle and sway.

It took a week to take care of everything in Athens, but it felt good to finally be back in Rosebrook Valley. Back home, where the smell of magnolias carried on the breeze and Spanish moss swayed from live oaks all around town. It settled something restless inside her that hadn't relaxed in three months since she'd been away.

Aiden stood with her outside the small three-bedroom, two-bathroom house she called home sweet home her entire life.

Vertical white siding made up most of the exterior walls of her childhood home, with board and batten gray shutters. Brick and thick wooden columns accented the covered porch.

Simple shrubs and lilyturf that required little upkeep lined the front of the house. Her mothers weren't home often enough to look after elaborate flowerbeds like other houses on the street, so this was their way of having something nice with minimal effort. The lilyturf plants added a pop of color amid a sea of green.

They walked up the paved walkway to her porch. Aiden carried a large box of her necessities, like her bathroom products and gaming consoles, while she rolled a suitcase full of clothes and carried a backpack with her books on her shoulder.

He set down the box, then returned to the car for more. She knocked on the glass of the exterior door. The inner wooden door stood wide open, offering her a dim glimpse into the home's interior.

Moments later, her mom came into view. Her smile brightened, crow's feet wrinkling the corners of her eyes when she opened the door. "I'm so glad you're home," she said, pulling Charlotte forward in a warm embrace, making her drop her backpack.

Her mom's bangle bracelets clinked together as she pulled back and held Charlotte at arm's length, looking her over. The way her mom's lips pressed together in a disapproving way made Charlotte's shoulders tense.

Her mom's bronze skin looked radiant under the sunlight. She didn't look a day over thirty, despite pushing fifty.

Dark eyes settled on Charlotte's face, and a soft sigh escaped. "You're not well."

She never knew how her mothers did it, but they had an uncanny ability of knowing when she wasn't at her best. Maybe it came from being together for years, or maybe it was a mother's intuition—if that were possible without blood relations.

"Good to see you too, Mom."

"I didn't mean that as an insult, sweetheart. You don't look sick or unsightly, just… a hunch. Come in, let's talk." She motioned with her hand to the open door, silver rings catching in the sunlight. "Hurry inside before Molly gets out."

"Molly? I didn't know you had a sister."

Charlotte turned as Aiden approached with another box. "Molly is Ma's cat. The owner abandoned her at the clinic, and they fell in love with each other."

Her mom's warm laughter made her smile. "It was love at first sight, that's for sure." She looked at Aiden, a soft smile lighting up her face. "Little fire. It's good to see you."

Her mom once told them the name Aiden meant "little fire" and held roots in Irish mythology.

"Mrs. Walsh," Aiden said with a confident smile.

It warmed something inside of Charlotte to see him so relaxed. When he first met her mom, Aiden acted cagey. Skittish. Nervous. When she asked him why, his anxiety grew until he finally admitted he felt like her mom could see through him.

She didn't mock him or even say it wasn't believable, because like earlier, her mom picked up on things others didn't and had a knack for reading people.

"I've told you time and time again to call me Sara. It gets confusing when Liz is around and you're calling us both Mrs. Walsh."

"Yes, ma'am," he said, his hand moving to the back of his neck in a gesture Charlotte had seen plenty of times before.

"Come on. Let's get this stuff to my room. I don't wanna leave my computer in the car too long in this heat."

Aiden picked up one box and followed her into the living room.

The space looked the same as she remembered it. A large sectional couch covered in throw blankets and a ton of pillows in a variety of bold colors formed an L-shape around a large, square coffee table decorated with tiny plants and candles in cute gemstone holders.

"That's Molly," she said, pointing to the long-haired black Persian cat sauntering into the room from the kitchen. The cat walked up to them, brushed herself along Aiden's leg, and then sashayed away to the front corner of the living room, jumping up onto her custom cat tree her mothers commissioned.

They had it designed like an actual tree growing in the corner of the room with carpeted platforms in various places for climbing, scratching, and lounging. The tree had one long branch with a flat surface to allow Molly to lord over her loyal subjects. The platform branch spanned one wall of the living room, passing over the entertainment center decorated with more candles and plant life, and another went in the opposite direction over the bay window facing the front yard.

"Will you be joining us for dinner, Aiden?" her mom called from the kitchen as Charlotte led Aiden toward her bedroom.

His gaze met Charlotte's, his brows flexing, indecision crossing his face. She chose to save him from the awkwardness. She didn't want him to stay if he didn't want to be around. His job was done. He got her home safely.

"I think he probably needs to settle in back at the academy before he does anything like that." She gave him a tight smile. "Isn't that right?"

"Yeah, I haven't seen Riley yet. She's going to give me an earful."

Her mom frowned, placing the romaine heart she took from the refrigerator onto the cutting board. She peered across the kitchen island separating her from where they stood. "Why would she do that? She sees you every day."

Discomfort settled in Charlotte's chest, tightening behind her sternum. She hadn't told her parents that Aiden had stayed with her yet. She forgot to mention it when she called and said she was coming home, only mentioning Aiden was going to drive her. She planned to explain everything once she settled in.

Sighing, she said, "It's a long story. I want to explain it when both of you are here."

Her mom hummed an acknowledgment, looking satisfied with the answer—for now. She returned to the refrigerator. "It's taco night." She straightened, holding two tomatoes. "Did you want soft or hard shells?"

"Both?"

Her mom smiled. "Both, it is."

Charlotte led Aiden into her room, her shoulders slumping as she crossed the threshold. The happiness she felt at being home burst like a bubble, evaporating into nothingness.

"What's wrong?" he asked, placing the box on the floor near the foot of her full-sized bed.

She climbed across the bare mattress to pull back the sheer black curtains that matched the black and silver celestial bedding she'd taken to her apartment. Opening the window to let in air to refresh the room after her absence, she turned to him and sat on the bed.

"I forgot to mention you were staying with me. All the times we spoke before I told them I was coming home, it never dawned on me to say anything."

Aiden's jaw muscle twitched. "You don't have to tell them. About me, I mean. You should definitely tell them about what's going on though."

"You don't want them to know?"

"I don't want to cause you any problems." He smoothed a hand over the side of his neck. "I'm gonna go get your computer and the other box I left on the porch." Without another word, he turned away and left her sitting there, confused and more than a little hurt.

He hadn't brought up their night together once in the last week, not since the morning he'd checked on her before her shower. Nor had he attempted to make any physical contact. Not even a hug. It was like he made a concentrated effort to put as much physical distance between them as possible.

It hurt.

What hurt more was that he acted like everything was fine—at least until they returned home. He had been attentive. Talkative. Anticipated her needs before she realized she needed something. It was like he was overcompensating for distancing himself.

All of it would be fine if she hadn't become so attached. If she didn't see the heat in his eyes at night when she got ready for bed. She didn't understand what held him back, beyond what she suspected would be a problem. He came from a different lifestyle than she did. Expectations and lineage.

She tried to tell herself it was all in her head. Insecurity. He wasn't the type to act that way, but she didn't know how else to explain the sudden shift.

Did he regret sleeping with her?

As they crossed into town, he seemed to grow colder, more distant than before. It was a side to him she'd never experienced, and it made her regret ever sleeping with him.

Of course the best sexual experience of her life gifted her with the most painful memories.

She stood and walked over to the desk on the left wall of her room, sweeping dust off with her hand to clean a spot for her computer accessories. She wouldn't get new plants to decorate. After the break-in, she didn't replace them, but now it seemed pointless. She didn't know how long she would be in town. If she were honest, she didn't care anymore.

Aiden came back into the room carrying the smaller box, setting it on top of the long dresser with an attached mirror on the right wall before turning and leaving again to get her computer.

He wouldn't even make eye contact anymore.

If this was how the solstice changed her life, she didn't like it one bit. She wanted the old Aiden back, if she had to choose between the him now and what she had before.

She took a long, slow inhale through her nose, counted to ten, and exhaled through her mouth. Her eyes stung.

After another few minutes, he returned with her computer, setting it on her desk and rubbing at his breastbone in quick, hard sweeps.

"Are you okay?"

He swung his head to look at her. His narrowed eyes looked red and glassy.

She took a tentative step toward him. "What's wrong?"

"I need to go," he said, voice thick and strained. He sounded like he was about to cry. She'd never heard him sound like this.

"Wait." She reached for him, but he pushed around her and strode out the door without a backward glance.

When she heard the front door shut, she didn't move. She dropped her hand to her side and stood frozen, staring at the empty doorway he disappeared through.

How had she messed up so much?

She didn't want him to hate her.

Did he?

"So what's the big news?"

Charlotte looked across the small, four-person dining table at her ma. She still wore her scrubs from the clinic, and her mousy brown hair was in a messy bun at the nape.

"I wanted to wait for you both to be home before I told you what I planned to do for school."

Her mom placed her half-eaten taco on her plate. "I was confused when you wouldn't tell us why you were coming home."

An undignified snort sounded across the table. "You weren't confused." Her ma looked at Charlotte. "As soon as we hung up the phone, I had to distract Sara from driving up there to see what was going on with you."

Her mom waved her hand, the clink of her metallic bangles filling the air. "It wasn't that bad, Liz."

"She was a mess. Swore something bad was happening."

"Don't discount my intuition. Something happened, didn't it?"

Charlotte looked between her mothers. It had been so long since she watched their playful banter that tears filled her eyes as homesickness crashed into her with force.

"Sweetheart?"

"Char?"

Chairs scraped, and comforting, familiar arms wrapped around her. She sobbed like a baby. Her mothers cooed and rubbed her hair and cheeks.

"I missed y'all so much," she said, hiccupping.

"We missed you too, sweetheart." Her mom wiped Charlotte's left cheek. The bandage around her fingertip, likely from a sewing needle, scraped Charlotte's skin.

Her ma took the chair to her right, forgetting her plate on the other side of the table to sit next to Charlotte instead of her wife. "Tell us what's going on."

The dam had broken. She told them everything about her homesickness, how she wanted to do a program to be able to help with the businesses, but there were no options local to them where she could commute. How she planned to take a break until fall and make a final decision on what to do then. She needed time. She wasn't ready.

She told them about Aiden and how he stayed with her.

Her ma assumed the reason was to keep her company while she finished up her coursework to help with her homesickness. While she didn't lie, she didn't correct the assumption.

She even told them about starting antidepressants again because it got so bad.

The two things she didn't tell them about were her stalker and what she saw in the alley. They already looked concerned for her.

"I just wish you told us how much you hated accounting before now," her ma said. Her pale cheeks appeared flushed. If anyone were to look at her, they would think she felt anger, but her mild rosacea always flared up when she felt stress, giving her a deep blush on her cheekbones. "We could have helped you figure something else out."

"I didn't want to bother you."

A smooth, tanned hand covered hers. "That's what we're here for."

She was glad now she pushed through the midterms. If she hadn't, and left earlier than now, all the time she spent feeling terrible would have been for nothing.

"There aren't any schools around, really," her mom said. "I don't think you should go back, though. If this is a homesick thing, it'll happen again. Even if you went to Atlanta to be closer, you would still need to move. It's still three hours away."

"What about Savannah State?" her ma asked.

Both Charlotte and her mom looked up at that.

"You could attend and be close enough to commute," her ma explained. "We're twenty minutes outside of Savannah. What's another fifteen to the other side of town?"

Charlotte picked at the shell of her taco, breaking little pieces off. "I completely missed that place. I thought the only local options were the art school or Blackthorn Academy." There wasn't a lot of reason to keep looking after qualifying for grants to attend UGA for their accounting program. She didn't think she needed to. If she had looked harder, would she have found Savannah State? Had she seen it and forgotten?

Standing from the table, her mom tucked her long black hair behind her ear. "I wondered why you didn't apply to the academy." She walked over to the kitchen, grabbed another can of Diet Coke from the refrigerator, and then placed it on the table. "Rumors or not, Blaire goes there. Aiden and Riley, too. Why not apply to go with them?" She picked up the pan in the center of the table, carrying it to the stove to warm up the now cold meat.

"That's not a bad idea." Her ma looked at Charlotte. "Do they have any business-related courses?"

She looked between her mothers, not sure how to answer their questions. She didn't want them to be ashamed of the fact she wasn't good enough to get into the school. No one was.

There was a reason the rumors existed.

The only local she knew to get accepted was Blaire, and only because someone handed her a scholarship on a silver platter. Charlotte still didn't understand how that happened. She only knew she wouldn't be so lucky.

Even Aiden's family wasn't from Rosebrook Valley. According to Riley, her family moved to town from Atlanta when Aiden was a toddler. She didn't know if others from the academy were local or not. Lukas's family was from Finland, and Riley told her Seth and Kai's family was German. She didn't know as much about Layla, and never asked where Mera came from.

Local families attempted to enroll their kids into Blackthorn Academy. Both into the college campus in town and the lower grades placed in what they called branch schools located outside of town.

If students from the private prep school, Magnolia Heights, couldn't do it, she didn't stand a chance.

"I don't even know what course to take," she said, diverting attention from not applying to Blackthorn. She could look into Savannah State to avoid further questions.

"For now, we'll keep your apartment. It's only another month and a half until the fall semester, right?" her ma said, sliding her plate across the table.

Charlotte nodded.

"Then it isn't much difference to deal with the cost. It'll save time in case you change your mind. In the meantime, you should check into Savannah State and see if they have something that appeals to you more here."

Her mom brought the pan back to the table and placed it on the heat mat. "Blackthorn Academy, too."

"Okay," Charlotte mumbled.

No way to avoid that one.

As they refilled new tacos, she realized that despite everything feeling strained between Aiden and her, it felt good to be home. Unfortunately, that made the idea of returning to the empty apartment in Athens alone even more daunting.

20

Friendship

Bells banged against the glass door as Charlotte entered the diner she used to work at.

Now called The Sizzlin' Griddle, the atmosphere felt so different after ownership changed hands a second time since her old boss Ricky left.

They'd done a lot in the time she'd been away.

Fifties music played from a jukebox in the corner, with records hanging from the ceiling. The entire diner now had a fifties theme. It suited the original style of shiny red leather booths, black-and-white checkered flooring, and chrome-wrapped bar. She often wondered why Ricky never embraced the concept.

Lazy, that's why.

The staff appeared diverse, no longer limited to pretty girls under nineteen. Her old boss had a type.

Gone were the skimpy server outfits, replaced with the cutest black hoop skirts with white poodles on them, big belts in the same color as the frilly petticoat the server wore—pink, blue, green, or yellow, and dainty shirts with glittery name tags matching the server's color. Other servers wore pressed slacks and white button-down shirts with black suspenders. Their bow ties and name tags also varied in color.

They made her feel underdressed in her white denim shorts, lavender tank top, and matching short-sleeved overshirt.

"Charlotte!"

At the sound of Riley's voice, she whirled around from her focus on the new dessert display.

On her knees in the booth, Riley waved her arms as if Charlotte weren't looking right at her. She looked so out of place in the bright and vibrant diner in her black band T-shirt over a fishnet undershirt. Charlotte couldn't see what else Riley wore, but she would put big money on it also being black—and some kind of boots, definitely boots. At least her pink pixie haircut fit.

Blaire sat across from her, laughing at Riley's antics. Layla sat next to Riley, peering over the booth's back with a soft, sympathetic smile, doe eyes wide.

Charlotte approached their booth and slid in next to Blaire, but not before she caught a glimpse of the cut-off, black jean shorts Riley wore over sheer black stockings and short combat boots. *Called it.*

"Ooh, new earrings?" Riley leaned across the table and flicked the tiny purple cloud earrings dangling from Charlotte's ears.

"Nah. I've had these since high school. Found them when reorganizing my closet last night."

Riley slumped back in her seat. "I still want those bat earrings you used to wear."

"You can have them."

"Really?" Riley's face brightened, mouth parting with all her top teeth showing as a wide smile overtook her face.

Charlotte nodded.

After her run-in with a vampire, she didn't want to have a reminder like that hanging around. *Can vampires actually turn into bats?* It wasn't like the man flew after her, so she had her doubts.

"So, how did Sara and Elizabeth take the news?" Blaire asked, turning to face her.

"They weren't disappointed in me."

"Told you it'd be fine," Riley said.

Layla looked between them, confusion lining her forehead. "What's going on?"

Riley turned to Layla, propping herself up on her knee, resting her arm on the back of the booth. "So you know how we said Charlotte is coming back for the rest of the summer?"

"Yeeeeah, but I didn't know why."

"How about let Charlotte explain it," Blaire said with a soft smile.

"Crap. Sorry, sorry. I'm just really excited you're home, and like, there's so much you've missed..." Riley trailed off, lowering herself back into her seat. "Sorry. Just excited," she repeated with a mumble.

Charlotte laughed. "You're fine." It had been too long since she experienced Hurricane Riley—as Aiden so affectionately called her—in person.

A server approached, her black hair twisted into a French knot with a big pink flower on the side that matched her flamingo pink petticoat. She wore Hollywood glam makeup that made her appear younger, but Charlotte suspected she was closer to her ma's age. "Hey there, hon. I'm Jessica. Will you be having something too?"

"What's good now?" Charlotte asked, looking at the others.

"Layla and I got chicken fingers and waffle fries," Blaire said.

"Cheese fries and milkshake," Riley added. Her lips twisted, and she turned to the server. "Actually, can I get another shake? Dreamy

Creamy this time."

"Yep." Jessica scribbled a note on her notepad.

Charlotte looked up at her. "Do you have honey mustard?"

"Sure do. The creamy kind, not that tangy stuff."

"I'll get the chicken fingers too, then. Can I get cheese on waffle fries?"

"Don't see why not. Just like putting it on the regular ones. Potato's a potato, darlin'."

"Okay, that. Oh, and maybe a soda? Whatever you have. Pepsi or Coke."

"Want a filler?"

She blinked. "A what?"

Jessica gave her a patient smile. "We have a bar with all sorts of goodies you can add to your drink. Lemons, limes, syrup shots like strawberry, cherry, caramel…" She tapped her blood-red lips with the end of her pen as she mulled over the options.

"Do you have cherries?"

"Yep. I usually put a shot of cherry syrup with a handful of maraschino cherries in my soda. Want something like that?"

"Yes, please. If that's okay."

"Sure it is. I'll get that right out to you."

When the server turned away and went to put in the order, Layla muttered, "I like the tangy honey mustard."

Riley and Blaire chuckled.

Charlotte preferred the creamy stuff. It wasn't as strong of a mustard flavor and tasted sweeter, but she wouldn't tell Layla that. Instead, she asked, "What's a Dreamy Creamy?" It sounded like a candy popsicle, but she didn't know how they turned it into a milkshake.

"Creamsicle ice cream turned into a milkshake. It is so good. It's new on the menu. I mean, they revamped the whole thing when the last owners bought the place, but they added this a few weeks ago," Riley said, once again rambling, her volume rising with her excitement.

The mention of Creamsicle made her mood sour. It sucked to wake up that morning to her pillows not bearing the scent of the creamy orange dessert.

"What's wrong?"

She looked up at Riley. "Hm?"

"You look sad."

"I'm good."

Hoping to distract Riley, she looked at Layla. "I'm back because I don't like my major. I don't know what I want to do, but staying up there is too hard. I want to be with my family."

She left it simple. Explaining it a dozen times was getting old.

Layla nodded. "I get that. I've never been away from home either."

From what she remembered, their situations were very different. Layla's parents were apparently overprotective and didn't see her as an adult until she turned twenty. She still had a couple of years to go.

In Charlotte's case, she didn't want to leave her family. They weren't pushing her out, but they wanted her to feel confident in the world without restrictions. Quite the one-eighty to Layla's upbringing.

"Oddly enough, my parents want me to look into enrolling at Blackthorn Academy," she said, shaking her head. The idea still sounded silly.

When no one spoke, she looked up at the others. Layla's eyes had rounded in frozen surprise, and Blaire and Riley were staring at one another. They looked to be communicating something without words. A sharp sensation pinched Charlotte's chest. She didn't have that connection anymore with Blaire.

"At least I don't have to deal with my unwanted friend," she said, changing the subject now that the mood turned tense.

She knew the reality. Blackthorn Academy wasn't for people like her.

Riley stared at her while she dipped her waffle fries in gooey cheese. "What unwanted friend?"

"Blaire didn't tell you?"

"No."

She set down the fry and dusted salt from her fingers as she prepared herself to inform the two girls staring at her in question about the things she didn't tell her mothers. Everything except the crazy run-in with Mr. Fangs.

By the time she finished explaining the hellacious experience, Riley's mouth gaped, for once speechless.

"And you *didn't* tell your parents?" Layla sounded as horrified as she looked.

"No. I didn't think it would be worth it to add the extra stress. Especially if I never go back to Athens." She picked up the fry again. "Besides, if I decide to return, they'll talk me out of it if they know there's a stalker up there." She took a bite of the cheesy fry.

"No shit," Riley said, scoffing. "You're not going back up there. I don't get why you didn't come home sooner."

"I wanted to finish my classes, so I at least kept my credits. I couldn't leave before the twenty-first, or I couldn't transfer everything."

Blaire set down her drink. "Why the twenty-first? Your classes were only a couple months?"

"Classes started May fourteenth. My midterm presentation happened on June twenty-first. If I didn't pass, I couldn't leave until I did remedial work. My advisor said I could transfer my credits, since I passed, so I don't have to stay through July for the rest of the extended summer session."

"You're still not going back," Riley muttered.

Charlotte laughed. "You know, you sound like your brother."

"Ew. Don't say disgusting things like that."

"Well, if I didn't agree to let him stay, he would have made me come back," she said, lifting the glass of specialty cherry Coke and taking a sip. The cherry syrup gave it an extra kick she liked.

"Made you?" Layla tilted her head in question.

"Ah… um." How did she explain the weird feeling she experienced around Aiden that made her want to do what he told her to? His protective instincts made him a little overbearing and a control freak, but something about it stirred an instinct of hers to either defy or yield to him, depending on the circumstance. "He has a way with words?" That sounded lame to her own ears.

Riley stirred her straw in her milkshake. "Don't let him push you around. He means well, but when he cares about someone, he is like a dog with a bone. Won't back down, even when he's wrong. I've been living with it for eighteen years, I know."

"He's not pushing me around," Charlotte said, frowning. "Anyway, he's acted really weird since we got back into town, so I don't think there's much to worry about."

"What do you mean?"

She looked at Blaire. "Well, before he came up to see me, we would talk most every night."

"Hold up." Riley leaned on the table with her elbows. "Every night? I knew something was up between y'all."

"It wasn't like that. We played games together, were friends. He kept the homesickness at bay. Kept my mind occupied."

Layla looked at her empty plate as the table fell silent.

Blaire leaned back against the wall. The sunshine streaming through the window made her blonde hair glow. "What was it like having Aiden stay with you?"

"Well, he's come up before, but never overnight. He only stayed the first night because we lost track of time, but then the next day there was the break-in, and well... you know the rest."

Riley quirked an eyebrow. "So what's the deal now?"

Charlotte looked at Riley. "What deal?"

"I think she means with him acting weird," Layla said.

"Yeah, that."

"I don't know."

She hated lying to her friends. She wanted to be closer to them and have something meaningful again, like she once did with Blaire, but if she couldn't tell them the truth, what kind of foundation was she creating?

"Why do I not believe that?" Blaire reached out and grabbed Charlotte's hand resting on the table. "I know you, Char. It's all over your face. What happened when he was there?"

Her eyes burned, and she willed her body to absorb the liquid emotion brimming in her eyes.

"Did he hurt you?" Riley said, rising. "I will kick his tail. Then I'll let Mama kill him."

"No!" Charlotte shouted, then looked around at the packed diner. A few people looked at her and she shrank into the seat. "No," she whispered. "He didn't hurt me... Not physically." At least they couldn't see the faded bruising from his bites on her stomach and breast. The marks on her hips were gone, and the one on her neck she covered well enough with makeup.

"Then what did he do?" Blaire's hand squeezed hers.

"Nothing. He was there for two weeks, and everything was great for the first week. I mean, except for the stalker stuff. Everything changed the day before I decided to come home."

"What happened?"

Her elbows thunked on the table, rattling the silverware as her hands cradled her forehead. Her food sat forgotten. "We slept together."

"You already said that," Layla said, lifting her water and taking a sip.

"I don't think she means sleeping in the same bed," Blaire said with caution. "Do you?"

Riley smacked a hand on the table, leaning forward, whisper-yelling. "You banged my brother?"

"No one says banged anymore," Blaire said, suppressing a laugh.

"Fine." Riley rolled her eyes, waving her hand from side to side with each euphemism she uttered. "Bumped uglies, boned, did the horizontal tango, rode the skin bus into tuna town—"

"Stop!" Blaire threw a fry at Riley.

Layla's eyes were so wide she looked like a cartoon character.

"Don't put it like that," Charlotte grumbled, cringing. "Any of that. But yes, we had *sex*. And it was amazing, and I hate myself for it."

"But she can't—"

Riley's hand clamped over Layla's mouth. "Nope."

Charlotte's eyebrows rose, mouth parting. "What in the world?"

"Nothing, nothing." Riley waved a hand, dismissing the odd interaction as Layla looked at her with exasperation, brushing her ruffled mocha hair from her face. "But seriously. You had sex?"

"Yes. I *just* told you," Charlotte said with a groan. "He had a nightmare, and when he woke up, he… He acted in a way I'd never seen before."

"Nightmare? Shit. He's still having them?" Riley's face fell. "I thought it got better."

"He said he didn't have as many when he was up there, but he still had them occasionally."

"That's good, at least." Blaire let go of Charlotte's hand and propped her head on her palm, elbow on the table. "You said he acted different? What did you mean?"

It felt weird. Her friends were looking at her like an anomaly. Asking questions that didn't feel intrusive but bordered on clinical. Asking what happened, how Aiden was different. She expected silly questions from maybe Blaire, like if he was good in bed or something, but this felt different. They seemed concerned and a little put off by the idea she and Aiden had sex.

"I've just never experienced him so aggressive and intense before. Not that it was a bad thing. Just new." She shrugged. "I mean, everyone acts a little different when they sleep together, right?"

"Sometimes," Blaire conceded.

Riley's cheeks tinted. "Yep. Absolutely."

Blaire laughed. "Apparently, Seth is *very* different behind closed doors."

"Huh?"

"He's a dom."

Riley swatted Layla's arm. "No, he's not!"

"It sounds like it from the way you describe him."

"How the hell do you know about doms?"

"I have access to the internet, you know. Just because my parents shelter me doesn't mean I'm ignorant."

"Bless your heart," Riley muttered.

"Anywayyy," Blaire said, trying to get the conversation back on track. But Charlotte didn't mind the detour. It felt so good to sit and joke with her friends and ignore the awkward situation she found herself in. To be happy for once in what felt like ages. "So what went wrong? If it was so good, then why are you upset?"

She sighed, slumping against the squeaky leather booth. "The next morning, he seemed fine. Touched me. Seemed affectionate… but then, nothing. He kept his distance but acted like he always did. Then when we hit Rosebrook Valley? Bam. It's like someone put up a wall between us. I haven't heard from him in a couple of days since he drove me back home."

"He didn't seem like anything was wrong, did he?" Blaire asked Riley. "Lukas said he seemed weird, but I thought nothing of it. Figured he was getting settled back in."

"I've only seen him once. He seemed fine, but I wasn't paying attention honestly. I kinda chewed him out for being gone so long and not letting me visit." Riley at least had the good sense to look embarrassed by her behavior.

Layla shook her head. "I haven't seen him at all."

"I'll get Seth to talk to him," Riley said. "Maybe he'll mention something."

Charlotte's stomach clenched when Blaire and Riley shared one of those looks again. She wondered if they knew more than they were sharing.

21

Hot and Cold

The walk from the diner relaxed Charlotte's frazzled mind. The girls acted weird about not only her possible inquiry into Blackthorn Academy, but also her intimacy with Aiden. Did they not want her around him? That made little sense to her.

She took her time walking through the evening crowds in the Valley Center Plaza, a sprawling outdoor shopping mall with dozens of stores and restaurants with pathways branching in different directions lined with small businesses. The smell of popcorn drifted on the warm breeze coming from the theater on the corner close to the diner.

It had been three months since she visited the town. Nothing changed except for the diner. Kids still climbed all over the massive marble fountain in the center of the plaza, while teenagers hovered near the theater, clustered together as they decided on their next movie. Couples held hands while carrying shopping bags in the other, moving from one store to the next.

The temperature had finally dropped, so the entire area was filled to the brim with life.

Had she expected anything different in the small town? Her life had turned upside down, but her hometown remained undisturbed by the outside world. It further backed her desire to stay.

Her phone chimed, and she shifted her Styrofoam box containing leftovers into her left hand to pull her cell phone from the back pocket of her shorts. Her stomach swooped when she saw the sender.

Aiden:

You busy?

Charlotte:

No. Walking home from the diner.

Aiden:

Diner?

Charlotte:

I had dinner with Blaire, your sister, and Layla.

What she didn't say was she only ate a single waffle fry. The whole interaction regarding Aiden made her stomach ache, and the idea of greasy diner food lost all appeal.

She tucked her phone away when he said nothing more. It was the first time he'd contacted her in two days, and that was it? Why did he need to know if she was busy?

She squeezed past a group of guys all dressed alike in baseball hats, tight jeans paired with cowboy boots or work boots, and T-shirts with designs about fishing, hunting, or some other form of country sport. They stood in front of a small sporting goods shop that sold everything from fishing gear to hunting rifles. It wasn't the kind of shop she visited, but she knew the owner. A nice middle-aged man who frequented the diner when she worked there. His wife worked as a receptionist for the dentist in town.

Her phone chimed again, and she stopped at a corner, setting her leftovers on the windowsill of a closed antique shop. She swiped the screen of her phone.

Aiden:

I need to see you.

Her face screwed up. Did he leave something at her house? She thought he left all his stuff in his mother's car when he dropped her off.

Charlotte:

I'll be home soon. I'm heading through the plaza now.

Aiden:

I'm in the plaza. Where are you? I'll find you.

Charlotte:

I'm coming up on the side path Mom's shop is on.

Aiden:

Wait for me.

She tucked her phone away and picked up her food, turning the corner to weave through the thinning crowd. The bright purple sign for Uniquely You, the boho chic clothing store her mom owned, came into view.

Stepping around a young couple looking in the window of a store with baby items, she saw him leaning on the wall, arms folded over his broad chest, hugged by a gray Henley with the top two buttons undone. His muscular thighs strained against his black jeans where he had one leg bent, booted foot propped on the wall.

She was sure the phrase tall, dark, and handsome was invented with Aiden Easton in mind. He looked as good as she remembered.

It's only been two days. Get a grip.

It felt like much longer now that he was in front of her.

As soon as she caught his eye, he pushed from the wall and stalked toward her. It was the only word to describe the way he moved. Tilting his head forward, he narrowed his eyes on her, holding her captive with his forest green gaze. She felt like prey in the eyes of a predator. A shiver ran the length of her spine, making her entire body shudder as she remained rooted in place.

Was he angry? No. Something sparked in the air that she couldn't explain that made her feel his approach meant something different.

When he reached her, his hand lifted to touch her cheek; the tendons in his forearms where he had the sleeves pushed up to his elbows flexed with the movement. She leaned into the featherlight touch he gave her with his fingertips, but he pulled away so fast she wondered if she'd imagined his touch.

"I needed to see you," he whispered.

"Why? What's wrong?"

"Everything." He took a step back, and she gripped the takeout container to restrain herself from chasing his retreat. "I drove all over trying to clear my head, and it's not working."

"What do you mean?"

"After I left, I went back to the academy, but when I couldn't sleep, I left. Hit the interstate. Drove to Atlanta, then down to the coast. Drove all the way up the South Carolina coast and back this morning. I ended up parking down at Lukas's parent's house at Tybee Island. Tried to sleep in the car midday, but it didn't work."

"Didn't work for what? I don't understand."

A group of young girls moved around them, laughing and talking loudly, but she couldn't make out anything they said. She focused all her attention on Aiden.

"What did you do to me?" he rasped, confusion and conflict waging war for control of his features.

"I didn't do anything to you," she said, frowning. "Have you slept? Eaten anything? If you've been driving… Wait. Have you been away from the academy since last night?"

"Haven't had anything. No food, no bl—*drink*." His jaw ticked. "Nothing. I left around three in the morning."

"Jesus, Aiden. You're gonna end up dehydrated. Let's go back to my place." She grabbed hold of his hand, only then noticing the tremble in his fingers before he tightened his grip on her hand. "I'll make you something. Mom had an appointment this afternoon, but Ma is still at work. No one will be there if you're worried about them."

"Why would I worry about them?"

"I don't know. I wouldn't want anyone to see me if I hadn't eaten or slept. I'd be hangry and antisocial."

His low chuckle slid over her like silk. She missed that sound.

"Oh!" She stopped, whirling to face him. "Here." She thrust the takeout container forward into his hands. "Eat this while we walk."

Aiden's dark brows twitched. "What is it?"

"I didn't eat all my food. Chicken fingers and waffle fries with cheese."

He opened the lid. "This is a lot. Did you eat at all?"

Was he seriously showing concern about her well-being when he was the one who hadn't eaten since yesterday? It was near seven o'clock. That meant he'd been on the road for sixteen hours. How was he not sick? It explained his hands trembling.

"Eat."

His eyes narrowed at the command.

"Please," she added in a rush.

He lifted a chicken finger from the container and took a bite, giving her a "there, are you happy?" look.

"Okay, let's go." She turned and led him down the street toward the outskirts of the plaza where the residential area was. Her house wasn't far from the plaza, which was convenient for her mom. She didn't have to walk far into the heart of town. Her ma, on the other hand, had to use the car to drive around the plaza and park behind the clinic.

The entire Valley Center Plaza was only accessible by foot traffic, so locals walked everywhere, since most everything anyone could ever need was in the heart of the massive outdoor shopping mall. Charlotte and her mothers only drove to the far side of Rosebrook Valley for groceries, the mall, and a few other businesses that didn't get retail space in the plaza.

By the time they reached her house, Aiden had polished off the entire container of food. It made her happy to take care of him for once.

She pulled out her keys and let them inside, beelining for the kitchen with the empty container to whip up something for Aiden to eat.

"You don't need to make anything else. I'm full."

Her hand paused on the handle of the refrigerator. "Full? You've barely eaten."

"Trust me, that's a lot."

For his large size, she didn't quite buy it, but she wouldn't argue with him. He was talking to her. That's what mattered.

"Well, at least get something to drink. You said you hadn't had that either, right?"

He gave a tight nod, looking down at Molly, who chose to grace them with her almighty presence, once again rubbing her scent all over his ankles.

"Molly," Charlotte chided, rounding the counter with a can of Diet Coke. "Sorry about her." She handed him the drink. "It's all we have. Mom is all about reducing sugars after the doctor told Ma she was pre-diabetic."

"It's fine." He opened the can and took a long swallow, his throat working with the motion. She couldn't stop staring at it. When he lowered the can, he raised an eyebrow. "What's wrong?"

"Nothing," she said, and the cat meowed at her as if to call her a liar, sauntering off after a tail flick in her direction. *Yeah, boo on you too, Princess Molly.*

"Want to watch a movie?" she asked. "It'll give you a chance to relax after driving around. If you get hungry again, I can whip up some dinner. I'm sure my moms would appreciate it if I did."

"Sure." Aiden shuffled over to the couch and lowered himself to sit.

"I'm gonna go put my sandals away, then I'll show you what we have." She turned and headed for her bedroom.

She still didn't understand why Aiden decided to leave the academy and drive all over two states, but she wouldn't push him in case it made him uncomfortable. The fact they were talking was a step in the right direction. Maybe he would tell her what the deal was the other day. Maybe it wasn't anything at all, and she read too much into it.

Either way, she wanted to understand so they could be friends again. The contingent loss of their friendship brought another sinking wave of despair that only exacerbated her low mental state.

As she approached her room, she paused at the sight of her open bedroom door. She closed it when she left earlier to keep Molly out. She was sure of it. Did one of her mothers return home while she was out?

Pushing the door open, she let out a gasp, and her hands began shaking violently.

"What's going on?"

She shrieked, jumping at the sound of Aiden's deep voice behind her.

"What?"

She spun around, hand on her chest to will her heart to stop beating so fast so she could answer his questions.

"What's wrong?"

How did he know something was wrong? He was just on the couch. He wouldn't have heard her gasp.

She stepped aside, allowing Aiden to look into her bedroom where a bouquet of pink roses lay on her bed. "How did he get into my house?" she whispered in horror. She spun to look up at Aiden, wide-eyed. "He followed me here. I knew it!" She wrapped her arms around herself. "I can't let him hurt my moms."

Aiden cursed, and unexpectedly wrapped her in his embrace from behind. He pulled her flush against him and buried his face in the top of her curls. "He won't. I'll kill him first."

Her breathing stuttered at his words. Words she believed.

Something about Aiden told her he would do whatever was necessary to protect those around him, even if it meant crossing lines people were never meant to cross. At least those who wanted to stay out of prison and whose hearts weren't corrupt. His heart was good, and she'd never see it as anything different.

Her cell phone rang in her back pocket, and they sprang apart like someone caught them in the middle of having sex in the doorway.

She pulled the phone from her pocket and looked at the screen. Her eyes met his questioning ones. "It's Ma."

"Which one?"

"*Ma.* Elizabeth."

"Right," he said, staring at the roses. "Sometimes I get it mixed up."

She didn't blame him. Her mind wasn't in the right place right now, either. Answering the call, she tempered her voice, hoping not to sound as freaked out as she felt. "Hi, Ma."

"Hi, dumplin'. Are you still at the diner?"

"No, I'm at the house. Aiden's here."

"Oh, that's good."

"Good?"

"Yeah," her ma said before the sound of shuffling and murmured voices came over the line. She seemed distracted. "Listen, Sara and I need to head up to Atlanta."

"What? Why?"

Aiden looked up from where he sat on the edge of her bed, looking through the roses. She suspected he was checking for a card.

"Your *puse* is in the hospital, and we need to go."

When it rains, it pours. "I'll come with you," she said, her mind racing with potential reasons for her grandmother's hospitalization. She didn't know her adoptive grandmother well, but she was still family.

"No. You need to stay home. The hospital where she is has restrictions on the people allowed in. You wouldn't be able to go back, anyway. I'll be lucky if I can even go back. They've buckled down on the kinds of visitors they allow in recent years. But I need to be there for Sara."

"Is she gonna be okay?"

"Oh, yeah. She's fine. Stable. They are only keeping her for observation. Rina just wants her daughter there, so we're going to drive up and stay in a hotel nearby until she's released."

"Okay," Charlotte mumbled, unsure of what else to say. She couldn't do anything for her mom, and she didn't even know if her adoptive grandmother would remember her. Her memory had been slipping in recent years. "Tell Mom I love her, and *Puse* too."

"Of course. We'll keep in touch. There's money in the jar on the fridge for groceries if you want anything special."

When she hung up the phone, she looked at Aiden, who sat on her bed in silence.

"Everything okay?"

Aiden's lips tightened in response to her explanation, and he lowered his head, the long, black strands on top of his head falling forward out of place. He clasped his hands between his thighs as he sat with his forearms resting on his thighs. He seemed to struggle with whatever was on his mind.

With a sigh, he looked up at her. "I can stay with you again. If you want." His eyes cut to the roses. "Because of this," he added.

The stalker. Right.

She almost forgot about it with the news about her grandmother. *Of course he's only staying for that.* She really needed to get herself together. *Priorities.*

She didn't want Aiden to feel obligated to stay with her because of some creep again, but she seriously feared being alone given her stalker had accessed the inside of her house. Having company was prudent.

Calling one of the girls didn't seem reasonable. They were on summer break. Blaire was spending time with her boyfriend. Riley was with Seth. And Layla couldn't do much if a stalker showed up—

even if her parents let her stay off campus. Plus, Charlotte didn't know her as well as she did Blaire and Riley, and even then, if they both didn't have boyfriends, they probably couldn't do anything to defend against a stalker either.

If she didn't want to be alone, Aiden was her only option.

"I don't want to bother you with it," she said, giving him the opportunity to back out of the offer even if she hoped he wouldn't.

"If it was a bother, I wouldn't offer."

Something about the look on his face made her question how true the statement was. Something had shifted between them after they slept together, and she didn't think she could reverse it.

"Okay, then. If you don't mind staying."

"It's not a problem." He looked at her bed. "I can sleep on the couch. It's big enough."

Her heart sank.

"So, movie?" She moved to her computer chair and sat down, trying to ignore the sadness sneaking in. She slid her sandals off and rubbed her feet. They ached after the walk home. Served her right for wearing a pair of sandals she had worn only twice. When she let go of her foot and looked up, she found Aiden watching her movements with a furrow to his brow.

He stood from the bed. "I'll wait out there."

She wasn't sure what that was about. Her feet hurt. Nothing wrong with giving herself a foot rub. It wasn't like they didn't have all night to watch the movie.

Sighing, she put her sandals in the closet and walked into the living room.

The sky had darkened to almost night while she was on the phone with her ma. She felt exposed by the big bay window. The feeling would only get worse once night fell.

Moving to the window, she jerked the curtains closed. If she was going to sit in the living room, she wouldn't give some creep in the bushes a front-row seat to her leisure time.

"I'm gonna grab some drinks. Want anything specific? There's beer, mixers, coolers..."

She wasn't twenty-one yet, but her parents allowed her to drink at home with them. She didn't do it outside of that except for the time she went on vacation with Aiden and their friends. Her parents wouldn't care if she had something as long as she stayed home.

"I'll take a beer."

He normally had liquor, from what she learned when they went to the beach, but her ma kept the hard liquor in a cabinet in her parents' bedroom, and she didn't want to invade their private space. They respected her personal space, she would respect theirs.

Grabbing a few beers and fruity drinks in a bottle, she brought them back to the living room and placed them on the table.

"Thanks," he said, grabbing a bottle and twisting off the cap.

"Can you open one of the fruit ones for me?" She never mastered popping off caps. She either had to use a bottle opener or have her mothers do it.

She moved around the sectional and crouched down to open the bottom cabinets of the entertainment center. She scanned the few options on hand then shook her head. "Nope. Let's see if Netflix has something."

When she turned around and grabbed the remote, she paused, gaze darting from where Aiden sat in the middle of the main couch to the sectional on one side that was shorter and had the attached ottoman. That was probably the better option, but she didn't want to make things awkward, either. She wanted to shift their relationship back to where it used to be. Distancing herself wouldn't do that.

"Gonna sit?" He looked up at her and cocked his head to the side.

"Oh, yeah, um." She'd been standing there longer than intended. Moving around the coffee table, she flopped down on the main couch, leaving a cushion between them. She picked up her bottle and took a drink. "What kind of movie do you wanna watch?"

"Horror?"

"I mean, as long as it's not about a stalking killer, sure. Oh, or vampires."

His brow rose, and he chuckled. "Alright. No stalking killers or vampires. What about zombies?"

"Zombies aren't good horror."

"Fine. You have a point," he conceded. "What about weird demonic possession?"

"Oh! I bet I know the one you're talking about." She flipped on the TV and loaded up the streaming service, navigating to the search bar.

"How do you know? There's a lot that fit that description."

"No. But. I saw the newest recently offered. I figure you're talking about that one. It's about the possessed hand, right? With the stupid kids who have to hold it and tell the spirits to talk to them, and then let them in and they become possessed? It came out a couple years ago, but just popped up for streaming."

"Yeah, that's the one."

She flipped her curls off her shoulder and gave him a smug smile. "Told you I knew the one you were thinking of."

"Alright, smartass." He leaned back and spread his knees wide, crossing his arms over his chest. "What am I thinking now?"

She set the remote down and turned to him. "That you're glad Riley didn't know you were coming over or she would turn this into a slumber party with a ton of candy and junk food and keep us up all night?"

"That's… oddly specific. I *wasn't* thinking that, but I am now."

"So what were you thinking?"

"I honestly forget. I'm stuck on the Riley home invasion."

"Don't worry, I won't text her." She smiled, turning back to the TV to find the movie and start it.

Settling back against the cushion, she pulled a throw pillow into her lap and wrapped her arms over the top of it as the movie began.

While the first movie was good, when they moved on to a teen scream flick, she quickly lost interest. The earlier parts were interesting, and she kept sitting forward to catch everything that happened, but as the plot progressed, it made less and less sense. Only half the things the kids did seemed reasonable.

She shifted on the couch, sinking back into her seat, and her arm brushed against Aiden's. When had she moved so close?

A glance on each side of them made her realize they both had moved to the cushion that once posed as a divider.

Clearing her throat, she moved her gaze back to the TV at the same time a jump scare happened.

"Jesus fuck!" She rose off the couch a bit, startled. Well, that sobered her up the rest of the way.

Aiden burst into laughter.

She spun on him. "What?" Her voice was breathless.

"I have never heard you curse like that."

"That's because I try not to. I curse, but not often. But *come on*," she said, throwing her hand out at the TV as she sat forward on the edge of the couch, grabbing the mixed drink and taking a swallow. "What did you expect?"

His hand rubbed over his mouth to hide his laughter.

"Go ahead, buddy. Laugh it up." *How is he not at least tipsy?*

"What do you want me to do? Protect you from the big bad TV monster?"

"No," she said with indignation, turning her nose up.

"Oh, come on, I'm just playing." He reached forward, and before she realized what was happening, his large hands hooked her by the waist and pulled her back to the couch. "Don't pout."

"I don't pout." She crossed her arms.

"No?" He directed a pointed look at her arms and then returned his gaze to her face, to her twisted lips.

Fine. She was pouting.

"Whatever." She turned her head to look anywhere but at him. She'd forgotten what this was even about, but she was having fun, so that was all that mattered.

"Charlotte." He caught her chin with his fingers and turned her face to his. "I mean it. No pouting."

"You're not the boss of me."

Something flashed in his eyes she didn't recognize, but she saw it. A slight twitch of his brow where his eyes narrowed, and a brief glimmer of a smile.

"That may be so, but I don't enjoy seeing you sad." His fingers moved from her chin to run down the side of her throat. "It unsettles me."

"Unsettles?" She swallowed.

"Makes me want to find whatever made you sad and make it regret ever crossing you." His hand dropped, landing on her knee.

This had gone somewhere she didn't intend.

Little sparks zipped up her leg from where his hand sat heavy on her skin.

"I'm not sad," she whispered.

"I know," he said.

"How?"

"A hunch. You don't pout when you're really sad."

Was she that transparent? He seemed to read her so well compared to others. Maybe he did that easily with everyone.

This close to him, she could see the golden ring around his pupil, flaring out into the green of his eyes like the sun filtering through the forest.

Was she seriously sitting there comparing his eyes to nature? *He's looking at you, say something!*

"Your eyes have gold in them," she said, leaning forward subconsciously.

Smooth.

He chuckled, low and deep. "They do. How much did you have to drink?"

Apparently not enough.

"One bottle. You've had more than I have."

"I hold my alcohol well."

She wouldn't drink more than one bottle. The doctor said her medicine wouldn't mix well with copious amounts of alcohol and advised against inebriation but said the occasional beer wouldn't harm her.

"Well, I'm not tipsy, just noticed that, is all."

"Alright," he said, his voice lowering into a soft cadence that relaxed her.

His head angled, and his gaze dropped to her mouth. His eyelids lowered to half-mast as his tongue traced over his lower lip.

"Aiden?" she whispered.

"Yeah?"

"You're going to kiss me, aren't you?"

"Yeah."

With that confirmation, he leaned in, closing the distance between them.

She feared alcohol was responsible for his abrupt change in behavior and worried he would regret everything as soon as the kiss ended. But that problem was for future Charlotte to deal with. Present Charlotte battled the urge to crawl into Aiden's lap.

His tongue swept into her mouth to tangle with hers, and he groaned. The sound made her nipples tighten, as if his vocal chords had a direct link to her body parts.

He shifted, his hand holding the side of her throat as his other gripped her waist, twisting her on the couch, lowering her down to her back, while never removing his mouth from hers. His body loomed over hers, hand gliding along her side as he used his other to angle her head where he wanted it, deepening the kiss.

Moaning into his mouth when his hand settled on her hip and squeezed, she canted her hips up to press against him where he nestled between her thighs. The answering grind of his hips against her made the denim of her shorts press against her panties and slide over her slit, making her ache to remove the fabric between them.

Her hands slid up his back, nails dragging over his gray Henley until she reached his shoulders. She moved one of her hands around to rest on top of his shoulder, and the other slid into his hair, raking over his scalp. He moaned into her mouth and bit down on her lower lip.

Breaking the kiss, he stared down at her. They were so close she could taste his breath, a strange mixture of beer and cream. His pupils were blown, but what caught her attention most was the green ring encircling them. The light from the movie on the TV made them gleam like jewels.

"Your eyes are so beautiful," she murmured, moving the hand on his shoulder to brush his stubbled jawline. "It's like they're glowing."

Those narrowed eyes that looked at her with such intensity rounded.

He shot up off the couch and stood above her, breath heavy, panic etched in every line of his body. She lifted herself onto her elbows and looked up at him.

"Aiden?"

He flinched, snapping his gaze to hers.

"Aiden, what's wrong?"

"I've had too much to drink," he muttered, his voice a rasp. "I'm sorry. I'm…" He looked all around the room, avoiding her eyes. "Can I go shower? It might help."

"Yeah," she said, feeling awkward. "Sure. You know where the bathroom is. I'll get you a blanket and pillow so you can rest after."

"Cool. Yeah."

He didn't sound like himself. That wasn't the way he spoke. But he didn't give her the chance to ask questions. He turned away and stormed out of the room, slamming the bathroom door behind him.

22

Recognition

Aiden's hands trembled as he squirted shampoo into his palm. He felt out of control. The question of whether he should stay with Charlotte, even though her stalker had come to town, lingered in his mind. Maybe he should call Riley after all.

When they returned to Rosebrook Valley, he distanced himself from Charlotte to get his emotions in check. After they slept together, they needed physical distance. He couldn't have her; couldn't keep her. Distance was the only way he knew to prevent devastation in the long run.

His nails scrubbed at his scalp; soapy water ran down his spine.

The problem came when not touching wasn't enough. Being in her presence, laughing… breathing the same air… it was too much.

It took everything in him not to take her every single night after the first time. An entire week of sheer torture.

He'd acted like an outright jerk the day he dropped her off at home, but he needed to get away. Needed distance before he did something stupid.

The problem came when putting greater distance between them did nothing to quell his need to be with her. In fact, he felt off-balance and out of sorts. Sleep eluded him, and the drive all over with no actual destination didn't ease the ache. The farther he drove away from Rosebrook Valley, the worse the pain in his chest became.

Now that Charlotte's stalker made his presence known again, he needed to protect her, but at what cost?

Rinsing the shampoo from his hair, he closed his eyes.

He shouldn't have kissed her again.

Alcohol wasn't the problem. With his preternatural healing, his body metabolized alcohol faster than a human's. Short of shotgunning beers, it took a lot to become inebriated. No, alcohol wasn't the problem. The problem was his growing need for her.

Why did he feel like this?

He understood his attraction to her. Their emotional bond sparked his interest, and paired with her beauty, it made sense his feelings grew into desire. But to feel like his world was crumbling and that cutting off a limb was preferable to being away from her? That wasn't normal.

He'd expect this kind of behavior if they were Korrena pairs, but that wasn't possible. For one, she was human. The Oracle explained the only reason Blaire could be Lukas's Korrena, while human, was her bloodline. She was the only one of her kind like that. Then there was the fact he'd had sex with Charlotte and tasted her blood. Sure, she hadn't consumed his blood, but was it necessary?

The textbooks stated that sealing a bond required sharing blood and sexual intercourse. But had anyone tested it? If only one half of a Korrena pairing consumed blood, would it stick?

He shook his head. *She's still human, so it's impossible.*

It had to be the reduced blood intake. It was the only other plausible reason he felt so out of control. The beginning stages of *sanguis manie* riding him hard, making him want to feed on a live source and act on primal instincts.

When he returned to the academy, he'd planned to return to a normal feeding schedule, but he was so depressed the day he came back, he only took what was essential to function. Then during the entire drive—for sixteen hours—he didn't consume blood. He didn't know how many hours had passed since he met up with Charlotte, but he still hadn't fed.

Now he stood in her shower shaking like a fiend withdrawing from a drug. His throat burned with hunger, and his cock jutted out, aching with the need to follow her smell that permeated the bathroom, made potent by the hot steam.

He thought he knew his limits. Thought he understood how long he could deny his body's needs. Thought if he surpassed those limits, he could control the hunger, control the monster inside him.

How wrong he was.

He shut the water off and stepped out of the shower, ignoring the ache below his waist. Lifting his jeans, he dug out his cell phone. If he was going to stay with Charlotte, he needed reinforcements.

Aiden:

Emergency. I need blood. Now.

Lukas:

What? Where are you?

Aiden:

Charlotte's house. Don't tell anyone. Can you bring me a few packets?

Lukas:

Yeah, but are you good?

Aiden:

No.

Lukas:

I know where she lives. Blaire showed me once. I'm on my way.

Lukas:

Sanguis manie?

Aiden:

Soon. It's starting.

Lukas:

Where you gonna put them?

Aiden:

I'll hide them in her fridge. Leave them on the porch and text me when you do. I'll slip out and get them.

Lukas:

K. On my way.

Aiden was thankful his best friend didn't push for more information beyond what was needed. He didn't have the mental fortitude for a long text conversation. It was hard enough to text with unsteady hands.

He toweled off the best he could with how severely his arms shook, slipped on his boxers again, and then lowered himself to the floor. He kept his back to the corner of the bathtub and wall, legs drawn up to his chest. Trembling hands threaded through his hair and clenched as he lowered his forehead to his knees.

He couldn't leave the bathroom until Lukas arrived.

He wouldn't put Charlotte in danger.

Even if his instincts clawed at his throat like a rabid animal at the edge of starvation. Even if the cravings for blood clouded his mind with sick thoughts, he would never act upon it.

After what felt like hours, his phone vibrated on the floor, and he snatched it up.

Lukas:

I'm here. Packets are beside the door.

Aiden scrambled up from the floor and peeked out the bathroom door. The house was dark. He had been in the bathroom so long Charlotte went to bed.

He stepped out of the bathroom and crept through the house to avoid making a sound and alerting her. Once he reached the door, he unlocked the deadbolt and doorknob, then eased it open. Pushing open the glass exterior door, he slipped out onto the porch. Lukas stood there with his hands buried deep in his pockets, a look of concern etched in his features.

"Thanks, man," Aiden rasped. "I didn't think I could stay all night like this." He held up his hand to show how violently he was shaking. Even his voice sounded borderline feral.

Lukas cursed under his breath. "Why did you let it go this far? Did you know your eyes are glowing?"

"Shit. No, I didn't." He dug his fingers into his eyes, as if applying pressure would prevent his body's natural reaction to the lack of blood from rising to the surface. When Charlotte mentioned his eyes glowing, he hoped it was a trick of the lighting, but he couldn't take chances. He had to get away from her. "I was stupid." A poor explanation, but the only one he had. He'd made a foolish choice by avoiding feeding. He lectured Riley about it often.

"Yeah, well, do I need to stick around? Send Blaire?" Lukas peered around Aiden toward the house. He wouldn't see anything. Charlotte had closed the curtains, and Aiden assumed she'd closed them to hide from the stalker.

"No." He crouched to pick up a blood packet, tore into it, and gulped down the thick liquid without stopping to breathe. The relief was instant.

"Better?"

"You have no idea."

"Actually, I do."

He wiped the corners of his mouth and raised a dark eyebrow. "What?"

"When they locked me in the dungeon, I sat there for around twelve hours, and it'd been a while since I drank before that."

"What time is it?"

Lukas pulled out his cell phone. "One. Why?"

He left the academy at three in the morning. His last blood packet was around ten the night before. He wanted to laugh at how foolish he'd been when the reality sank in of how long he'd gone without blood. "It's been twenty-seven hours since my last packet this size." He held up the empty bag.

"Are you fucking serious? What the hell, man?"

"Shhh, you'll wake her. She's already freaked out because of the stalker." He looked over his shoulder toward the house, listening for Charlotte. "But yeah, I know. You don't have to even tell me how risky it was."

"Why did you not drink something today? And why is she freaked out about the stalker down here? Didn't she move here to get away from him?"

"I wasn't at the academy. And that's one reason, but he followed her here."

"Where were you?"

"Here, there. Everywhere in between." His shoulders lifted in a shrug.

"You could have stopped at a clinic."

"Yeah, I messed up."

Lucas sighed, his hand raking into his hair. "You said the stalker followed her here?"

"Yeah, he broke in and left roses on her bed."

Lukas cursed and turned in a circle, rubbing his hands over his face. "And that's why you're here?"

"Yep. Her parents aren't here. I can't leave her alone, man."

"Yeah, I get it. But something has to give."

He bent to pick up the other two packets. "I know. Listen, I need to get back inside and hide these before she gets up and finds me missing."

"Alright. Call me if anything happens. If you need more, let me or Seth know."

"Yeah. Thanks, man. And keep this from Riley."

Lukas gave a stiff nod before turning and jogging down the paved walkway, disappearing into the night.

A scream tore him from the first peaceful sleep he'd had in days.

He untangled himself from the blanket wrapped around him and jumped up from the couch, running for Charlotte's bedroom ready to rip the throat out of the asshole who dared to come into her home while he was there.

Throwing the door open so hard it stuck to the wall, he froze, chest heaving.

Charlotte lay on her bed, tangled in her bed covers, thrashing in her sleep. Her cries and whimpers echoed in his ears and hit his heart like a kick in the chest.

He crossed the room in three quick steps, then knelt on the bed and grabbed her shoulders.

"Charlotte! Charlotte, come on, it's me!"

Her head thrashed from side to side as she clawed at his arms, tears running down her temples into her hairline.

"Wake up. I need you to wake up," he said, trying to sound soothing, but he couldn't mask the panic in his voice. He intimately understood the feeling of being imprisoned within one's own mind; defenseless and unable to escape the malevolent forces that sought to harm.

Charlotte's eyes flew open, but she stared up as if not quite back with him yet.

He lowered his forehead to hers and squeezed his eyes shut. "Come on, Kitten. You're okay. You're okay."

She threw her arms around his shoulders and dragged his body down on top of her, taking all of his weight. Crying softly, she buried her face in his neck, clinging to him, taking deep drags of his scent into her lungs.

"That's it. You're okay. I'm here."

She sniffled and let her arms fall from his shoulders after several minutes, allowing him to move to support himself on his elbow, still hovering over her in case she needed him again. "Don't call me a kitten," she said. Her words lacked heat, leading him to believe she didn't wholly dislike it.

"Did I call you a kitten?"

"Yes," she said, a pout on her face as if the name offended her sensibilities.

He brushed his thumb over her temples. "You remind me of one."

Her eyes rolled, and she squirmed. He sat up, tucking his leg beneath him, placing one foot on the floor, allowing her to move into a sitting position.

"So, you want to tell me what that was about?"

"Just a nightmare."

"Well, yeah. But what about?"

Her arms crossed beneath her chest, diverting his attention downward, revealing her choice of attire—a baggy T-shirt with no bra. The twisted covers, and her bare legs on display, made it obvious she wasn't wearing sleep shorts. Was she wearing anything underneath? He shook his head.

"You won't tell me about your nightmares, so why should I?"

He licked his lips, dragging his teeth over his lower lip before grinning. "You got me there, but come on. You scared the shit out of me."

"It was the stalker. He tried to kill me." She looked up into his eyes as hers welled with tears. "He had already killed you."

"Well, that didn't happen. I'm here." He thumbed away a tear that tracked down her cheek. "I'm harder to take out than you'd think, Kitten."

Her laugh sounded watery, and she sniffed. "Stop that."

"What?" He tilted his head as if he didn't understand, and she rose to the bait as expected. He wanted to make her forget about the nightmare.

"The kitten thing." She tried to look put-out, but the longer he stared at her, the more he saw the cracks in her armor—until she burst into laughter.

"You don't really hate it, do you?"

Her gaze moved to the wall. "No," she mumbled, a pout in her voice.

"What was that?" he teased.

"You heard me."

"Mm, nope. Sure didn't."

She pivoted and smacked his bare arm. "You did too!"

"So you *like* being called kitten?" The blush that spread across her cheeks made his brows rise. "Do you like it when *I* call you kitten? Or just the nickname in general?"

Her gaze lowered to her lap, and his heart sped up. She already responded to him in ways he didn't expect, but now this? Couples gave each other pet names all the time, but kitten hit different from how baby or honey did—and they weren't even a couple.

It wasn't a name he'd use in public knowing she enjoyed it instead of humoring it. The shift in her reaction made it feel sexual and almost kinky.

He took a chance, ignoring the warning signal not to tread into those waters. "Do you want me to call you kitten?" He paused, his throat clicking with his hard swallow. "*My* kitten?"

Her head snapped up at his last question. Her pupils had devoured her irises almost completely.

Holy shit. He swallowed the knot in his throat. Ignoring the way he felt about her wasn't working anymore.

He wanted her. *Needed* her.

He didn't know how he would navigate the divide between their species, but he would do it. Maybe one day she would grow tired of him, and he would never have to deal with it, but that was a future problem. Denying himself what he wanted now wasn't fair. He wouldn't do it. Not when he could see she wanted him too.

"I'm sorry," he whispered, leaning in and kissing her jaw, moving to brush his lips across her cheek. "I shouldn't have denied either of us what we wanted." His lips hovered over hers. "You do want this, don't you?" With a vulnerability he felt to his bones, he added, "Me?"

A tear fell. Her whispered confirmation mouthed over his lips was all he needed to know she was his—at least for now.

As he pressed his lips to hers, she whimpered at the touch. He loved the sound of her desperation. A desperation that turned from sound into action when she shifted, her hands moving to his shoulders as she rose to her knees. He twisted to plant both feet on the floor as she threw a leg over his thighs and straddled his lap.

The way heat radiated from her core against the thin fabric of her panties and his boxers made him shudder.

His hand moved to cup the side of her throat, his arm encircling her waist as he claimed her lips again, pulling her flush against him.

She rocked her hips, taking pleasure from the straining erection trapped snugly between them. Moaning when she angled just right, he slid his tongue into her mouth to duel with hers.

Her grip tightened on his bare shoulders, her nails biting into his flesh. "More. I need more," she breathed against his mouth, breaking the kiss.

Without making her wait, he worked her shirt up and off her body, tossing it to the side and freeing her breasts. His hands slid down her body, mapping the curve of her waist and the shape of her hips until he palmed her backside. Pressing her core to him as he swiveled, he lowered her onto her back, chasing after her with his lips devouring hers.

He rained kisses and bites over her neck, shoulders, and down to her breasts where he found the faintest trace of yellow where the bruising he left her with had all but vanished. That wouldn't do.

He dragged his tongue across her skin before latching on and pulling the soft flesh into his mouth, causing her to buck her hips. A throaty moan escaped. When he applied slight pressure using his blunt teeth with the suction, she mewled and squirmed beneath him, much like she had done before. A reaction seared deep within his core memories.

Worshiping Charlotte's body would never get old.

He lifted his head. Satisfaction with his work had a slow grin spreading across his face. "My mark looks good on you, Kitten."

She whimpered at the name.

He moved down, trailing his tongue lower from between her ribcage all the way down the soft flesh of her stomach until he reached the lacy line of the powder blue panties she wore. His fingers curled under the waistband, working the fabric over her hips and down her legs until he tossed them aside, baring her to him.

Before, he missed the opportunity to savor what she offered him, but he wouldn't make that mistake again.

His fingers traced a path across her hips, along where her leg creased at her pelvis. "You're so beautiful," he murmured, eyes trained on the pink, bare, swollen flesh glistening with arousal below a faint dusting of red hair.

When he finally allowed himself to have a taste of what he had yearned for since the night they slept together, a shiver ran down his spine. The sweet flavor of pineapple cake, much like the scent he'd grown accustomed to, burst across his tongue.

With his tongue pressed flat, he traced it over her slit, indulging in the irresistible sweetness that left his mind in a blissful haze. He flicked the tip of his tongue across her swollen clit, making her hips rise off the bed as she cried out, hands grasping into his hair and gripping with force, making him grunt.

To keep her still while he enjoyed her to his heart's content, he wrapped one arm over her trembling thigh and the other around her hip to press his palm to her lower belly. He angled his thumb down and toyed with her clit while he moved down, sucking her sensitive folds into his mouth in small increments until he reached her entrance.

She panted, moaning as she tried to grind her hips against his face, but his hold kept her still as he eased the tip of his tongue inside her, consuming the most potent source of her essence.

"Aiden, I need more," she whined, her hands falling away from his hair to squeeze the covers at her side.

He lifted his head to find not only her face flushed, but her chest had taken on a splotchy red tone. The sight made him grin. He loved making a mess of her.

Tightening his grip on her thigh, he continued the torturously slow circling of his thumb on her clit as he turned his head and sucked the flesh of her inner thigh into his mouth.

She let out a garbled sound that made his leaking cock twitch in impatience to get inside her. His teeth sank into her skin in response to the sound, and she wailed so loud he was glad her parents weren't in the house.

"Fuck. Shit." Her breath shuddered as he detached. "*Fuck.*" Her back arched when he bit again, crying out, "Fuck me, Aiden!"

It amazed him how crass her language became when lust overwhelmed her. Not that he minded it. Her losing all filters, allowing herself to surrender to her baser needs and instincts, gave him deep satisfaction. He longed to succumb to his instincts the same way, but he refused to harm her.

His tongue ran over the fresh mark on her thigh, soothing the sting he must have left behind.

Moving off the bed, he slipped his boxers off, freeing his aching cock, which twitched when she licked her lips. Her lust-drunk gaze locked on the leaking head. He didn't think she realized she was leaning toward it.

He gripped the base of his shaft and stepped forward to the side of the bed. Her gaze snapped up to his, and he gave her a lazy smile.

His knees buckled and hit the side of the bed when she surged forward, swallowing the head of his cock into her warm mouth. He didn't expect her to go for it so fully. She scrambled up onto her knees, one hand pushing his away from his shaft and taking its place, the other hand moving to grip his hip.

Watching her sink lower on his cock, his eyes drank in the sight of her hourglass figure bent in front of him on the bed, her knees tucked beneath her, her small feet the only thing visible past her rounded backside. He wanted to sink his fangs into the plush flesh. He groaned at the mental image while she swirled her tongue around the head as she withdrew.

Glassy, striking green eyes looked up at him, lips swollen and begging to be kissed. "I need," she started, her cheeks becoming rosier before she flicked her gaze down, falling silent.

He curled his finger beneath her chin, lifting her face to look at him. "Tell me what you need, Kitten. It's yours." Anything she wanted; he would give her anything within his power. He didn't know what was happening to him—why he felt the driving urge to handle her the way he did—but he didn't want to stop.

He couldn't stop.

Instead of speaking, she lowered her mouth back down over his shaft, her mouth open in a way that gave no suction. Her nails dug into his hip as she pulled him forward, pushing his cock farther into her mouth. Her gaze darted up to his as she gave another tug on his hips. A shudder ran through his body when he realized what she was asking for.

Both of his hands cupped her cheeks, holding her on him. "Tap my hip if you need me to stop," he said, barely able to hold back the growl working its way through his chest to his throat. Her hummed response vibrated through his shaft, making it pulse and leak against her tongue.

He dropped his right hand and curled the left into the mess of curls clipped to the back of her head.

Starting slowly, he eased her forward down his length, testing how far she could go. When she made a small sound of discomfort, he lessened the depth and held her still, letting her get used to the feeling. The apprehension didn't last long. As she accommodated to the thickness in her mouth, he increased not only the pace, but the force he applied to the back of her head.

Her moans, and the squirming of her hips, spurred him on. He knew she could handle it. Her movements and moans showed she enjoyed it.

The sounds she made as she slurped his cock like her favorite candy made him curl his toes into the carpet. Her nails biting into his flesh, breaking the skin, ignited his blood. The marks would heal soon, and the reality disappointed him. He wanted to carry her marks as much as he wanted her to carry his.

"Fuck, Kitten. This feels incredible." His hand tightened on her hair, and she moaned against his shaft, sending a vibration through him that almost made him come. "I have to stop, or I won't be able to bury myself deep inside of you, and I *need* to do that." He tugged her head back off his length, and she sat back on her feet, her hands dropping to her thighs.

Tendrils of flaming red curls hung around her face and stuck to her sweat slicked neck and forehead, fallen from the hair clipped on her head. Her parted lips looked swollen and red. Her chin glistened with the remnants of drool where she lost herself to giving him control.

She looked breathtaking. Debauched, marked, needy.

Before he could say anything, she crawled across the bed, lowered her chest to the covers, and then turned her head sideways on the pillow. With her back arched, knees planted on the bed, her backside swayed in the air, revealing her swollen lower lips to him. The silky arousal that he savored before now coated her bare core, inviting him for another taste.

He cursed to himself. "You tell me if it's too much." His instincts flared to life, making those words come out guttural and strained. "This is all for you. You control this. Do you understand?"

Her quick nod eased a tightness in his chest.

He needed her to understand she had the power to make him stop. No matter how much his baser needs took over, he would stop if she willed it. He might be the one taking the lead, but he would never take what wasn't freely given, and he wouldn't cross a line she marked in the sand.

Positioning himself behind her on his knees, he sat back on his heels. He leaned in and sucked the skin of her backside into his mouth like he wanted to do before, latching on with his teeth like he'd done to other parts of her. She cried out and slammed her fist on the bed, the other squeezing the covers in her grasp.

He lifted his head to admire the red and purple mark. He growled in pleasure, moving down to swipe her core with his tongue, indulging in another taste. She whined at the contact.

He lifted his head and placed his hands on the cheeks of her backside, squeezing tight. "Shhh. I just needed another taste. You're a temptation I can't resist." He stroked his cock slowly before gliding the head along her core, lubricating himself. "You have no idea how wet you are for me, do you, Kitten?"

Her soft whine in response made him smirk. She hadn't said another word since she begged him to fuck her. But her needy whines, moans, and desperate garbled pleas that almost formed words let him know he had her where he needed her. He would do anything to make her feel good.

Her knees spread farther apart as she lowered herself a little more, angling herself in line with his length as he pushed forward, nudging at her entrance but not entering her. Her frustrated whine when she tried to push back and didn't move made him smile. He held her hips still in a bruising grip, preventing her from sinking down on his cock.

"You want it, Kitten?"

She made a soft, needy sound, wiggling her hips, begging without words.

"No. I want more than that. I want you to tell me how much you want this." He slid the head in an inch, and she gasped. "Well?"

"Please," she said, looking up at him with one eye from where she held her cheek pressed against the pillow.

"Please what?"

"I want it."

"What do you want?"

"You know what I want," she pouted with frustration, but it lacked any bite, a moan following her words when he dug his fingers into the fleshy part of her backside.

"I want to hear it." His voice was a sharp command, but the rasp in his voice betrayed his need to sink deep inside her. He didn't know how much longer he could hold up a conversation.

"Aiden," she sobbed. "I need you to put it inside me. I need to feel you. I need it. I need it. I need it." Tears filled her eyes, making his widen at the naked longing in her voice as she repeated her plea over and over while choking on her sobs.

He inhaled long through his nose, taking in the sugary aroma of her scent floating in the air, pushing down the burn in his eyes. He never knew sex could feel like this.

No, this wasn't sex. This was a joining of souls.

Her need was so potent he felt it inside of him. Her longing and need for him hit on a visceral level, mirroring his in startling clarity.

With no further preamble, he punched forward, sinking all the way until his thighs met hers, making them both cry out in unison.

Her walls fluttered around him, but she wasn't coming, not yet.

Once again, he couldn't bring himself to take her slow and delicate, like she deserved. He needed to possess her. So he did. He thrust his hips, intending to mark her insides as thoroughly as he had done to her outer flesh.

His hands slid up to her waist, holding her tight beneath the ribs. He pulled himself closer to her as he ground his hips. Sweat glistened on her spine, and he curled himself over her to lick it from her skin. It tasted salty and sweet.

His size easily dwarfed her beneath him, and he took advantage of that, lowering his mouth to bite her shoulder as he pounded into her. She squirmed beneath him, moaning and pleading for more.

Before long, the taste of copper mingling with sweet vanilla sugar met his tongue. He hesitated, but she wasn't having it.

"Harder," she rasped. "Bite me harder."

Growling, he pulled her skin into his mouth, savoring the addictive liquid, driven by her demands. She wanted him to bite harder instead of urging him to stop. She didn't know what she was asking for. Did she know he was drawing blood? She had to feel it.

He rocked his hips against her, rotating them in a way that must have hit a spot inside her she liked because she shattered around him with a broken sob as he detached from her skin.

The walls of her insides choked his shaft, sending him flying over the edge into his own climax, pulsing inside her, painting her with the most intimate thing he could offer her.

Allowing a modicum of self-preservation to trickle in, he squeezed his eyes shut so she wouldn't see them this close up—in case they were glowing. He took a deep breath before opening his eyes again.

She lay still beneath him, panting, eyes closed.

He slid his tongue over the spot where he'd bit her. An angry bruise marred her skin that pacified something inside him, but confusion swept his mind when he didn't see anywhere he broke the skin.

Lifting himself from her back, he looked down at her, trailing his hands down her spine, relishing the feel of her sweat-slicked skin beneath his hands. Rolling her face to bury it into the pillow, she hummed a soft moan, responding to his ministrations. She truly acted like a kitten, purring for him when he petted her. So he continued, hoping to soothe her after such an intense moment between them.

As his hands slid up to her shoulder blades, he choked on his own saliva.

His chest seized and his hands trembled as he stared without blinking at the faded black tattoo beneath her hairline at the top of her spine. A circle with a straight line splitting the middle and an upside-down crescent slicing through the base of the circle.

He knew for a fact Charlotte didn't have tattoos. But he didn't need to know that to know what was staring him in the face.

The fading mark on her skin called to him, and his entire body responded. His nerves were alight with a mix of desire, fear, confusion, and need. His cock thickened again, still inside her.

Charlotte was his Korrena.

How the fuck does that happen?

The sound of rustling woke Aiden, breaching into the most peaceful sleep he'd experienced in a long time. A nightmare was trying to seize him, but it failed to take root. He rolled his head to the side to look at Charlotte, only to find her side of the bed empty.

His brows drew in, and he blinked a few times, focusing his vision on the darkness in the room. It took a moment for his mind to catch up with the present.

Charlotte was missing.

He bolted upright, and the air in his chest stuttered when he caught sight of her standing in front of the other window holding the sheer curtains open, looking out into the night.

She stood bathed in moonlight, unaware of his gaze on her, her naked skin ethereal under the luminous blanket of night.

"Come back to bed," he said, voice rough from lack of use. He cleared his throat. "You shouldn't stand in front of the window like that."

The curtain slipped from her fingers, and she looked over at him. "Why?"

"If someone's out there, I don't want them seeing you like that."

Her hands came up to rub up and down her upper arms, her arms wrapped around her like a shield. "I didn't think of that," she murmured.

He pulled the covers back, urging her to join him in the bed. He didn't like her so far away so soon after his discovery. "What are you thinking about, then?"

"I feel funny," she said, crawling from the foot of the bed to his side. He had to suppress a groan at the way her hips swayed with the movement.

"How so?" He pulled her into his arms when she reached him, pulling the blanket over their naked bodies. She put her hand on his chest, snuggling against him.

"My chest. I woke up because I felt panicky." Her finger trailed down between his ribs and swirled in circles on his abs. "When I snuggled up to you, it went away. I don't know what happened."

The thought crossed his mind that the feeling she picked up on was his own panic when the nightmare tried to take root. Did her making physical contact soothe it and drive the nightmare away? Was she already responding on instinct to the Korrena bond?

"Are you okay now?" His lips brushed the top of her head, his thumb stroking her upper arm.

"Mm," she mumbled, yawning. "Do you think he's out there?"

His grip on her tightened, and his teeth locked, jaw clenching. "Don't worry about him. I'm here."

As long as she had him, nothing would get to her.

She belonged to him now, and he would do anything to protect her. No one would take her from him. He'd kill them.

"Go back to sleep," he whispered. "I'll take care of you."

She wrapped her arm around him and nestled deeper into his hold as if his words settled her. He wrapped his other arm around her, tugging her closer as she drifted back to sleep. She hitched her left leg over his leg, bending it at the knee. The warmth from between her legs against his thigh made his cock twitch.

They'd had sex. He'd tasted her blood. Both were more than anyone he'd known who formed a bond did before sealing it.

Seth tasted Riley's blood before they sealed their bond, but they didn't have sex. Much to Aiden's displeasure, Seth explained how more happened between them, but they never went as far as intercourse prior to sealing the bond. Seth needed answers, so Aiden didn't fault him for oversharing.

Did having sex intensify everything?

He laid his head back against the pillows, closing his eyes.

He remembered learning that the more physical contact they shared, the stronger the bond grew. It was a reason many Korrena pairs couldn't resist touching one another prior to awakening. The instinct to be tethered to their mate was strong long before awareness set in.

That explained why it became frustrating not to touch Charlotte after they slept together the first time. Why he would find himself wrapped around her when he woke in the night if she wasn't thrashing about. How the urge to touch her arm or back as he moved about the kitchen when she cooked meals pushed at him.

His eyes shifted to the window as unease settled in his chest.

He said he was done refusing them what they both wanted, but how would he handle this newest development? It would be near impossible to hide their connection now that he knew she was his Korrena. The physical and emotional pain of going back to his dorm alone when her parents returned would be enough to drive him mad. He knew it. The bond between them had grown faster than it had for others he knew.

He couldn't tell anyone about the mark. A mark that wouldn't show at the back of her neck anymore because they weren't a sealed pair yet.

If he told them, and Charlotte found out the truth about what he was…

One small favor, he no longer had to worry about the Blackthorn Clan wiping her memories if she discovered the truth. The Korrena bond protected her from that. Forced separation of a Korrena pair violated their laws. Wiping her memory would force them to never be together.

The problem he faced now came down to his species.

Charlotte had been so upset about what she witnessed in the alley before he came to Athens that he felt certain she would reject him as a monster.

Korrena pairs could choose separation. She could choose to break their bond. After witnessing Blaire and Lukas have their bond stolen, he knew formed bonds could break. But if the bond was never sealed, then all Charlotte had to do was walk away. She didn't know the pain and suffering it would bring them.

Even if she knew, would she prefer it to being with a monster? Because that's how she viewed his kind after witnessing that rogue attack. Monsters who fed on poor, unsuspecting humans in dark alleyways. Like vampires on TV.

He'd finally found her. The person made for him.

And all because of his birth species, he would lose her.

23

Sickness

The walk through the courtyard from the dorm to the main building did nothing to relax Aiden. The scent of daylilies and magnolias filled the air with their pleasant aroma, carried on the midday breeze that made the rising humidity of early July bearable. On a better day, he might stop and sit on the edge of the marble fountain and drink in the sounds and smells that came with the peak of summer, but today wasn't a better day.

Charlotte left a week ago to see her grandmother Rina in Atlanta, and now he felt like he was dying.

His skin itched, and his chest ached. His head felt fuzzy and throbbed with an ever-present headache he couldn't shake. The urge to vomit tightened his throat. His healing did nothing to ease how his body seemed to revolt against him.

Stepping from the bright sunshine of the day, he entered the main building to make his way to the cafeteria on the second floor.

He kept his head down, avoiding eye contact with anyone he passed.

His eyes were bloodshot, and he probably looked like something the cat dragged in half dead. He didn't want to draw attention to himself.

In the cafeteria, he slunk to the buffet bar to grab a tray. The large buffet tables that wrapped around the center of the cafeteria held the spread of the day. Each meal they served had something new. With feeding all the students living on campus and catering to a variety of different cultures from all parts of the world, the amount of food that passed through the cafeteria was considerable, yet with minimal waste.

He grabbed the first things he saw. A small bowl of garden salad and a packet of the closest dressing, a small bowl of cantaloupe, and a serving of lasagna. Stopping at the beverage bar, he grabbed a cup and filled it with iced sweet tea before getting a blood packet from the refrigerators on the back wall. He would not neglect his health like before, not when he felt like this.

"Wow. You look like death warmed over," Seth said when Aiden approached the round table in the corner where his friends always sat at.

Riley sat between him and Blaire, who sat on the other side of Lukas. Dominic was on the other side of Lukas. Layla sat on the other side of Dominic. Three empty seats separated Seth and Layla. With Mera and Kai already gone to California, the vacancy at their table looked odd.

He placed his tray down and sat beside Seth. "Thanks, man, but death doesn't—" He cut himself short when awareness hit him.

The entire table fell silent. The conversation between Blaire, Lukas, and Dominic paused as they turned their heads to him.

He cursed under his breath. "Forget what I was going to say. It was a bad joke. I wasn't thinking." He slumped into his seat and ran a hand over his face. "I don't know why I said that."

"What's going on?" Lukas said, placing his fork on his tray.

He wouldn't lie. His physical appearance made it obvious something was off.

"I think I'm sick," he said. He opened the blood packet, making sure he had that first in case he couldn't stomach his food.

Riley put down her sub sandwich and turned in her seat. "Sick?"

"Something like that."

Layla's face screwed up, and with her doll-like appearance, it made her look more like a child. "But you can't be sick."

"Technically, he can," Dominic said, looking at Layla. "Long term he can't be, but for a brief period, if the sickness is strong enough—like cancer—he would fall victim to it for several weeks before his natural healing could conquer it." A frown lined his lips, and he put his elbows on the table, lacing his fingers and pressing them to his mouth as he studied Aiden. His empty tray sat pushed forward in front of him.

Blaire asked, "What do you mean by sick?"

"Sick. Like, headaches, the sweats, poor sleep, fatigue, my chest hurts… Should I go on?" Aiden gave her a half-hearted smile, so she understood he meant his sarcasm to be harmless. He wasn't sure he could competently convey his emotions today.

"You had enough blood?" Lukas asked, giving him a pointed look that made it clear he still wasn't happy with what transpired the week before.

Aiden didn't blame him. He wouldn't have been happy either to hear his best friend neglected himself to the point of becoming feral and possibly losing himself to mania.

He held up his blood packet. "Yeah, this is my second today. Had one at breakfast."

Lukas nodded, saying nothing more on the subject. Aiden trusted he would keep their secret.

"Have you been to the health wing?" Seth asked.

Aiden gave a brief shake of his head. "Nah. Not yet."

He knew the culprit behind the gradual buildup of sickness in his body. He needed his Korrena. Needed Charlotte.

Sara came back to pick her up before they transferred Rina to a care facility. While she was in hospital care for her broken hip, they discovered the accident was related to a neurological condition. The hospital said they couldn't in good faith send Rina home without round-the-clock care, and Charlotte's family lacked the necessary resources for the care Rina needed, so a long-term care facility became the only option.

Sara wanted Rina closer to Rosebrook Valley so she could see her often, but there weren't any vacancies, and the waiting lists were too long. They brought Charlotte to see Rina in case her cognitive functions diminished too far before they could make a trip again to see her while running two businesses.

"You need to see someone," Blaire said, breaching his thoughts. She scooped up a bite of lasagna. "If this isn't normal for you guys, you should at least see if you're okay." She took a bite.

He couldn't tell them the reason he felt like he was dying was because his Korrena was halfway across the state. The temptation to borrow his mother's car again and drive to Atlanta made his skin itch and tingle.

"Yeah, maybe."

"Maybe he just needs to get laid," Seth said, leaning back in his seat, popping a grape into his mouth. "Always makes me feel better." He winked at Riley, and her cheeks flamed in response.

"You're an idiot," she said.

"Well, you chose me, so what does that make you?"

"Also an idiot."

Dominic snorted, and Seth gave him a shrewd look. Even if Dominic no longer showed any attraction to Riley, Seth still acted like he was a mild threat. His attitude lessened the more time passed with Dominic making no moves to pursue Riley.

"So what are we doing for Lukas's birthday this year? It's the end of next week." Riley looked between the two guys. "Dom, you weren't here when we went to Tybee Island for spring break, but it was sort of this big celebration for everyone's birthday because with all the mess around here last summer through the last semester, no one got to celebrate."

Aiden wiped the sweat from his brow and took a long drink of his iced tea. Lukas gave him a look of concern, but he gave a brief shake of his head. He might talk to Lukas—and maybe Seth—about it, but later. Away from the rest of them.

Lukas's jaw muscle shifted, and he looked at Blaire, who was talking to Riley about his birthday. It was the only sign he understood. His best friend knew him. He knew when to wait.

His fingers dug into his eyes, and he forced down another bite of salad. The lasagna sat heavy in his gut, like the cheese had curdled in the stomach acid churning there. This could not all be from being away from her. He never heard of separation bringing this level of physical torment.

"I think we can save the birthday talk for later," Seth said, leaning in to get a better look at Aiden's face. "You need to see someone. You're sweating bullets."

Riley jerked her head around to look at Aiden, and the way her eyes softened and filled with worry hurt him. He didn't want to upset his little sister.

Blaire's hand rested on Riley's shoulder in a comforting gesture.

"He's gonna go see someone. Don't worry." She gave him a sharp look.

Sighing, he stood. "I'll take care of it."

He couldn't go to the health department. If he went and told them the truth, the domino effect would rock the school, throwing everyone's life into disarray. They were only now coming down from the chaos Blaire's arrival brought, and even then, they still faced issues because of a human Korrena. Charlotte also awakening as one, without the magical blood Blaire possessed, would be another situation where others would want to experiment.

He would be damned if he let anyone put their hands on Charlotte.

Suppressing the growl that rose in his chest, he picked up his tray. "I'll talk to you later," he said, looking at Lukas.

"Sure, man. I'll come by your room later and check on you."

"Me too," Riley said.

Seth shook his head. "I think he needs rest."

Lines settled between Riley's eyebrows, and she frowned at her Korrena. "Lukas is stopping by. Why can't I?"

"You can do whatever you want, but if you go, you'll hang out forever yapping your brother's ear off. If Lukas goes, he'll check on him and leave."

"Okay. Yeah. That's fair."

Layla laughed, and Dominic smoothed a hand over his mouth to hide his amusement.

"Let me know if it gets worse or you need anything," his sister said, looking up at him with a serious look on her face that looked out of place there. She must really be worried.

He didn't answer. He couldn't lie to her.

Stalking across the cafeteria, he disposed of his trash.

It felt wrong to be the weak one. He always supported the group. Always ensured everyone was okay and well. When something went wrong, he stepped up to either figure out the problem or solve the problem if it was known. It threw him off balance to not be in control of the situation.

The darkness of his dorm helped ease the prickly feeling skittering over his skin like insects.

He collapsed on his bed and reached beneath his pillow, pulling out the baggy T-shirt he'd stolen from Charlotte. She wore it the night he noticed his mark on her. When she threw it into the hamper the next morning, he snatched it out and hid it.

If he had to go back to the academy without her, he would take a piece of her with him. A piece that held her natural scent. It also held the sweet pineapple upside down cake scent that made his mouth water. He now knew the smell to be the pheromone unique to her, that only he could smell as her Korrena. No wonder he became addicted to the smell while living with her in Athens.

He lifted the shirt to his face and breathed her in.

The potent scent of her arousal still clung to the fabric, and it made his cock stir in his jeans.

He eased his shirt up over his abs and worked open the button and zipper on his jeans, freeing his thick length. He gripped it tight in his hand. The relief he felt when the sourness in his stomach receded was startling. The combination of her scent and the pleasure he derived from it made him feel better.

Lifting his hand to his mouth, he spit into his palm before grasping his shaft again and working himself in slow, long strokes. He twisted his hand at the head, making his toes curl in his boots.

His other hand held her shirt close to his nose as he took another hit of her scent. His cock jerked in his hand, balls tightening in response.

He wondered if she was thinking of him. If she touched herself thinking of him while they were apart.

Squeezing his eyes shut, he arched his neck as he let the mental image wash over him of Charlotte lying in bed naked, toying with her ample breasts, working her hand between her legs, bringing herself pleasure while thinking of him. He shuddered.

Did she play with her nipples and take her time? Or did she go straight for it and work herself into a frenzy without preamble?

His grip on his shaft tightened as he jerked himself in quick, short strokes to the mental image. He groaned his pleasure into the silence of the room. What was she doing to him?

He wondered if she slid her fingers inside, or only worked over her clit. Did she use toys? He recalled seeing a little purple device inside her nightstand. That thing had no purpose other than self-pleasure.

Leaving the shirt lying over his face, he pushed his jeans down farther, allowing his balls to be free. He cupped them in one hand, massaging as he worked his other hand over his length, slick with his natural lubricant and spit.

"Fuck, Charlotte."

The image in his mind shifted, and he saw her bent in front of him as he took her from behind, his mark prominent and permanent on her neck. He wanted it so badly. Wanted to claim and seal the bond.

In his mind, he reached for her and pulled her body flush with his, wrapping one arm around her waist and the other over the tops of her breast, giving her no escape from the cage of his arms.

She cried out at his brutal thrusts, his fingers pressing into her arm and waist in a way he knew would leave bruises, and it pleased him to know that because she was human, they would last.

When he sank his fangs into her, making her entire body convulse as her climax overtook her, he filled her with his seed. An anger settled in at her use of birth control.

He gasped, and his eyes flew open as thick, sticky ropes of cum coated his abs. Pulling the shirt from his face, he dropped it at his side, lying there in his mess in shock.

Had he seriously thought that? He didn't want children. Not yet.

It was just a fantasy. Only a fantasy, he told himself, trying to quell the panic seizing his chest that he'd come thinking of filling her and leaving more than a piece of himself behind.

His need to claim and own every part of Charlotte was invading every part of him, twisting his thoughts and revealing desires he never knew he had. So far, she hadn't been against any of it. Even the biting and blood thing. Though, unlike his fantasy, when he bit her and drew blood before, it wasn't with his fangs.

With the high of his orgasm fading, the itchy feeling came back. Sooner than later, something had to give. If a week caused this much internal conflict, how was he going to function long term without her?

Grabbing his phone, he opened their text thread. He needed to know she was okay.

Aiden:

Hey. How are you holding up?

Charlotte:

I'm alright. Grandma doesn't seem sick, but it makes sense. The issues only happen when she has a lapse in memory or focus.

Aiden:

I'm sorry this is happening.

Charlotte:

It's okay. We weren't very close. At least she's not sick. They expect her to be around a long time.

Aiden:

That's good.

He pulled his shirt over his head to clean off the cum drying on his stomach then tossed it into a hamper. He tucked his cock away and got up, going to the closet and getting a clean shirt.

Settling back on the bed, he tucked her shirt beneath his pillow.

Aiden:

So other than that, how're you doing?

Charlotte:

Fine. Why?

He frowned. Did the separation only affect Vasirian? He didn't think so. Blaire mentioned something about suffering while away from Lukas. Maybe it only affected a human if they had a sealed bond.

Aiden:

Just making sure things are okay.

He typed out "I miss you" then deleted it. He didn't want to be clingy, even if he felt that way.

Charlotte:

Okay. I've gotta go. Ma is calling me for dinner.

Aiden:

Have a good night, beautiful.

Charlotte:

:-)

He set his phone down on the bed and settled back. He hoped the physical release before texting her would make it easier for him to fall asleep.

After a few minutes of silence, his phone buzzed against his hip and he sighed, picking it up.

Riley:

We were thinking about going to Haven for Lukas's birthday. He doesn't want anything major.

Aiden:

Sounds good.

Riley:

I'm gonna invite Charlotte, so make sure you have a packet before we go.

Aiden:

Sure.

Riley:

I hope you're feeling better. I love you.

Aiden:

I will. Soon. Promise. I love you too.

It was the truth. Soon he would feel okay again. Once Charlotte came home.

He wondered if she would even be back in time for Lukas's birthday. The tightness in his chest at the thought of going another week without her around made him question if he could even survive it.

24

Coincidence

"Are you sure we don't need to take you to the doctor? They accept walk-ins." Charlotte's mom looked at her in the rearview mirror once she put the car in park.

"I'll be fine once I'm out of the car."

Her mothers shared a look before her ma turned in her seat and gave her a sympathetic smile. "You think it might be because of your medicine?"

She'd finally told them about the depression medication while they were in the hotel in Atlanta. She couldn't hide it from them and didn't want to. She didn't feel shame for needing a pill to sometimes help her get through the day, but she felt anxiety around whether they would look down on her or treat her differently.

"No. I've taken the pills for months now. If I were going to have side effects like this, it would have already happened."

Within days of leaving Rosebrook Valley, sickness had settled in and got worse as the days passed until her mothers took notice. She kept experiencing cold sweats, extreme lethargy, stomach upset, and pounding migraines the likes of which she'd never experienced.

"I just need to rest. I think being in an unfamiliar place after only getting back from college has been a lot to handle."

The only time the symptoms eased was one night after she got off the phone with Aiden a couple of days after she arrived in Atlanta. She called him after dinner while her mothers went to a show. She decided to stay in the room after vomiting twice; she didn't want to ruin their night.

After disconnecting the call, she got the strangest ache that spread through her body until her body burned with arousal. She took care of it the only way she knew how when on her own. When her legs became weak, she sat in the bottom of the shower as the sickness took hold again and she vomited down the drain.

It made no sense to her why her body wouldn't act right.

"Let's get you inside then," her mom said, opening her door and walking to the front door while her ma grabbed the luggage from the trunk.

Charlotte ambled up the paved walkway, rubbing at bleary eyes that wouldn't focus.

"That's so sweet of him," her mom said, facing the front door.

Putting the luggage on the porch, her ma asked, "What's sweet of who?"

"Aiden." Her mom turned, a bright smile on her face. In her hands was a crystal vase filled with a bouquet of pink roses, a tiny envelope with "Charlotte" printed on the front clipped on a plastic stem. "I always knew there would be something between the two of you."

Charlotte's stomach tightened.

"I thought so too. Charlotte, sweetheart, why didn't you tell us?"

Unlocking the door, her mom went inside carrying the roses while

Charlotte stood frozen in place on the steps. How did she explain those weren't from Aiden? How did she explain who the roses were from? Her chest tightened at the idea of facing what they would say to her for hiding everything from them.

"Charlotte?"

She yelped and flinched when her ma put a hand on her arm.

"What's the matter with you? Are you absolutely sure we don't need to take you to the doctor?"

"No!"

Her ma's eyebrows lifted.

"I mean, no ma'am. Sorry."

Her ma gave her a wary look, grabbing the handles of the two large rolling suitcases, her duffel bag balanced against the handle of one of them. "Well, let's get inside so you can rest."

Charlotte followed her inside the house.

"I put the roses in your bedroom on the dresser," her mom said from the kitchen where she stood filling two glasses with Diet Coke. "Want some?"

"No. I think I'm just gonna lie down and take a nap."

"Jen wanted us to go out with her and Beth for dinner," her ma said, giving Charlotte a worried look. "I think I'm going to call her and cancel."

"No, it's fine. I'm fine. Go out." At both of her mothers' twin frowns she said, "Seriously. If I get worse, I'll call you, I promise. I'm already starting to feel better now that we're home."

"If you're sure," her mom started but Charlotte held up a hand.

"I am. Go. Have fun."

Before they could say anything more, she retreated to her bedroom and shut the door, thankful she didn't have to explain anything to them. With cautious footsteps, she went to the dresser and pulled the envelope from the bouquet, opening the flap and pulling out a small card.

Soon, Cherry.
Be ready.

A coldness not brought on by the air conditioning made her body shudder. She shoved the card into her desk drawer. Aiden would want to see it.

Slipping off the ballet flats she wore, she climbed on top of the covers of her bed, curling on her side. The scent of cream and orange drifted into her nose, and she buried her face in the pillow to soak up the remnants of Aiden's scent. She missed him.

It's only been a week and a half.

She didn't care.

When her phone chirped, she pulled it out of the pocket of the black romper she wore. She loved it had pockets for things like her cell phone.

Noah:
Hey.

Her brows bunched. What in the world was Noah doing texting her?

Charlotte:
Hey. How are you?
Noah:
Good. Visiting my parents.

Charlotte:

No classes?

Noah:

Nah. After we finished our class, I'm done until fall semester.

Charlotte:

Oh. Same.

Noah:

But you're not sure if you're coming back, right?

Charlotte:

Right.

Noah:

I won't keep you, but I wanted to see if you wanted to meet up for dinner later.

Noah:

As friends!

Noah:

I promise. Only as friends.

She laughed at the messages coming in quick succession, cheered by the banter. She sat up on the bed.

Charlotte:

How can we have dinner? I'm not in Athens.

Noah:

I know. I'm in Rosebrook Valley too.

Charlotte:

Wtf?

Her brows collided. *How strange…* What were the odds Noah would come back to town after she returned home?

Noah:

My parents live here.

Charlotte:

I didn't know that.

Noah:

There's a lot you don't know about me. ;-)

Charlotte:

Touché. Fine. Where and when?

Noah:

I didn't think you'd accept. How about the diner you used to work at?

Charlotte:

It's got a new name, but it's hard to miss. The sign out front is flashy and neon yellow and red on black. Sizzlin' Griddle.

Noah:

In the plaza? I've seen it.

Charlotte:

Yep.

Noah:

Meet at 6?

Charlotte:

Sure.

Noah:

K

She looked at the time on her phone. She had three hours before she needed to meet with him. It would give her time for a nap and to get ready. She felt sticky and gross after the drive home while feeling ill and needed a shower. Hopefully the nap would ease the discomfort in her stomach enough that she could eat.

As she entered the diner, a smiling young server approached. His brown shaggy hair curled around his ears, falling in his eyes, giving him a boyish charm. The freckles helped.

"Hey there! I'm Alex." He tapped the sparkly green name tag attached to his suspenders. "You want a booth or the bar?"

"I'm actually meeting someone," she said, moving her gaze over the crowded diner. When her eyes locked onto a head of wavy dark brown hair, she pointed. "Him."

"Well, okay. If you need anything, I'll be here. I'll be the one running around like a chicken with my head cut off." He winked and turned away, sauntering across the room to a table that flagged him down. His perky greeting carried across the restaurant chatter.

She crossed the diner, her corkboard platform sandals clicking on the floor. She loved the shoes even if they didn't always love her. Her short white dress, similar to her favorite navy one with the sweetheart neckline and puff sleeves, matched the white ribbon around her ankles. The lack of color would help combat the humidity and also prevent any sweat stains from showing when, inevitably, the cold sweats from whatever made her so ill set in. She hoped it wasn't contagious. Maybe it was a bad idea to be in public. But her mothers seemed fine, so maybe not.

"Noah?"

Twinkling blue eyes met hers as he turned in the booth and smiled at her. "Hey, I'm glad you showed up."

"I said I would, didn't I?"

"Well, yeah. But I dunno. Was worried you'd think this was me trying to get a date." He paused, his gaze sliding down. "You look fantastic."

She shrugged, trying to play it off. She hadn't worn the outfit to impress him. It was a strategic maneuver for physical comfort. Sliding into the booth across from him, she smiled. "Thank you. So why didn't you tell me your parents lived here when you found out I'm from here?"

His smile faltered, and he gave a light shrug. "I didn't think it was important. Didn't think either of us would be here at the same time. Didn't think you were leaving."

"Well, here we are."

"Here we are," he echoed with a grin.

Before he could say anything else, the fine hairs on her arms stood on end and, as if a magnet pulled her eyes, her gaze moved to the front entrance.

Her eyes met Aiden's, and his eyebrows lifted in surprise as a smile bloomed on her face. She hadn't contacted him since she returned. She planned to do that after her nap, but she overslept and hardly had time to shower before the walk to the diner. Her mothers were already gone, so she couldn't get a ride from them.

She lifted her arm and waved for him to come over, excitement bubbling inside that she could finally see him again. Noah turned to see what had caught her attention.

As Aiden approached, his expression turned thunderous, making her smile fall.

She slid over to allow him to sit, and he didn't miss a beat, scooting until their bodies pressed together. His muscular arm looped over the back of her neck, hand cuffing her shoulder in a proprietary move. She didn't want to admit it, but she liked this new side of him.

"So you're back in town?" he asked, never taking his eyes off Noah, who looked uncomfortable.

"I am. I got home earlier this afternoon."

"That so." His voice was cold, hard. She didn't like that part of this new side, but was glad it was not directed at her.

"I didn't let you know because when we got there, I had a…" She paused, her eyes moving to Noah and then up to the side of Aiden's head. "A delivery."

His gaze shifted to her, and a flicker of concern passed through his eyes. She nodded, understanding what he wanted to know. His jaw clenched, and his hand tightened on her shoulder.

"Then I took a nap because I wasn't feeling good before I came here."

"You're sick? You didn't have to come out and meet me," Noah said, his eyes shifting from her to Aiden, as if he didn't know who to keep his attention focused on.

Aiden leaned over and pressed his lips to her temple. "I'm not mad," he whispered. "I missed you. Are you okay?"

Her breath caught at his words. She wanted to tell him she missed him when they texted a few nights ago, but she resisted the urge to do it. Didn't want to seem too clingy.

Sinking into his hold, she sighed. "I'm okay now." It felt weird. The unpleasant feeling that made her want to vomit and curl into a ball had subsided so remarkably that she could almost argue it all had been a dream.

An older woman with hair coiled on top of her head in a retro style, wearing the same poodle skirt uniform as several other servers, approached the table. "Hi there. Welcome to the Sizzlin' Griddle. Our special today is the Rock Steady Burger. A half-pound patty with all the fixin's and sauteed mushrooms. Comes with fries smothered in cheese and mushrooms. What can I start y'all with?"

Noah looked between Charlotte and Aiden in question. She wondered if he thought their meet-up was over now that Aiden had arrived. She didn't like that.

She looked down at her menu and then at Noah, smiling. "What do you think you'll have? I couldn't eat that much burger if I tried."

Noah's shoulders relaxed. "Yeah, me either. I like food, but not a lot of mushrooms. I think I'll get a club sandwich with plain fries and water."

"You got it. And for you darlin'?"

"I'll have the Disco Fries and one of those cherry cokes with the syrup and maraschino cherries."

"What are Disco Fries?" Aiden asked.

She handed her menu to the server. "Fries with mozzarella cheese and brown gravy."

"Sounds like the thing Dom called poutine."

"That's with cheese curds," Noah said, drawing Aiden's sharp gaze. "Poutine, I mean. I tried it when I visited Toronto last summer. Same thing almost though, yeah."

"Huh." He looked up at the server, dismissing Noah. "I'll take a regular cheeseburger and an order of Disco Fries. I also want a Cherry Coke, but not like hers. The actual flavored soda."

"Sounds good." The server bundled the remaining menus and smiled. "I'll grab your drinks now. Bear with us, we're a little packed this evenin'."

"So you two are a thing now?" Noah asked, tilting his head.

Aiden's fingertips trailed over her upper arm, causing the skin to pebble. "We are. That a problem?"

"Nope. No problem." Noah's gaze flicked to her and back to Aiden. "I'm happy for you both."

She felt a twinge of guilt in her chest. She told Noah she wasn't ready to date anyone, and here Aiden was, openly claiming her. She swallowed down the feeling. "Yeah, with not having to be in school, I didn't have the added stress."

It was true. One reason she avoided dating was school took too much of her time. Also, she couldn't involve anyone in the mess with the stalker. Aiden understood that.

"That's cool. So you're not going back to school then?"

"Why wouldn't I go back to school?"

"I mean, since you're dating, and you weren't because of school stress… If you go back—"

"If she goes back, we'll make it work," Aiden said, voice sharp.

She didn't know why he despised Noah so much. This seemed stronger than simple jealousy.

Noah pushed out of the booth. "Bathroom." He thumbed over his shoulder when she looked up at him in question.

She sat up when the server brought their drinks, taking a sip. Looking over at Aiden, she studied him now that they were alone.

He looked handsome in his medium-wash jeans and navy T-shirt, but something about him seemed off, and it wasn't the angry looks he kept sending Noah. His hair appeared flatter, his eyes were bloodshot, and around his eyes seemed darker than usual. When he caught her staring at him and raised his brows in question, she blushed.

"Are you feeling okay?" she asked.

Aiden's lips turned down at the sides, and he set his drink down. "Why?"

She looked him over once more, noticing the sweat dotting his brow. He looked like she had all week long. And while sitting in the cool diner seemed to help, it still weighed on her.

"You look like you're sick," she said, her hand coming to rest on his.

His nostrils flared, and his lips pressed together. "I'll be alright," he muttered, reaching out to pull her against him again.

She sank into his embrace, and she felt him relax and bury his face in her curls, inhaling deep.

"So we're all thinking of taking Lukas to Haven for his birthday."

"His birthday?"

"Yeah. This Friday on the twelfth. It's his twenty-first birthday."

Her face screwed up. "I didn't know he was older than you."

"Only by seven months." He took a drink of his soda as Noah approached the booth. "Anyway, Riley thought we should go celebrate there since he doesn't like a big deal made of it. You coming?"

"Of course. I'd love to come."

25

Need

The bass thumped and red lights swept over a crowded dance floor filled with bodies grinding to the strains of a techno and metal mashup. Flashing lights and fog from machines in the corners made the dancers look like they moved in slow motion.

Charlotte had been in the gothic nightclub Haven once before, when she turned eighteen the fall before last. Blaire hadn't been able to go, but the other servers at the diner took Charlotte one weekend. There was always a theme with colors to suit it. Tonight, red dominated the space, making it look like a seedy castle.

She stood at the top of the set of black stairs lined with red strip lights and black candles on wrought iron candelabras. Her gaze swept the room, scanning for familiar faces. The dance floor offered limited visibility, so she switched her attention to the lounge area where tiered candles flickered atop hardwood tables. Patrons in various states of inebriation sat in black leather booths, drinking, making out, and having a good time.

The song shifted to something with a heavy beat as she descended the stairs into the throng of people.

She hadn't seen Aiden in two days since they left the diner. His mother had roped him, Lukas, and Seth into doing some house repairs for her, so they only had the nighttime to FaceTime with each other. It became a challenge before the end of each call not to stoop to the level of phone sex.

Her need for him had become a problem. She felt like a fiend. Never had she yearned for someone as intensely as she did Aiden.

Gentle hands came to rest on her shoulders as she reached the bar area lit underneath with red lights. Her eyes darted up to see Blaire's reflection in the mirror wall behind the bartenders.

She turned to face her friend and smiled.

"About time you got here!" Blaire shouted over the music. "You look amazing!"

Charlotte looked down at herself with a smile. "That was the plan," she said, more to herself than Blaire. She knew Blaire didn't hear her.

She'd worn a pair of black, high-waisted, leather shorts that came down a couple inches below her backside. The shorts had an open-front, mesh maxi skirt that flowed behind her when she walked fast enough. A black, slinky cowl halter put her entire back on display. She paired the outfit with strappy heels. Wearing her hair up on top of her head, she secured her curls with pins and two black hair sticks. She finished the entire ensemble with a smokey eye but left her lips bare. She wanted them free from anything intrusive.

The goal was to appeal to Aiden, but she wasn't too confident in her look until Blaire's expression set her at ease.

"You look awesome too," she said as Blaire led her away from the bar.

Blaire laughed. "This is all Riley's doing." She smoothed her hand over the long blonde waves cascading down her back.

Riley had dressed her in a long-sleeved crop top fitted to her like a second skin and a miniskirt with a slit up the front of the thigh.

Blaire led her over to a table next to the dance floor where Lukas sat with Seth, Riley, Layla, and a handsome guy with dyed platinum hair showing dark roots and sides. His eyebrow piercing caught her attention. She always thought those looked cool on guys. Blaire caught her looking and leaned in. "That's Dom. He's a new student."

Charlotte nodded. She remembered Aiden mentioning him. "Where's Aiden?"

An animalistic growl behind her made her spin around with wide eyes. *What in the world?* Her curiosity died when she saw Aiden standing a couple feet away, resembling all her wildest fantasies made flesh.

He wore a pair of fitted black slacks that hugged his muscular thighs. His black, button-down shirt with the sleeves rolled up his tight forearms was tucked neatly into his slacks, accented by a black leather belt with a simple metal buckle. The top two buttons of his dress shirt were undone, giving a peek at the muscles he hid beneath.

Her lips pressed together before her tongue could run over her lips.

Blaire leaned in to whisper, "He never dresses like this for the club. Always T-shirt and jeans."

Charlotte wondered if he had the same idea as her when he planned his outfit.

He approached her, his eyes heated with a promise of all the things she wanted him to do to her. She could still feel the marks on her skin, even though they were long gone.

"You look amazing," he said, voice gruff.

"You don't look so bad yourself." She smiled up at him and then turned. He settled his hand on the bare skin of her lower back. She shivered.

"Dom, this is Charlotte," Riley said, hopping up, her layered tulle skirt almost swallowing her. "Charlotte, this is Dom."

"Nice to meet you."

"Likewise," Dominic said, lifting his glass in a toast. "Cheers."

She turned to Lukas. "Happy birthday."

He shook his head and sat back in the seat, pulling Blaire down on his lap. The corner of his mouth twitched, but he tucked his face into Blaire's hair before anyone could see the embarrassed smile.

He didn't like birthdays and wasn't used to attention. They'd had the conversation once before. But he never went against Blaire's desire to celebrate with him because of how she felt about it. They compromised with smaller celebrations or celebrating multiple birthdays together, so he wasn't the sole focus of attention.

Aiden guided Charlotte over to the empty side of the booth, letting her slide in first, moving to sit close to her, his thigh pressed alongside hers.

She hadn't told Blaire or Riley about the development in their relationship. Hadn't told them about how they slept together again or how Aiden seemed to openly acknowledge there was more between them than friendship now. She wondered if Aiden wanted anyone to know—besides Noah.

His arm went over the back of the booth and his fingers grazed the back of her neck, making her shiver.

After several drinks, she felt good. Sitting with Aiden touching her, even if only through hidden brushes of his skin against hers, made her body feel hot. No longer did she feel sick, she felt needy.

The mood in the club shifted, and the lights lowered as the fog increased on the dance floor. The heavy bass cut through the air followed by a sensual beat.

"Dance with me," Aiden whispered in her ear, making her skin pebble as his breath caressed her ear. He slid out without waiting for her to answer, and she followed, glancing once over her shoulder. No one paid them any attention, lost in conversation with each other.

Once he led her to the dance floor, not too deep into the mass of writhing bodies, he pulled her close to him. She gasped when his hard length pressed against her lower stomach, straining against his slacks. Her eyes met his, and he slowly turned her to face away from him so he could wrap his arms around her from behind.

Hands splayed across her stomach, bunching the fabric of her slinky top as they swayed with the music. His lips trailed over the side of her neck, moving over her shoulder where he scraped his teeth across her skin, making her moan. She didn't have to worry about anyone hearing her, the music was too loud.

"You were made for me," he whispered into her ear. His breath fanned over the back of her neck as his lips ghosted over her skin.

The line would sound cliché and overdone coming from anyone else. It sounded like something a dudebro might say to sweep an unsuspecting girl into a one-night-stand. From Aiden, it sounded like he believed those words with every fiber of his being. Maybe he did.

She was starting to believe he didn't see her as beneath him, even though their social status was leagues apart.

He bent forward, and his hands moved down over her hips and back up, sliding beneath the slinky material of her top. His fingers brushed along her ribcage until he took the weight of her breasts in his firm hold. He massaged the sensitive skin, making her moan. She laid her head back against his shoulder.

Her skin prickled with awareness of their surroundings. Heat made her skin tingle in response to the bodies close to them. To anyone around them, unless they looked hard enough, they'd never know what he was doing. Her top gave easy access, but the dark fabric hid any of his movements.

"Did you wear this for me, Kitten?"

The nickname murmured with reverence in her ear made her shudder with desire.

She pretended to hate it. Fought him on using it. But since he didn't waver when he discovered she enjoyed hearing it—wanted to be his kitten—she didn't protest anymore.

It wasn't like she was into pet play. This was different. She wanted to belong to him, to be taken care of by him. To give him what he needed. She wanted him to praise and lavish her with attention. She loved being his kitten.

"Tell me," he rasped, nipping her earlobe.

"Yes." Her voice sounded breathy, and she squeezed her thighs together against the pulsing sensation in her core.

"That's my good kitten." He ground his cock against her backside as if rewarding her admission. She liked being rewarded. "Fuck. What are you doing to me, Charlotte?" His grip tightened on her breasts.

Her heels made it possible for him to position his length against her ass and not her back. As he nibbled at the skin on her neck, her eyes fluttered open. She caught Blaire's eyes first, then noticed the others were watching them with varying degrees of surprise.

Well, the cat's out of the bag now.

She didn't care if they watched. Part of her had invited someone to catch them. Now they had, and the rush went straight to her head.

Blaire lifted her hands, turning to everyone as if to make them stop staring. As they looked away, Charlotte's eyes slid closed again as Aiden's teeth sank into her skin.

Would he make her bleed again?

She hadn't talked to him about it since it happened, but she knew when he bit her before that he broke skin. She had felt something wet trickle over her skin, and it wasn't his saliva. He drank her blood. She didn't know he was into that sort of thing, but for some reason, it didn't put her off.

It made her curious and more than a little aroused. The realization startled her when the haze of lust over her mind cleared, but only because it didn't repel her.

She didn't think she would be into something like blood play, especially with what she'd witnessed back in Athens. Something about Aiden consuming her in more ways than one, taking a piece of her inside of himself that would never go away, made her mad with need.

She needed to tell him.

Gasping when he pinched her nipples, she pushed back against his thick length. She was ready to go home and take him with her. But it was his best friend's birthday. She couldn't do that to them.

His lips trailed up her throat as his hands slipped away from her breasts, sliding down to rest on her hips, fingertips digging into the leather of her shorts.

"If we don't stop now, I'm going to end up taking you on the dance floor," he growled against her ear.

She turned in his arms and looked up at him. His pupils were so large they overtook his irises. Only a sliver of the dark green on the outside glimmered against the red light.

He stooped and captured her lips with his, tangling his tongue with hers for only a moment before he pulled away from her. "Come on, let's go see the birthday boy." His voice remained strained, but he encouraged her forward with his hand on her back.

"I need to go to the bathroom first," she said. "I'll be right back. Go ahead."

The bathroom wasn't as crowded as she expected, but she was still hot, so she decided to step outside to get a little fresh air before she joined the others. After what happened on the dance floor, and the tipsy feeling buzzing through her veins, she needed a breather.

"Hey, Charlotte!"

She spun on the stairs and saw Noah approaching in black jeans and a black T-shirt. "Noah?"

His eyes swept her body, and his upper lip curled. His eyes narrowed. "I didn't think you'd be here." His voice sounded rough.

She frowned, but instead of addressing his statement, she asked, "What are you doing here?" He wasn't at the table in the diner when they talked about Haven. Had he heard when Aiden asked her?

"Just hanging out." Something sounded off in his voice. She couldn't pinpoint it, but he sounded nervous and uncomfortable. "Wanna come over and sit with me?"

"No, I can't. I'm with some friends who are waiting on me."

The muscles in his jaw worked as he looked to the side. Looking back at her he said, "Only for a little bit. I wanna catch up without your boyfriend hogging all your attention." He tried to laugh it off like a joke, but it sounded choked.

"I don't think that's such a good idea. He's waiting for me."

Without letting him say anything else, she turned and finished the quick jog up the stairs out into the open night air of the plaza. Moving over to the side of the building on the sidewalk, she rubbed her hands over the sides of her neck, laying her head back and sighing.

"Charlotte!"

She dropped her arms and watched as Blaire, Riley, and Layla came toward her.

"You okay?" Layla asked when they reached her.

"Yeah, just a little tipsy. Needed some air."

"I bet you did," Riley said with a huge grin on her face. "I didn't know things were like *that* between you and Aiden."

Charlotte lifted one shoulder in a half-hearted shrug. She couldn't deny it.

"I want to know *everything*," Blaire said, grabbing her by the arm.

Riley held her hands up. "Whoa. Hang on. I do *not* want to know everything. You're forgetting that's my brother."

Layla giggled.

They all turned toward the alley beside the building when the sounds of a fight echoed in their direction.

"Drunk idiots," Riley muttered.

"I don't think..." Charlotte squinted as the light caught the face of one fighter. "Are his eyes—" She couldn't say it. If she mentioned she thought the guy's eyes were glowing, they would think she was crazy. This was merely the residual association of alleyways with the vampire she thought she saw. Nothing more. Nothing less.

"Charlotte! Where are you going? Don't get involved."

"What?" She turned to look at Blaire, and that's when she realized in her curiosity about the person's eyes, she had stepped toward the alley.

When she looked back, a man was approaching her, but not any man—Noah. Had he exited through the side door?

His eyes were wide, and the blue in them seemed to glow beneath the streetlight.

"Charlotte, you need to get—"

He grunted as a blond man slammed into his back, snarling. Noah crashed into her, making her lose her balance and stumble. The man zipped around Noah and grabbed Charlotte by the arm, yanking her up with surprising strength.

"Sweet Cherry, so good of you to join us."

She knew that voice. The nickname made her shudder in fear.

Her gaze met the eyes of her stalker. An obvious amber glow dominated his irises as his canines elongated.

26

Monsters

Stepping out of the club into the nighttime air, Aiden looked around in search of Charlotte. Riley said she saw her go out the door and followed her with Blaire and Layla in tow. That was ten minutes ago.

Lukas, Seth, and Dominic trailed behind him. Both Seth and Lukas were eager to check on their Korrenas as much as Aiden was his. Though his friends still didn't know her importance to him beyond what they witnessed on the dance floor.

He hadn't realized his friends saw them. At least the fog, lighting, and the dark outfit Charlotte wore camouflaged what he did to her.

As much as he tried to resist temptation, he couldn't stop himself from touching her like he had. After being apart for a week and a half, only to spend another two days unable to do more than talk on the phone, his body was angry with him, and his need for her dominated his every thought—especially when he saw her in the outfit she wore for him.

When a scream rang out through the air, his blood turned to ice in his veins. He knew that scream, but never accompanied by a blanket of fear.

Pushing through the few stragglers making their way into the club, he rounded the building toward the alleyway where the scream came from.

He saw the backs of Riley, Blaire, and Layla first.

As he approached them, panic grasped his heart, digging its claws in. He stopped short, gagging and struggling to breathe against the dread overtaking him.

"Are you okay?" Lukas said, stopping beside him, putting a hand on his back when Aiden doubled over, gasping for breath.

"It's Charlotte," was all he managed to choke out. He felt as if he was being strangled by an unseen force.

Seth stopped on his other side. "What are you—"

Another scream pierced the air.

Forcing down the overwhelming emotions he recognized to be Charlotte's, he staggered upright and rushed forward past the trio of girls at the mouth of the alley.

Terror of his own seized his lungs as the scene came into view.

Halfway down the alley, another man had Charlotte's arm held high near his face in a tight grip. His eyes were wild, ablaze with the fury of his primal side. He grinned, fangs on display as he said something Aiden couldn't hear.

Charlotte's head thrashed back and forth in denial of whatever he said.

Noah leaned against the wall, cradling the arm hanging limp at his side. Blood streamed down his face, leaving a distinct smear on the wall where his head had made contact. His glowing blue eyes narrowed on the man holding Charlotte. She recoiled when the man stroked her cheek with his thumb.

"Let her go!" Riley shouted.

The rogue Vasirian's head snapped up, his blond hair sticking to his forehead and temples with sweat. He snarled at Riley for interrupting him.

Seizing the distraction, Aiden sprinted toward the pair with everything he had, but it proved futile. The man brought his head down as Charlotte sobbed, begging him to let her go. Aiden's chest tightened as the rogue's fangs sank into her skin.

Her screams echoed in the dim alley, and if there were people outside at this time of night, it would draw unwanted attention.

Layla's hands went over her eyes, and Blaire screamed.

The sight of the rogue's fangs tearing into the skin of his Korrena triggered something inside him to snap. The frenzy consumed him as he closed the distance between them.

Someone would die tonight, and it wouldn't be him.

He glanced sideways as Lukas flanked his left side. His friend had his back.

He collided with the rogue. Pressing his shoulder against the rogue's torso, he put all his strength into the move to dislodge the bite from Charlotte's arm. When the rogue fell backward from the force, Lukas scooped up Charlotte into his arms and rushed her over to the others.

Aiden and the rogue hit the ground, snarling at one another.

Bloodlust had consumed the rogue, causing amber eyes to flare and his pupils to dilate. He tried to twist out of Aiden's grip, but he couldn't match Aiden's strength.

"Get off me," the rogue said, struggling against Aiden. His head turned toward Noah. "Get her, you piece of shit!"

Aiden's attention pivoted to Noah. The rogue took advantage of the distraction, disentangling himself and slamming his boot into Aiden's shoulder, sending him off balance. He fell to the side, a growl ripping free from his chest. Red blanketed his vision as he stared down the rogue.

No one would take Charlotte from him.

He used his position to his advantage, lunging forward and bear-hugged the rogue's waist, pushing forward until they slammed into the brick wall of the side of the nightclub. Bits of debris fell to the ground at the contact.

Searing pain greeted him when he stood, as the rogue's fangs dragged over his cheek, splitting the skin with deep gouges. The pain made his vision spot, but he didn't release his grip. If he let go, Charlotte would be lost. He only hoped one of his friends would dispatch Noah before he got to her.

Blood poured from the wounds on his cheek, fueling his rage.

He leaned forward and shredded the side of the rogue's throat with his teeth. The rogue shouted in pained fury before grabbing Aiden's head, dislodging him before he could rip into a vulnerable spot and end things. Saliva dripped from the rogue's bared teeth onto Aiden's shirt as they tussled. Blaire shouted at Lukas to do something while Layla's panicked scream cut through the frenzy.

His friends interfering in the fight would not only put them in danger but endanger him as well. Too many bodies posed a threat. Rationally, he knew they didn't want to hurt him, but if they interfered and took his prey from him—the one who tried to harm his Korrena—they would become his enemy as well.

Blaire didn't understand that as a human, but the others did.

When the rogue lunged for his jugular, Aiden grabbed him by the throat. His fingers dug into the torn flesh on the side of the rogue's neck, making him howl in agony.

Aiden staggered to his feet with the rogue's throat in his tight grasp. His body vibrated with the energy from his unsuppressed preternatural strength. He had no desire to hold back.

He wanted blood. He wanted vengeance. He wanted to rid the planet of the filth that dared to lay a single finger on his Korrena.

With a snarl, he threw the rogue. His prey collided with the wall and nestled into the bricks, leaving an imprint that cracked like lightning.

Aiden closed the distance with little effort. His need to avenge his other half dominated him.

With a strong grip, he seized the rogue by the hair and jerked his head sideways.

"Aiden, no!" Riley screamed, but her warning came too late.

His fangs tore into the rogue's throat and ripped out his jugular. He spit the torn flesh from his mouth and dropped the lifeless body at his feet—a testament to what he would do to anyone who tried to take his Korrena away from him.

He turned to deal with Noah, but he had vanished.

"I've called reinforcements to clean this up," Dominic called, striding forward.

Aiden's chest heaved, and he trembled violently. The fury coursing through his body hadn't diminished. When Dominic got close enough, Aiden snarled at him in warning.

Hands lifted, Dominic canted his head to the side. "It's me, Dom. Listen to me," he said in a soothing tone like one would a rabid animal.

"We need to get you out of here. This is bad." He motioned to the corpse on the ground. "You've committed a crime punishable by death. As a member of the Blackthorn Clan, I'm obligated to take you in."

Aiden growled at him but stopped himself from stepping toward the new threat.

Dominic lifted his hands again. "Listen to me. I'm not going to," he said, voice softening. "You think I don't recognize what's happening?" Dominic looked over his shoulder at Charlotte, prompting another growl.

"You protected what you cared for, so I won't do it, but you need to get out of here. I'll do what I can to cover this up. I have someone local who can dispose of the body before word gets back to Blackthorn Security or the clan, but I can't hide what you look like. Go. Clean up and heal before you return."

After seeing them on the dance floor and witnessing Aiden's response to the rogue biting her, Dominic clearly saw the truth of their connection.

"You need to run," Seth said, coming forward, concern etched in his features.

Charlotte moved forward, catching Aiden's eye. He stepped around Dominic to look at her. He had to know she was safe.

The first thing that hit him was the overwhelming fear radiating from her. She looked paler than normal, her eyes glossy and red, streaks of black mascara staining her cheeks.

He stepped forward, reaching up to touch her face. When she flinched and stumbled back a step, the rage that fueled him evaporated into nothing. Her fear sobered him.

Of course she feared him. He was the monster, and she was the innocent human. Prey to devour—at least through her eyes. He was nothing more than a predator.

He knew his eyes were glowing in the alley's darkness. Blood ran down his chin from killing another Vasirian. His fangs grazing his lip added to the terrifying visage. The gouges in his cheek undoubtedly looked horrific.

His gaze flicked to Lukas, and he barked, "Get her to the academy."

"She can't! They'll wipe her memory!" Riley protested, glancing at Dominic as if he would call on the clan to charge in and do it there and then.

"W-what?" Charlotte sucked in a breath as she stepped away from both Dominic and Riley. "I don't want my memory erased," she said, voice hitching with alarm.

"No one is touching her!" Aiden roared, startling them all. His voice dropped to a low rasp as he fought to get his demons under control. "No one touches her," he rasped, voice guttural.

Lukas positioned himself behind Charlotte, not physically touching her in an effort not to provoke Aiden, but showing his commitment to protect her in Aiden's place.

He nodded his thanks to Lukas and then his gaze settled on Charlotte's face. "No one is going to hurt you. I'll die before I let that happen."

The tears rolling down her cheeks combined with her fear split him open.

Part of him wondered if it would be a good thing for her to forget. To forget him. He didn't want her to know fear at this level. Didn't want this night to traumatize her further and bring more nightmares. Didn't want her bound to someone she would fear her entire life.

The mere thought of her forgetting him hurt.

Not able to look at her any longer, his gaze swung to Riley, and he said the words he dreaded sharing from the moment it became his reality.

"They won't wipe my Korrena's memory."

Turning from the sounds of everyone speaking over each other, trying to express their shock and thoughts all at once, he disappeared down the dark alley.

He would heal, but he didn't know if his heart would ever recover.

Charlotte saw his monster, and she feared him.

27

Truth

Charlotte kept her eyes trained on the jasmine plant sitting on the massive desk with ornate carvings of thorn-covered vines. The plush, black leather chair she sat in did nothing to alleviate her uneasiness.

Blackthorn Academy.

She didn't understand why her friends led her onto the academy grounds through the enormous black gate with the letters "BA" in ornate script welded into the bars. For years, she wondered what the campus looked like beyond the road leading from the plaza lined with live oaks dripping with Spanish moss, but shock overloaded her system, and she recalled nothing of the trip across campus aside from the panicked ramblings of Riley and the others trying to calm her.

Her gaze moved down to the bandage on her inner forearm.

When Lukas led her into a building on the right side of campus, Dominic took charge, providing hurried direction to a pair of women wearing latex gloves who appeared uncomfortable with Charlotte's presence. They tended her wound and bandaged her up before Lukas and Dominic whisked her away to this office filled with the smell of old books from the floor-to-ceiling bookshelves lining the walls.

Dominic's authoritative tone toward staff members seemed odd coming from a student, but she had more pressing matters on her mind than worrying about why everyone, including her friends, seemed to defer to him.

Faint red tinted the pristine bandage, showing her wound still bled. A wound caused by a bite.

A bite from a vampire.

A vampire like Aiden.

Aiden.

Aiden is a vampire.

It explained the strange growls she found peculiar but never questioned further. Some people expressed strange ticks, made odd noises, and displayed involuntary behaviors. She wouldn't put a spotlight on something he might feel self-conscious about. Maybe she should have.

It also explained the blood he drew during the last time they had sex.

Oh god.

She had sex with a vampire.

The thought should terrify her. It *should* have made her want to run away in terror, but it didn't. *Well…* Her nose wrinkled. Anyone else *besides* Aiden would terrify her, but he didn't.

Even faced with the truth that he wasn't human, she didn't feel afraid. Her mind replayed what he looked like standing before her covered in blood, eyes glowing, sharp fangs stained with the blood of a man he'd killed.

A man he'd killed. For her.

Aiden didn't hesitate to eliminate the man who bit her. The man who had made the last several months of her life a living hell. Why had a vampire wanted to stalk her?

If she were honest with herself, once the terror of the threat disappeared, knowing Aiden would protect her to that extent felt exhilarating. He wouldn't hurt her.

Sitting back, she rested her head against the back of the chair as the adrenaline thrumming through her system receded.

The chandelier overhead cast amber light over the room, reflecting on the large window behind the desk, allowing her to see the trees and garden on the other side steeped in moonlight. She wondered what lurked in the darkness outside.

Was the campus safe?

UGA wasn't. Noah attended, and he was a vampire. The blue glow of his eyes confirmed his lack of humanity, leaving no room for confusion.

Her eyelids lowered, and she sighed.

How had she believed him to be human? Shouldn't there have been warning signs? She recalled how he liked to touch her a lot more than others, and Rachel's apprehension. While none of it screamed "I'm a vampire!" it made her pause. She rationalized that his behavior developed from his attraction, but there were things he did that normal humans didn't. Like, how did he know where she lived?

Aiden didn't show any red flags, she reminded herself. *Except the growls and the blood drinking.* He also acted more aggressively than how he acted in everyday life when they fooled around. Was that a vampire thing? She was all for that side of vampirism, if so. *Maybe it's an Aiden thing.* Either way, she liked it.

So he showed more vampire red flags than Noah. Why didn't it bother her like Noah's behavior did?

The sound of the heavy wooden doors behind her opening startled her out of her thoughts. Thoughts she should *not* be having while facing a crisis. *Priorities.*

Her libido made her an idiot.

She sat up straight, turning in the chair to see a slim Asian woman dressed in a black pencil skirt, jade chiffon blouse, and sky-high stilettos that Charlotte would break her neck attempting to wear. Her shiny black hair rested at her nape in a simple chignon accented by a pearl clip.

Russet eyes settled on Charlotte, making it hard not to squirm under the intense scrutiny. "I never in a thousand years thought we would encounter this situation again," the woman said, her voice calm and measured.

As she moved across the room, she didn't make much sound.

Lowering gracefully into the high-back leather chair behind her desk, the woman pressed her lips together, a scant breath escaping her nose. "At least this time, I hope you remain conscious."

"Conscious?"

"The last time we explained the truth to a human, she passed out. With your previous encounter with our kind, you've seen our fangs and glowing eyes. I don't foresee fainting."

Charlotte's brows flexed, pulling in at the center. "To a human? Our kind? Does that mean you're also a vampire?" Her spine stiffened. The woman didn't seem dangerous, but Noah hadn't either.

"Settle yourself, Miss Walsh. I have no intention of harming you. My name is Soomin Velastra, Headmistress of Blackthorn Academy." She laced her fingers across her lap, lowering her elbows to the arms of her chair. "And no, I am not a vampire. I am a Vasirian."

"I've never heard of that before."

A faint smile pulled at the headmistress' pale pink lips. "Then we've done our job properly. The world cannot know about our existence. It's dangerous."

"Why? Would we be in danger if we knew?"

"No. My kind would. Humans fear what they do not understand, Miss Walsh." The headmistress gave her a pitying look. "They hunt and eliminate the things they don't understand. Sometimes capture and experiment on them. My kind lives alongside humans in peace, and we want to keep it that way."

The scene from the alley in Athens flashed through her mind. The poor human was attacked by one of her kind. Her eyes slid down to her arm. Another attack on a human. Somehow, she found the talk of peace almost laughable, all things considered.

The headmistress tracked Charlotte's gaze.

"There are some who live to cause discord. Like with humans, our species also have members in our society that go against our laws. It doesn't matter the species, Miss Walsh—"

"Charlotte, please."

The headmistress inclined her head. "Very well. All species have troublemakers. Law breakers. The rogues live outside Vasirian law. They believe humans are nothing more than chattel to use for feeding, manipulating, and gratification."

"And the person who attacked me?"

"A rogue." She lifted her hand, waving it to the side. "The closest I can think of to compare them to as a human equivalent is gangs. Human gangs tread the bottom rung of society, bucking the system, and taking what they will with no regard for human decency."

"You're really not a vampire?"

"I can see where you get that impression, but the Vasirian are a different species from humans. Vampires do not exist." She smoothed a hand over her knee. "It's speculated that the myths and legends surrounding the blood drinking, fang-bearing creatures of the night who attack in a frenzy of bloodlust relate to a condition Vasirian suffer when they haven't fed in a long time."

Charlotte's eyes widened a fraction. They had fangs; Aiden drank blood from her. Her shoulders sagged as the rational part of her brain took over. Of course they fed. But if they were different from rogues…

"You don't drink human blood?"

"We do." A hand lifted to stop Charlotte from asking questions in panic. "Through donations received from clinics. We drink from blood bags freely given by humans, though they don't know we are one of the recipients of their donations. It is against our laws to consume blood from a live source—hence the rogue's disregard for the law in attacking you."

Charlotte didn't mention Aiden tasting her blood. She didn't want him to get in trouble for breaking the law.

"Now, to my point." Headmistress Velastra tapped a manicured nail on the arm of her chair. "The media's display of rabid monsters likely relates to *sanguis manie*—blood mania. This condition occurs when a Vasirian goes for an extended period without blood. The time varies for each of us, and the younger we are, the shorter the timeframe is. While we need normal food and drinks like you do, we also require blood, or our body shuts down."

"Shuts down?" She frowned. "Like dying?"

Headmistress Velastra nodded. "That is the end result. We experience several stages before that happens. Tremors, anger, weakness, fatigue… We eventually begin a descent into madness, where we hallucinate and become nothing more than rabid beasts searching for blood. The final stage if we don't get enough blood to stop the madness before it overtakes our brain is death."

Charlotte sat back in her seat. The illness sounded terrible. When

Aiden lived with her, he seemed fine. She wondered where he fed because there weren't blood bags anywhere in her apartment—not that she could see at least. Wouldn't blood bags need proper storage?

"Now, we need to discuss why you're here tonight."

Her chest tightened.

The casual conversation lulled her into a false sense of security, allowing her to push aside all the unpleasantness of the night to learn something new about a species she had never heard of before. It aligned with her interests. She loved the obscure and unexplained.

"We believed Blaire was the only human capable of bearing a Korrena mark until the Oracle's prophecy came to fruition. But now that you've—"

"I'm sorry, ma'am. I need to ask… What is a Korrena? I heard it mentioned before they brought me here." Her face screwed up. "Oh, and prophecy? What Oracle? I haven't heard about that."

As much as she wanted to ask where Aiden was, and mention he was the one who used the terminology, something told her not to. Dominic said he did something punishable by death. Was he on the run? Was he okay? Her stomach soured as fear for him threatened to take over.

Headmistress Velastra closed her eyes for a moment and then nodded. "I apologize. When I explained everything to Blaire, I threw her to the wolves by thrusting the information at her all at once and left her with a packet of paperwork I composed before her arrival." She sighed in a way that sounded defeated. It didn't suit the put-together woman. "Admittedly, that wasn't the best way to approach the situation, but I was new to it. In this case, I've had no time to prepare, so I will do my best to answer your questions. If I go too fast, please interject. No apologies expected."

Blaire knew all this? Why did she know? Before Charlotte could follow that line of thinking, the headmistress spoke again.

"First, the Oracle is the oldest living Vasirian. She is four hundred years old."

"Holy crap." Charlotte blinked repeatedly. "Are you guys immortal like they say vampires are?"

A soft chuckle that seemed out-of-place coming from the reserved woman before her filled the air. "No, that would be a myth humans perpetuated. We live for a very long time. Hundreds of years. Our physical aging slows to allow for such longevity. The students here range from their late teens to their mid-twenties, and it is during this period that the aging process initially decelerates. When we're in our seventies, we appear as young as someone in their early to mid-thirties, and our aging slows further, allowing us to resemble a forty-year-old human at one hundred." She paused. "As an example of it in action, I'm seventy-five."

Charlotte's mouth gaped. The headmistress didn't look a day over thirty-five, so seventy-five surprised her.

"Again, the aging process slows until we cease aging upon reaching the age of one hundred and fifty years old, appearing no older than sixty."

"That's convenient."

"What is?"

"Well, if you look like a sixty-year-old human, then you're near retirement again, right?" At the headmistress' nod, she added, "Well, you can avoid questions then. I mean, unless you go out in public in ten or twenty years."

"We have our ways of handling that."

Charlotte's lips twisted to the side. She wanted to ask what those ways were, but she already felt overloaded with information, and she knew the headmistress was far from done. Her eyes went big as something dawned on her.

"Oh my god, wait a minute. You said something earlier!"

"Yes?"

"The students here. Are they Vasirian too?"

The soft chuckle slipped again. "That's correct."

"So that means…"

The headmistress crossed her legs, waiting Charlotte out, allowing her to come to her own conclusions.

"It's not just Aiden. The others are Vasirian too. Holy crap! Is Blaire a Vasirian? How can they come out in the sun? Come to think of it, how did Noah do it?"

"Myths, Charlotte. Sun can't harm us. And yes, your friends—with the exception of Blaire—are Vasirian."

Charlotte slumped in the chair, sliding down with her hands over her face, muttering into her palms. "I can't believe it. No wonder I never fit in with them. They were keeping secrets from me."

"To be fair," the headmistress said, "it is against our laws to reveal the secrets to humans. If a human finds out, we have to wipe their memory to protect ourselves. Your friends were protecting you and following the law."

"Does this mean you're going to take away my memory now?" She didn't want to forget.

"No. The issue of the Korrena throws a wrench in that."

"Oh yeah, that. You were gonna tell me what that was. Sorry. This is so much."

"I told you. Your apologies aren't necessary. This is foreign territory for you, and in some ways, it is for us as well. While we went through it with Blaire, we didn't expect another human to manifest a Korrena mark until the prophecy fulfilled itself."

A knock sounded on the door.

"Come in," the headmistress called.

When the door opened, and Blaire stepped inside, Charlotte jumped from the chair. She stared at her best friend, emotions ricocheting around in her chest like balls in a pinball machine. Relief at seeing a familiar face, confusion, and a small tendril of betrayal hovered in the back of her mind like a wraith.

"I thought it wise to bring her in to help in this situation. A friendly face—someone like you."

Blaire came forward and stopped in front of Charlotte. "I'm so sorry we couldn't tell you." A tear trailed down her cheek. "I wanted to tell you so many times. I wanted you to know the truth."

Charlotte looked at her feet. She still wore the strappy heels from the club, her sexy outfit feeling out of place and uncomfortable in the light of the cozy office.

"I was about to explain to Charlotte what a Korrena is and about the prophecy. Your timing is perfect," the headmistress said, motioning to the other black leather chair beside Charlotte's that Blaire took.

Charlotte sat back down. She would have to face the emotions she felt about not knowing everything later. Right now, she couldn't do it.

"A prophecy was given long ago foretelling Blaire's arrival in our world. Only recently have we uncovered her connection to an ancient bloodline dating back many centuries. A bloodline filled with magic, linking to the witches and warlocks of old who were eliminated in a mass genocide to appease a king's lust for power. Blaire is the only descendant of this bloodline, and her becoming one of our kind will herald the awakening of any human with dormant magic in their blood, allowing them to find their Korrena mate."

Blaire looked at Charlotte. "The Vasirian have a king who rules over them and sets their laws. I met him when we went to Europe. There's an entire family in power and extended courtiers called the

Blackthorn Clan."

"Like the school?"

"Yeah. It's named after them. Dominic is a distant cousin of the royal family. He's part of the clan."

Well, that explained why everyone followed his lead without question.

She turned in her seat toward Blaire, resting her hand on the arm of the chair. "But witches? Seriously? Magic? That's a thing?"

Blaire suppressed a smile, but her lip kept quirking. "'fraid so."

"*Jesus,*" Charlotte breathed. "Wait. Does he even exist?" She didn't consider if she believed the Christian faith, but was it wrong to even use the word?

Blaire's face scrunched.

The headmistress shook her head. "We've believed for many centuries that multiple gods governed our existence and that humans got it wrong—and right on some levels. It felt like the Greeks got closest to what we thought to be the truth, but even they were incorrect. The Oracle informs us the stars created us and watch over our actions."

"The stars?" Charlotte deadpanned.

"Celestial Conclave, to be precise. Similar to gods but manifested in stars. Beings without corporeal form like you would believe gods to have."

"This is crazy."

Blaire laughed. "How do you think I feel? I'm supposed to save an entire species."

"What?" Charlotte winced when the headmistress' eyebrows rose in surprise at her high volume.

"Yeah. The prophecy. If I don't become a Vasirian, the species eventually dies."

"Are you serious?" Charlotte caught an odd note in Blaire's tone. "How do you become a Vasirian?"

"A very risky process—Lukas and I have been forbidden to attempt it while the rogues are a problem. Failing means death, so I'm kinda motivated to obey."

"Why you?"

"The magic."

"You're a witch?"

"The last one alive."

"I'm dreaming. This has to be a dream."

"I would say it's not so bad, but if you'd been here over the last year..." Blaire shook her head. "That's for another time. I promise to explain."

Charlotte jumped when the headmistress clapped her hands.

Blaire laughed. "Don't worry, she does that a lot."

"Well, sometimes I must redirect wayward students," the headmistress said with a slight smile. "Now, our kind is in danger, yes, but that's not what is important right now. At least not for you and why you're here. That information is what we need to focus on."

Right. Why *was* she here? Why were they letting her in on all the secrets now? Were they going to kill her?

"Please don't kill me," she blurted.

Blaire looked at her in horror.

The headmistress frowned. "Why would we do that?"

"For knowing your secrets."

"We're choosing to share them. You're in no danger of death. Relax."

Blaire reached out and touched Charlotte's arm. "I wouldn't have brought you here if I thought they'd kill you."

Charlotte rubbed her eyes, and her fingertips came away black.

She'd forgotten about her smokey makeup. She suspected she looked like a swamp monster.

"Aiden informed me he saw his Korrena mark on you," the headmistress said.

She perked up at the use of Aiden's name.

"A Korrena is what our kind calls a mate—a pair. The word Blaire used to best understand it was what humans call a soulmate."

"Soulmate?" Charlotte glanced at Blaire.

She nodded. "Lukas saw his mark on me one day when I left work. Headmistress Velastra came to see me the next day, you remember?"

Charlotte thought the headmistress looked familiar. "Yeah, sort of. I thought she was a professor though."

"My title has changed, but we have encountered one another before."

"Anyway, the mark"—Blaire pointed at the tattoo on the side of her neck that matched the one Lukas had—"isn't a tattoo. Apparently Korrena pairs have a unique marking to them only. Yours won't look like this. It won't even be in the same spot."

"Where will it be? What does it look like?"

"I don't know. Aiden didn't describe it or say where it was."

"I haven't seen a mark anywhere."

The headmistress laced her fingers over her knee. "The mark isn't permanent until you seal the bond with your pair."

"That's done by sex and blood sharing," Blaire said, leaning over.

"But we've had sex, and he's—" Charlotte bit the inside of her cheek and winced.

Blaire blinked. "He's? What?"

"I don't want him to get in trouble."

"Whatever he's done, I would like to know," the headmistress said. "It will help me guide both of you through this transition. I am aware of what he did to the man in the alley who attacked you." She inhaled deeply through her nose, sitting forward and placing her arms on the desk. "Charlotte, I protect my students. I understand what drove him to commit the crime. Having Dominic Harrison's backing made it easy to cover what Aiden did. But no one outside of those involved can ever know. Understand?"

"I understand," she whispered. The unspoken consequence of the headmistress' words settled over her like thick tar, stealing her breath. Aiden would die. She looked at Blaire, unable to look at the headmistress when she admitted what happened. "Aiden drank my blood. When we had sex last time, he bit too hard or something and I bled a little." She drew a breath and rushed to add, "He didn't use fangs! I would have noticed the difference. He's… bit me other places where I could see. I know what it feels like when he uses his normal teeth."

Her face flamed. It embarrassed her to admit something about her sex life in front of the headmistress of Blackthorn Academy. It was weird to discuss her sex life with a stranger at all, but she had the feeling this was normal for them. If it had been Blaire alone, she wouldn't balk at having a conversation about it. It wasn't like she knew what his fangs felt like, but she suspected there would be pain. Aiden's bites never hurt.

"So not only have you engaged in sexual activity, but he's tasted your blood?"

She nodded.

Blaire didn't seem to bat an eye at the clinical way the headmistress asked intimate questions. If sex was part of whatever the sealing a bond thing was, it made sense. She had to learn about it somewhere. Was it so different from counselors and sexual education classes? At least she wasn't in a classroom full of students talking about sex.

"Then you've come close to sealing the bond without realizing it." Before Charlotte could ask what it would take, the headmistress continued. "The mark is special to your pairing and is a symbol of your lasting bond. Pairs who have formed deeper connections can see their mark on occasion, but the visual is fleeting. It is the bond calling to the other, making itself known."

"So what does a bond mean?"

"Korrena pairs have a special connection no others share. You will connect on an emotional level where, if the emotions are intense enough, you will sense them. No other person can ever bond with you this way for as long as you live. It's the greatest love you'll ever know."

Love? If she was Aiden's Korrena, did that mean he loved her?

As if reading her mind, the headmistress said, "Many Korrena pairs sense their bond before it reveals itself. The pair may have already formed a romantic relationship prior to their awakening. In some cases, they don't know each other, and they adapt and get to know one another. In some cases,"—she gave Blaire a pointed look—"they might dislike one another."

Blaire scoffed. "There was a lot more to it than that. We didn't actually hate each other." She rolled her eyes.

"But wait. Are you saying if the mark shows up you *have* to be with the person? What if you're enemies? What if the person is a bad person? Like one of those rogues?"

"The bond is a magical thing, choosing pairs that are compatible but might need to get to know one another and allow a connection to form organically. You don't have to accept the bond, but it's painful to be away from your pair. It can make you physically ill."

Charlotte laughed. "Well, that explains a lot."

"How so?" Blaire asked.

"Recently, both Aiden and I were sick."

"I remember he was. I didn't know you were."

"I went to Atlanta with my mothers. We didn't see each other but once in two weeks until tonight."

"Well, you won't be ill anymore if you choose to accept what I offer," the headmistress interjected.

Charlotte turned to look at her as russet eyes narrowed.

"Like I offered Blaire, I am extending a scholarship from the clan to attend the academy so you can be close to your Korrena, preventing the illness associated with your separation. You may enroll in any program you wish and obtain a legitimately recognized degree like any other university in the country."

Blaire smiled. "That solves the issue with being away from your moms."

"My moms," Charlotte mumbled. Lines etched her forehead. "What about my mothers? What do I tell them?"

"They cannot know about us," the headmistress said. "In Blaire's case, she could abandon her old life, but based on what Blaire, Aiden, and Riley have shared with me, I understand you are very close to your mothers."

Charlotte nodded.

"They can know of the scholarship, and that one stipulation in receiving a full scholarship is you must live on campus. We will provide all your living expenses and additional money for anything you need or want within reason as an allowance."

She hated the idea of lying to her mothers, but what other choice did she have? If she refused, they might wipe her memory. If she refused, she wouldn't see Aiden again. She finally had the chance to get a degree close to her family, be with her friends, and maybe experience a relationship worth having.

Straightening in her seat, she took a deep breath.

"I really like Aiden, so I'm willing to see where all this goes. I mean, I wanted to change majors anyway, so this is good timing." She shrugged, hoping to convey a lighthearted confidence, but she didn't know if she had succeeded.

"I'm really sorry I never told you anything," Blaire said, a look of regret overtaking her features. Her eyes sparkled with liquid emotion.

"I understand it now."

"Come in. She's accepted," the headmistress said, looking over their heads. Had someone knocked?

"You're staying?"

Charlotte twisted in her seat, eyes widening as Aiden strolled into the room in jeans and a T-shirt instead of the clothes from the club. He didn't have any blood on him, and the wound on his cheek was nowhere to be seen. He looked like himself again. When she didn't say anything, too caught up in looking him over for injury, his expression shuttered, and his Adam's apple bobbed. Her chest tightened as hopelessness gripped her.

"Is that you?" she whispered.

His dark brows lowered over his eyes. "What do you mean?"

"Are you sad?"

His head flinched back, his beautiful green eyes widening.

"I'm staying," she said, hoping to quell the sick feeling in her stomach. A feeling her instincts screamed were Aiden's feelings echoing through her.

"You feel me," he murmured, reverence in his voice.

"I think so. If you were sad." Her teeth sank into the edge of her lip as she drew it into her mouth.

"I can't believe this is happening." He laughed to himself. "I've waited for you for so long."

"What?"

The headmistress spoke up, breaking their connection. "We spend our lives learning of the Korrena bond and our mate to prepare for the awakening, which only happens in the latter teen years. Aiden is twenty and is past the age where normal discovery happens. Not everyone finds their pair, so many his age without a bond often feel despair at the possibility it'll never happen. His own mother didn't discover her pair until eighty-one years of age."

Charlotte looked back at Aiden, and he offered a sad smile. She couldn't imagine growing up knowing there might be a soulmate meant for her—someone destined to be her other half—and then discovering they didn't exist.

"It's because you were human," he said. "I don't know how it's possible, but it happened."

"I need to speak to the Oracle," the headmistress said. "This development needs to be explored. We need to know how it plays into the prophecy. For now, show Charlotte to her room. Classes are not in session and won't be for another three weeks. This should allow you time to acquaint yourself with the campus and the student body. It should be easier for you since your relationship with your Korrena is less volatile than someone who shall remain nameless experienced with theirs."

"Me. I'm nameless," Blaire said with a self-deprecating laugh.

The headmistress looked up at the ceiling as if asking for guidance.

"Listen, if I couldn't laugh about it, I don't know what I'd do." Blaire looked at Charlotte. "You have it easy. When I first came here, Headmistress Velastra was stone cold. Nothing could crack her poker face."

The headmistress arched a perfectly manicured eyebrow. "Poker face?"

"You never laughed, sighed, or anything. Riley even said you were like that. Now you smile and show your frustration with us."

Headmistress Velastra smoothed her hand over her pencil skirt, clearing her throat. "Well, you are a frustrating bunch I have grown rather fond of." Before Blaire could say anything else, she turned her attention to Charlotte. "Again, your relationship is stable with your Korrena, and you have friends already at the academy. Your transition should be easier than it was for Blaire."

Aiden stepped forward and motioned for Charlotte. "Come on. I'll show you to our dorm room."

"Our dorm room?"

"Yeah. Did you tell her about the sickness?" He looked at the headmistress.

"I did."

He scratched his jaw. "To curb the discomfort of being apart—the sick feeling—they let us share rooms." She recalled their conversation about coed dorms. Now it made sense. Somewhat. "We have our own bed each, though," he added, and she wondered why he felt the need to mention it. It seemed normal for a dorm room to have two twin beds.

"Unless you want a big bed to share," Blaire said. "After you seal your bond."

Aiden sighed. "Yeah, or that." He motioned toward Blaire with his hand.

Charlotte looked at him, unsure why he sighed or why he looked uncomfortable. His cautious demeanor made little sense. Whatever connection she felt before wasn't working. She couldn't feel anything. Maybe whatever he felt wasn't strong enough?

"We can discuss any changes you would like to make to your dorm at another time. For now, it's late and you need to get settled in. We will get your belongings from your home tomorrow."

28

Hope

The quiet walk across the darkened academy grounds and up the stairs to his—now *their*—dorm room set Aiden on edge. Charlotte remained silent after they left the staff building, eyes darting everywhere the lights around campus touched. He didn't like it.

Once on his floor, she hesitated in the doorway leading from the stairs, eyes scanning the different doors lining the hall with apprehension.

"I won't let anyone hurt you." He moved to stand in front of her, his back to the hall. Meeting her wary eyes, he added, "No one will lay a finger on you." It felt like barbed wire raking his throat as he swallowed and forced out words he didn't want to say, but she needed to understand. She needed to know she wasn't in danger with him, despite what she saw. "Not even me."

He turned before he could see the look on her face. He didn't want to see her revulsion and rejection. While she may have accepted a place at Blackthorn Academy, it didn't mean she accepted his species. At least not on a romantic level.

It didn't mean she didn't fear him.

He couldn't shake the terror he felt radiating from her in the alleyway when she looked at him. He caused that. No explanation of Vasirian being civilized would quell her natural instincts to run from a predator.

She followed him. Her footsteps echoed his. *Better the monster you know.* He wanted to cringe as soon as the thought crossed his mind.

Opening the door to the dorm room they would now share, he stepped aside and let her enter first, flipping on the light switch.

How did Lukas do this?

When Blaire woke up in the dorms after fainting at the sight of Headmistress Velastra's fangs, Lukas had Riley and Aiden with him. It helped with the transition. The way Lukas put it, as soon as Aiden and his sister left the room, everything went to hell. He acted like an asshole, and Blaire retaliated. It laid the foundation for a long, drawn-out tug-of-war between the two of them. Blaire didn't fear their kind, but she and Lukas experienced their own problems.

He sighed. He wished his sister was here to act as a buffer. He didn't know how to act around Charlotte anymore.

He closed the door behind them and locked it to add an extra layer of security for her. He didn't think the students would attack her, but he wouldn't take any chances. If it helped her feel at ease, then all the better. That her stalker had been one of his kind probably didn't help her acceptance of everything. At least he was dead. They couldn't even celebrate her freedom from the man because it would force her to recall the awful things she saw. He didn't want to remind her of his latent monster.

"The bathroom is through there, if you want to take a shower or anything," he said, breaking the silence.

Standing in the middle of the room, as though reluctant to touch anything, Charlotte turned to face him, gaze following to where he directed with his hand to the ensuite off the entrance hall of the dorm. "So this is what you meant about the school being okay with girls and guys sharing rooms," she said. With how low she spoke, he thought she said it to herself, but he answered anyway.

"Yeah."

She looked at him. "And you've never had another girl in here?"

His head angled to the side, and his brows tightened. "No. Well, other than visitors like Blaire, Layla, and Riley." He looked up. "Oh, and Seth's flings before he and Riley discovered they were Korrenas."

"Wait. Seth and Riley are mates?"

"They are," he said in a halting voice. He wondered what she thought of that. She had to know that Blaire and Lukas shared a bond, but it surprised him no one had mentioned Seth and Riley.

"That makes so much sense. The tension between those two before they started dating seemed so intense." She laughed. "I guess dating isn't the right word. Boyfriend and girlfriend, either. I've been calling Lukas Blaire's boyfriend for months."

"It's similar."

"Is it?"

She walked to the side of his bed, looking across it out the only window to the courtyard below. He moved to stand at the head of his bed after moving a pair of dumbbells from the floor near the foot of his bed so she didn't trip. He wanted to give her space, but he felt uncomfortable too far away, as if she'd disappear if he looked away a second too long.

His Korrena stood in front of him, and he didn't know what to do. If he touched her, would she scream and run away? He never thought a pair bond would happen for him, and even now, it wasn't guaranteed, not with her fear so potent.

"Aiden?"

He blinked. She stood staring at him, no longer focused on the window.

"I asked you a question."

His hand ran over his face. "Yeah, it's similar. But it's also not. It's more." Not able to stand any longer, he sank onto the edge of the bed and clasped his hands together in front of his mouth, putting his elbows on his thighs. He stared ahead at the opposite wall where his TV sat, video games strewn around the stand. She probably hated how untidy his space looked.

"I don't know what all they told you, but sometimes Korrena pairs connect right away. Either they were former lovers, friends, or had some strong connection that made it easy to accept the bond. Then whatever relationship they had going into the awakening grows into something more. Pairs who develop romantic relationships could call themselves boyfriend and girlfriend, but it's deeper than that."

The bed shifted as Charlotte perched on the edge of the mattress at the foot of his bed, which formed a corner with the head of the second bed. She still wore the slinky outfit from the club, which looked out of place in the dorm room. He'd need to get her something else to wear soon.

"Sealing the bond is similar to what you experience with marriage, except there's no divorce. Not without a lot of pain. We didn't know it was even possible to break a bond until it happened to Blaire and Lukas when she was kidnapped."

"What?" Her voice pitched high, and he looked over at her again.

"Remember the psycho TA who kidnapped her? Everything we told you was true. He was obsessed with her, but the former heads of the academy covered his actions because he was stealing her blood for them to experiment on."

Charlotte's hand flew to her mouth when a gasp escaped.

"He ended up severing their bond in some fucked-up ritual."

Charlotte lowered her hand from her mouth. "So they don't have a bond now?"

"They do. It's restored. It's a long story, and I'm sure Blaire will fill you in on it, but that tattoo on their neck is a symbol of their sealed bond."

"So they are sort of married?"

"It's the closest thing I can compare it to in human terms. Our kind marries. My parents are married. It's the same thing you would do. The sealing of a bond is an extra layer of commitment. Where marriage has rings as a symbol, the mark shows the binding of souls."

"That actually sounds incredibly romantic."

He scoffed. "Think so?"

"Binding yourself to someone forever? The headmistress said you live for hundreds of years. To have someone who loved you and connected with you on that level always by your side? That's a hopeless romantic's dream."

When she put it like that, it sounded wonderful. It was how he felt about it. But he didn't think she considered the long-term ramifications associated with binding her soul to another's; to his.

Charlotte toyed with the tip of her thumbnail. "What if you get angry with each other, though? What if you get tired of one another? What if the other person cheats?"

"You work it out, just like you would in a marriage."

Charlotte shook her head, the curls that had fallen from the bundle on her head swishing around cheeks still stained with black tears. "Not everyone works out their problems."

"I've never heard of a Korrena pair not working through their issues. As for cheating? It's unheard of. The intense yearning for your other half is too great."

Silence descended as Charlotte looked down at her hands, flicking her thumbnails against each other. He didn't know what was going through her mind, and her feelings weren't strong enough to give him any insight into her emotional state.

With both sex and blood passed from one side of their pair, their connection had already surpassed that of others. After speaking with Seth while Charlotte was being treated by the medical team, he gained greater insight into how close their connection had come to a fully sealed bond. It wasn't far off at all. All she had to do was drink his blood while he was buried deep inside of her. While he claimed her body. *Stop. She's not going to do it.*

He didn't need to get his hopes up.

When he stood from the bed, her gaze snapped up at him and he gave her an apologetic look. He didn't mean to spook her with the sudden movement.

"Uh…" His hand cuffed the side of his throat as he rubbed at it. "I know it isn't ideal, but until they can bring you your clothes and stuff, I'll loan you something to sleep in, so you don't have to stay in that." He motioned to the outfit she wore, unable to resist letting his eyes roam over the skin on display.

"Yeah, thanks. I don't think I ever want to wear this again."

He shook his head. She looked phenomenal in the outfit, but he didn't blame her; it probably wasn't comfortable. He retrieved a pair of boxers and a T-shirt from his closet and returned, passing them to her when she stood. "My regular shorts would swallow you. These are going to be big as it is, but it's better than anything else I have."

"It's okay."

"You can shower or take a bath and get some sleep. The door's locked from the inside so no one can get in." He nodded to the bed on the opposite side of the room. "The bedding is new, added while you were in the staff building. That whole side of the room is yours. The desk and all. You also get half of the closet. Before the summer is out, they'll provide you with a uniform and all the things you need."

She laughed. "I still find it so weird you wear uniforms in college."

"It's just the policy. I don't understand it, but I know some religious and military schools have similar things. I guess it's the Blackthorn Clan's way of keeping the elite appearance to discourage humans from applying."

"Yet they still try."

He chuckled.

She looked down at the clothing in her hands and then up at him. "Thank you, by the way. Not just for the clothes, but for everything else. You saved me. I didn't thank you for that."

His fingers twitched at his side with the need to touch her. Instead, he gave a tight nod and clenched his fist. "I told you I wouldn't let anything happen to you."

Stepping forward, she used the arm not holding his clothes to wrap around his waist, resting her cheek against his chest.

His heart lodged in his throat, and it took swallowing several times to force it back into his chest cavity. He couldn't take it anymore, he had to ask. Her actions since they entered the room made no sense. "How are you not afraid?"

She tightened her grip on the back of his shirt, and she sighed. "Because none of you have ever hurt me, or even Blaire, and she's been with the academy for over a year." Her head tilted up, her chin resting against him like she did when he first arrived in Athens—it felt like a lifetime ago. "And you've always kept me safe. No matter what, you didn't let anyone hurt me. *You've* never hurt me."

His hand lifted slowly, giving her the chance to step away, but she didn't move. He cupped her cheek, and she leaned into the touch. "I would never hurt you." He took a deep breath and closed his eyes against the burn in his eyes. "I will never hurt you as long as I breathe."

Charlotte didn't say anything to his words, giving only a small nod as she separated from him. He hated the loss of her warmth.

"Take your time," he said. "I'll be out here if you need me."

When she disappeared into the bathroom, he collapsed onto his bed and pressed the heels of his hands against his eyes. It boggled his mind how she wasn't afraid of them. It gave his fearful heart hope, and that was a dangerous thing.

He couldn't deny the ever-present demon in the back of his mind reminding him that to her he was nothing more than a monster once his canines descended and his true hunger showed itself.

29

The Past

A violent crash startled Charlotte awake. Blinking away the exhaustion weighing heavily on her body, she looked at Aiden's bed, perpendicular to her bed. Moonlight from the window illuminated his tossing and turning.

Her gaze moved around the room for the source of the noise that woke her. A broken lamp lay on the floor between their beds. Aiden must have knocked it over with his thrashing.

She pushed her covers down and put her feet on the floor, rolling her neck. She felt stiff and her arm throbbed. The stress that kept her muscles taut hadn't abated in sleep. She didn't feel a threat in the room, but she couldn't shake the events of earlier in the night from her tired body.

Her stalker was dead. She was free. Noah ran when Aiden attacked the stalker, but she didn't think he could get onto academy grounds. Dominic told her he had people searching for him.

Pushing to her feet, she adjusted the boxers she'd rolled at the waist several times to fit and crept over to Aiden's bed, climbing onto it from the bottom corner to avoid the broken glass.

His face was twisted in pain, and she hated it. She knew he had nightmares, but he never told her what they were about. It made her question if he trusted her or not. For him to keep what he was a secret from her should have given her the answer to that question; by their laws, he couldn't tell her before.

Maybe he could share now.

"Aiden," she whispered, crawling up beside him, kneeling on the bed, her hand touching his shoulder as he squirmed. When he didn't respond to her voice, she put her other hand on the other shoulder and shook him. "Aiden!"

His eyes flashed open, and he jackknifed up in the bed, causing her to fall back. In a swift movement, he caught her around the waist before she could fall off the bed. Lowering his forehead to her shoulder, he shuddered.

She didn't dare move. Her hands rested on his large shoulders, her legs straddling his thigh, but she didn't sit. She wasn't sure if he had his wits about him yet. Her heart hammered in her chest from the near fall into the pile of broken glass.

Taking another long inhale, he lifted his head to meet her eyes.

She brushed away the pieces of his disheveled hair that stuck to his sweaty forehead. His eyebrows drew in. Did he not want her to touch him? The thought made her feel sad.

"I wish you'd tell me," she whispered.

"Tell you what?"

"What you dream about when it hurts."

His arms tightened around her in response to her words, and she expected him to retreat, but he surprised her. "Alright." He shifted her to his side and slid over to make room for her on the bed.

The covers were damp with sweat, so she pushed them down with her feet and sat with her back to the cool wall, crossing her legs and putting her hands in her lap. He moved to sit beside her, and she did her best not to enjoy all the naked skin on display, since he wore only a pair of athletic shorts.

"Since you know the truth now, I don't have to keep this from you." He bent his left leg, wrapping his hand over his shin. His other hand rested on the right thigh of his other leg that extended over the side of the bed. "When we went to Europe, it wasn't a school trip. Well, it was, but it wasn't something like a field trip. We went there to meet the Blackthorn Clan, the leaders of our kind—"

"They told me about them."

"Did they tell you about Europe?"

She shook her head.

"Well, we went there to see them because the Order got arrested for the shit they pulled with Blaire."

"Who is the Order? What did they do to Blaire?"

Aiden tapped his leg. "Technically, there are three Orders in the world, but they go by different names. A group of Vasirian who oversee the area of the world they are located. The members on this side of the world also acted as the administration for Blackthorn Academy. There are a few schools like ours in the world, and each leadership group oversees them." His eyes cut to hers. "Until now. After they experimented on Blaire trying to discover the secrets of how she could be a Korrena as a human, and their role in helping Vincent with Blaire's kidnapping, they got apprehended and removed."

"I remember the administration got in trouble, but I didn't know they were the Order."

He nodded. "We went to Europe to back up our witness statements, but a lot of things happened. While we were there, Riley and Blaire were captured and nearly died. If it wasn't for Dom finding them, there's no telling what would have happened."

She didn't know anything. All this time she spent at UGA stressing if accounting was the right career path, her friends were on the other side of the ocean fighting to survive. It made her feel useless and guilty for thinking her problems were actual problems. They didn't compare to what happened to Blaire.

"The rogues — Did they tell you about them?" At her nod, he said, "They attacked Blackthorn Manor to capture Blaire while we were meeting in the throne room. They don't want her to live. They don't want the prophecy to come to light."

"The magic thing?"

"Yeah." He nodded, his gaze unfocused across the room.

She was glad they'd explained the history and prophecy to her. Something told her Aiden was having a hard time relaying everything to her. The information was a lot to digest. She couldn't fathom trying to explain it all to someone so utterly clueless.

It made little sense to her for people to want to kill Blaire if she was destined to save their species. Did they want their kind to go extinct?

"During the attack, the clan and the rest of us had to fight. There were so many of them," he said, his voice going distant as he stared forward, unblinking. She suspected he wasn't in the room with her anymore, but back in the manor, in his mind.

"Someone knocked out Lukas. They caught Blaire. When I tried to help…" The rise and fall of his chest grew heavier, his breaths becoming shorter. "Riley tried to get to me, but Seth and Dom wouldn't let her. She had to watch," he said, his voice rough with restrained emotion. A single tear slid down his cheek, sparkling in the moonlight. "She watched me die. Watched them press a gun to my temple and put a bullet in my head."

His tongue peeked out of his mouth, moving over his lips to moisten them. "Blaire's magic brought me back. I don't know where I was. It felt like a sort of limbo. Floating in space, waiting on wherever I was supposed to go." His burning gaze turned to her. "I heard you crying."

She blinked. "What?"

"I thought it was Riley crying for me, but in my dreams since, a voice told me my Korrena was waiting for me. I just knew it was my Korrena mourning me. *You* mourning me. I think it was symbolic, not literal. I mean, you knew nothing about us or what a Korrena was." He shook his head and looked across the room again. "When I woke up, Blaire had passed out. She used all her strength and magic to heal me. To bring me back from the dead. She doesn't even remember it."

The silence that fell was heavy, only broken moments later by his meek laugh. "I'll tell you what, though. They told me what Blaire did to the man who shot me." He put his head against the wall. "Her therapist told her it might have resulted from shock, but I think it was also the strength she's gained being in our world. Not physical strength, mind you. Mental. She went off. Stabbed the rogue to death until Lukas pulled her off him."

She tried to imagine Blaire killing someone in cold blood, but she found it difficult. Blaire had been afraid to even defy her stepbrother before she came to Blackthorn Academy. Had she really changed so much in a year? Considering everything they told her she went through, it wasn't out of the question.

"So yeah. My nightmares for months have been reliving that moment on my knees with the gun to my head, or the after where I waited in limbo." His heavy sigh sounded defeated. "I don't know how to make it stop."

Her stomach cramped, and her eyes stung. She couldn't stop her emotions from taking over as her vision blurred with unshed tears.

The more she heard about their world, the more her curiosity grew, but it sounded scary. Not in the "monsters waiting in the dark" sort of way, but in a "This world is dangerous and if you're not strong enough, it'll eat you alive" sort of way.

His head turned when she hiccupped, and he pivoted his body toward her. "Why are you crying?"

She sniffed and wiped her nose. Tears streamed down her face, making her swipe her chin. "I didn't know… I didn't… I never knew anything." She sniffed. "God Aiden, I've liked you for a long time now. To think you might have died permanently, and I wouldn't have gotten the chance to really know you the way I have this last little while…" The tears fell faster, and she hiccupped as her chest tightened.

His arms wrapped around her shoulders, drawing her to him. She didn't resist, burying her face in his chest, wetting his skin in the process. He made a gentle shushing sound. "It's okay. I'm safe now. I'm here."

"No, it's not!" Her fist balled against his arm and hit his bicep. "It's not okay. It's not okay. I didn't know. It's not okay someone shot you in the head. None of this is okay!" Her soft cries turned into heartrending sobs that racked her body, making him hold her tighter.

"No, I guess not." His hand moved up to cup the back of her head, burying his face in her sleep-mussed curls. "But I'm here now. I'm not going anywhere. I won't leave you."

Aiden held her tight, comforting her as she poured out her grief over the potential loss of the time they shared. She didn't understand the anguish she felt. Although she hadn't lost any time, the mere thought of it caused her chest to flutter in a panic.

It felt like she was grieving his death, even with him right in front of her.

His heart beat thunderously in her ear and he spoke low. "Charlotte. You're breaking my heart."

Her head popped up, and she looked up at him, sniffing. "What?"

"Your emotions are wide open to me right now. They are so strong that I feel all your sadness and panic." When her heart tripped over itself with anxiety at the idea her feelings were hurting him, his eyes softened. "I'm not upset with you. I'm worried about you." His thumb swiped her cheeks. "I'm really not going anywhere."

It had been a long time since she'd cried like that. A long time since something hit her with such a force that she felt helpless to stop the waves of heartache from crashing in. Even before starting depression medication, she didn't react like this. Depression made her pivot between anger and emptiness. It affected everyone differently but had usually been consistent within her.

Releasing a calming breath, she wiped the remaining wetness from her chin and cheeks and looked up at Aiden's face. "How often do you have the nightmares?"

"Almost every night. Less when I slept with you."

Her face felt hot. "Have you talked to anyone about your nightmares?"

"Not really." He leaned back against the wall, and she turned on the bed to put her back to the room, facing him. "I've told some of our friends that I have them, but not the details."

"What about a professional?"

"Like a therapist?"

"Yeah. It helped me way back. I don't see one now because I know what's going on and the medicine does enough to help with it, but if it got too bad, I'd start therapy again."

She wondered if maybe before long she could stop taking pills, but she wasn't sure. She quit when she felt better years ago, but as soon as anything shook her foundation enough, she needed it again. It was possible quitting wasn't an option. Was it healthy to start and stop depression medication whenever the need arose, like cold medicine, or did it make sense to take it as a preventative measure? She needed to at least ask the doctor that much.

He sighed. "I haven't, no. The others have been seeing the therapist in the psychology department, but I haven't. It really messed with a lot of them, witnessing what they did and all. I guess if I saw my friend or sibling—" His jaw tightened, and she reached to grasp his hand, squeezing.

She knew without him having to finish. He didn't need to keep reliving it.

"I think it might be a good idea," he conceded. "Especially now that I have the Korrena bond to contend with, too."

"What do you mean?"

Aiden laced his fingers with hers. "The bond can make you volatile. Aggression is common, for example. You wouldn't know it to look at them now, but Lukas and Blaire fought like cats and dogs in the beginning. The jealousy was intense. Lukas and I almost—"

When he didn't continue, she squinted. "What?"

"He thought I was trying to take Blaire from him. We almost got into a fight."

She reared back. "What? Why? What happened?"

The chuckle following her rapid-fire questions held no amusement. "Yeah, about that… I made a pass at Blaire." He shook his head at the shock no doubt twisting her facial features. "She and I developed a connection. A friendship. While she and Lukas fought against their bond, she relied on me, and I did what I always do. Look out for people." He shrugged.

She didn't see how that equaled making a pass at someone spoken for—or were they then? She didn't have the chance to ask because he continued.

"I grew to feel attraction toward her. I didn't find her physically attractive when we met. I mean, I didn't think she was ugly. I just didn't consider her in a sexual way."

Her eyes widened. Aiden wanted to have sex with Blaire? Her belly flip-flopped with an unwanted sour feeling, and she tasted bile. Something coiled tight inside of her and she pushed it down, unwilling to acknowledge it as jealousy toward her best friend.

"They weren't getting along, and I figured if she didn't want a bond with him, and he didn't want one with her, then it wouldn't hurt to shoot my shot. I wouldn't have even bothered if I knew they felt anything for each other." He scratched his leg, averting his eyes. "Turns out they did, and I felt like an ass. Lukas forgave me, and Blaire and I remained friends, but we still have this weird connection that even Lukas can't deny."

That creeping sting of jealousy resurfaced. She hated it.

"I mistook my feelings for her, though. It was a combination of a couple of things."

"What things?" She hated that she sounded pissy.

His brow rose. "You're jealous? I knew I felt something… but it didn't make sense."

She bit the inside of her cheek and looked at his pillows.

"Charlotte."

She looked at him.

"There's nothing romantic between Blaire and me."

Intellectually she knew that, but she couldn't stop the feeling.

"That's another part of an early bond. Jealousy. It'll always be there, but it's never more potent than in the early stages of a bond. For me, it'll always be there. I know it. I'm not even going to deny it." He shifted and bent his knee again. "But yeah, nothing between her and me. The Oracle—"

Before he could ask if she knew who that was, she held up her hand. "I'm familiar with her." She smiled when he laughed, nodding.

"So, the Oracle revealed Blaire and I share a connection. We all do, actually."

"What do you mean?"

"Sort of like kindred spirits. We've all found each other in some way or another throughout the years. Except Dom, Layla, Mera, and Kai. Be it as siblings, lovers, friends, or whatever. Lukas, Blaire, Riley, Seth, and me. She said there was a sixth, and I'm starting to believe that was you since you're my Korrena."

Her hands twisted in her lap.

To be tied to someone's soul—five other someones—to exist over and over, finding them and sharing a lifetime, only to repeat the process again when the time was right, sounded so surreal. *Any more surreal than magic, resurrection, and another species not documented by humans?*

"Blaire and I share a different connection though, and it influenced my actions. I felt drawn to her because centuries ago, two lovers were murdered, and in their final moments, their pleas to never part were heard by whoever is watching over us. Their will was pushed forward through time until Blaire and I were born."

"Wait. You're reincarnated?"

"No. I thought that at first too. The connection of the six of us is a reincarnation thing, but not this. We carry the will of that couple to never part from each other, in whatever way that may be." He shook his head. "It's crazy to think about. They loved each other so much that they couldn't accept death without leaving that love in the world to never die."

"So that's why you wanted Blaire?"

"Yes and no. It helped push it along, but really, I can't feel attraction to someone without having an emotional connection with them."

"You're demi?"

"That's what Mera says, but I don't put a label on it. I just know what I read about it fits."

She knew about demisexuality. Her ma was demisexual. When Charlotte looked into it, because she didn't understand how her ma could be a lesbian and demisexual, she discovered that being demi wasn't about which gender a person felt attraction to. It helped her learn more about her ma, and now it helped her better understand Aiden.

"Blaire and I got close while I kept watch over her when she first arrived. When you sprinkle in the weird tie the magical connection adds, it was a recipe for attraction." He shrugged. "I don't feel attracted to her now, though. I still felt it for a bit after I backed off. It's not like an attraction can turn off like a light switch, but I grew to understand how much stronger my desire to be her friend was than desiring her sexually."

Her nose scrunched. "Does that mean you didn't feel anything for me before we became close friends?" That's how it would work if he was demisexual, but she felt something for him from the moment they met. At least, physical attraction.

"Oh, I did." At her raised brows, he laughed. "The first time I saw you, it felt so strange to get a hard-on from just seeing you in that mini-dress uniform at the diner. I had to hide it from the others."

Her mouth gaped. "What? I don't understand."

"I think my body recognized you as my pair before my mind realized it. Even your scent seemed familiar."

"Scent?"

"Yeah, you smell like pineapple upside down cake."

"I do not." She lifted her shirt and sniffed. All she smelled was Aiden's laundry detergent. "I don't even have anything that smells like that."

He chuckled. "No, you wouldn't. It's a pheromone unique to you that only I can smell. There should be one for me that only you smell, too."

There was so much to learn about this Korrena stuff she couldn't keep up.

"You usually smell like a blend of orange Creamsicle lotion and the cologne you put on at my apartment." She'd smelled the bottle one day when he sprayed it. "Oh, and my bathroom supplies."

"I don't wear lotion."

"Really?"

"Really. So I smell like ice cream to you?"

"Like Creamsicle, yeah. That's not something you have?"

"No. That would be the pheromone I have that would appeal most to you. Probably why I slept better beside you than not. Your scent calms my mind. It's supposed to soothe you and draw you in. "

"All it's doing right now is making me hungry. Cake and ice cream? Yes, please."

Aiden laughed. "I haven't eaten either since before the club. We were planning to grab something from a late-night restaurant afterward, but things went… Well, you were there."

The last thing she wanted was to think about the rogue who attacked her. She didn't want to burst the bubble of comfort and peace they had at that moment, but the look on his face let her know unpleasantness had already seeped in. She put her hand over her bandaged forearm and winced.

"It hurts?"

She moved her hand and grimaced. "A little, yeah."

Heavy black brows speared together over forest green eyes, swimming with insecurity. "I'm sorry."

"Why?"

"For what you went through. Because I'm a monster? Take your pick."

"No. No, you're not." When he looked away from her, she snapped her fingers. He wouldn't do this to himself. "Aiden, look at me." His gaze slid back to hers. "Monsters hurt others. Monsters steal, kill, torment, and destroy without remorse."

"But you were afraid of me."

She reared back. "When?"

"In the alley. After I killed that piece of shit who hurt you. You were terrified. I felt your fear."

"I wasn't afraid of you. I was afraid of him, not you. You surprised me, but I wasn't afraid."

She watched the muscle in his square jaw jump and flutter with his clenched teeth, and she sighed, reaching out with her bandaged arm and placed her hand on the side of his face. The anxiety on her chest lifted when he leaned into her touch.

"Aiden, never be sorry for who you are. For what you are. And what you are is no monster. You're beautiful."

He kissed her palm. "I wish I could heal it for you."

"What?" Her brows raised, lowering her arm. "Don't tell me you have the ability to heal," she said in a flat voice. That would be overkill.

"I do, but only my bites. A Korrena's saliva holds healing properties. It's why when I broke your skin before you had no wound. I didn't use my fangs, but I was rough." He grimaced. "Sorry about that."

"Why? I'm not." Her skin heated. "I liked it. A lot. Is that a

Vasirian thing?"

"What?"

"The roughness. The marking and the way you talk." The more she said, the more she felt like her skin might catch fire.

The corner of his mouth tilted up and his eyes narrowed. "No. It's not a Vasirian thing, Charlotte. It's not a Korrena thing either. It's what you do to me. You drive me mad. I can't help but want to devour you."

Her breath caught in her throat. The temptation to tell him to do it buzzed inside her. But that might be too much after everything they experienced tonight. Instead, she redirected the conversation.

"I don't understand all this. Magic, Korrenas, Vasirian—not vampires… but I won't run away. I want to learn more."

"Yeah?"

When she nodded, he reached out and put his hand on the back of her neck, pulling her forward to seal his mouth over hers, making tingles spread over her skin. She moaned, and he slipped his tongue into her mouth.

Kissing Aiden was addictive.

Leaning in, he lowered her down onto the bed. Her head nestled against his pillow and the smell of him surrounded her from beneath as his body covered her front.

Breaking the kiss, he worked his way over her cheek to her neck, kisses alternating between gentle and firm with a bit of suction.

When he lowered his hips between where her legs bent to cage him in, his erection pressed against her core, making her moan.

"Is this okay?" He kissed across her neck and up to her lips where he hovered over them, waiting for her answer.

She didn't know if she liked his hesitation. She wanted the uninhibited Aiden. The one who didn't hold back and succumbed to his wants without overthinking it. Overthinking was something she did; she needed him to be certain. Although she was open to tenderness and savoring the moment, she sensed only caution from him.

Her hands came up to bracket his head from both sides, the stubble from the day's growth on his face scratched her hands. "I need you to stop worrying about me being afraid of you."

"But—"

"No. Aiden, I want you." Her eyes narrowed. "*All* of you. Stop holding back."

He lifted his hands to grasp her wrists. "You think I want to hold back? I don't." When her brows lifted in surprise at the sudden harsh tone, he kissed her palm, tempering his voice. "When I said I wanted to devour you, I meant it."

"So devour me, then."

Aiden moved her arms over her head on the bed, putting her hands together. "Don't move them."

Clasping her hands together, she watched as Aiden rose, kneeling between her thighs. He didn't move, and the longer he stared at her lying beneath him, the heavier her breathing became until she felt like a needy mess. He wasn't even touching her; at least, not with his hands.

His gaze roamed over her body, clad in nothing but his T-shirt that fell to her mid-thigh and boxers. The heated look in his eyes made the slow drag of his gaze feel like a sensual caress.

When it felt like she would combust if he didn't touch her, his hands slid beneath the T-shirt and worked it up her body until it bunched above her breasts. Steady hands grazed the sides of her breasts, thumbs moving across the nipples but not lingering.

"Do you know how obsessed I am with these?" he asked, giving her breasts a firm squeeze, making her gasp.

Even though she always hated the size of her breasts, and considered a reduction at one point, the hungry way he touched and looked at them made her second-guess doing anything about their size. The way he handled them, like they were something to cherish, made her rethink her opinion. She didn't mind his focus on them.

He bent, leaning in to glide the flat of his tongue over her nipple as he pinched the other between his thumb and forefinger. "Do you know how lucky I feel?" he murmured against her skin, before kissing the peaked bud. "To have you here, knowing the truth, and not running away? It feels unreal."

She moaned when he took her nipple into his mouth, sucking tight to her skin while flicking her nipple with the tip of his tongue until she squirmed.

His lips grazed across the valley between her breasts before he dragged his teeth over her left nipple. Her responding groan bordered on embarrassing.

Clenching her fists to avoid lowering her hands to touch him, she wiggled her hips, seeking friction, but his lower half hovered too far from her reach.

Aiden's teeth sank into the tender flesh of the side of her breast, pulling her skin into his mouth and sucking. Her breath caught, and she arched into his mouth. The thought of him marking her again sent shivers of delight down her spine.

Moving lower, he kissed across her stomach to the rolled waistband of her boxers. He hooked his fingers beneath the fabric and tugged them down, moving aside to shimmy them down her legs. Once they were discarded, he moved between her legs again, lowering his upper body to trail his tongue over her inner thigh.

"Your skin tastes as good as it smells," he murmured before

sucking the sensitive skin of her upper inner thigh into his mouth.

She whined, wriggling her hips while he marked her.

His fingers slid over her swollen and sensitive core, and the sound of her arousal made her cheeks boil with heat. It surprised her how much he affected her.

Slipping a thick digit inside her channel, he cursed against her thigh. "You really want this, don't you, Kitten?" He twisted his hand to rub his thumb in circles over her clit, sliding in another finger alongside the first.

When he increased the pressure with his thumb, her neck arched, and she cried out.

Moving to her other thigh, he lavished her skin with open-mouthed kisses and small nips until he neared the crease of her thigh. Her eyes flew open, and she yelped when he bit harder than he had the other side.

His head lifted. "Too much?"

She lifted her head, looking down at him while panting. "No."

"Good." His wicked grin intensified the pulse between her legs. Fresh arousal pooled at her core. "Fuck, the way you squeeze me…" His head shook from side to side.

He angled his fingers upward, and he touched a spot inside her that caused her to see stars at the same time as he closed his mouth over her clit.

She screamed at the dual sensation, lowering her hands and burying her fingers in his hair, pulling. She didn't know if she wanted to make him stop or if it was her body acting on reflex at the overstimulation.

Pulling his fingers free, he lifted his head, disentangling her hands from his hair. He *tsked*. "Kitten," he chastised, a low growl to his voice that made her shiver. "I thought I said not to move."

He couldn't be serious. How did he expect her to maintain her position in that situation?

At her silence, he tilted his head from side to side in consideration, a slow and mischievous grin spreading across his face. His lips glistened with her wetness. "Do I need to make you stay still?"

"What do you mean?" Her hesitant voice made him frown.

"Nothing." He bent to kiss her knee, gentle again. Gone was the need in his voice she heard before. If she wasn't mistaken, he was retreating again. He misunderstood her.

"No, please. What?"

"It's too much," he said, hands sliding over her thighs. "I got carried away."

Her head rocked from side to side against the pillow. "Please. I like it when you talk like that. I was… confused."

Turning his head, lips still brushing her skin, he squinted as if assessing the truth in her eyes. "Do you? Like it, I mean."

"Yes," she said, her fingers toying with the bedding at her sides as her skin flushed.

"What if I kept you from touching me?"

"How?"

His gaze cut to the burgundy and black plaid tie hanging on the back of his desk chair and the air stalled in her lungs. He asked so low she almost didn't hear, "Do you trust me?"

She had a feeling her answer would do more than bolster his actions in a sexual context; he needed to know she trusted him on the most fundamental level. Did she trust him?

"I do," she whispered.

With those two words, he pushed off the bed and moved to his chair, grabbed the tie, and settled back between her legs again. "You need a safe word."

"A safe word?"

"You know, for if it's too much. I don't want you to feel like you can't stop me."

She frowned. "I could just say no."

"Sometimes it's hard for people to say no in the moment. I wouldn't want you to feel like you couldn't. So tell me something you wouldn't say in normal conversation."

"Creamsicle."

"What?"

"That's the word."

He laughed. "My pheromone?"

Her cheeks flushed.

"Creamsicle, it is."

He leaned over her, lifting her arms above her head, crossing her hands. She licked her lips, watching him wrap the tie around her wrists several times, lacing it through the center and looping it over the metal bar that traversed the length of his wooden headboard. He smirked when she tugged at the restraints, unable to get free.

Moving back down her body, he nipped, kissed, and sucked at her skin until he positioned himself between her thighs again. "You are so beautiful, Kitten. And all mine." His mouth covered her clit again, tongue flicking at a rapid pace.

Her back arched, a guttural groan escaping her mouth. She couldn't do anything with her hands restrained above her head. He knew it. She knew it. And he took advantage of it.

Two fingers slid into her heat again and she whimpered, trying to hold back the moan in her throat, failing when he sucked at her slit. The wet, popping sound when he pulled away was lewd and made her toes curl.

His left hand gripped her thigh in a bruising grip as he lavished her with kisses, licks, and bites that pulled at the sensitive flesh between her legs.

The noises he made as he lapped up her liquid arousal sounded obscene. If she weren't out of her mind with pleasure, she might feel embarrassment, but with the way he possessed her body, she couldn't think of anything other than how amazing she felt.

Her legs trembled, and her hips bucked against his face. Her orgasm was approaching fast, but she needed to resist surrendering. She wanted him inside her first.

"Aiden, please."

He hummed against her in question, never relenting on his assault on her clit. The vibration made her gasp.

"I want you," she said with a whine.

His left hand gripped her thigh, and he rose to smile down at her, pulling his thick fingers from inside her. She thought he would give her what she wanted, but she was mistaken. He lowered his face again, watching her with an intensity that made her squirm.

When his slick fingers grazed over her other hole, making a riot of butterflies erupt in her belly, she gasped. A single brow rose in an unspoken question.

She'd never let anyone touch her there, not even herself. Now, here she was submitting to another thing she never thought she would have desired until Aiden Easton came into her world.

At her nod, he swirled around the tight, puckered skin until she relaxed, and he pushed the tip of his ring finger in. The fit felt tight, and a little uncomfortable, but he rocked at a gentle pace until her muscles loosened, allowing him deeper. When she felt his first two fingers slide inside her core above the one in her other hole, the fullness made her choke on a moan.

She tugged on the restraints, keening like a dying animal when he sucked her clit into his mouth, flicking his tongue in a punishing frenzy as he worked his fingers in sync, taking both of her holes at the same time.

The sensations were too much. Too raw. Too everything.

She would hyperventilate if she didn't come soon.

Her trembling thighs squeezed his head, and he growled against her, vibrations making her whimper and beg for him. She recognized the noises pouring from her mouth to be possible words, but their meaning eluded her.

His head lifted, and he spoke, his voice nothing more than a guttural rumble. "Come for me. Come all over my fingers and face."

Aiden didn't give her a chance to answer; he probably knew she couldn't. Instead, he resumed dragging his tongue up her slit and swirling it around the swollen bundle of nerves that pulsed in time with her pounding heart.

Pulling off her clit, he growled a command her body was helpless to resist. "Come for me, Kitten."

Her back arched, and if he wasn't pressing his face against her lower half, still lapping away at her, the force of her climax would have made her hips come off the bed. She screamed; eyes screwed shut as tears escaped over her temples.

He worked her through the aftershocks of her orgasm, the feeling of both of her channels tightening and fluttering around his fingers prolonging the sensations.

When she collapsed in a boneless heap, he slowly extracted his fingers, careful of hurting her. He grabbed the boxers at his side, using them to wipe his fingers clean before crawling up beside her and untying her wrists. He inspected them for marks, trailing kisses over the now sensitive skin as he praised her.

"You did so good, Kitten." Another kiss. "Thank you for trusting me." He lowered himself down onto the bed, pulling the oversized shirt down her body, tucking her into his side.

She snuggled into him. A foggy sensation settled over her mind, making her feel borderline nervous, and she didn't know what was happening to her body. The intense reality of what they did trickled through the fog, and she clung to him, a soft whimper muffled by his chest.

"Shhh," he said, kissing her temple. "It was a lot, but I've got you. You're not going anywhere. You're safe."

After several minutes wrapped around him while he whispered soothing reassurances to her, she looked up at his face. "I don't understand what just happened."

His fingers toyed with her curls, and he nodded. "I've never experienced it, or seen it before in person, but I've seen it talked about when I've watched stuff online."

"What?"

"It can happen to anyone. Doesn't have to be BDSM, or anything like that. They call it subdrop."

"Subdrop?"

"An adrenaline crash after a particularly intense sexual session. It happens a lot in the BDSM world, but it can happen to anyone." He stroked her head.

"You like BDSM?" She felt silly asking the question. He'd bound her wrists; of course he did.

"Not exactly. The only reason I saw anything about it was because of Seth. He was doing research for something he wrote—I'll let him explain to you about that—and he had me help find some information. I kinda got lost down the rabbit hole reading about it." He chuckled. "You're the first person I've ever wanted to tie up, and the first I've ever been aggressive with. I haven't been with many, but I've never felt the need to…" He looked up as if searching for the word. "Own someone so completely as I do you." His eyes met hers. "Did you hate it? Are you okay?"

The laugh that escaped her sounded nervous, but she wasn't. "I loved every minute of it. I just didn't understand the anxious feeling that followed." She looked down at his lap to the bulge straining against the front of his shorts. "What about you?"

"Tonight isn't about me." His lips touched her forehead. "You've been through a lot and had a lot of information dropped on you. I wanted to take your mind off it."

Burrowing deeper into his hold, she hummed. "Mission accomplished."

He smirked. "Good to know."

30

Sickness

The next day Charlotte gained the opportunity to explore the campus without too much scrutiny, since classes were not in session. She wasn't confident in going alone yet, but Aiden wasn't leaving her side, and all their friends were eager to show her around.

Students stared when she walked past, and she wondered what they thought of her being a human in their domain. Were they afraid of her, or did they hate her?

Blaire and Lukas led Aiden and her into the cafeteria for breakfast, the first time she got a decent look at most of the student body.

Aiden placed his hand on her lower back to guide her to the buffets to the left of the entrance. The abundance of food overwhelmed her. Biscuits, grits, porridge, rice, sausages, bacon, eggs, fruits of various types all littered the space. Some foods seemed normal for breakfast, but others not so much. Who had fish for breakfast?

When Aiden noticed her looking at the grilled fish, he said,

"Blackthorn Academy has students from all over the world, so they try to provide foods similar to what they are used to back home."

It made sense. She didn't think she would enjoy moving away for school and not having at least some comforts of home, but Blackthorn Academy went all out. Rich people things she didn't understand.

They grabbed trays and picked out their preferred breakfast before Aiden led her to the beverage table, allowing her to choose her favorite. Picking up a can of grape soda, she turned and squinted.

"Aiden?" she said, making Lukas and Blaire halt ahead of her and turn around at the sound of uncertainty in her voice.

"What's wrong?"

She looked up at him and then back to the refrigerator units on the wall. "Are those what I think they are?"

His hands tightened on his tray, knuckles turning white. "They are," he said, voice measured and slow.

Her swallow made her throat click. "You need one?"

"I will, yes."

Her eyes shifted to Lukas, who watched her with wariness. "And you?"

"I was going to wait until after breakfast, so you didn't have to see, but yeah."

Blaire gave her a sympathetic smile. "It's hard at first, but you get used to it."

She scanned the cafeteria, taking in the students laughing and eating. Some were drinking from blood bags like the ones in the refrigerator units.

"You don't drink human blood?"

"We do. Through donations received from clinics. We drink from blood bags freely given by humans. It is against our laws to consume blood from a live source..."

The conversation with the headmistress played in her mind, and she looked between Aiden and Lukas. "Do you want me to get you both one? It's okay."

"You don't have to—"

"It's not—"

She laughed as they spoke at the same time.

Lukas shook his head. "I'll grab them when we sit down, if you're okay with it."

"I'm not going to stop you from doing what you need to live," she said, letting Aiden guide her to a large round table in the back corner where Riley, Seth, Dominic, and Layla were already seated.

When she put her tray down, Riley jumped up and wrapped her in a big hug. "I'm so glad you stayed!"

She stiffened, taken off-guard. She gaped at Riley. "Did I have a choice?"

"Well, yeah, you did. I just thought…" Riley looked around at everyone and then back at Charlotte.

Aiden tensed at her side.

"I didn't mean it bad," Charlotte clarified. "I mean, I thought with the attack and me knowing everything, I couldn't leave if I wanted to." She looked at Aiden as he lowered himself into his seat. "I don't want to, just so you know."

He slid her chair toward him when she sat down, his arm banding around her waist, fingers tightening on her hip. He leaned over to whisper in her ear, "I wouldn't let you go, anyway."

"Not another one," Dominic grumbled.

"What?" Layla asked, looking at Aiden and Charlotte, then back to Dominic, who focused his attention on them.

"Korrena couples." He shook his head. "Horny rabbits."

Layla flushed, poking her eggs with a fork.

Seth smirked. "Don't be jealous, *Dom*. Aiden's twenty. He's waited long enough."

Blaire frowned and looked at Seth. "Dom's also twenty."

He looked at Dominic and then at Blaire and grimaced. "Shit. Sorry, man."

Charlotte sympathized, having learned that a Korrena pairing usually showed itself by the late teens. If Dominic was already twenty, he was long past due, like Aiden. She wondered if his Korrena was human too.

Lukas sat down, sliding a blood packet in front of her to Aiden. She looked between them. Everyone at the table stopped what they were doing to look at her.

"If you don't stop acting like I'm going to freak out and run from the room screaming or faint, I'm going to… I dunno… scream and not run from the room."

Lukas laughed. "Blaire did faint."

Blaire rolled her eyes. "Not at the sight of blood."

"No, at the sight of fangs," Aiden quipped.

Charlotte stared at Blaire as her cheeks bloomed pink.

Seth swallowed a mouthful of orange juice and looked at Blaire. "Didn't you say you had a panic attack when you first saw someone drink blood?"

"How would you feel if you had no prior knowledge and hadn't seen it before?"

"She's right," Charlotte said. "I've seen it before. I saw a rogue attack someone before."

"Well yeah," Riley said, twisting her lips. "We all saw what they did last night."

"No, I witnessed it in Athens."

The table fell silent.

"What did you witness?" Layla asked.

"At first, I thought it was a couple making out, but then I saw the rogue man's face. He was drinking from a human guy. I thought he was a vampire."

"Always vampires," Lukas mumbled.

Dominic set his fork down. "The headmistress knows about it?"

"I told her," Aiden said.

"Well, I've already sent word to the clan about what happened, and Gabriel touched base with me this morning."

"Who's Gabriel?"

Dominic looked at her and smiled. "My cousin. One of the members of the Blackthorn Clan, which I know you're aware of from the headmistress." When she nodded, he continued. "He told me the king is interested in what this means, that another human is a Korrena. He's sent for the Oracle."

"Does that mean I'll have my memory erased?"

Aiden growled, and she put her hand on his thigh in reflex at the sound. "Over my dead body," he said.

"It won't happen anyway," Dominic insisted. "Korrena pairings are sacred to our kind. The clan would never wipe your memory strictly on the grounds that you're Aiden's Korrena."

There was so much she didn't understand about their world. The laws, the culture, the Korrena bond. She'd spent the morning while they got ready asking Aiden questions she suspected were odd to him, but with all the stuff about vampires out there, she didn't know what was real or not. Stuff like how they are fine in the sun, garlic, strength, and other things.

It stunned her to learn they had preternatural healing, especially knowing their kind was able to die and that Aiden had died once already. Learning that most injuries healed in minutes to hours, while diseases like cancer could be gone within the month, fascinated her. But like humans, any fatal injury spelled certain doom. If they couldn't heal fast enough, it would claim their lives.

Their strength outmatched humans, but only if they used it with intent. That explained the frightening grip the rogue had on her.

"Do you mind?" Aiden asked, holding up the packet. "After last night, I'm kinda…" His lips flattened.

She remembered the headmistress explaining the condition *sanguis manie.* It scared her to know that without blood, Aiden would die. She would never deny him what he needed.

"Don't make yourself sick," she said. "Any of you." She looked at the full blood bags on every tray but Blaire's. None of them had touched their packets, and Charlotte suspected it was because of her. "I don't want you to suffer, so please."

One by one, they picked up their packets and consumed them as she asked. It didn't scare her. It didn't turn her stomach to see blood move up the tubing into their mouths. It wasn't different from her ordering a steak and consuming a cow. They weren't feeding off a human directly. They weren't killing anyone. In a way, humans did worse by killing animals, but in the end, it was all for survival. Not sport or the desire to harm like the rogue from last night.

She stirred the grits on her plate as a thought occurred to her. "I forgot to ask you about Shark Week," she said, looking over at Aiden.

His brows tightened in confusion. "What's that?"

Layla swallowed a sip of blood before speaking. "Is it that thing on the Discovery Channel? My parents have old episodes on their computer from the nineties."

"I think it still airs," Riley said.

Seth nodded. "It does. I still watch it."

"No, that's not what I mean." Charlotte's cheeks turned pink.

"Maybe I shouldn't talk about it at the table."

"Oh my god, I know what you mean," Blaire exclaimed, turning saucer-eyed, drawing attention from nearby tables. "I forgot you called it that." She giggled with glee.

Lukas observed her with a raised brow.

Blaire turned to him. "Remember when I got my period, how I freaked out?"

"Don't remind me," he muttered.

"That's what she calls it."

When Lukas looked at Charlotte, her face turned molten.

"Sharks aren't actually attracted to human blood, you know," Seth said.

"What do you want to know?" Riley asked, elbowing Seth in the ribs.

He grunted. "What? It's true."

She held her hand up in front of his face. "Anyway, Blaire thought everyone would want to eat her until we talked." She laughed at Blaire's incredulous look. "Hey, it was cute."

Charlotte toyed with the tab of her soda can. "I mean, won't they? Won't it attract attention when it happens?"

"Nope," Riley said, taking another drink of blood. "We have them too. Unless you're bleeding from a wound exposed to air, most of the time we won't notice. Or unless the covered wound is bad enough." Her smokey blue eyes shifted to the bandage on Charlotte's arm. "Like that, I can't smell it. I did last night, though."

It made sense. So as long as she kept herself clean and sanitary—which she always did—there wouldn't be an issue.

Layla put her empty packet on her tray and pushed it away. "Do you think more humans will awaken like Charlotte has?" Everyone looked at her.

The prophecy was clear that Blaire becoming a Vasirian was the key to other human Korrena discoveries, but Charlotte's awakening contradicted that.

"I wondered the same thing," Charlotte whispered.

"All we can do is speculate," Dominic said. "And with you needing to settle in and get used to this new world, it's best not to dwell on it until we hear from the Oracle."

As much as that sounded like a good idea, it was hard to not think about.

"Speaking of settling in," Riley started, and Charlotte looked at her. "What about your parents?"

"My moms had to return to Atlanta to finalize some paperwork for my grandma, but I told them on the phone this morning about the scholarship, and that I've been staying with you and Blaire."

Blaire leaned back in her chair. "So they don't know about you and Aiden?"

"What am I supposed to tell them?"

"You're dating?"

"Oh. Well, they suspect that already." Exhaling a long sigh, she looked at Aiden. "I don't know what to do. Even though I'm grown, they are a big part of my life. Will they ever be able to know? I mean, if things actually work out where I stay with you and we don't break up, what then?" Her gaze moved to the others. "What am I supposed to tell them when school's over?"

Dominic shook his head. "Breaking up really isn't how it works with Korrena pairs. Once you two seal the bond, you're bound until death."

"Okay," she said, tone casual. "I'm not put off by that at all. Aiden explained how it works. How it's stronger than marriage. I just wondered if it was ever possible."

"Only the breaking of the bond ritual, which was explained to you," Aiden said, low, but Lukas flinched at his words.

She glanced at both Blaire and Lukas and the turmoil in their expressions. Watched how they moved closer to one another to comfort each other. Was that how the bond worked?

"Listen," Dominic said, stealing her attention. "Your parents can never know. The clan will wipe their memories if they find out anything about our world. And if they discover the information was given intentionally, there would be punishment for the guilty party. I can't cover everything up." His eyes met Aiden's across the table. It reminded her of his words in the alley last night. He covered up the murder for Aiden.

"When you're done with school, and start your career, you wouldn't be living with your mothers anyway," Blaire reasoned. "They won't know the difference because you can still visit them and everything. Look how often we go to town, and Riley is working for Sara."

Maybe she put too much emphasis on sharing things with her mothers, but if it would put them in danger, she would keep their secrets.

31

Adaptation

Several days passed without incident before Charlotte asked Aiden to accompany her back to the apartment in Athens at the end of the week so she could pack everything and talk to the landlord.

She would take the most important things she couldn't do without, like video games and her favorite decor, and donate the rest to those in need. She didn't want her mothers forced to keep stuff when she already had a room there, and it all wouldn't fit in the dorm.

Once they finished in Athens, she and Aiden returned to Rosebrook Valley to meet her mothers for dinner to give them the details about her scholarship. She had only given a brief explanation during a quick phone call when she'd given her mothers the news before they set off for Atlanta to take care of her grandmother's paperwork.

The news that she would stay close to home thrilled both of them, and neither questioned the stipulation of living on campus. If the elite university would pay all expenses, who were they to question the policy, her ma had said.

She still hadn't decided on a major, and classes started in two weeks. The headmistress understood and told her to take her time, that even if she started late, they would help her catch up. The college credits she'd already accumulated both in high school and at UGA met the criteria for her to start as a third-year student alongside her friends.

It helped ease any concerns her mothers had, knowing she had friends like Blaire and Riley there. The subtle mention of her boyfriend, Aiden, didn't hurt either.

It made her feel guilty to hold things back from them. She went from hiding her discomfort about accounting, to hiding the stalking situation, to now keeping a dangerous secret that put them all at risk.

Aiden tried to reassure her when they left her mothers—he literally sensed her frustration—but it didn't stop the gnawing pain in her chest and the growing uncertainty surrounding her place in a world where her family stayed on the outside.

Now, as she sat on the edge of the large fountain staring across campus at a flowering apricot grove in the distance, she wondered what it meant in the long run for her family.

If they aged differently from humans, her mothers wouldn't miss it when Riley and Aiden remained youthful while she didn't.

"You look like you're thinking really hard," Riley said, swinging her legs, the heels of her knee-high boots tapping on the marble, making the buckles clink and rattle.

"Thinking about the future."

"What about it?" Blaire said, taking a large bite out of the taco in her hand.

"My moms. Aging. What's going to happen."

Instead of eating lunch in the cafeteria, they came outside to have a bite to eat while the girls could have her to themselves. Aiden had a meeting with the student liaison about adjustments to his schedule for the fall semester.

Blaire finished her taco and looked at the container beside Charlotte. She'd eaten two hard tacos already but couldn't stomach the third.

Her diet since arriving at the academy had been full and consistent instead of her usual grab-and-go breakfast to ensure her medicine didn't make her sick, a quick bite for lunch if she thought of it, and a sensible dinner. Now, with Aiden needing to manage a regular schedule of blood intake, they went to the cafeteria or canteen for every meal and occasional snack.

Breakfast wasn't a single-banana affair anymore; she had an entire buffet at her disposal. She didn't even have to worry about the costs, either. The headmistress said her meals were part of the funding from the Blackthorn Clan for her use.

She didn't know if she could get used to not pinching pennies, but she wouldn't snub the hand that feeds, either.

"You mind?"

She passed the container to Blaire. "Knock yourself out."

They used to share food all the time when they worked together at the diner. She didn't have the appetite Blaire did. Her best friend was a foodie through and through.

"You're the best." Blaire scooped the fully loaded taco from the container and took a big bite.

Charlotte suspected Blaire's intense love of food came from her youth. She once read that kids who rarely got fed grew into adults obsessed with food. Something about food insecurity.

It wasn't like Blaire had starved as a child, but her mother struggled from time to time as a single parent before finding a good job, later marrying into the Wilcox family when Blaire was older.

Charlotte met them when Blaire was in high school, so she didn't know firsthand of their struggles from when Blaire was little.

Blaire had told her they never went without, but it wasn't uncommon they turned a pack of instant noodles into a full meal. Not uncommon for college students, but not the best for a developing child.

"So you're the new human?"

Charlotte blinked against the sunlight, focusing on the trio of girls standing in front of them. "I guess that's me?" She side-eyed Blaire and Riley.

"What's your name?" the middle girl asked, her head angled, shoulder-length strands of honeycomb brassy hair falling to the side. She wore tailored jeans and a fitted, soft-looking blouse that, while pretty, looked too heavy for the humidity.

"Charlotte," she said with hesitation.

The shortest girl on the left, who looked not much taller than Charlotte, smiled. "I'm Piper."

Returning her smile, Charlotte said, "Nice to meet you. I like your shoes."

The girl wore a pair of velvet platform Mary Janes in cherry red. They looked stunning with her pencil dress in solid black. Her jet-black hair was in a high ponytail tied off with a big red ribbon. She screamed rockabilly, and if Riley hadn't returned her attention to whatever distracted her on her phone, she'd no doubt have said something about the girl's fun style.

"Lindsay," the tallest one on the right said. She looked uncomfortable, twisting the end of her loose blonde braid between her fingers. Did Charlotte make her uncomfortable, or was it her friend in the middle who seemed standoffish?

“Right. Names aside,” the middle one said with a dismissive wave. She didn’t give *her* name.

Whatever. These types were everywhere, and she could spot them a mile away. For some people, high school never ended.

“Why are you here, exactly?”

“Because I have a scholarship.” She didn’t know if it was safe to mention the whole Korrena thing or not.

The girl scoffed, not even attempting to disguise her disdain. “Scholarship? You didn’t even pay to be here? At least this human did, and she has a reason to be here.”

Riley’s head jerked up. “Charlotte has every right to be here, so why don’t you go on and leave her alone, Alex?”

“Besides, I didn’t pay to be here either,” Blaire said, giving Alex a shrewd look. “The Blackthorn Clan funded my way because my Korrena goes here.”

“Well,” Alex started, and Charlotte didn’t know if the red spreading over her cheeks was from embarrassment, anger, or overheating from the outfit she wore. “What’s her excuse?”

“Noneya,” Riley sniped.

“None-what?”

“Noneya. None of your business,” Piper said with a snicker.

Alex gave her a scathing look. “Thanks for clearing that up.”

“You’re welcome!”

The bright and bubbly voice counter to the sarcasm made Charlotte want to laugh. Piper knew what she was doing. It was clear she didn’t agree with Alex’s mean girl routine any more than Lindsay did. In fact, Lindsay looked like she wanted the ground to open up and swallow her whole.

Having enough of this after seeing how uncomfortable Alex made her own friends, Charlotte squared her shoulders and said, “I think I have the right to be here.”

“Oh yeah? Why’s that?”

“Because my Korrena also attends. Why else do you think my memory is intact?”

The way Alex’s face flickered through a series of emotions from shock, to confusion, to disgust made Charlotte laugh.

“You have a Korrena? That’s so cool! I wish I had mine,” Lindsay finally said, smiling with a dreamy expression.

“Who?” Alex demanded in a sharp voice.

“My brother, now go away.”

Alex snapped her gaze to Riley. “Aiden?”

The girl’s tone shifted swiftly from angry to nervous. How well did she know him?

“Mmhm.” Riley didn’t look up from her phone, as if Alex wasn’t worth her attention.

“No, but he’s—”

“Still not interested in you.” Riley tapped her heels on the fountain, unable to sit still. She looked over at Charlotte. “She had a crush on him when we were kids, and while she doesn’t talk to him that much, she never got over it.” She looked at Alex again. “If you didn’t bother talking to him for years, why would you expect him to be available whenever you were ready?”

Alex spluttered. “I didn’t!” She crossed her arms. “I just thought…” She glanced to the side. “I talk to him now,” she said, almost too low to hear.

Riley lifted a brow, the glitter in her eyeshadow catching the sunlight.

“Forget it.” Alex huffed, spinning on her heel and storming away.

“We’re really sorry about her. She’s weird about humans,” Lindsay said, giving an apologetic smile. "It really was nice to meet you."

"Yeah. Welcome to the academy. Lindsay and I share a dorm on the first floor of the third building down." Piper pointed in the direction of the dorm buildings. "Fourth room on the right side. If you ever wanna hang out, come find us."

"Sure. Thanks. I'll do that."

"Great!" Piper grabbed Lindsay's arm and pulled her in the direction Alex had disappeared toward the dorms.

Charlotte watched them until they rounded the main building and turned to look at Blaire, who laughed.

"Well, I'm impressed."

"What do you mean?"

"My first day around the students, I got attacked and almost bitten. I'd say your introduction to the academy is going a lot smoother than mine did."

"Almost bitten?" She looked around with caution. She thought the students didn't drink from live sources because of the ample supply of blood packets.

Riley hopped up, the chain belt of her pleated black skirt tinkling. "Not everyone is nice, but you're not in danger. Those guys aren't here anymore, and they were asshats."

If Charlotte could meet others like Piper and Lindsay, maybe her time at Blackthorn Academy might not be so bad.

"So none of them have a Korrena?"

Riley shook her head. "No, that's why Piper and Lindsay room together. Alex's roommate moved out recently when she found her Korrena. They're in my building now."

Charlotte looked up at the fluffy white clouds moving across the blue sky. "They looked our age."

"Piper is twenty-three, actually. She's in her last year. Lindsay is eighteen, though. Alex is twenty-one."

Turning her head to look at Riley, Charlotte asked, "Why are there so many students without Korrena mates? If you're supposed to find your pair by your late teens, how come so many college students are without one?"

Blaire and Riley shared a look.

"The magic that keeps the cycle of Korrena pairings going is dying," Blaire said, a serious expression crossing her face. "It's part of the prophecy. If I don't do what I'm supposed to, the entire thing falls apart."

"Over the years, the number of our kind who discover their Korrena at the 'right age' has taken a nosedive." Riley shifted from foot to foot. "Mama didn't get hers until eighty-one. I don't know why they haven't updated the books. It'd feel less damning if they officially raised the average age, but no one knows anymore what's normal." She looked up at the stained glass windows on the front of the main building. "Besides, if everything fixes itself when Blaire does her thing, it'll go back to what they teach us, so I guess that's why they don't change it. But who knows."

"Do your siblings have theirs?"

"You know about Heather's husband, right?"

"Yeah." Charlotte remembered Riley's older sister had a husband and kids, but wasn't sure if they were paired.

"Yeah. Greg is her Korrena. Our other brother hasn't found his, though. It's why he's so focused on his restaurants."

Blaire put down the napkin she used to clean her fingers. "I hate that everyone is suffering because of me." Both Charlotte and Riley turned to look at her at the same time. "What? Like you said, if I do my 'thing'—if I were a Vasirian—the magic would be strong enough to make others find their pairs."

"Maybe," Riley conceded. "But none of us really know that. The Oracle said you were the only human who could be a Korrena, and well..." She held her hands out to Charlotte as if presenting her as a prize on a game show. "Exhibit A of how wrong that is."

Something didn't seem right. If everything in the prophecy she learned from the others came to pass so far, then why, when she and Aiden connected, did it all go topsy-turvy?

32

Vulnerable

A breeze blew through the courtyard as Aiden led Charlotte from the main building after dinner. The sounds of the bubbling fountain and low conversations from other students returning to their dorms filled the air around them.

He didn't know how to address the topic he wanted to with her. Of all his friends, he always had the right words, and gave advice to everyone, but with Charlotte, he felt on unstable ground.

"It smells so good out here," she said, stopping to look at the perennial flowerbeds lining the front of the main building.

He tucked his hands in his jeans. "Depending on the time of year, the smells change. Dogwood trees bloom, the apricot blossom trees in the grove over on the other side of the drive, the cascading jasmine on the other side along the hedge maze… There's always something in bloom."

It dawned on him how weird it might be for a guy to know so much about the flora on campus, but his mom rambled on and on about it when they first took a look at the academy grounds before his freshman year.

She smiled and shook her head. "My moms would love it. They don't have the time to keep anything alive in our yard with the businesses taking up so much of their time."

They continued their walk to the dorm buildings in silence.

He sniffed and looked over at Charlotte. "So, how are you adapting?" *Smooth.* "I mean..." He groaned, bending his head back and closing his eyes. "I don't get why this is so hard."

"What's wrong?" She looked up at him as they walked. "I'm doing fine. Probably because we're not in classes yet, so I'm not interacting with as many people outside of our circle, but I have met a few people. Most of them are nice."

"Most?"

"Well, all but this one girl named Alex." The puckered expression on Charlotte's face, where it looked like she swallowed a lemon, made Aiden think there was more to it. "I think she likes you."

There it is.

"I don't know if anyone does around here, but I'm not interested in anyone else. I told you it doesn't work for me like that, and besides, I have you. You're my Korrena. No one else matters. They didn't matter before I knew."

"What do you mean?" Charlotte stopped and turned to him.

He licked his lower lip and pulled it into his mouth, his teeth showing as he tried to sort out how to say what he felt without scaring her away. *Screw it.* "You were mine before I saw my mark. It wasn't the Korrena pull. I felt something for you. Genuine. I know this whole biology thing heightens it, but I wanted you even without it."

Her lips parted as she looked at him in surprise. He wanted to kiss her, but he needed her words more than her lips in this moment. Did she feel the same?

"Well, I don't get the whole Korrena thing yet, so I know my feelings for you aren't influenced by anything else. At least that I'm aware of. I thought you were cute when I first met you."

"Cute?" The corner of his mouth ticked up in a teasing smile when her eyes went big and her cheeks flushed pink, making her freckles stand out. Did all redheads blush so easily?

"Not cute like a baby! I mean. Um. You were handsome. Hot." She spun on her heel and started walking toward the dorm. "You're mean."

He rushed to catch up to her and slid his arm around her shoulder. "I'm not mean. I was only teasing."

The cute *hmph* sound she made in response settled his nerves about how she felt about her time at Blackthorn Academy. If she weren't happy, she wouldn't be able to joke with him this way. Blaire and Riley were right. She would be okay.

Approaching the door to their dorm, Charlotte stopped short, and the shot of fear hit him with all the subtlety of a bucket of ice water to the face.

"What's wrong?" he demanded, stepping around her and drawing up when he saw what lay in front of their door.

A pink rose lay on a piece of paper in front of their dorm door on the floor.

"I thought you killed him," she whispered, her voice breaking.

I thought I did too.

He marched forward and snatched up the rose and paper, unlocking their dorm and letting Charlotte in ahead of him.

He skimmed the note.

Sweetest Cherry,

I see you have found your way into our world. I hoped to keep you away. To protect you from all this as the only gift I could give you. The only way I could show you I love you, even though I can't have you by my side. Unfortunately, it isn't possible now. Now that you know everything, you will face the consequences of your association with your blonde friend. A pity when childhood friendships turn into nightmares.

Sweet dreams for now,
J

J? Who the fuck is J?

He folded the note and put it in his pocket. Charlotte didn't need something more to upset her right then. He'd show her, but after he settled her fear.

Stepping inside their dorm, he found Charlotte pacing in front of her bed. The trembling fear radiating from her set his teeth on edge. He wanted to throttle the threat, but the threat wasn't here for him to unleash on.

Throwing the rose into the wastebasket next to the door, he approached her, hands coming up to rest on her upper arms from behind. She stopped and sank into his embrace when he slid his arms around her front and held her close, face buried on the top of her head, breathing in her scent.

"He's not dead," she whispered.

"He is."

"No." Her curls brushed his lips as she shook her head negatively. "He must've healed."

"I tore his throat out. There's no coming back from that."

She spun in his arms and looked up at him, taking a step back from his hold. "Then how?" She motioned to the door. "How did they know to deliver a rose? A *pink* rose. Not many know about the stalker, and I know y'all didn't do it." She sniffed and swallowed hard. After a moment of silence, she looked up at him with widened eyes. "Maybe you didn't kill the stalker."

"What do you mean?"

"The guy in the alley outside the club called me Cherry, so I assumed he was the stalker, but so did idiots at the diner. I've always hated the name. Maybe it was a coincidence."

With the note also referring to Charlotte as Cherry, it didn't sound illogical. He didn't think the use of the name was so common, but if two different people used it, and people at the diner… What did this mean for them? Who was the man he killed other than a rogue who bit his Korrena? Whoever the man in the alley was, he still deserved his fate. He seemed so determined to capture Charlotte with the way he demanded Noah get her.

Aiden cursed under his breath. *Noah.* Noah stayed close to Charlotte in Athens, and now he showed up in Rosebrook Valley when she did? Something about that rankled him and had his instincts on high alert. Noah knew more than he let on. Was he her stalker? Then who was J? Did he use the letter to throw them off his trail?

"Aiden, how did he get on campus? I thought the security here was tighter than Fort Knox."

"It is. I don't know how he got in, but we have to tell the headmistress so she can inform Blackthorn Security their safeguards are compromised."

He tried to tell himself her fear of the rogue Vasirian wasn't a generalized fear of his kind, but that ugly black feeling in the back of his mind became harder to ignore when he felt her apprehension on a visceral level.

Charlotte said she didn't see him as a monster after seeing him at his most primal—had shown him she accepted him—but did she harbor lingering hesitation about his world? She didn't balk at their consumption of blood. Didn't seem opposed to a lot of their way of life. But when faced with his fangs, the prophecy in action, and the violence of the rogues, would she still keep such confidence in her ability to handle it? He had to trust her the way she trusted him.

Hoping to ease her mind, he said, "They won't get to you here. I don't know how he got on campus to deliver that, or if he had someone deliver it, but I won't leave you."

She blinked several times in rapid succession. "Um. Hate to break it to you, but a rogue bit me before and Riley was *right there*." Her mirthless laugh made him tense. "What makes you think the stalker won't get to me?"

His voice hardened. "Because I won't leave your side until that piece of shit is found." The thrum of his pulse increased as his blood pressure rose. Did she think he wasn't capable of keeping her safe?

Charlotte flinched at his tone, and his spine stiffened.

"I'm sorry." He turned away and stalked across the room before he said something in anger he would regret. He collapsed in his chair and sighed when the bathroom door closed behind him.

Tugging the note from his pocket, he shook his head. He didn't get a chance to talk to her about it. Tossing it on his bedside table, he pulled out his phone and called Lukas. "We have a problem," he said before Lukas even said hello.

"Charlotte?"

"Her stalker."

"Isn't he dead?"

"I thought so, but there was a note and rose left at our door for her."

Lukas cursed, and Aiden heard movement before Lukas said, "I put it on speakerphone. Blaire, Riley, and Seth are here."

"What's going on?" Riley asked.

"Charlotte got a rose and a note from her stalker. At least I think it's him. The rose was pink, fitting the stalker's MO. I don't think the rogue I killed was the guy."

"The fuck?" Seth said, his voice incredulous.

Blaire asked, "What's the note say?"

He grabbed the note and read it to them before tossing it back on the bedside table.

"Who's J?" Riley asked.

"That's what I want to know. I need to ask her," he said, rubbing a hand over his face as he tilted his head back.

Lukas muttered, "I want to know how they got on school grounds."

"Did you call the headmistress?" Seth asked. "Riley, stop moving. I'm about to fall off the bed."

"I'm trying to get close enough to listen."

"You can hear just fine right there."

Aiden couldn't even find amusement in the back-and-forth between Seth and Riley. His fingers scraped through his hair, and he tugged at the crown of his head in frustration. "I think the rogues are trying to get to Blaire through Charlotte."

"It sounds that way from what the note says," Lukas said.

"Though it sure sounds like one of them has taken an extra liking to Charlotte." Riley's words made sense. The additional words of love and obsession weren't necessary if this was all about Blaire.

"I haven't showed Charlotte the note yet, but when I do, I think we should take it to Headmistress Velastra."

Riley asked, "Why haven't you shown her?"

"She was upset, and I said something that made it worse. I think she's still afraid of us, even if she doesn't act like it."

Riley's loud yell and incoherent rambling came rapid-fire-fast through the tinny phone speaker, and rustling sounded on the line until Lukas's voice became clearer.

"I took it off speakerphone. Riley is having a fit about proving we are safe. Seth's trying to calm her down."

"I don't blame her."

"Why?"

"Because our world isn't like Charlotte's. You went through this with Blaire, remember? You tried to drive her away from here because you were afraid *for* her yourself."

"True," Lukas conceded. "But things are different. We understand this situation now. I don't think Charlotte's afraid of us, but she has every right to be afraid of the rogues and a stalker. I mean, fuck, you were killed, man." Lukas's voice cracked on the last words.

The reminder of what happened threatened to trigger memories he didn't want to experience. He closed his eyes and counted backward from ten until he exhaled heavily, focusing on the truths he knew: He was alive. Charlotte didn't fear him. He didn't represent his world, just like Charlotte didn't represent the human world as a whole. There were bad people to fear in both.

"Listen, she'll be out of the shower soon. I need to get off here."

"Call us if you need."

"Yeah. Tell Riley not to confront her, though. I don't want to make things worse."

"I got you."

"Oh, I'm gonna run and grab a blood packet. Can you come down and hang out on this floor until I'm back? I don't feel comfortable leaving her alone."

"No problem. I'll head down now."

He stood. He suspected Charlotte might wait him out in the bathroom until he went to bed, so grabbing a packet now to give her space sounded like a good idea. If it made her comfortable to go to sleep without him around, he wouldn't wait on her, but he wouldn't leave her vulnerable—not more than she already was.

The problem with not being able to sleep meant finding himself experiencing a different form of torture than what awaited him in his nightmares.

Lying in the darkness, he tried to keep his attention off the girl lying in the other bed who stole his heart. It took all his willpower to fight the urge to go to her in her bed. The need to be close to her made his skin itch.

The ache radiating through his chest from missing her body heat and the feel of her smooth skin brushing against his when they slept together made the possibility of sleep a fleeting fantasy.

He wished he could crawl into her bed and feel her curl against his side.

He closed his eyes as visions of their nights in Athens together trickled into his mind. Sometimes she would unconsciously sling her leg over his and wrap her arm over his chest in a full body hug.

He even missed the nights where she seemed less relaxed, and he ended up with her foot jammed into his ribs or a set of toes in his face.

Sure, they were in the same room together, but the longing to be physically touching made it hard to breathe sometimes. It felt like desperation. Ever since they returned to Rosebrook Valley, the distance became painful. Now sharing the same room, the pain lessened, but it brought little comfort.

He tried to match his breathing to her soft, deep breaths. Tried to relax. He really tried. But the longer he watched her chest rise and fall with every deep breath she took, studied the way her legs looked bathed in moonlight from the window, and listened to every little sigh that pushed past her soft lips, the more his cock thickened.

He pressed the heel of his hand against the base of his erection to ease the ache.

Seeing her in his T-shirt did things to his lizard brain that he wouldn't admit to anyone. She had plenty of her own clothes now, but every night she stole the T-shirt he'd worn for the day before going to bed. Except tonight. Tonight, his hamper stood open. She'd grabbed another one he wore recently, since she'd gone to bed before he changed.

He knew it was his scent. While it might not all be biology making her want to surround herself with his scent, he understood the need. They taught them all about it in the Korrena education classes growing up.

He wondered if she sought it for comfort or something more.

Either way, the action did nothing to quell the growing desire he felt.

When she rolled over, putting her back to him, hitching a leg over the blankets, he bit the inside of his cheek to hold back the groan at the sight of her sleep shorts riding up and exposing the bottom of her backside and the expanse of her thigh.

The position, with her leg forward, thighs slightly spread, teased him with a shadowed view of a place he knew all too well felt like heaven on earth.

Gripping his shaft through his athletic shorts, he willed himself to calm down. She didn't need to wake and find him in this state. He needed sleep or he wouldn't be able to protect her like he should.

When she murmured something soft and breathy in her sleep, he groaned.

It was going to be a long night.

33

The Oracle

Waking with the intense urge to empty her bladder, Charlotte climbed out of the bed on wobbly legs. She felt so tired. All the stress with the recent changes to her life had steamrolled her brain. She worried everything would finally catch up to her, and the depression that had receded to manageable levels upon her return to Rosebrook Valley would return with a vengeance.

After finishing her business, she stepped back into the moonlit room, her gaze drifting to Aiden lying tangled in his covers.

She didn't fully understand what had happened earlier.

The antagonistic way she spoke to him made her feel terrible. She didn't mean to sound like she didn't trust him. She did. Fear had taken over, and she freaked. Not only because her stalker lived, but also because he'd found his way onto Blackthorn Academy's campus like he did at UGA.

Aiden's frustration was justified. She didn't hold it against him.

It hurt her heart to put him in danger by having a stalker. From her understanding, rogues weren't an everyday part of their lives. One so focused on her, who had attacked her, put a target on Aiden as much as it did her mothers. Even if they were both Vasirian, it still didn't change the reality that her being at the academy put Aiden and her friends at risk.

She banded her arms around herself.

No one had ever made her feel the way Aiden did in her entire life. She had never felt for anyone the way she did him.

Walking across the dorm room, she lowered herself onto the edge of his bed, trying not to wake him. Her gaze moved across his face, studying his features.

She wondered if agreeing to stay at Blackthorn was the best thing for him.

Reaching out, she traced his cheekbone and stubbled jaw with her fingers. He groaned, turning into her touch, his brows flexing.

With everything that happened to Blaire since that fateful day where the headmistress came to the diner and offered her an escape, and how out-of-the-loop Charlotte had been through it all, she didn't truly feel like she belonged in their world.

Her presence brought more danger, and she was an inconvenience for being naïve to their ways.

Lowering her hand to her lap, she went to stand, but paused when she saw an open letter on his bedside table that hadn't been there earlier.

She wasn't a nosy person, and wouldn't touch it in normal circumstances, but seeing the cursive "Sweetest Cherry" at the top had all her senses on high alert. Snatching up the paper, she began reading.

Blaire? Blaire was the only blonde friend she had. It made sense.

They wanted to hurt Blaire for her role in the prophecy. What did this have to do with her stalker, though? Never had he said anything about love. *Who is J?*

Placing the paper back on the table, she stood and crawled into her own bed.

Why did Aiden keep the letter from her?

A sick, oily feeling settled in her stomach.

Even with the stalker being a Vasirian, and his ultimate goal getting to Blaire, his obvious sick fascination with Charlotte made one thing clear to her: if she stayed, she put them all in danger.

She needed a break. A break from feeling like the walls were closing in. Away from the gnawing need to crawl into bed with Aiden just because he made her feel safe.

Not wanting to wake him, she decided not to change clothes. No one walked around the campus this late from what she noticed from the window, and with the heat, her sleep shorts and his T-shirt would suffice.

She crept over to the closet and pulled out a pair of flip-flops, carrying them to the door. She wouldn't put them on inside the dorm to avoid the noise.

Leaving the room, she wandered out of the dorm building and across the campus until she found herself at the back of the main building, looking at the dark forest looming in front of her.

Did they have fences somewhere in the forest or on the other side? She sure didn't see any keeping her out of the forest, so maybe someone could get on campus that way. *Nope. Not going in there.* She shook her head and stepped back from the forest, ready to go back the way she came.

"What brings you out here, child?"

She shrieked, spinning on her feet, and almost falling when her flip-flop caught on the edge of the cobblestone.

A few feet away from her on the path stood a woman with hair as black as night shot through with silver strands pulled tight in a bun at her nape, dressed in a long dark robe with glimmering chains. Charlotte couldn't make out many details with the limited lighting at the back of the academy, but the robes had some sort of design along the bottom, hood, and draped sleeves.

"I'm sorry for scaring you."

Straightening, she smoothed her hands over the front of Aiden's T-shirt to give her something to do while she composed herself. "I'm fine. Um." She looked around the empty path and the darkened forest behind her. "Can I help you?" She didn't want to be rude, but even with a school full of fanged students, someone wandering around at night in robes seemed weird.

"Maybe not, but you might be able to help me." The faceted jewels at the ends of the chains around the woman's waist glittered red when the moonlight caught them as she walked past Charlotte over to the edge of the forest, looking into the shadowed depths. "You know only the peak of the iceberg of secrets in our world. In order for you to understand your place here, you need to know the truth."

"Who are you?"

"I am called the Oracle."

Charlotte angled her head to the side, trying to get a better look at the woman's face. The age lines discernable by moonlight and gray in her hair said she was maybe fifty or sixty, but she was supposedly hundreds of years old. It wasn't that Charlotte didn't believe the headmistress when she had explained how Vasirian aged, it simply seemed too unreal at the time, even with her claim of being in her seventies. Seeing a living person as old as the Oracle helped solidify the reality of it all.

"You are aware of the Blood War, but not everything."

"The Blood War?"

"A time when our king's great-grandfather Rosendo Blackthorn ordered the execution of every witch, warlock, and pregnant Vasirian woman to prevent their powers from growing or their children overtaking the Blackthorn bloodline."

She knew it by description, but not by name, and not in that much detail.

"The humans with magical blood knew of our existence then. We lived in harmony together and found our Korrena pairs among them. The severance of power when Rosendo sought to destroy the bloodlines resulted in many of my kind no longer being able to find the one destined for them. As you know, Blaire is the key to restoring that bloodline."

"How do you know what I know?"

"Because, child, I know and see many things." The Oracle smiled over her shoulder the way a mother would when indulging her child. "I've also been kept up to date through Dominic and your headmistress."

Charlotte curled her fingers around the bottom of Aiden's T-shirt. "So when Blaire becomes a Vasirian like you, everyone will find their Korrena again?"

"Among other things."

"Like what?"

"The magic that lives in her blood—the blood of a witch—will spread upon her awakening, rousing dormant magic in those like you. The magic that keeps the Vasirian strong and alive will strengthen. As it is, we grow weaker with every year that passes."

The Oracle turned fully to face Charlotte.

"If Blaire doesn't become a Vasirian, our future dies with her. Not only do we not find our pairs, but our preternatural abilities will fade away, reducing our lifespans to that of a human. Without magic, those older—like myself—will become dust."

Charlotte gasped.

The Oracle shrugged. "Human organs cannot survive hundreds of years. It is only natural it would happen."

"That's awful."

"This is true. It is a terrible fate, but one we might face. I foresee mass hysteria arising among humans who witness those they work alongside aging at an alarming rate as their bodies catch up with their organs. The ripple effect across the world will be devastating."

Charlotte curled her toes against her flip-flops. The thought of people around her small town withering away and dying in minutes sounded terrifying. She didn't want to imagine people with friends and coworkers witnessing that. She couldn't picture the headmistress as an old woman.

"With our preternatural abilities gone, we then become susceptible to human ailments without the ability to heal. There will be no children born when our reproductive functions fail without the magic that keeps us existing. But none of that will matter to most of us when the time comes."

"What? I don't understand."

How could the Oracle say it didn't matter if their kind didn't have children anymore?

If they started dying without their magic, wouldn't they want to reproduce to restore their population? That's what humans did with animals on the verge of extinction. Her nose wrinkled when she considered the comparison to humans, but it was the best parallel she could draw. Humans had entire breeding programs to restore animal populations on the verge of disappearing because of disease or human interference.

"Blood, child. Blood."

"Huh?"

"While we will be similar to humans in most every way, our existence still relies on the consumption of blood. No matter how our magic dwindles, this need will never extinguish. Without magic, blood will become like a poison to our bodies until we can no longer consume it. At that time, we will succumb to *sanguis manie* and—"

"You'll go mad and die," Charlotte finished for her, her voice flat.

"Precisely."

"Where do I fit into this? Why am I here? They said Blaire was supposed to be the only descendant."

The Oracle smiled and her gaze moved over Charlotte's head, staring up at the stars in the clear night sky as she spoke.

"The stars have revealed new truths. A danger to both your kind and mine. The balance and restoration are at risk, saved only by a friend's sacrifice. An untapped, lost power is the conduit for a bond deeper than that of lovers to overcome even death itself. But the heart must be open."

"What does that mean?"

"It is one of the prophecies that has come to fruition in Blaire's path to restore our rightful bloodline."

Charlotte tried to remember the words, picking them apart and fitting them to any information already shared with her, but she hadn't known the words were related to some prophecy or she would have paid better attention.

Sensing her struggle, the Oracle stepped closer. "Aiden sacrificed his life to save Blaire. Only he would be strong enough to do that. With his death, and her unfailing devotion to him—her open heart—unwilling to give him up in the face of everyone resigned to the loss, a door unlocked on Blaire's magic, and she was able to bring him back to us." With a soft smile, she said, "Your awakening was made possible by that door unlocking."

"I don't understand. You said others with dormant magic like me… does that mean I have magical blood? Am I a witch?"

The gears in her head worked overtime as she tried to make sense of all the information dumped on her tonight when all she wanted was fresh air to get her head on straight. She never imagined her entire perception of everything would turn upside down.

The Oracle moved to stand beside her, turned opposite to the direction Charlotte faced. She lowered her voice. "Even if you were to remove yourself from the path you are on now, it will not thwart what is to come. The wheels are set in motion. But know this: the others are stronger with your presence. Never doubt your place with them. Your soul was meant to be alongside theirs. You may not see your own strength yet, but it exists."

Charlotte started, head snapping to the side as she met the Oracle's knowing gaze. Somehow this mysterious being knew of her insecurity.

"You belong here, Charlotte. They need you."

With those final words, the Oracle stepped away along the path that followed the back of the academy toward the staff buildings.

The enigmatic woman hadn't answered the questions about Charlotte's blood or if she were a witch, or even how her presence tied to the prophecy, but one thing the Oracle did for her was give her reassurance. If she had the power to receive and give prophecies that shaped the future, then maybe her words held merit.

Squeezing her eyes shut, she took a long, steady breath and nodded to herself. She had to try. If she made the others stronger, then she had to try. The Vasirian needed Blaire. Blaire needed her. She didn't think she could let go of Aiden, anyway.

She only hoped the strength she gave them overrode the danger she brought by bringing a stalker and other rogues to their doorstep.

34

OUTSIDER

With the new day came a new resolve. If the Oracle believed Charlotte belonged in their world, then something had to give. It wasn't only by her own hand that she felt like an outsider. Her friends had kept her in the dark about everything; and while that might have been for her protection, it still stung. They could have given her *something*.

Trusted her.

It did more than make her feel bad that they didn't trust her to not say something. It made her feel excluded and alone.

Aiden was in the shower when she woke up, so she got dressed and took the note from his bedside table. She needed to confront him about it.

Another item on the take-no-prisoners agenda of the morning.

Now, standing in the cafeteria watching her friends talk amongst themselves with smiles and laughter, she questioned if she should say anything at all and risk bringing down the mood.

Her crescent moon earrings slapped her neck when she shook her head from side to side. *Focus.*

One thing her ma always taught her was sometimes to make progress you needed to ruffle a few feathers.

Aiden had already grabbed a tray with breakfast and his blood packet. She had told him to go ahead while she got her drink, needing to get her head in order before she did what needed to be done.

With a tight swallow, she strode toward the table, her resolve in place.

Everyone fell silent when she approached, making her shoulders tense.

"What now?"

Riley and Blaire exchanged a look, and Charlotte gripped her tray. Placing it down on the table, she sat, movements stiff, and it took all her self-control to regulate her breathing.

"Are you okay?" Layla asked.

"Why wouldn't I be?"

"Well, the rose…"

Charlotte glanced at Aiden. He'd told them. Instead of waiting for her, or even asking if she would be okay with sharing something that scared her, he'd taken it upon himself to share information without her consent.

She tucked her lower lip into her mouth, taking a long inhale through her nose and blinking several times.

"Charlotte?" Aiden turned in his chair, his warm hand landing on her arm.

Of course he sensed her emotions. Even if she tried to school her features, her heart cried and bled at the feeling of betrayal. It didn't matter if the subject revolved around her, they still kept her out of their discussions.

"So I met the Oracle," she said, her voice pitching sharply before she cleared her throat. "Nice woman. A little cryptic. Wandering around in floor-length robes in the dark seemed a little unhinged, though." She hoped the change in subject would both calm her and deflect attention from her internal pity party.

Did she take her medicine last night or this morning? She felt worse than she had in days. With the news of her stalker still being alive, she hadn't paid enough attention. It only took one missed dose to mess with her mood.

Blaire stirred crumbled bacon into her cheese grits. "When did you meet the Oracle?"

"Last night."

"You were with me last night," Aiden said, confused.

"I woke up to go to the bathroom and needed some fresh air. Took a walk around campus and ran into her." She spread butter over the silver-dollar pancakes on her plate.

Aiden's fists clenched on the table. "It's not safe for you to go out by yourself."

Pausing her pouring of syrup, she looked at him, her upper teeth bared in a small sneer. "I've been going out for months in Athens while a stalker roamed around. With both humans and rogue Vasirian wandering around there, I probably was in more danger there than wandering around a closed university campus behind iron gates." She set down the syrup. "Unless there's something more I'm unaware of?" She looked around the table, meeting everyone's eyes, a challenge in her own.

"No. But…"

"Aiden. Nothing happened." She sat back in her chair. "The Oracle expanded on the things the headmistress told me. The things y'all've told me."

"Did she say anything new?" Dominic asked, opening a blood packet. "Something to explain all this?"

"Some of it was vague."

Blaire snorted. "Surprise, surprise."

"But she did say my soul belonged with all of yours."

Riley squealed, clapping her hands, bouncing in her seat. "She's the sixth!"

"What?" Lukas said, looking over at her.

Her hands came down on the table as she sat forward. "Remember? The Oracle said we were all supposed to be together. Like kindred spirits or something. Reincarnated."

"I remember that, but what the hell do you mean by sixth?"

"She told us there was a sixth person who had yet to find us," Blaire said.

Charlotte looked around the table. "But there are…" She counted with her finger pointing to each person. "Seven of you before I came along."

"I'm not part of that revelation," Dominic said, sitting back and crossing his ankle over his knee. "But I'm apparently connected to her future." He nodded his head in Riley's direction.

Seth grumbled and took a bite out of his biscuit.

Charlotte's lips pulled in. *Ookaay. A sore subject to avoid. Got it.*

"I'm not either," Layla said, her French tip manicure tapping on the side of her water bottle. "I'm learning things like you are. I mean, I obviously know all about our species and Korrenas, but all this prophecy stuff you're finding out about?" Layla paused, swallowing the tasty pancakes.

Charlotte nodded for her to continue.

"It's new to me. I didn't start hanging out with them until last semester—something like that."

"So you think it's Charlotte?" Seth asked Riley.

"I do. It's the only thing that makes sense. She's Aiden's Korrena. Besides, the Oracle said her soul is connected to ours, so that's like writing it in the clouds with a plane by Oracle standards."

"What?" Charlotte had no idea what Riley meant.

"The Oracle can be incredibly vague," Aiden said.

"She often talks in circles because she can't tell us information directly unless the Celestial Conclave grants the right," Dominic added. "It risks upsetting the balance of things, which could influence a change to fate."

"Did she say anything else?" Riley asked.

Charlotte explained everything she could remember from last night, hesitating to say anything about her awakening and blood. The Oracle wasn't clear on the information for her to understand it enough to explain.

"Listen, there's something else we need to talk about," she said after they absorbed the information about the Oracle.

"What's up?" Riley said.

All her earlier resolve wilted and turned to dust inside. She didn't feel as comfortable broaching the subject after their productive conversation about the Oracle. She should have confronted them first, but she didn't need Aiden knowing he'd hurt her. The familiar tightening in her chest made her realize she needed to do this or nothing would change.

Keeping her eyes on the last bites of her tiny pancakes, her words came out soft but clear. "I've felt left out. I always felt that way before I came here, and I know there's a reason for it now, even if it still feels bad, but…" She looked up, meeting Blaire's eyes. "Even though I'm now in this world, you're still excluding me."

Blaire dropped her gaze down to her tray.

Riley looked at Seth before looking back at Charlotte. "You're not excluded. You're our friend." Layla nodded her agreement.

Lukas leaned over, his shoulder bumping Blaire's. "I know Blaire has felt guilty leaving you in the dark for a long time. Even without her telling me, I felt it." His hand went into his hair to push it away from his face. He had a habit of doing that. She wondered why he didn't cut his long hair if it kept bothering him. "I'm not good at this sort of thing, but Riley's right. You're our friend. You were important to Blaire, and that made you important to us. We got to know you, and—"

"Now you're one of us!" Riley said, voice firm, but her eyes looked sad.

"I don't know you, really, but you seem nice," Dominic added.

They all sounded so sincere, so why did it feel like it wasn't true when they kept things from her? She needed to know why. Before she could say anything, Aiden spoke.

"You belong here, Charlotte. With me. With them. No one excludes you anymore. We had to before to protect you. It hurt us to do it, but we needed to make sure you were safe. If they wiped your memory, they would have to take away your memory that we even existed. What we had before wouldn't matter. You wouldn't know us."

Aiden's words made her feel guilty, but she couldn't stop the weird feeling that he still was keeping her separated from his world. She might exist in their world now, but they still all treated her with kid gloves, shielding her from knowing things or handling things they deemed not appropriate for a human.

Blaire was human, but she was a witch with magical blood. If Charlotte understood correctly, Blaire's magic protected her.

As a lowly human, Charlotte was a liability.

Steeling her courage, she slipped her hand into her pocket and pulled out the note from Aiden's bedside table, tossing it on the table, open for Aiden to see the words on the page. "You all clearly know about this too, if you know about the rose," she said, tone flat and accusing.

He cringed.

She turned in her seat, forcing him to make eye contact with her. He wouldn't look away from her when he gave her the answer she needed. She needed to see the truth in his eyes. "Do you even want me in this world or not?"

He gaped at her.

"You never asked me to be part of this world. Never said that's what *you* wanted. You've gone with the flow, accepting whatever has been laid out for you. You haven't even told me how you feel about it." Her hands tightened into fists on her thighs. "I've only heard the older adults like the headmistress tell me we're soulmates, but I haven't heard once if it's what *you* want, or anything else."

She shook her head.

"I understand the concept of it. The Korrena pairing. I don't read the books Blaire and Riley do—video games are my hobby—but I'm familiar with the mythical world of true mates." Her laugh sounded hollow. "Well, it's not so mythical, after all." She forged on, even though it looked and felt like Aiden was on edge. Something tingled at the edge of her consciousness. An uncomfortable awareness that felt a little dark. "I don't know your feelings, and I'm not sure how you feel about all this."

"You know I want you," he said, voice hard.

"A lot of men have wanted me in my life. I'd be stupid to think you weren't attracted to me, considering what's happened between us, but your heart doesn't have to be in it to..." Her gaze shifted to the others at the table, as if realizing they were still listening. "Well, you know." She had gone on a tangent in her frustration and forgotten them. The varying degrees of surprise made her tense.

"I've told you about how I am with relationships." His eyes tightened at the corners. "With sex."

But was that really him or the Korrena bond? The more she learned, the more she wondered if the bond overrode his sexuality. He admitted to attraction before they had any form of emotional connection. It left her confused and unsure of his true feelings. He couldn't be angry with her for that. Her concern was valid.

"I know that, but is it not the bond?"

"Oh boy," Riley said, drawing Charlotte's attention. "We went through this," she said, glancing at Aiden with sadness in her eyes. Seth put his hand on hers on the table. "Seth hated the idea of a Korrena bond because he thought it was forced biology. We both almost rejected the bond when it presented itself because of it."

"Really?"

"Yeah. Biology makes your existing feelings stronger, and makes it easier to fit together, but if your heart isn't in it, it won't ever develop."

"The bond chooses pairs who are compatible and who fit together," Dominic added.

Charlotte looked back at Aiden. He still looked mad, but she wouldn't apologize for her worry. She said nothing that wasn't true. She didn't know what he wanted. He had said nothing. That wasn't on her. Even now, he remained silent.

She repeated her earlier question. "Do you even want me in your world?"

If she had to pinpoint the look on his face, she would say he seemed offended, but his tone sounded furious when he snapped, "Do you realize what all I've done to keep you safe in this world?" His voice dropped an octave, a sharp precision to his tone that cut into her like a knife. "What I did to keep you safe before you even knew about this world, when we thought a human was stalking you?" His jaw worked as he ground his teeth.

His anger and resentment mingled with her confusion and insecurity, a potent cocktail of turmoil in her belly that turned into something poisonous.

Her nose wrinkled as she narrowed her eyes. She couldn't mask her impertinent tone if she tried. "Don't confuse your savior complex with a genuine care for me."

Riley gasped.

"Aiden," Lukas said, a warning in his tone.

Charlotte looked up into Aiden's eyes. His shoulders shook with anger, his fist clenching and unclenching on the table as he stared down at her. His eyes flashed with a flare of glowing green at the edges of his iris. She looked at Lukas, not sure what was happening.

"It's the bond. We don't have the best control of our primal urges when it's new or unsealed."

She swallowed. He wouldn't hurt her, would he?

Aiden jerked in his seat as if she'd struck him.

Seth stood abruptly and strode around the table to stand behind Aiden, grabbing his shoulders and holding them in a firm grip. He lowered his head. "Calm down. She didn't mean it."

"You both are feeding each other's negative emotions," Dominic said, his gaze moving between her and Aiden.

"We've been through this with two pairs already," Lukas said. "First with me and Blaire, then with Riley and Seth. This is all too familiar."

Riley said firmly, "He won't hurt you."

Aiden's gaze snapped to Riley, a divot forming between his eyebrows.

"Aiden, you look five seconds away from tearing her head off," she scolded. "She needs to know that even like this you won't hurt her."

He looked back at Charlotte, and a pain tore through her chest as his features crumpled. "Never," he croaked. It seemed like he had trouble finding the ability to speak.

Licking her lips, she looked up into his eyes. "I'm sorry. I didn't mean what I said. I do genuinely want to know if the reason you did the things you did for me was because of a misplaced need to save anyone and everyone." She shook her head. "Maybe not misplaced, but a need to do those things. It's your nature. You take care of people. Protect the people around you. That doesn't mean you feel something else for them."

The cafeteria had cleared out at some point in their conversation, and she hadn't noticed. Her words sounded so loud in the vacant space.

Aiden took a measured breath, his shoulders lowering as Seth let him go. She could still feel his anger. He didn't like her questioning him. Was he upset she was questioning his feelings, or was he upset she'd put a spotlight on his protector habit? Had she done wrong in confronting him this way in front of the others? It put him in a vulnerable position, but he wouldn't be able to avoid answering her with all eyes on them. She needed those answers.

"You know, I've always joked about being the protector of the group. It's been a joke with everyone, so I go along with it, but I would *never* go out of my way like this for someone outside of the people in my circle—which you are now a part of, anyway. You weren't part of that when I made the choices I made. You were a friend, but you weren't deep in our world yet, and I didn't think you ever would be, and I still did what I did."

His fist clenched again, and his Adam's apple bobbed, but he pressed on.

"I wasn't even going to tell anyone, not even my best friend, about the mark I saw on your skin—to protect you," he snapped. "Even if it meant I'd never have you in the capacity of a Korrena mate, I was going to hide it to keep you safe."

"No," Riley whispered. "The sickness alone might kill you. Why would you do that?"

"Because I would do anything to keep her safe." Aiden's intense stare met Charlotte's. "*Anything.*" His gaze moved down to her mouth when she licked her lips, not sure how to respond to his enmity. "I've felt so much for you for such a long time. I can feel the bond growing, but I can feel my true feelings growing the more we're together."

He hit his chest with his fist where his heart resided. "If you can't see how I care about you and that I want you around, then I don't know what to say." His tone grew indignant. "I don't know how to be any clearer. You were made for me, I told you that. I mean that with every fiber of my being."

It was too much.

As much as she tried to process his words, the anger flowing from him to her overwhelmed her senses and she felt like she would drown in the sea of emotions if she didn't get away.

Pushing her chair back, she stood. "I'm sorry," she whispered. "I need a moment." Without waiting for any of them to respond, she left her tray and escaped the cafeteria. She needed a quiet place to think.

35

Amends

Aiden leaned against the wall in the hallway of the bottom floor of the main building. After Charlotte left the cafeteria, the turbulent emotions burning through him like a wildfire finally abated.

With her there hitting him left and right with confusion, sadness, guilt, and her own anger, he couldn't process his own emotions properly.

Never had he struggled with keeping his temper in check before.

When he killed the rogue in the alley, his fury was justified. But this? This felt wrong. Snapping at Charlotte for asking questions she had every right to ask him left him feeling like scum.

He didn't like the queries because they called his feelings for her into question, and he had no doubts how he felt about her. But she was right. Other than in moments of shared passion, he hadn't been crystal clear in his words. He'd thought the things he said and did would speak for him, but it seemed Charlotte needed something direct. It wasn't her fault. He'd misunderstood.

His friends tried to help him when she left. Seth and Lukas understood what he was experiencing more than anyone. Even Blaire on some level. She had her own struggles with anger. The only one of them who didn't have a strong affinity for anger was Riley.

Every Korrena struggled with their most volatile emotions, their strongest desires and needs riding them to act in ways they normally wouldn't to obtain them.

He wondered what that was for Charlotte.

Considering the overwhelming rushes of insecurity and emptiness that sometimes took his breath away, he wondered if the bond made the depression she spoke of worse. Did she struggle more now that she was with him? He hated that. He hoped as the bond grew he could counteract that with the love he could show her.

He pulled his phone out of his jeans.

Aiden:

Where are you?

When she didn't answer for five minutes, he grew impatient and worried.

Aiden:

I'm serious. Please tell me where you are. I'm worried. I'm sorry.

Another several minutes. He gripped his hair.

Aiden:

Charlotte don't do this to me.

Aiden:

come on

After finding out a rogue snuck onto campus, he didn't want her to be alone; but more than that, he didn't want to leave their encounter in the cafeteria unresolved.

His eyes burned. The blurred screen made writing texts difficult. He blinked away the moisture in his eyes. If he weren't running on sheer panic, he might feel embarrassment for texting her like a needy child, but he needed to know he hadn't messed up.

He couldn't mess up; he'd just got her.

Aiden:

Where are you

Charlotte:

I'm in the woods.

He stuffed his phone in his pocket and ran down the hall until he burst through the back doors of the academy into the shaded back path that ran between the forest and the back of the academy.

She could be anywhere in the forest.

Aiden:

Where in the woods?

Charlotte:

The benches across from the back doors. I went straight back from those. Are you coming out here?

He didn't want her to run or try to stop him. If she asked him not to come, he would respect her wishes, so he didn't answer to avoid being put in that situation.

Stuffing the phone back in his pocket, he ran into the forest, looking left and right, searching for any sight of her. She shouldn't be in the forest alone with rogues about.

He'd moved so deep into the forest he wondered if he'd passed her when a shock of vibrant red hair caught his eye. His steps slowed, and he rubbed his chest. He needed to make things right. After witnessing how the unstable bond between his friends came close to tearing them apart, he would do anything to avoid it with his own bond.

"Why are you all the way out here?" he asked, voice low as he approached with cautious footsteps.

He couldn't even see the academy from where they were. Pine trees surrounded them deep in the forest. The sizeable gaps overhead between the skinny pines reaching high above them allowed the sun to filter through and make it easy to traverse the dense foliage.

Climbing over a fallen log, he came to a stop a few feet in front of Charlotte.

"I've come out here a couple of times when you've been busy." Her lips twisted to the side. "Before the stalker, I mean. When I thought he was dead and I was safe." Her shoulders sagged, and the defeat she felt echoed his own. "I probably shouldn't be out here now that we know otherwise." She cleared her throat, holding a hand up to shield her eyes from the sun that hit her face when she looked up at him.

"Can we talk?"

When she nodded her agreement, he moved to sit next to her, gauging if she felt uncomfortable about it. She didn't react negatively, so he took it as a win.

"It's peaceful out here," she said. "I've always looked at the academy's surrounding woods from down in the plaza and wondered what it was like around the campus. I like how it feels separated from the hustle-and-bustle of town."

He took a moment to study her while she talked. She seemed relaxed now that she had gotten a break from him. Her bare legs were curled beneath her, hiding the cute sandals tied at her ankles that he liked so much. Her denim shorts riding high on her legs showed off the small beauty mark at the top of her thigh. A navy-blue blouse hugged her body, with a neckline high enough to not expose too much of her cleavage. He wasn't sure if that disappointed him or not. While he didn't want others to look, he couldn't deny his fascination with her breasts. He didn't even know he was a breast guy until her.

Shaking his head to rid himself of his thoughts before he derailed his purpose for being out here, he said, "I'm sorry." When she looked up at him, he elaborated. "I'm sorry if I scared you."

She pulled her hair up high on her head, clipping it in place. The heat wasn't as bad in the forest, but he imagined having dense curls down one's back would make anyone hot. "I'm sorry if it seemed like I don't believe you care. I do. I just…" Her lips tightened in a frown as if she were trying to think of how to word her thoughts. "I just feel like if you need to hide things from me when I've already witnessed so much—experienced so much, then what else could you hide from me? What else *would* you hide from me?"

He cursed. She was right.

"I didn't think of it like that. That was a mistake on my part. I understand where you would draw that conclusion, though. I probably would too." He rested his head back against the tree trunk. "I want you to know you can trust me. I thought I was protecting you, but now I understand I was only isolating you further when you're already so different in our world."

"Which isolates me enough as it is."

"You're right." He rubbed a hand over his thigh, the feel of the denim scraping his palm distracting him from focusing on his emotions too much. "I planned to talk to you about the letter after I helped calm you down when we found it, but things went sideways, and you went to shower. You were already asleep when I got back from the canteen… I didn't get the chance." He closed his hand into a fist. "I called them while you were showering. I wanted them to know what we were facing, too. I should have consulted with you first. But I did it to protect you. Everything I've done has been with your protection in mind."

He met her eyes.

"I'm sorry. I promise it won't happen again. If I discover anything, I will tell you everything I know." He turned toward her, lifting a hand to brush his thumb over her cheek as he cupped her jaw. "I do care about you. I want you to try to not give up on me. I know this whole Korrena thing is a foreign concept to you, and I'm not asking you to commit to sealing the bond and completing the bonding ritual, but I want you to consider what life might be like with me. Give me the chance to show you."

Charlotte's brows rose, and the way her lips parted distracted him. "What's a bonding ritual?"

"We've already done most of it," he said with a shake of his head, unable to hide the smile it brought to his face. "To make the bond permanent—which would make our marks permanent like you've seen on Lukas and Blaire's neck—we have to have sex."

"Which we've had. And you've tasted my blood before," she added confidently, as if she knew the steps to sealing a bond.

He couldn't hide the full body shudder the memory of the taste evoked. Nothing on this planet compared to the silky, sweet taste of her lifeblood.

"The headmistress said we almost sealed it, but I didn't get a chance to find out what the other step was. What is it?"

This was the point he would know for sure if she could handle being with him. She'd witnessed him kill and didn't falter. Could she do the thing it took to complete their bond? Even if their life would be short together, he wanted whatever time fate would allow him.

"You need to drink my blood too."

Her head raised; bewilderment, and a hint of curiosity took over her features. "I do?"

"We share blood. I drink yours, and you drink mine. At the same time."

"The same time?"

"It has to be an exchange of our life essence flowing between each other without interruption. It's kind of like a link. My blood entering you, and yours entering me concurrently. While also being . . . connected."

"Connected? What do you mean?" Her head angled, her mouth working as if she were talking to herself. She looked back at him. "I mean, wouldn't we have a connection through blood and biting?"

"Sex," he said, smirking at the way her brows climbed. "When we share blood and make love at the same moment, the bond locks into place. It's the ultimate connection we could ever have with one another. It has to happen all at once." His gaze dropped to her mouth when her tongue peeked out over her lips. He wondered if she realized she was doing it. "It binds you to me, and me to you." Their gazes connected. "You'll own me for as long as I live," he whispered.

"You mean as long as I live, right? I won't live hundreds of years."

The flicker of sadness in his chest he knew didn't belong to him made a spark of hope light in his heart. Did she want something more? It killed him to know he couldn't give that to her.

"When you're… gone," he started, swallowing when his voice

cracked as he forced the last word out. “there will never be another for me. I’ll always belong to you.” He brushed his thumb over her cheek, stealing the tear that rolled over her fair skin. Leaning in, he stole a tender kiss from her lips.

It surprised him when her arms came around his neck, chasing his retreat. She deepened the kiss, pivoting her body to swing a leg over his lap, straddling him.

“Hello,” he said, chuckling.

“Hi.”

He loved how breathy her voice sounded when affected by him.

“I really am sorry if I hurt your feelings,” she said, lowering her gaze. Her fingertips slid up and down the back of his neck, making his skin pebble. “I don’t know what happened, but I was feeling so many awful things, and then I could feel your anger and it just fueled the fire. It became this endless loop of misery.”

Hooking his finger beneath her chin, he angled her head to look at him. “I’ve never had such a hard time controlling myself, but it wasn’t your fault. You know that don’t you?”

She shook her head from side to side, and he closed his eyes. He suspected she blamed herself for it. Between her emotions and her retreat, he gathered she blamed herself for his inability to keep his primal urges at bay. Seeing her confirmation did nothing to make him feel better.

“First of all, my behavior is never your fault. No matter what you might say or do, I’m in control of my own actions. I choose if I react poorly or not. I might have a hard time with impulse control, but in the end, it was my decision to respond the way I did and not another way.”

When she tried to look away, his fingers tightened on her chin.

“And second? You have every right to call me on it. Like I do you. This might get worse before it gets better. Even when we seal the bond, it won't be the end of it. Young bonds aren't the most stable. We get the chance to learn about it from childhood until high school, but nothing they teach us prepares us for the actual experience."

"Does it get better?"

"Yeah. I know you haven't spent much time with Mera and Kai, but they are the longest-bonded pair in our group. Since we started here at the academy, I haven't seen them fight. I think it was the end of their junior year in high school that they bonded. I honestly can't remember." He settled back against the tree trunk, releasing her chin. She slid her arms around his neck to rest on his shoulders. "But the point is, they got it under control. Lukas and Blaire still struggle sometimes, but they are significantly better than they were a year ago."

"What about Riley and Seth?"

Aiden laughed. "I think they're a special case." He smiled when her face pinched, not getting the joke. "They've known each other their entire lives, so it helps them come down faster from a heated situation, but they still have their moments. In fact, Seth's jealousy rivals Lukas's, but he keeps it so suppressed, you wouldn't realize it."

"He's jealous of Dom."

Putting his head back against the tree, he laughed louder. "Yeah, he is. Even though he knows he has nothing to worry about—he's told me—he still can't help the way his body responds to Dom like a threat. Dom tried to date Riley, so I don't blame him, but I wonder if it isn't a situation like it was for Blaire and I."

"What do you mean?" She shifted on his lap, her hands sliding down to rest on his abs. They tightened at her touch, sending a delicious shiver up and down his torso.

"The Oracle said he's connected to Riley's future. What that means, none of us know. But he's important to her future, so Seth has to accept Dom's here to stay."

Charlotte giggled. "That must be hard for him."

"I get it, though." He lifted a hand and brushed a few curls back from her face. "I'm just as bad—probably worse."

"Huh?"

He chuckled and shook his head. "You have no idea how much I wanted to kick Noah's ass."

"Well, I don't blame you. He was with the rogue who attacked me." She frowned. "I never suspected he wasn't human."

"That's because we're good at hiding it. We grow up learning how to integrate into society." His hand tightened on her hip. "But what I meant was when I saw him for the first time. Not only did I feel threatened because he was like me and hanging around you, but also, I could see his interest from the jump."

Her mouth parted. "What? How did you know that?"

"Oh, he didn't hide his contempt for me that first day on campus when I drove up to visit you." Aiden smirked. "You didn't notice?"

"I knew you two seemed to really dislike each other, but I couldn't sus out why."

"Other than the natural reaction to seeing our kind around someone of interest to us that is human, we could each see the other's intent. I don't think I did a good job hiding my feelings, either."

He remembered their first encounter where he suspected Noah felt the same apprehension about a Vasirian hanging around the human he had his sights on that Aiden felt toward him. Their kind didn't take special interest in humans; it went against the natural order of things. Unless they had ulterior motives.

"I know he was involved with the rogues, that he was one himself, but—"

"He's a rogue?"

The corner of Aiden's mouth slanted. "Yeah. If he's hanging around with a rogue, he's a rogue. The only things that differentiate a rogue from a regular Vasirian is their disregard for the law and/or their association with other rogues. They aren't a different subspecies or anything. It's like saying 'he's mafia' in reference to a human."

"Oh." Charlotte's gaze dropped again.

He didn't stop her from taking a moment to herself. He wouldn't enjoy hearing someone he thought he could trust, or at least considered a friend, was someone different from what they led him to believe.

Her fingers curled into his shirt on his stomach. "So it was all an act? Did he do all those things to get to me because of Blaire, like the stalker wanted to do?" Her eyes met his, and the vulnerability there stole his breath.

He lifted his hands to cup both her cheeks. As much as he loathed to admit it, she needed answers to reassure her. "Noah liked you. It's hard to mistake genuine affection. I don't know what his intent was, but there was more to his actions."

It crossed his mind that his words meant to reassure might make the betrayal hit harder, knowing Noah wasn't faking it. That her friend sold her out. Maybe he shouldn't have said anything.

When she leaned forward, resting her head against his chest, he looped his arms around her, placing a hand on the back of her head.

He didn't know what it felt to have a friend betray him, but he didn't need to know firsthand. Charlotte's emotions flowed into him, giving him an intimate understanding of the pain it brought.

36

Noah

Charlotte watched as Riley cut into another swath of orange fabric. She had a pile of different shades of orange and pink around her on the floor of the craft room in the back of the clothing shop. Riley had said they needed to create an ombré effect with sunset colors for a beach wedding next month.

When she first asked about going with Riley to work so she could see her mom, Blaire and Lukas seemed hesitant about her leaving the academy grounds, but even Aiden reassured them that Riley could protect her. Riley might be smaller, but she wasn't human. Her preternatural strength would be enough to ensure Charlotte's safety.

Leaning forward, resting her elbows on her knees, she bit the edge of her thumbnail. In the couple of days following her conversation in the forest with Aiden about Noah, she replayed the events of her time getting to know him while she lived in Athens. The correlation between events that happened regarding the stalker and times she saw Noah seemed too convenient.

Was Noah her stalker all along?

She sat up, sliding her hands across her thighs, tapping her fingers where they came to rest.

Her theory made sense but didn't. The biggest flaw in her theory came from Noah's lack of issue with expressing his interest in her. He'd approached her like a normal person who wanted to date her. A stalker wouldn't do that. Would they? A stalker would act unhinged and send stupid notes with flowers, make phone calls, and escalate to threats. The behavior of the stalker didn't align with Noah's attempts at a connection with her.

But the stalker showed up in Rosebrook Valley when she did, just like Noah.

She huffed, slumping against the wall.

"You're gonna hurt yourself if you keep thinking so hard," Riley quipped.

Charlotte groaned, slapping her thighs, and standing. "I know. I *know*." She paced to the other side of the room near a drafting table covered in various sketches of different dress designs. "I just can't figure out who this guy is. It's obvious he's after Blaire, but I don't understand his interest in me. Why not go straight after her?"

"Because his job and his interests are different?"

She spun around. "What did you say?"

Riley set the fabric scissors down, looking at Charlotte. "If he's supposed to get to Blaire, then he'd do that, but if he's interested in you, then that's different."

She put her hand on her forehead, placing the other on her hip. "Huh?" Nothing about what Riley said made the least bit of sense to her.

"Okay, so the rogues don't work alone. Like gangs, right?"

"Yeeeeah."

"So he's not the only one after Blaire. I mean, there were two of them in the alley."

She had told them all about Noah after everything that had occurred, so they knew he shared a connection with her.

"Now, he might be the big kahuna, or he might be low on the totem pole, but if the dude in the alley wasn't him, and that guy Noah isn't him—which I'm still on the fence about—then that means someone else is stalking you."

"What's your point?"

"Uh." Riley looked up at the ceiling. "Oh!" She dropped her gaze back to Charlotte. "Right. That shows you there are more people."

"Uh huh," she said, dragging out the last word. Where was Riley going with this?

"So like, if they all are going after Blaire, then he got sidetracked. Which ended up in all the roses, notes, and all that jazz."

"So you're saying the stalking behavior has nothing to do with trying to get to Blaire through me? It's separate?"

"Yes! That!" Riley snapped her fingers, pointing at Charlotte. "You get it!"

"Why didn't you just say that?"

"I did," Riley said, looking puzzled. "Weren't you listening?"

Charlotte's phone chiming in her pocket saved her from playing ring-around-the-point with Riley any further. She gasped when she saw the sender.

"What is it?" Riley scrambled to her feet, moving over to peer over Charlotte's arm. "Ew. Why is he texting you?"

"I don't know," she said, voice low. She swiped the screen.

Noah:

I owe you an explanation.

"No, he doesn't. He's a rogue, working with other rogues who hurt you. Block him."

Before she could do that, her phone rang, Noah's name flashing on the screen.

"Put it on speaker," Riley said, hitting the button to accept before Charlotte could decide if answering was worth the hassle.

Tapping on the speaker icon, she held the phone in front of them. "Noah?"

"I didn't want you to find out about me that way," he said in a rush.

"That way? Did you plan to tell me what you were?"

"I…"

"That's what I thought. No one was going to tell me anything," she said, a bitterness to her voice she couldn't mask. It still irked that she was kept in the dark. She didn't think she would ever be okay with it, but she accepted it as the necessary evil to keep her safe.

"Charlotte," he said, pleading. "You don't know what my kind does to humans who know the truth."

"Actually, I do."

"What?"

"Memory wipe. I know everything."

A beat of silence.

"How do you know?"

"She's my brother's Korrena, asshole," Riley interjected, a smug smile on her face.

"You have a Korrena? You're human."

"Apparently that isn't a thing, except with one friend of mine."

"Blaire," he said. He already knew; she didn't have to acknowledge it. "Who's with you? Who is that talking? Who's brother?"

"It's Aiden. The guy you met in Athens. And she's a friend—his sister."

"He's your Korrena?" He blew out a sharp breath. A stilted laugh filtered through the phone's speaker.

"That's what she said," Riley snapped. "Why are you calling?"

"Listen, Charlotte. I really like you." When she sighed, he rushed to add, "As a friend! As a friend. I was trying to look out for you."

Riley nudged her arm and when she looked over, she mumbled, "Ask him why." She darted across the room to grab a notepad and marker.

"Why? Why were you looking out for me?"

"I was trying to protect you from something bad."

Riley scribbled on the paper and held up the notebook. It said, *why did he attack you?*

Charlotte made a face. She didn't think Noah had attacked her. He'd said something, but she couldn't remember what, not after everything that happened. She distinctly remembered the panic in his voice, though. It didn't align with someone attacking her.

Riley nudged her again. She'd been silent too long.

"Um. Why did you attack me?"

"What? I didn't." He paused and then his voice dropped, insecurity suffusing his tone when he asked, "Did I? Please tell me I didn't hurt you."

Why wouldn't he know? Something seemed off.

Riley glared at the phone. "Dude. Are you playing dumb?"

"No. I—"

"If you're not going to be honest, she's hanging up," Riley said, a fierceness to her voice that Charlotte hadn't heard before. Riley's protective behavior made her feel warm inside.

"No! Wait! Please don't hang up, Charlotte. Let me explain."

"Get to it then," Riley snapped.

"Okay. Okay. He gets it." Charlotte turned slightly, keeping the microphone end of the phone closer to her. She fixed her gaze on Riley. "I want to hear what he has to say."

Riley huffed, and when she nodded, Charlotte angled back toward her.

"Thank you," Noah said, exhaling in relief. "I was suffering from *sanguis manie*. It's this… condition that—"

"I've heard of it."

"Okay, that makes it easier." He cleared his throat. "That's why I wasn't sure if I hurt you. I was trying so hard to fight against it when I approached you. I wanted to get you out of there before Brent got to you."

She shared a look with Riley before asking, "I still don't understand why you wouldn't know if you hurt me."

"I don't respond well to lack of blood. It only takes a few hours and I start experiencing adverse effects."

"A few hours?" Riley asked. "But aren't you older?"

"I'm twenty. I know that's still old enough I should be able to go at least most of the day without issue, but I've never handled it well. I know my limits."

When Charlotte met Riley's eyes again, she asked, "I don't think I understand this part."

"Younger Vasirian struggle more than older ones with lack of blood consumption. *Sanguis manie* sets in earlier for us."

"There are cases of older Vasirian—much older than me—who have similar struggles to me. No one really knows why, though," Noah added.

Riley shook her head. "I didn't know that."

"Anyway. I had gone almost twenty-four hours without blood. I was on the edge of madness. I barely remember the events of that night."

"What?" Riley set down the notepad and scratched the back of her head. She'd made notes about some of the other things Noah said, not just the answer to her question. "Why did you go that long? No. You know what? Give me that." She snatched the phone from Charlotte's hand and pressed the button to start a FaceTime call.

When the call connected, Noah's face, covered in a dark layer of scruff, came into view. His curls looked disheveled, and dark circles stained the skin beneath his eyes.

"Jesus, Noah. You look terrible."

"Good to see you too, beautiful."

Riley grumbled. "Listen, bud. That's my brother's Korrena, so off limits." She nodded, satisfied when he lowered his gaze in response to her reprimand. "Now." She took a breath, then unleashed, yelling, "What the flying fuck?" She tempered her voice, but the sharpness remained. "What were you thinking coming to a crowded nightclub like Haven if you were suffering from *sanguis manie*? Why didn't you get blood from a clinic?"

She looked at Charlotte. "To prevent this very thing, and to uphold the law of not feeding from live sources, the Blackthorn Clan has granted us permission to go to any blood donation center to get blood whenever we need it. Humans donate more than you realize."

"Really?" She hadn't thought it was so common.

"Oh yeah. Millions of units a year. Not only does it help us, but it's used all the time in medicine. Mera told me all about it."

Riley focused back on the screen where Noah was looking between the two of them in silence. "Your story isn't adding up." At least she wasn't yelling at him anymore.

He ran a hand over his forehead, pushing his curls off his face. "I wasn't alone at the club."

“We know. The asshole attacked Charlotte.”

“Brent isn’t—wasn’t—the only one you need to be worried about.” He sighed as if what he needed to say brought him discomfort. “The man who ordered us to watch you kept me locked in a room without blood for the day prior to coming there. That’s why I couldn’t get blood when I needed it most, and why I couldn’t avoid going to the club. He’d have killed me, or made Brent kill me.”

“My stalker did that to you?”

Noah ran his tongue over his front teeth. “No. The guy in charge of the local group isn’t the one stalking you. That was Brent.”

“What? He’s dead. She’s still getting stupid notes and roses.”

“She is?”

“That’s what I said.”

He looked at Charlotte with concern. “What did the note say?”

“I can’t remember everything,” she said. She wasn’t sure if she should show her hand, but she also didn’t remember. “He signed it with a J, though.”

“James.”

“James? I thought you said her stalker was Brent,” Riley said, looking at Charlotte. “Do you know a James?”

“No, I don’t think so.” She looked at Noah. “Is he a classmate?”

“Not that I’m aware. I haven’t actually met him. When he kept me locked up, he had other guys check on me. I’ve only talked to him on the phone, so I don’t even know what he looks like. I don’t know anything about him, but I knew Brent. And yeah, Brent was her stalker. He lost his Korrena in an accident a few years back. He’s never been the same. You kinda look like her. She had curly red hair and a lot of freckles, not the few you have.”

“So he became obsessed with Charlotte, redirecting his longing for his Korrena at her,” Riley surmised.

"Yeah."

Charlotte had done a little reading about the Korrena bond. For sealed bonds, losing a Korrena often drove the other to follow soon behind them because of their inability to cope in the world without their pair. Physical pain, mental anguish… it made her feel so terrible for those who'd suffered that loss.

To not only lose their soulmate, but then have to suffer the swift deterioration of their mind afterward? How could fate be so cruel? What did that mean for Aiden when time took her away from him? Were all Vasirian who lose their mated pair destined for such a terrible future, if they saw one at all?

It still didn't excuse her stalker—Brent—but it made her understand the madness behind his actions.

Did she forgive him? No. She didn't know if she could.

He tried to kill her Korrena. Tried to force her to endure the same loss. Maybe if he hadn't tried to kill Aiden when he came to her defense, she could, but she only had it in her to dredge up a morsel of sympathy.

Noah's voice pulled her out of her thoughts.

"James must have picked up where he left off to keep you scared. He's been directing our movements, but someone else is controlling his actions. I've never met them and don't know their real name. I don't even know if what I said will get me killed or not." He slouched. "I don't want to be part of this anymore. I want my life back. What little life I had. I never wanted this, but I didn't have anyone."

"What about your parents? They're in Rosebrook Valley."

He met Charlotte's eyes. "They hate me."

"But why?"

"I don't know if I ever told you if I had siblings or not, but I had a sister."

Riley tilted her head. "Did?"

"When we were kids…" He sucked in his cheeks, lips pursing as he breathed in through his nose. "I went camping with some friends on the Savannah River. Trudy wanted to come along. I didn't want her to go. You know, annoying little sister and all."

Riley rolled her eyes.

"She was two years younger, so it wasn't like she was out of place with us." He shook his head. "Anyway, she wouldn't let up until I agreed, and my parents told me I was responsible for her since there were a bunch of boys around. The first night there, we'd all settled into our oversized tent to sleep. She slept next to me because Dad would kill me if I let her near the other guys." He laughed. "She woke up and had to go pee. I fell back asleep before she came back. Everyone else was already asleep."

Charlotte didn't like where this was going.

"The next morning, we all got up, and she was nowhere to be found." Noah swallowed. "My buddy Shane went down to the riverbank and…"

"Oh no," Riley said, hand going over her mouth.

"Yeah. Trudy was half on the shore, half in the water. She'd drowned. We have no idea how she ended up in the water. She couldn't swim."

"You can't heal from drowning," Charlotte whispered.

"No. You can't," he confirmed, his voice hard and distant. "Anyway, my parents blamed me for not watching out for her hard enough. They've never forgiven me."

"That's stupid," Riley said, anger in her tone. "It wasn't your fault."

It amused Charlotte how quickly Riley could flip her point of view regarding someone. She wasn't shallow or fickle, but she didn't dwell on the worst in people.

"Well. Enough about all that. It's not relevant."

Charlotte frowned. "You should come to the academy and talk to the headmistress. See if she can help you. You don't have to live like that if you don't wanna."

"I can't do that. I exposed myself to a human. Not to mention I worked with the rogues who are trying to get to Blaire." He scoffed. "They'll ship me off to Cresbel Asylum so fast I won't know what hit me."

"What's that?"

Riley looked at Charlotte. "It's where criminals of our kind go. Whenever Vasirian commit acts that go against our laws, they usually have a trial in front of the Blackthorn Clan, and if it's bad enough, they are sent there. Sometimes they are sent straight there if they do something stupid like kill someone."

It made little sense for Noah to go to prison over what he did. He didn't hurt her. Prison? The punishment seemed extreme. But trusting him to come to the academy… Could she trust he wouldn't sell her out to the rogues? He first befriended her under false pretenses. Who was to say he was telling the truth now?

Still, his life was in danger. She couldn't stand by and allow him to be killed when he seemed sincere.

"You need to do it, Noah. I won't press charges against you."

Riley laughed, and Charlotte turned toward her. She didn't see anything funny.

"There's no charges." At Charlotte's confused expression, Riley added, "It's not your call. If Blackthorn Security is aware of an attack on a human, they normally do the thing with the trial, just with the Order—which is temporarily disbanded as you know. So instead, they would haul them off to the clan."

"So Noah would face your king?"

"Yep."

"Can't we just..." She looked at Noah. "Keep it a secret?"

Noah grimaced.

"The headmistress already knows what happened," Riley said. "My brother and Dom told her. That's why she knows about that guy Brent's death."

"Yeah, but she's keeping Aiden's secret."

Riley shook her head. "The problem is Blackthorn Security *knows* a rogue attacked you, but they don't know who. They don't know he's dead. They'll likely pin it on Noah if we bring him to the academy."

"What? No!"

"Hey," Noah said softly. "It's alright."

"No, it's not. You're not taking the fall for a crime you didn't commit."

"That's not what I meant. I mean, don't think you need to vouch for me. I did something stupid, and this is the price I pay for it."

"Screw that," Charlotte snapped. She was tired of the people she cared about getting hurt and being forced to sit idle while it happened. "We can say the rogue got away or something. No one has to say anything about anyone dying."

Riley nodded. "We could talk to the headmistress and see if she would keep it under wraps. No promises, though."

"That's treason," Noah said.

Charlotte and Riley shared a look. Was there no way to save Noah?

"Still gonna do it," Riley said, dismissing Noah's look of surprise. "Anyway, I got a question."

"Okay," he said, dragging out the word.

"Why are the rogues really targeting Charlotte? I mean, it seems like it's about Blaire, but why bring Charlotte into it?"

It was a question Charlotte had asked herself over and over since she realized they wanted Blaire.

"Well, you know why Brent focused so hard on her, but the original reason is trying to get to the human of prophecy, which you also know. The thing you don't know is that they believe Charlotte would be an easy way in, with her being a human and not aware of our existence." He sighed, his kind blue eyes meeting Charlotte's. The immense remorse in them pained her. "You were originally an assignment, but I grew to like you so much. You were funny and smart. I enjoyed spending time with you."

"Sucks for you. She's my brother's Korrena."

"Yeah, I get it." He laughed. "You really are protective of him, aren't you?"

Riley crossed her arms and raised a dark brow. "Problem?"

"None at all. I'd be the same way about Trudy if she were still here." He cleared his throat and looked at Charlotte. "Are you bonded?"

Her face warmed, and she shook her head. "We've not done the ritual, no."

"Doesn't matter though, right?" Riley asked tartly.

She looked at Riley and nodded. "I'm not leaving Aiden."

"I know," Noah said. "That's not why I asked. Just curious. Korrena pairs are special. I didn't think another human could be one. I only want to be your friend."

Charlotte moved to sit on the bench behind them along the wall. Riley joined her. She needed to be honest with Noah.

Closing her eyes to recenter herself, she opened them and said, "I need time. I'm not sure about what friendship we could have after all the manipulation."

"I understand that, but I need you to know something."

She didn't respond, instead waiting for him to continue.

"Everything I said and did was real. Everything. I just didn't tell you who I was and my original intent when I approached you."

"Yeah, and what was that?" Riley asked. "You got near her while no other rogues did. Why?"

"I got close to learn how much contact she had with Blaire. At first. I didn't know where the others were gonna go with that information. I was only told to find out how close she was to Blaire now."

Charlotte wouldn't lie and say hearing how innocent his job had been, and how little he knew of the rogue group's intent, didn't affect her opinion of him. She wondered if he knew how far they wanted to go—hurting Blaire, attacking Charlotte—if he'd still have joined them. He couldn't back out halfway through, even if he did like her. She understood the threat to his life if he did.

"Girls," her mom said, pulling back the curtain of rainbow beads separating the craft room from the back hallway. "I'm about to close."

"Okay, Sara. I'll put the fabric away and we'll get going." Riley stood, moving to clean up the mess on the floor.

"It's looking great, by the way," Sara said, her gaze moving over the mannequin in the corner already accented with orange and pink fabric.

Riley bloomed under the praise, wiggling a little as she put the cut material neatly into a plastic bin.

"I have a dinner date with Liz tonight. We're going out with a few friends. But I'd like to get together sometime for dinner with you and Aiden soon. If classes are starting soon, that academy is going to have you too busy for us."

"Sure, Mom." Charlotte smiled at her mom before she slipped through the curtain and back down the hallway.

"I guess you have to go," Noah said when she returned her attention to him.

"Yeah. But we'll talk to the headmistress."

Riley rushed over and put her hands on the bench, looking down at the phone. Charlotte recoiled to give her space. "Lie low. Don't meet that James asshole."

"I'll try. I can't ignore him if he calls me."

"Well, don't meet him. If you don't really know him, there's no telling what he'll do. But we won't leave you hanging long. I don't think you're so bad. That's high praise, so accept it." Riley stood and sashayed over to the mess she'd made.

Charlotte laughed.

"She always like that?"

"A little bit."

37

CONTROL

The smell of vanilla and orange stirred her senses, pulling Charlotte from the depths of a dream where Aiden lavished her body with attention. She didn't want to open her eyes, afraid of losing the last remnants of the dream.

When a masculine groan sounded too real to be a dream, her eyelids fluttered open at the same time Aiden kissed down from her knee, over her inner thigh. At the sound of her moan, he looked up, meeting her eyes.

"Good morning," he said, voice low and rough. He must have woken up not long before her. She loved his sleep altered voice.

"Morning," she said with a smile.

Her eyes trailed over him. He sat between her legs on the bed wearing a pair of loose athletic shorts and a T-shirt she planned to steal before bed later tonight.

His hand cupped the calf of her bent leg; her other leg lay across his lap. She still wore her sleep shorts and his T-shirt, so he hadn't done half of what he did in her dream. Still, the simple touches over her exposed skin made heat pool at her core and goose bumps rise on her skin.

The hand not holding her bent leg slid up her outstretched leg to her thigh, pausing at the hem of her shirt, his gaze flicking up to hers. She squirmed and slid down, forcing his hand to move up her skin and slip beneath the fabric.

His fingers curled against her flesh, biting into her skin. "Words." He leaned over and kissed her knee. "Tell me what you want, Kitten."

That familiar tension in her chest hit at the sound of the nickname, her nerve endings coming to life as tingles spread over her. Her heart fluttered inside her chest, her breathing quickening.

Most of the time, she talked little when they had sex until he reduced her to a babbling mess of obscenities and unfamiliar noises. It seemed he wasn't having any of that today.

"Touch me," she whispered.

"I am touching you."

His wrist twisted to where his thumb rested on her inner thigh, and his other fingers remained on the outside. He tightened his hold on her thigh enough to bring the smallest bite of pain, making her moan. The grip only lasted a second, but he still soothed the area by brushing his thumb against her skin.

"See? If you want something different, you're gonna have to tell me."

The devil. Aiden was the devil.

His deep chuckle made her think he could read her mind, or her thoughts were written all over her face. She didn't know. None of her mental faculties were operating at full capacity at the moment.

She rolled her lips in and lifted her chin. His brows shifted up in momentary surprise before a devious grin spread across his face. Her swallow sounded loud to her ears.

"I guess if you have nothing to say, I'll take care of this myself."

He shifted, putting her foot onto the bed and rising to his knees. He pulled off his T-shirt with one quick movement and settled back against the wall. His erection pressed against his shorts obscenely. Without looking at her once, he reached inside and pulled out his thick length, pushing his shorts beneath his balls.

His left hand cupped his sack while he stroked the other hand down his shaft, a groan falling from his lips as his head dipped back, thunking against the wall behind him.

Rising onto her elbows to look at him, she licked over her lips as he gave himself slow, sensual strokes, twisting his hand with every pass over his darkened cockhead.

"Fuck, Kitten," he breathed. His chest rose and fell faster, the tendons in his throat standing out in his arched neck.

She wanted to see him break, but at the same time, she wanted him to give that to her.

"I could come like this," he said, voice strained. He grunted. "I could come all over my fist just thinking of burying myself deep inside of you. Fuuuuck." His strokes grew faster, his other hand massaging his balls, pulling them away from his body.

Her gaze latched onto his toes curling where his legs hung off the side of her bed. She'd had enough.

"Aiden," she whined, squirming her hips. Her wet panties pressed against her overly sensitive core.

He rolled his head on the wall to look at her with hooded eyes, slowing his movements. His chest heaved, a shudder passing through his body when he twisted his hand again. He squeezed the base and held it, waiting for her to say the words.

"Please," she whispered. Her fingers curled into the comforter when he didn't move. "Please touch me." She worried her lower lip. Even though he had her aching for him, she wasn't lost to her desires, so expressing her needs proved challenging.

He stroked himself again once. Twice. Three times.

"Fuck me," she said, her voice so low she wasn't sure he could hear, but he sprang into action, moving to his knees and shucking his shorts off, proving he had.

Fingers gripped her waistband and yanked her sleep shorts and panties off in one quick movement. His gaze latched onto her core. The bed beneath her must have a small puddle from how drenched she was. Her thin shorts did nothing to prevent her from soaking through the fabric to the sheets.

She lifted her hand to reach for his cock that leaked a steady stream of his natural lubricant, but he stopped her by grabbing her wrist in a tight hold.

"No," he said, a growl to his voice that made a shiver dance down her spine.

She fell onto her back, and he pulled the shirt up her body until her arms lifted above her head, tangled in the fabric. The neck of the shirt stopped right above her nose, covering half of her face. Her lips turned down when he didn't finish pulling the shirt off and stopped moving.

"Aiden?"

"What's the word, Kitten?"

"What?"

"Your safe word."

Her breath caught, and she swallowed. "Um. Creamsicle."

"Good girl. Don't move," he commanded with a light smack to her hip.

Her breath hitched again in response to both the command and the touch.

She sucked in her stomach, back arching, when his teeth dragged down between her breasts and across her belly. The sensations were magnified because the shirt held her not only bound, but also blindfolded to what he did to her. She trusted him, and he knew it, so she didn't fight him on this new dynamic they'd fallen into. She liked it.

He didn't touch her or do anything else for a moment, but then his body heat cloaked her body, his breath fanning over her lips. His lips hovered inches from hers. What did she look like to him like this?

Her lips parted on a whimper at the bruising grip of his hands on the back of her thighs beneath her knees, pushing her legs up. But nothing she felt before compared to the explosion of pleasure that came when he sank himself deep inside her in one hard thrust.

Aiden wasn't gentle.

He rutted into her like a feral beast, hips slapping against her backside as he pressed his entire body weight into her, pushing her knees to her chest.

She cried out when he slammed into her and rotated his hips, lifting his body from hers to angle himself inside her to brush across that sweet spot.

Moving his hands to her waist, he slid her down the bed, positioning her into his lap with her upper body lying on the bed. Her limp legs draped over his thighs, forcing her back to arch. She could do nothing to stop it with her arms bound, and she loved it. The way he manhandled her body like she was his own personal plaything made her core clench around him.

He cursed, pausing his thrusts, holding himself deep inside her.

A sharp smack rang out into the room, and she yelped as a mixture of pleasure-pain flared out over her hip. He didn't spank her hard, but enough that she felt the sting.

"The things you do to me." His hands settled above her hipbones, giving her a little squeeze. "I want to ruin you. Make you unable to walk or sit down without remembering what it felt like to have my cock buried inside of you."

She moaned and rocked her hips against his lap, encouraging him to move. The new sensations from his spanks to the added thrill of losing one of her senses, heightening all the others, brought her close to the edge.

Another smack.

"I'm in control here, Kitten. I'll fuck you when I'm ready to."

Her eyes widened behind the blindfold. The way he spoke when he let himself go sounded dirtier than she ever did.

"You like that, don't you?" Judging by the way he flexed his fingers and his muttered curses when her walls clenched around him and fresh arousal pooled at his words, he already knew the answer. Slowly, he slid almost out of her. "Being my kitten." He punched his hips forward, and she gasped. "Me telling you all the depraved things I want to do to you." Another thrust. His voice lowered. "You like me in control, don't you?"

She squirmed against him as he slowly rocked into her.

"Don't you?" His voice hardened. "Tell me. Say it."

"Yes," she moaned, arching her back when he began thrusting into her hard and fast.

"Good fucking girl."

The brief vulnerability he showed when he first asked her about being his kitten was long gone. Was it because their bond was growing? Was it the grip a Vasirian's primal side had ramping up his natural personality? There might be some truth to that, but they had since grown comfortable with one another. Comfortable enough to let go and show the other parts of themselves they hadn't shown another.

In her case, she didn't even know she was into any of this until he opened her mind to it. Now, she couldn't imagine things any other way. But she knew deep down she could never submit to anyone else like she did to Aiden. Even if he left her tomorrow, she didn't see herself surrendering to another man the way she did him.

His hands roamed as his movements slowed again. If she didn't know any better, she would think he was edging her, or himself. Every time her insides fluttered, he would slow. Considering the way he jerked himself before sliding inside her, she found it surprising that he hadn't come. She suspected the brief moments of reprieve gave him a chance to calm down.

"I need to see you."

She gasped when he pinched her nipples as his hands made their way up to her shirt, slipping it over her head, freeing her arms. Her eyes met his, and her mouth dropped open.

The once dark forest color that made up his irises now looked like deep emeralds glowing against his dark eyelashes. Breathtaking.

Every muscle in his body appeared taut, as if even though he wasn't gentle with her, he was still holding himself back. What would it be like if he succumbed to his most primal urges?

She swallowed. She knew why he was holding back.

Aiden had the strength to hurt her without tapping into his preternatural side. To anyone on the outside, it would seem like he was losing control with her, but he had the ultimate control. Not just over her, but over himself. He had the power to kill her, but he didn't. He pulled his bites, his smacks, his grip. He might leave bruises she would cherish for days, but he would never hurt her with the intent of causing genuine harm.

Her heart swelled as a feeling she'd never experienced before washed over her. His eyes widened, but he didn't say anything. Could he feel what she was feeling at this moment?

She'd never been in love before. She wondered if this was it.

Feeling too raw and exposed, she didn't say anything, turning her head on the pillow, breaking eye contact.

Maybe it was too early to say it when she wasn't sure if that feeling of being wrapped in a warm blanket fresh out of the dryer on a cold rainy night was actual love, but she couldn't deny something warmed her chest when she thought of how he took care of her in so many ways.

"Eyes on me," he said, slowly rocking into her again.

She looked up at him. His eyes were still glowing, and she wondered if he realized it. Could Vasirian feel it?

He bent over her, running his tongue across her ribcage and along the underside of her breast. He nipped the sensitive skin there, making her moan. His mouth closed over her nipple, and he sucked it tight, flicking his tongue against the tightened bud, strengthening the force of his movements as he increased his speed.

Her neck arched as she babbled curses at the ceiling.

When a familiar tingle started building again, pulsing through her core, she wrapped her legs around his waist, hooking her ankles over his firm backside. "Please let me come," she begged. She didn't want him to stop again.

She felt him smile against her breast and that's when she knew he was not only holding himself back, but also controlling her release. Had he waited for her to beg?

He sat up, pulling her body with him. Before she could wrap her arms around his neck, he banded his arms over the top of hers, fingers digging into her back as he thrust up into her body, bouncing her against his lap.

She wailed and hung her head back as the new angle took her to greater heights.

His mouth closed over the sensitive area where her shoulder met her neck, and she felt the scrape of teeth sharper than she ever had before.

Her head snapped up, and she met his wide, wild eyes.

He stared at her, and she knew he was waiting for her to use the safe word.

She wouldn't.

As much as the idea of fangs piercing her skin made her nervous after the painful bite from the rogue, she couldn't pretend she didn't want to know what it felt like to have Aiden bite her with his fangs. Blaire told her it wasn't like another Vasirian biting when Korrenas bit one another. The pleasure was supposed to be incredible. She wanted to feel it. She already felt okay when he tasted her blood before; this was just another step.

Her head fell to the side, her curls falling away from her neck and draping over her opposite shoulder.

His dark brows drew in, and his eyes flashed. "Say the words, Kitten." His voice was nothing more than a guttural rasp.

"Bite me," she whispered.

Without hesitation, Aiden lurched forward, his fangs sinking into her flesh. Her mouth fell open, her body shuddering in ecstasy when her climax overtook her body after the brief pinch of pain dissipated. When he sucked her sensitive skin into his mouth, her blood filled his mouth.

All too soon, the intoxicating feeling fled, leaving her feeling drunk.

With a few quick thrusts while her body slumped against his, limp and unable to hold on for the ride, he grunted, stilling inside her.

Warmth spread through her core as he filled her.

He wrapped his arms tighter around her, his forehead pressed against the area where he bit. It didn't hurt. He'd probably healed her. "Thank you," he whispered in a shaky voice.

She didn't understand what he was thanking her for. Her head remained foggy, and she whimpered a little.

"Shhh, I've got you." His hands smoothed over her back, soothing her as her mind came back to her. "You did so good for me. You're so beautiful." He continued to praise her until she felt strong enough to lift her arms and wrap them around him, hugging onto him.

Tears streamed down her cheeks, and when they dampened his skin, he pulled her back from him to look at her face.

"Why are you crying?"

"I don't know," she said, hiccupping. "I just feel really good." She sniffed.

He chuckled and wiped her cheek with his hand.

"Are we bonded now?"

He blinked. "What? Why would you think that?"

"Because you drank my blood while we had sex."

He licked his lips; her blood stained his tongue. It made her insides tighten around his semi-hard cock, and he winced. "Sensitive," he answered her questioning look. He swallowed. "No. You have to drink my blood too, remember?"

"I forgot," she mumbled.

She'd been so caught up in the moment, she forgot there was another step to seal their bond. She only thought he had to drink and be inside her at the same time.

After a minute or two, he squinted at her as if something perplexed him. His hands came up to cup both sides of her face. "Did you ask me to bite you thinking it would bond us forever?"

When her hips squirmed, and her gaze drifted to the side as embarrassment colored her cheeks, he smiled so brightly it stole her breath. His pure elation punched into her chest and washed over her entire body.

He kissed her tenderly, turning the kiss into something slow and passionate as he held her face in his hands.

When they separated, she asked something that had been on her mind. "Will you biting me turn me into a Vasirian if Blaire isn't one?"

"No. There's a long process around that."

"What is it?"

He slowly lifted her off his softened cock and laid her back on the bed, getting up and walking into their ensuite. After a few moments, he returned with a warm washcloth, cleaning her body of their blended fluids. She was a mess. After he cleaned himself, he crawled onto the bed beside her and pulled the sheet over them, pushing away the damp, soiled comforter.

He turned toward her, propping himself up on his elbow, and traced his fingers across her stomach on top of the sheet.

"In order to become a Vasirian, you have to lose enough blood to be on death's doorstep, either by me draining you myself or by some other means, like an accident or something. The only person who can make your change possible is me. I'd have to feed you my blood at that point, and you would have had to go into the process of accepting the transition. Once that happened, you'd go into something like a coma until the transition completed." He shook his head. "I don't know how safe it is. With you and Blaire being the first human Korrenas to show themselves in hundreds of years, we don't know what happens from that point. We only know the starting process."

Losing all of her blood—or most of it—sounded frightening, but if humans did it hundreds of years ago successfully, why couldn't they do it now?

"Is that something you're interested in?" He tried to keep the hope out of his voice, but she felt it thrum through their bond as clear as spring water.

"I've always been fascinated with legends, myths, and the unknown. To live for what would feel like forever knowing those I care about would be there with me? It opens up so many possibilities." She traced his knuckles with her fingertips.

Mundane human life hadn't done her many favors, but it hadn't been terrible like for some people. If she were honest with herself, she didn't mind the idea of trading her humanity for a longer life with her friends and Aiden. It would give her more years to get it right.

She didn't think telling him without a sealed bond was wise.

What if he changed his mind?

38

Instability

Aiden splashed water on his face, willing his breathing to calm and his body to settle. Minor tremors troubled his fingers as he settled unsteady hands against the counter on each side of the bathroom sink and stared into the mirror.

Another nightmare.

The lines around his eyes served as proof of the frustration weighing heavily on him. Frustration that even though he'd met with the counselor in the psychology department like the others, the nightmares persisted.

He understood two therapy sessions after Charlotte suggested it wouldn't be a magical fix-all for his situation, but he expected to have a better handle on the after-effects. Less panic. Maybe the ability to fall back asleep without struggling. Talking about the trauma and coming to terms with what he went through should have made it easier to get control of himself once he was awake enough to realize the nightmares weren't real. At least, it should be that way. The therapist had given him techniques to ground himself once awake, but they weren't helping.

The nightmares weren't as frequent with Charlotte nearby. With the bond growing between them because of their openness to one another and the physicality of their relationship, the nightmares weren't as intense. Instead of a vivid reel depicting his death and the subsequent events, the nightmares transformed into a hazy and disjointed sequence reminiscent of normal dreams.

He grabbed a hand towel to wipe water from his face before tossing it back on the counter and leaving the bathroom.

Charlotte slept without a hint of awareness of his nighttime struggles. For that, he felt grateful.

Tonight was one of those nights where she decided to be a gymnast. She lay with her upper body hanging off the bed, arms stretched over her head, and both legs propped on the wall. He didn't know how she found comfort in the weird positions she contorted her body into. At least this position appeared tame compared to others. Still, if she slipped lower to the floor, her neck would hate her come morning.

"Alright, Kitten. Time to sleep like a normal person," he whispered, lifting her from her peculiar position and placing her onto the bed proper. She snuggled into the bedding, a smile on her face. His chest tightened at the sight.

She had burrowed under his skin and made a home, and he wasn't sure he wanted anything different. He wanted her as enamored with him as he felt for her. He questioned if his obsession with her was normal, but at least he wasn't stalking her.

Of course, she never gave him a reason to.

Shaking the strange thought, he pulled the covers over her and turned to go back to his bed. He paused when her phone chimed on the nightstand.

It took him a moment to realize the growl disturbing the peaceful quiet of the room came from him. The sight of Noah's name on her phone tossed rationality out the window. He snatched the phone from the nightstand. He couldn't see the complete message, but he saw the preview.

Noah:

Did you talk to the headmistress? I haven't talked to...

He gripped the phone. After what happened in the alley, and with Noah's identity exposed, he didn't think Charlotte would have anything to do with the guy again. What did he mean by talking to the headmistress? Had Charlotte spoken with him about the academy? Why would she want anything to do with him? The questions swirled in his mind, inflaming his irritation.

Trusting her had seemed like an easy decision. He didn't have any reason to doubt her feelings or suspect her of anything. Now, he couldn't ignore the uncomfortable thing slithering in his gut, agitated at the possibility something was happening between her and the rogue.

He didn't have those answers, but he knew one thing without question: Charlotte was hiding something from him.

She wanted him to not hide things from her, but here she was hiding things from him. He wasn't about to allow a double standard to cause a rift between them.

Tomorrow, he would get answers.

The entire time he sat on his bed playing with his phone waiting for Charlotte to finish her shower tested the limits of his patience.

He wanted to go in there and demand answers, but acting like a neanderthal would get him nowhere.

He witnessed enough of the asshole posturing from his friends to know the kind of damage that behavior would do to his fragile bond. Even if he felt like throwing a fit, he wouldn't do it.

The problem with good intentions was they tended to fly out the window when faced with reality and heightened emotions.

The bathroom door opened, and Charlotte stepped out into their dorm room. Her shoulders inched up, and she froze, looking at him with trepidation.

Lifting her phone from where it rested against his leg, he said, "What's this about?" His voice was calm, but her body language hadn't changed. His irritation flowed to her through their bond without restraint. He couldn't hide it from her if he tried.

"What do you mean?"

She hadn't checked her phone when she woke up, instead going straight to the bathroom. The unread message remained on the screen, taunting him.

He held the phone out. Afraid if he said anything, or moved, he would do or say something he would regret. While he would never harm her physically, he didn't trust himself not to say something stupid and hurt her heart. The jealousy trying to steal his rationality surrounding the situation strangled him.

Closing the distance between them, she took the phone from his hand.

Her face fell, and confusion swept her features as she looked back up at him. "Are you upset Noah messaged me?"

His eye twitched. He closed his eyes and took a calming breath. His words were measured and slow as he said, "Of course I'm upset a rogue who had the audacity to attack you is texting you like you're friends."

She put a hand on her hip and angled her head. "We *are* friends—sort of. He didn't attack me, though."

He dropped his phone on the bed and stood, towering over her. She didn't shrink back. Her chin tilted up so she could meet his eyes. He wasn't angry like in the cafeteria, but her casual way of addressing the situation contributed to his volatility.

"How can you stand there and say that when he was with the rogue who bit you?"

"I talked to him the other day with Riley at my mom's shop."

His voice rose with anger infusing his tone. "You talked to him?" He only had so much patience.

Her eyes narrowed. "That's what I said."

"No. Absolutely not."

She blinked. "Excuse me?"

"He has no business talking to you again."

"Aiden," she said, hand lifting to take his, forcing him to unclench the fist at his side. "He's my friend."

The soothing way she ran her thumb over the top of his hand grounded him and allowed him to temper the aggression he felt. He couldn't understand why she wanted to be Noah's friend after everything, and he told her as much.

"Because things didn't happen like you think."

"What?"

"I'll explain, but first let's sit down."

He let her lead him to her bed. When he sat down and scooted back against the wall, she sat perpendicular to him against her headboard, putting her phone on the nightstand beside her. Before she could cross her legs, he lifted them and draped them across his thighs. He massaged her bare feet, giving himself something to do to give himself a fighting chance at keeping his emotions settled.

"I meant to tell you we talked to Noah. You were already asleep when I got home from dinner with the girls, so I couldn't tell you then. And then yesterday morning… well, with what I woke up to, I didn't get the chance."

Her face flushed pink, and he smirked in satisfaction, more of his tension deteriorating at the memory.

He loved knowing she enjoyed herself. Loved knowing what he did to her. He'd never felt a desire for the kinds of things they did, but with her… Charlotte unlocked a side of him he didn't know existed. It freed him of all his worries to be like that with her. It felt like in those moments, he could let go, and she allowed him to control every aspect of the situation with complete and utter trust. He needed it more than he realized.

"I didn't want to mention Noah when we went out with everyone, and then at dinner last night, because I wanted to talk to you first, but when I got back to the room after stopping by Riley's room, I was so tired I didn't get around to it." She flicked her thumbnails against one another. "I'm sorry I didn't tell you sooner. I just really didn't get the chance. I planned to tell you, though." She looked up at him.

"I believe you." He squeezed her foot. "I just don't understand why you talked to him."

She proceeded to detail how Noah reached out to her and told her about the man named James who directed them to get close to Charlotte to see how close she was to Blaire. How the other rogue who bit Charlotte was, in fact, her stalker. A man who lost his Korrena and went off the deep end upon seeing a redhead like his wife. She explained Noah's erratic behavior was an attempt to get her to run, but he was suffering from *sanguis manie,* so he appeared unhinged instead.

By the time she finished, Aiden didn't know what to think.

In most situations, he would have doubts, but with how Charlotte explained the way Riley tore into Noah, and the questions she had, he wasn't sure he had much of an argument. Still, he would refrain from complete trust.

"So the headmistress is going to help him?"

"I talked to her yesterday before we went out with everyone. She told me that Noah is right. It's treason if she keeps it quiet. But with my willingness to forgive him, and in exchange for information that would help them against the rogues, the clan might make a concession."

He put his other hand on her thigh. He didn't think Headmistress Velastra would risk herself like that for someone she didn't know. She already put herself in a dangerous position by hiding the murder Aiden had committed.

"She said she would speak to Dom and contact the clan to see what'll happen." She stared at her nails. "I hope it'll be sooner rather than later because from the way Noah talks, he's in danger. If they'll punish him by denying what he needs to live…"

Her eyes met Aiden's, and he hated the sadness he saw there.

"Maybe it's wrong of me to want him to be okay after what he did, but I'm not the type of person to let someone in trouble stay in that situation if I can help it. Even if they've wronged me, I can't knowingly allow someone to suffer."

"And that makes you a good person. I love that about you."

She looked down at her knees.

"So what's he said?" Aiden motioned to her phone on the nightstand.

She grabbed her phone and opened it. "He's asking if the headmistress said anything and said that he's not talked to James. He hasn't contacted Noah."

"It's only been a couple days."

"Yeah, but I don't know how often they talked on the phone. He's never actually met the guy in person."

His hand rested on her ankle as he studied her twisting a curl in her fingers while looking at her phone screen in concentration.

Guilt gnawed at him for his assumption of the worst. The lack of patience and knee-jerk anger wasn't his default setting. He wasn't that type of person. With the nightmare still fresh in his mind, the lack of sleep the night before, and the bond's influence heightening his jealousy, his emotions were unstable.

"I'm sorry for the way I acted," he said.

Charlotte lifted her head to look at him, placing her phone down beside her.

"Or rather, the things you felt coming off me. I knew you could feel it, and I still couldn't control my emotions enough to make it easier on you. For that, I'm sorry."

Her lips drew in, and her nose screwed up adorably, eyebrows smashing together. "I just don't understand it."

"What?"

"What has you on edge?"

"It's nothing serious." He squeezed her leg.

"That's not what I wanted to know. Serious or not, if it's bothering you enough that your emotions are that intense, I want to know." She wriggled and her toes curled on his thigh. "I care about you. You can talk to me, you know that, right?"

"I know." He laid his head back against the wall and rolled it to the side to look at her, resigned to admit to her his problems. If he expected their relationship to flourish, he needed to not be so rigid in his control and let her in. "I had another nightmare last night, then saw the phone message. I didn't sleep much because of it all. I think it didn't help the way I responded."

"Is there anything that makes it better?"

"The nightmares?"

When she nodded, he said, "Sleeping next to you."

Her mouth parted.

"When we touch, they tend to lessen." His hand slid to her foot again, massaging the heel. "At least, more so since you've come to the academy."

"Maybe we should start sleeping together, then."

"You move like a contortionist in your sleep," he said, laughing at the incredulous look on her face. "You do. I think for my own physical safety, we should have a bigger bed first."

She leaned forward and smacked his arm. "You're mean," she said with a pout. "Fine. I'll just sleep all by myself. More room for me." She smiled brightly, all her teeth on display. He loved seeing her smile.

He grabbed her chin with his forefinger and thumb before she sat back and gave her a soft kiss. When she sat back, he asked, "Do the others know now?"

"I told Blaire, Layla, and Riley what the headmistress said when I went by Riley's room last night after dinner. Blaire and Riley said they'd talk to Lukas and Seth. Dom probably knows by now from the headmistress. Blaire didn't know a James either."

"We'll have to ask Dom if he knows anyone important by that name."

He didn't get angry that she talked to them. Riley already knew. It didn't bother him if the others knew about the situation, or about Noah. Before he knew the full story, the only thing that bothered him was thinking she kept in contact with Noah after she learned who he was.

He hoped by letting Noah in, she didn't end up hurt again.

39

Unexpected Allies

Charlotte hadn't visited the library on the top floor of the main building of Blackthorn Academy before. With classes still not in session, she had no reason to until now.

Floor to ceiling bookshelves filled the massive library's interior on all the walls except for the far wall lined with windows. The windows of the library weren't stained glass like the front of the building. Arching into elaborate points with decorative circular shapes along the upper portion of the window, the windows maintained their tracery design, but the panes of glass were clear, allowing students to view the horizon.

Their group, composed of Aiden, Blaire, Riley, Seth, Lukas, Dominic, and Headmistress Velastra, sat at a long table away from the windows near an archway leading away from the main chamber near a couple of freestanding bookshelves.

Charlotte looked up at the beautiful chandelier overhead. Spherical and teardrop-shaped sparkling crystals covered the many tiers, refracting the light from their faux candles and casting the room in amber ambient lighting.

She jolted when Blaire touched her arm, giving her a questioning look.

She shook her head, offering a smile.

Ever since Aiden told her about how he still struggled with his nightmares, she wondered what she could do to help him. It wouldn't be a hardship to sleep by his side if it helped him attain peace. It surprised her he hadn't already requested it. Then she remembered his apprehension about his species despite her assurances.

She hoped allowing him to bite her with his fangs would show him her sincerity—that she wasn't afraid of what he was. Reassuring him wasn't why she allowed him to bite her and drink her blood, but she wondered if it would double as reassurance for him.

The headmistress clapped her hands at the head of the table, drawing their attention, halting the chatting amongst them. "Dominic and I spoke with the other members of the Blackthorn Clan through conference calls after we became aware of the situation with the young rogue." She rose from her seat and her manicured nails tapped the table when she steepled her fingertips against the surface. "I have met privately with the young man to discuss his situation and the clan's decision."

Riley stretched her arms in front of her, the many bracelets on her wrists clattering on the surface of the table. "What did they say?"

"King Adrian has accepted the information we provided and with the caveat that the young man remains under strict surveillance in the interim, he may seek asylum at Blackthorn Academy. If he indeed desires to reform himself and integrate back into our world, we will grant him the same opportunities as the rest of you to obtain a degree and move out into the world, but only if he proves his sincerity during his time here."

"That's it?" Seth asked, his steel eyes narrowing. "He just gets away with being with the rogues who are after Blaire and hurt Charlotte?"

Lukas leaned back in his seat, crossing his arms. "I don't know why he gets a free pass to go to school. He puts the rest of us at risk."

The headmistress leaned forward, narrowing her russet gaze on the two who spoke against Noah. "I expected more understanding from you two, considering I've been made aware you know the full account of why he behaved like he did."

"I still don't know if I can trust him," Lukas muttered.

"You're correct," she conceded, standing upright. "This is why Blackthorn Security will monitor his behavior and interactions on campus. Furthermore, this is not a slap on the wrist situation. Noah Black will be required to meet with the clan at a future date and provide a detailed debriefing of everything he knows about the rogue group or groups operating in this region. That information isn't pertinent to this discussion, so I didn't think I had to inform you, but since you both were willing to accept Mr. Black so graciously…" She cut her gaze between Lukas and Seth, the disappointment in them clear on her face.

"With all due respect, I don't blame them for their mistrust," Dominic said.

"Nor I. I am not one hundred percent settled in the choice myself, but I feel with the details provided, punishment when he seems unaware of the role of those he surrounded himself with is unjust." She settled her gaze on Lukas. "For someone who knows what it's like to be labeled guilty on assumptions, I expected more from you."

Charlotte leaned over and whispered, "What is she talking about?"

Blaire frowned, ducking her head. "When I was gone, students treated him like he'd killed me, unaware of the actual story. Rumors ran rampant, and some outright called him a murderer."

Lukas slid his gaze over to the two of them. Blaire hadn't been as quiet as she thought.

"That's exactly what I'm talking about," the headmistress said. "Thank you, Blaire."

"Look, I'm sorry. I didn't mean he should be crucified for it, but I'm tired of seeing these assholes walk, get their memory wiped, or go to Cresbel while Blaire suffers, and we get pegged as the ones in the wrong."

"If you knew what happened behind the walls of Cresbel Asylum, you wouldn't say that," Dominic said with a shake of his head. "The reports I've seen during meetings with the clan would shake you to the core. It is not a place you want to end up." He looked over at Aiden, catching his eye.

Dominic had stopped Aiden from ending up there or being executed. Charlotte had more to thank him for than she realized.

Headmistress Velastra said, "I understand you feel this is unfair, Lukas, but there are procedures we must follow. There are things you've all done that have been overlooked for the sake of the greater good, but if the clan proceeded with harsher punishments above what another would receive for the same laws broken, anarchy would erupt in our world. There's already enough discourse surrounding Blaire's awakening as it is." The headmistress rounded the table. "We need to try to mitigate the discord." She waved a hand at someone out of sight before returning to the table. "I expect you all to behave yourselves."

Noah rounded the corner of a bookshelf with his hands tucked deep into the pockets of his dark jeans. He wore a leather jacket over a charcoal gray hoodie with a white T-shirt underneath. He offered the room a hesitant smile, but it didn't meet his eyes.

Aiden stood, and Charlotte followed, reaching out for his arm to keep him from going after Noah. A muddled mess of emotions hit her chest like a gunshot the instant Aiden noticed him. She couldn't decipher his feelings. The only thing she knew for certain was that Noah was the target of his intensity.

Aiden moved to position himself in front of her when Noah noticed her and rounded the table. "Stay away from her," he said, voice like ice. When Noah froze, he added, "Give me a reason and I'll end you."

His lack of trust in Noah was unmistakable now. While he didn't express his mistrust as candidly as Seth or Lukas did before, his words carried a deadly promise that everyone in the room knew he was capable of fulfilling. He had killed for her before.

Noah held up his hands and took a step back. "I get it."

"Aiden," the headmistress said, voice stern. "Sit down and control yourself or you will be asked to leave. All of you show a bit of decorum. I expect better than this."

Riley tapped her hands against the table. "I didn't say anything. I trust the guy."

Charlotte's mouth popped open, and Riley laughed.

"What? I didn't. But he said all that stuff. He's a sad boy."

"A sad boy?" Noah's dark brows disappeared behind his shaggy curls.

"Yep," she said, sitting up.

Riley didn't elaborate on her assessment of Noah, and he shook his head. If he planned to be a part of the academy, he would need to get used to her eccentric behavior.

The headmistress gave her an exasperated look.

"What?"

"Read the room."

"Okay," she said, groaning. "I promise I'll stop teasing."

"She's not going to stop," Seth said.

"Oh, ye of little faith."

Headmistress Velastra cracked a small smile, and Lukas snorted.

Charlotte found it amazing how Riley could completely transform the atmosphere, defusing the tension without even realizing it. She studied Riley's face as she stuck her tongue out at Seth. Maybe she did know what she was doing.

The headmistress clapped her hands, diverting attention back to her again. "Have a seat, Mr. Black." Her gaze moved across the table, her tone sharpening to a reprimand. "Aiden."

Aiden slumped into his chair, but not before grabbing Charlotte by the arm and pulling her with him. She yelped in surprise until he pulled her into his lap, placing one hand on her thigh and the other on her stomach. She looked at Blaire with wide eyes.

"Get used to it."

Noticing Charlotte's uncertainty, the headmistress softened her voice and said, "A threatened or insecure Korrena will do things to soothe their negative feelings and assert his or her position to anyone they feel is a threat."

Aiden sucked his teeth.

"Lukas still does it," Blaire said, offering a smile.

Lukas shrugged. "Whatever."

Riley giggled. "You're not so calm yourself." She looked at Charlotte, hooking her thumb at Blaire. "You should have seen the way she pushed past this girl at Haven trying to talk to Lukas. Blaire planted herself right in his lap and stuck her tongue down his throat."

"Talk about asserting her position," Dominic mumbled, trying not to laugh.

Aiden chuckled behind Charlotte, and his body relaxed.

Blaire's face turned as red as a tomato, and Lukas smirked.

Noah slid into the seat Charlotte vacated and looked at Aiden. All eyes moved to Noah, questioning his choice to take the seat next to Aiden. Did he have a death wish?

"It's fair you don't trust me." He ignored the rumble in Aiden's chest. "We've not had the most pleasant interactions, and now you've found out all this about the rogues, but I didn't know half the shit going on, I swear it. I would never want to hurt her."

"Why?" Seth asked.

"Truth be told, I liked her. Not as a friend, but more."

Aiden tightened his fingers on her belly. She squirmed and leaned into him, hoping her weight would ease him.

"I don't feel that way anymore. I mean, she's cute and all, but I'm not about to lose my head over her. The most that happened was a kiss, and—"

"The fuck you say?"

She gasped at Lukas's outburst and looked up when he moved to stand between where Noah sat and where Aiden held her in a vise-like grip. He'd moved to intercept Aiden before he could even stand.

The overwhelming emotion of rage passing through their bond made her want to vomit. Aiden trembled beneath her. Lukas didn't have a direct line to Aiden's emotions like she did, but they were best friends. They looked out for one another, knew each other well enough to know when the other would react badly.

Even though Aiden knew about the kiss, his potent anger made her question how intense his fury had been when she first told him about the kiss before the bond started to develop. Hearing Noah say the words himself likely had an effect similar to pouring gasoline on a bonfire.

Riley leaned forward on the table, her knees on the seat, peering around Lukas, who remained a silent sentinel between Noah and

Aiden. "When'd that happen?"

Charlotte took a breath. Even though she could taste his anger, he moved the hand from her thigh to stroke her arm with the gentlest touch. "Before Aiden came to visit. The night I saw the Vasirian in the alley."

Riley's eyes narrowed. "Did he force you?"

"No! Noah's not like that. I pulled away and told him I only wanted to be friends. Nothing happened." She didn't understand why she needed to defend herself or Noah. She wasn't dating Aiden then. Still, she wanted to ease their worries. "We're friends. Nothing more."

Aiden grunted.

Lukas looked back at him. "We good?"

"Yeah," Aiden said, voice no higher than a strained whisper.

Charlotte turned to give him a quick kiss on his lips to make him feel better, but he startled her by putting his hand on the back of her head, sliding his tongue into her mouth, and tangling it with hers. When she moaned, he pulled away, cutting his eyes to Noah. *Well, then.*

"Talk about asserting his position," Riley said, echoing Dominic's earlier words about Blaire. He snorted a laugh.

"If everyone is done acting like children, I'd like to finish this," the headmistress said.

Aiden scoffed, sitting back and pulling Charlotte against him.

"Mr. Black. With the danger you will face turning your back on the local gang of rogues you have been with, I have been advised to inform you that you are under strict orders by the Blackthorn Clan not to leave campus until they can send for you to come to Europe to discuss what you know."

"Don't gotta worry about that. No way am I going back into town and getting myself killed."

She nodded, satisfied with Noah's response.

"So I have a question," Aiden said.

Headmistress Velastra looked at Aiden, who sat watching Noah with intense scrutiny. "Very well."

"How'd you have the black eye and split lip for so long?"

Noah scratched his head, fluffing his curls. "Brent."

"Brent?" Seth asked.

"Yeah. The rogue who stalked Charlotte. The one Aiden—"

The headmistress cleared her throat.

"The one who disappeared," Noah corrected. "He injected me with Folinarin before he kicked my ass for kissing Charlotte. I couldn't heal for a while. He wanted me to suffer."

"He sounds like a sadist," Charlotte said. *And to think I felt a little sorry for the guy and his loss.*

"You're not far off the mark. One of the other guys told me that after he lost his Korrena he wasn't the same. I didn't know him before that. Brent said he wanted me to remember my place and have a reminder not to touch what is his."

Riley's face scrunched. "What's his?"

Noah looked at Charlotte. "Her."

Aiden's hands tightened on her; an inhuman growl rumbled in his chest.

Riley, ignoring her brother, asked, "Why are the rogues after Blaire? It's the one thing we've tried to understand. Like, why would they try to kill her if she'll be able to save them?"

"What are you talking about?"

Everyone looked at Noah.

"The prophecy," Riley said like it was obvious.

"I don't know much of their motives, but if Blaire becomes a Vasirian and the ancient magic awakens and kills us all, I don't blame them for being concerned." He looked at Blaire. "I don't think you should die or anything, but there has to be something to avoid destroying us."

"What the hell are you talking about?" Lukas snapped, sitting up.

"The prophecy."

"That is *so not* the prophecy," Riley said. "Is that what your gang thinks?"

"Not my gang."

"My bad." Riley waved a hand. "*Former* gang."

"Anyway, it's what's spread throughout the rogue communities and created the panic."

Lukas slumped back, releasing a string of curses. Blaire placed her hand on his arm.

"Your sources are very wrong, Mr. Black. The prophecy is the exact opposite of your belief."

"What?"

Charlotte saw the confusion in Noah's eyes. He didn't know the truth. It would seem none of the rogues did.

"If Blaire *doesn't* become a Vasirian, then the magic keeping us alive disappears and we all die," the headmistress said, clasping her hands in front of her.

"What in the… What?" Noah looked around the table at everyone. They all held varying degrees of frustration and resignation. "You're serious?"

"I don't joke, Mr. Black."

"I… I didn't know." He swept his gaze to Blaire. "I swear I didn't know."

She nodded but said nothing.

"Is there a way to inform the other rogues?" Charlotte said, sitting up in Aiden's lap now that he'd calmed down. "Maybe put an end to this?"

Seth shook his head. "We can't just put out an all-broadcast bulletin like an international emergency. Humans can't know. It would create a panic like we've never seen."

"We need to speak to the Oracle," Headmistress Velastra said, looking at Dominic. "Perhaps the Celestial Conclave has provided her insight into this dilemma. If she's unaware, she needs to know as well as the rest of the clan. The rogues believing Blaire is a threat to them, and not their salvation, makes this a treacherous path to navigate."

"Speaking of the Oracle," Blaire started, and everyone looked at her. "I had another dream last night."

"A dream?"

Blaire looked across the table at Charlotte with a nod.

Blaire had shared before about a magical place that she could only access in her dreams if the Oracle pulled her there. The place was real but cut off from their plane of existence because of the loss of magic. It sounded like the stuff of fairytales, but she knew Blaire wasn't lying about it. Too many things aligned with other events they'd explained to her.

The coolest part of it all was Blaire had a guardian wolf named Ciro that the Celestial Conclave granted her with her father's will for her to be safe. A guardian wolf was another thing to add to the top of the pile of unreal things Charlotte had to believe if she expected to survive this world.

"What happened?"

Blaire looked up at the headmistress. "The Oracle told me about Charlotte and why she became a Korrena."

"What? When?" Riley pushed to her knees again, unable to sit still. "Why?"

"In my dream last night. I've been with Professor Sinclair all day, so I couldn't say anything."

"The Oracle didn't tell Charlotte when they met," Aiden said. "Why did she tell you?"

"The Celestial Conclave gave her more information since then. The magic that saved your life left a piece of itself inside of you. That spark of magic called to the dormant magic in Charlotte. It was supposed to happen this way."

"What do you mean?" Riley asked.

"Aiden's death was part of the prophecy, but what wasn't said—but was still meant to happen—was if my heart opened enough to save him, then it would facilitate Charlotte's awakening. She was meant to awaken before the other humans. So even if I chose against it, she would be with us. My magic reverberating through Aiden awakened Charlotte."

Dominic let out a low whistle.

"Chose what?" Charlotte asked. "What choice?"

Lukas looked at Charlotte. "If Blaire doesn't become a Vasirian, the magic won't come back. Our kind then becomes kind of…"

"Doomed?" Riley finished for him, and Lukas winced.

"Why don't you want to become one?"

Blaire's gaze shifted to Noah with apprehension. "I do, but the Oracle told us it isn't safe to do it yet. With the threat of the rogues, Lukas can't safely turn me. I'll be too vulnerable during the transition. I used to not know if I wanted to do it, but I do now."

His hands went up in a sign of surrender. "Hey now. Now that I know the truth, I don't get why the others would be against it. At least, the ones who know. I know the gang I ran with doesn't know this. I fully support you joining us."

"Dominic, can you contact one of the members of the Blackthorn Clan to have the Oracle reach out to me? I would like to speak to her about this new information to see if it holds any bearing on the prophecies she's already laid out for us. I want to know if there is any additional information we can glean about the rogues' actions."

He nodded, looking at the headmistress. "I'll get on that after this meeting. Nothing new has come forward so far about who's controlling their movements. Adrian has tried to get inside information with no luck. The groups are way too organized across multiple countries to not have someone in a position of power running them."

Noah scoffed, drawing everyone's attention. "Oh, there is absolutely someone above the rogues. I've never seen them, but James always reported to someone. When Brent talked with him on speaker phone, James seemed afraid whenever they talked about making his reports."

"Mr. Black, I want you to meet with our security team after this and give them all the information you know about the members of the gangs that operate in this region."

He sat up and put his arms on the table. "Sure, but I gotta warn you…" He tapped his fingers a couple times. "There are several in the area. I only really know ours—well, my *former* one." He gave a shake of his head, his chin-length waves brushing his cheeks.

"Several?"

He nodded at Riley.

"That's outrageous," the headmistress said. "How have we been able to remain in the dark about this? The Blackthorn schools and local associations keep us well aware of what is happening in the region concerning everything in the human world. We have to know to keep our schools protected."

"Hey, I'm not lying."

"We don't think you're lying," Dominic said, giving Noah a sympathetic look. "We're concerned. Only a couple of months ago, we believed there weren't any organized rogue cells in the States."

"How wrong we were," the headmistress said, lowering herself into the seat.

40

Breaking Point

Aiden squeezed Charlotte's hand before unlocking the door to their dorm room. The meeting with the headmistress took a turn he didn't expect when she brought Noah into the room. Allowing him to join the school hadn't settled well. Aiden couldn't decide if he trusted Noah or not.

The guy seemed sincere, but too many times people his friends thought they could trust had proved them wrong.

"I'll be out in a sec," she said after slipping her shoes off, disappearing into the ensuite while he went to his bedside table to put his phone down.

Knowing Charlotte favored a neat living space, he picked up his discarded T-shirt and placed it on the bed, freezing when a blood-curdling scream broke the silence.

Charging into the bathroom, he jerked to a stop to avoid running into Charlotte. She stood in front of their smashed mirror. Shattered glass littered the counter's surface and the floor. Among the shards were dead pink roses and petals everywhere.

Her hand pressed to her forehead, and she spoke with a fearful voice. "Why is he doing this if the stalker is dead? What does he want?"

When she turned to seek comfort from him, she shrieked and stumbled back, almost stepping onto the broken shards with her bare feet, until he pulled her against him.

Turning with her in his arms to look behind him and see what frightened her, he couldn't suppress the snarl that escaped at the message on the wall crudely written in blood:

Charlotte sobbed, clinging onto his chest as her body shook violently.

Of everything they experienced together, he never felt her fear like this. It wasn't even because he could physically feel the fear with their growing bond. He'd never seen her respond so poorly, even with the break-in.

She had reached her breaking point.

There were limits to how long someone could remain strong before they eventually broke.

He bent, putting his hands on the back of her thighs, lifting her. She threw her arms around his neck and wrapped her legs around his waist. He carried her into the bedroom and sat down on the bed, holding her to his chest, grabbing his phone from the bedside table and placing a call.

Even though he wanted to destroy the room in a fit of rage after someone came into their space and made his Korrena feel unsafe, he had to remain calm for her. Although she sensed his fury, he refused to display it. He noticed she responded better if he didn't make an outward display of anger.

"Hello?"

"Lukas," he said, clenching his teeth, voice tight.

"What's wrong?"

"Get over here." Aiden ended the call before Lukas could respond and tossed it to the side.

Minutes later, his best friend burst into the room. Charlotte screamed, her entire body jolting.

"Fucking hell," Aiden said when her nails dug into his skin through his shirt. He'd forgotten to warn her they were coming. He put a hand on the back of her head, tucking her face against him as he rocked her like a child, making gentle shushing sounds against the top of her head. "I've got you, Kitten. I've got you."

Blaire shoved Lukas out of the way to get over to the bed, crawling beside Aiden. "What's wrong with her?" Before he could say anything, Seth and Riley piled into the room behind Lukas. "They were with us when you called."

"What's going on?" Riley demanded at the sight of Charlotte. She joined Blaire on the bed.

"The bathroom," he said, keeping his voice calm and low while continuing to rub Charlotte's back and cradle her head.

Lukas turned and went into the ensuite, Seth trailing behind him.

"What the fuck?"

Riley hopped up at the tone of Seth's voice and rushed into the bathroom. "Holy shit." She gaped from the doorway.

Blaire glanced over her shoulder and then back at Aiden. "What is it?"

"I'm going to kill Noah, that's what."

Charlotte whimpered.

All this time they thought the stalker wasn't dead after finding a rose on campus, only to have Noah waltz in and change their perspective. Was it all a ploy to lure them into a false sense of security? Noah's arrival brought with it the biggest disturbance they'd encountered since the break-in at Charlotte's old apartment. It hadn't escaped Aiden's notice that the blood in the bathroom was human blood. Where had he gotten it?

"Why do you think he had anything to do with that?" Riley asked, coming over and taking Blaire's place when she got up to see what everyone had already seen.

Aiden didn't have it in him to explain his theories, not when he needed to focus on the frightened girl in his lap. "It's too convenient that on the night he arrives, this happens."

Charlotte lifted her head, sitting up on his lap now that her trembling and tears had abated. Black streaks marred her cheeks from runny mascara, and her nose looked red and irritated. He took the T-shirt he'd dropped on the bed and wiped her nose. "The rose and that note came before Noah ever joined. It's that guy James."

That made him pause and rethink his position. If James didn't know they were aware of Brent's identity as the stalker, his continuation of the ruse after Brent's death wouldn't seem strange. Still, the convenience of Noah's arrival and this incident struck him as odd. Maybe James used him as a distraction. Did Noah provide that distraction willingly or was it mere coincidence? He didn't want to trust the guy.

"I get you're upset, man." Lukas leaned against the back of Aiden's desk chair, crossing his arms as Blaire took a seat. "I know what you're going through with the new bond. It makes things chaotic, and anytime the worst happens, you're going to suspect someone you see as a threat to her."

"It makes you irrational," Seth added, scratching the back of his head.

Aiden was glad they had been through the bond's trials already. He didn't know what he would do if they hadn't. In situations like this, he would be the one to point out that James was the likely culprit, but instead, his emotions were too volatile to allow him to focus and not think of Noah—the guy who showed interest in his Korrena—as the real threat.

He needed to get his head on straight.

Lukas ground his teeth together. "If the rogues are getting onto the campus and doing things like this without being noticed, Blaire is in danger, too."

"Isn't everyone?"

He looked at Riley.

Like Aiden, Lukas only thought of his Korrena when the situation became dire. No one could expect otherwise—young bond or not. The protective instincts around the Korrena bond ran deep.

The rogues didn't care about Vasirian law. They would hurt any student who got in their way. They could easily slip in amongst the students and no one would blink. It was still summer break, so no one wore their uniforms. It made infiltration easier—especially if the rogues were young like Noah. Even then, with aging at a snail's pace, older rogues would blend in just fine.

A hard knock sounded on the door. Charlotte pressed herself against Aiden, gripping the back of his shirt, and he tightened his hold to soothe her.

"It's probably security," Seth said. "I called them from the bathroom."

Riley opened the door, and several members of Blackthorn Security stepped into the room, crowding the space. Their eyes scanned the room's occupants.

"Who's dorm is this?"

"Ours," Aiden said.

"You and who? Her?" The man nodded at Charlotte.

"Yeah, my Korrena."

The bearded man decked out in all black combat gear, complete with a tactical vest, grunted. "What's going on?"

"Their bathroom is destroyed," Lukas said. "Someone wrote on the wall with blood."

"You sure it's blood?" the man asked. "What'd they write?"

"'You're mine,'" Riley read aloud, frowning at Aiden, her gaze sliding down to Charlotte in his arms.

Whoever wrote the message was sorely mistaken if they thought Charlotte belonged to them. The porcelain-skinned goddess in his arms belonged only to him. Only he could worship at this altar. She was his, and he would die to protect her and ensure his place at her side.

"Not sure who or what it belongs to, but the smell is definitely blood," Seth said, his nose wrinkling. "I don't think it's Vasirian blood. Maybe human."

"What makes you say that?"

"I'm not good with human blood."

The man nodded in understanding. Not everyone had an iron will. Those who didn't avoided putting themselves in positions that made them susceptible to weakness.

Aiden looked at Seth. His eyes had a faint white glow at the edges of his silver irises. He remembered how hard he had it when Blaire bled on multiple occasions. He wouldn't attack anyone, but he

struggled around copious amounts of human blood.

A female security guard with brunette hair tied back in a low ponytail stepped forward. "The headmistress has debriefed us about the other human on campus and about her circumstances with the rogues. This related to that?"

He nodded.

"Alright," another man wearing a black ballcap said, coming out of the bathroom, "I want y'all to go elsewhere for now while we secure the location and clean up the mess."

The woman guard stepped to the side. "We'll let the headmistress know of the situation and have her contact you all when we're done gathering evidence and running a check on the blood on the wall to confirm if it is human DNA and if we can find a match in the local law enforcement's database. In the meantime, avoid letting anyone know about this."

"We don't need a bunch of panicking kids running around," the bearded security guard said. He didn't look much older than Aiden, but that didn't say much for his age.

Aiden hoped taking a walk and getting fresh air would ease the prickly feeling crawling over his skin. He needed to remain calm and not go after Noah. He hated that he needed to continuously remind himself that the real threat to Charlotte wasn't the curly-haired guy with smiling blue eyes.

41

Family

Charlotte looked at Aiden as he led her from the dorm building. She didn't understand why seeing the bathroom wrecked made her break down the way it did, but she couldn't handle it all anymore. She looked down at the cobblestone beneath her feet.

Through the entire ordeal with her stalker, she kept her wits about her. She contacted the police, secured her home, did everything right. Now she felt like a blubbering damsel-in-distress running to Aiden to save her from the big bad.

Her mouth parted as a thought dawned on her.

"What's wrong?"

She looked up at him, knowing he felt the shockwave of panic that went through her system. "What if he went to my mom's next? What if he's with them now? What if he's hurt them?"

Riley angled toward her as they walked. "I can call Sara." She pulled out her cellphone.

"No!" Charlotte lifted her hand. "I thought they couldn't know."

"I'm not gonna say anything stupid. I'll ask her about my hours this week. I mean, I don't actually remember them anyway, and it wouldn't be the first time I've called her about it. She's used to it at this point." Riley shrugged. "If something is wrong, she either won't answer or will say something."

Charlotte listened as Riley carried on a lively conversation with her mom on speakerphone. They were at home watching a movie and eating takeout Chinese food. The panic and tension in her muscles eased. She didn't know what she would do if James hurt her mothers.

After the phone call ended, and they started walking again, she said, "I feel stupid."

"Why?"

She looked up at Aiden. "Instead of doing the right thing and contacting security like Seth did, I turned into a mess and made you take care of me. And now Riley is checking on my moms instead of me. I feel kinda useless right now."

Aiden stopped, forcing her to stop too or let go of his hand. She turned to look at him. The others came to a stop around them.

"Don't do that." He squeezed her hand. "You're allowed to stop and have a moment. You're allowed to break down." He stepped forward and cupped her cheek. "I'm here. Break, scream, cry. I'll still be here. I will hold you up until you're able to stand on your own again." His thumb swiped a tear from her cheek.

"We're here too," Riley said, and Lukas and Seth nodded.

"You don't have to be alone anymore, Charlotte. We love you. You've always been my sister, and I hated you weren't with me through this."

Charlotte turned and threw her arms around Blaire's shoulders, sobbing. "I thought you didn't care about me anymore. I thought I'd lost you." Blaire's shoulder muffled her cries. Later, she might feel embarrassment about her emotional outburst, but right now, it felt cathartic to let it all out.

Blaire hugged her tightly and laughed. "You haven't lost me. Never will."

"I love you so much."

"Me too, Char."

"How cute. Isn't human love wonderful?"

Charlotte released Blaire, and they all turned to see five men and two women standing across from them near the side of the main building that faced the dorms.

"What do you think, Lee?" A woman on the far right sporting skinny jeans and an army green T-shirt looked at the man beside her dressed in baggy jeans and a red T-shirt.

"Only love that matters is yours, babe."

"Ain't he the best?" She smiled, and they shared a quick kiss.

"Will you two shut the fuck up?" the man in the middle said. He stepped forward. His sun-kissed brown hair was pulled back in a low ponytail that fell down his back. He wore light-wash jeans with a white T-shirt and a leather jacket similar to Lukas's and Noah's. Were they not hot? "Ignore those two. They just bonded, and we've been subjected to their fuckfest all week." He swiped a hand down his face. "I don't get paid enough for this shit."

Lukas glanced around. "How the hell did they get on campus?"

"What do you mean?" Blaire looked up at him. "Who are they?"

"Rogues."

"How do you know?"

Riley crossed her arms. "Who else would approach us in the middle of the night after their room got trashed?"

"I don't know. Students?" Blaire's voice faltered. It sounded like she didn't trust her own judgement.

A woman near the end laughed, drawing Charlotte's attention. It was the deputy from the police station when she reported her stalker—Madeline, if she remembered right. She knew something seemed weird about the officer. "Oh you delusional little human. I wouldn't be caught dead attending one of the clan's institutions."

Movement on the other side of Madeline caught her attention. It was the intimidating officer built like a mountain she met the day of the break-in. *Brooks.* She sure remembered *his* name. His catlike eyes now glowed an eerie shade of chartreuse and lingered on her.

These people weren't students. Not at all.

"What do you want?" Seth said, stepping in front of Riley to join Lukas and Aiden, who already stood blocking Blaire and Charlotte from the rogues in front of them.

The man with the ponytail pulled a handgun from the back of his jeans and pointed it at them. Aiden let out a strangled noise. "The blonde and the redhead. Give 'em to us and we'll leave nice and peaceful-like." A couple of men behind him laughed.

"Seth, go get the security guys at the gates," Lukas said.

The man with the ponytail threw his head back and laughed. "Oh, now that won't do. I doubt they'd be much help. Not with being dead and all." This time, all the others laughed.

Charlotte looked around the empty courtyard. No one was around to help them. Her gaze darted to the dorms behind them. If they tried to call for help, would the guy shoot them? Did the others have guns? She didn't want to put other students in danger. Still, they needed help.

Following her gaze, the man with the ponytail waved his gun at her when she opened her mouth. "Don't get any ideas, Little Red. You'll be dead on the ground before anyone hears you."

Madeline smirked. "Silly girl thinks someone can help them."

Charlotte's eyes moved to Aiden as fear that wasn't her own paralyzed her, distracting her from the taunts of the rogues. His hands shook at his side, his gaze focused on the gun in the man's hand.

She moved behind him, resting her hands against his back where the rogues couldn't see her. She didn't want to point out his fear for the rogues to see, but it felt like she was drowning in it. How he stood under the weight of that terror was beyond her.

"Why don't you go away!" Riley yelled from behind Seth, and he groaned.

A woman wearing army fatigue pants and a white tank top rolled her eyes and popped a gum bubble, swinging a baseball bat loosely at her side. She scratched her buzzed hair and mocked Riley's voice with a laugh, glancing at Madeline and Brooks to her left.

"While this is fun and all," the bearded man on her other side said. "Let's get this show on the road. I got cold beer waiting for me at home."

The man with the ponytail that Charlotte deduced was their leader hooked his thumb in their direction, and the others sprang into action, running toward the students.

Brooks went straight for Blaire, and Lukas intercepted him. They crashed to the ground in a tangle of limbs and grunts.

Seth slammed his fist into the face of the man with the beard. He dropped like a sack of bricks to the ground, surprising Charlotte with how weak he was. He hadn't looked very muscular, but she expected more of a non-human. The rogue lay on the ground clutching his face, groaning, and blubbering as blood poured through his fingers from what she suspected was a broken nose.

Lukas struggled against Brooks, trying to free himself from beneath the mountain of a man. He narrowly avoided having his hands and neck shredded by the sharp fangs gnashing in his face when Seth rushed over, using the momentum of his sprint to knock Brooks off Lukas, giving them the opportunity to tag team the man.

Riley grabbed Blaire's arm, pulling her away from everyone. The man with the ponytail focused his attention on them. He chased them toward the tree grove when they broke into a sprint across the front of the courtyard.

The mouthy Korrena pair and the woman with the buzzed hair corralled Aiden and Charlotte toward the side of the main building. Madeline joined them while Seth and Lukas fought behind them.

The male half of the Korrena mates didn't hesitate to go for Aiden, throwing a fist into his jaw, followed by a sucker punch to his gut. He grunted and doubled over before righting himself, a bruise blooming on his jawline. He snarled and lunged at the man when the woman with buzzed hair took advantage of Charlotte's distraction over Aiden's fight and sprang at her.

She screamed, turning and running in the only direction where rogues weren't in her path—the forest. She couldn't fight at all, but she was fast. Blaire used to force Charlotte to go running with her all the time. It nearly killed her, and she hated running, but she was faster than Blaire.

Madeline's voice called out, "Run away, Little Red! The big bad wolves are coming for you!" A chorus of howls and whooping laughter followed her declaration.

She wasn't used to the forest at night. She'd come out here several times since joining Blackthorn Academy when she thought her stalker was dead, but she avoided entering the forest at night. Bobcats, coyotes, rattlesnakes, and copperheads were some of the predators she had to worry about in the forest.

Tonight, she had a new predator to fear, and she was their prey.

The longer she ran, the more she worried she wouldn't find her way back. She no longer heard the pursuing rogues or the sounds of the fight she ran from.

Stopping to catch her breath, she placed her hand on the bark of a pine tree and bent at the waist, coughing.

The forest wasn't as dark as usual with the full moon overhead. It illuminated a clearing a few feet away from where she stood. A small group of fallen trees at the center blocked her view from the other side, casting eerie shadows.

Entering the clearing would put her on display and make her easy pickings.

"Charlotte!"

She staggered when Aiden bellowed her name. Before she could call back to him, she heard the sounds of crunching foliage drawing closer. She didn't know if it was Aiden or not.

Staying still would end in disaster; she had to take her chances by crossing the clearing.

As soon as she broke the tree line and progressed several feet into the open space, a man stepped out from behind the fallen trees. She screamed, and Aiden called her name again. He heard her. The man grinned at her with his teeth showing as several others joined him.

She called Aiden's name. The others called for her, too. They would find her. She knew it.

Her heart rate increased when Aiden yelled, "Keep making noise! I'll find you!"

The man *tsked* several times like scolding a child as she continued to call their names, telling them she was in the clearing. He moved closer, away from the shadows, and the moonlight caught the shock of red hair on his head.

Several feet to her left, her friends burst through the trees into the clearing. Noah and Dominic were with them. They rushed over, and Aiden enveloped her in his arms. Blood stained his arms and shirt. His lip looked busted, and drying blood crusted around his nostrils.

"I'm okay," he whispered when she touched his face. "Dom was showing Noah to their dorm since they'll be sharing so Dom can keep an eye on him. They showed up mid-fight. Security is handling it now."

That explained why the other rogues hadn't gotten to her and she didn't hear them anymore.

"Such a touching sight. So, you're my daughter's Korrena?"

She spun, and Aiden kept his arms locked around her from behind.

"I'm sorry," Riley said. "I think I just had a stroke. Did you say daughter?"

The man's gaze slid to Riley. "I did."

Lukas swiped the blood from his cheek.

"Charlotte doesn't have a dad," she said, crossing her arms. Riley didn't intimidate anyone standing there in a skirt with hot pink tulle underneath and a little T-shirt with a pink pixel heart on the front. She looked like a goth Care Bear. "Sperm-donor, sure. But you expect us to believe that's you?"

"I think I know my own child." He turned his attention to Charlotte.

She tried to step back but couldn't because of the wall of man behind her. He tightened his hold in reassurance.

Her father was Vasirian? How was that possible? The Oracle would have said if she wasn't human, so she knew he wouldn't have been a Vasirian at her birth. He would have needed to be reborn Vasirian. The only thing she knew for certain was turning humans went against Vasirian law and only Korrena pairs could do it. Did this man have a Korrena? Did that mean Blaire and Charlotte weren't the only humans with Korrenas?

"What do you want?" Aiden called out.

"My daughter, of course."

Seth stepped forward next to Charlotte and Aiden. "We're supposed to believe you're her father? What the hell are you doing with rogues?"

Lukas stood at her other side. "He's not a Vasirian," he said, glancing at Charlotte. "He shouldn't know about us. Shouldn't be with rogues."

Her eyes widened, and her gaze snapped to the man claiming to be her father. He smirked. There went the rebirth and Korrena theory.

"Well, when you run the biggest rogue cell in the Southeast, what do you expect? I know all about this world, and I have for over twenty years."

Lukas cursed.

"Of course, we weren't always in Georgia. Your area has smaller groups, not comparable to my empire." He held a fist in front of his mouth. "No, definitely not comparable. But absorbing them into mine proved easy enough."

"What are you talking about?" Riley snapped.

"After we heard about Blaire's place in the Vasirian world, I moved us from Florida. You see, we can't have her around ruining everything."

"She's saving us, you moron!"

The red-haired man glared at Riley.

"She is a plague." He looked at Charlotte again. "My sweet girl. You understand that I had to keep my identity from you, don't you? Before you knew of Vasirian, I had to stay away. I knew about you, though. When your mother died, I was heartbroken. I couldn't keep you. I couldn't stand the thought of raising you alone without her. A reminder of what I'd lost."

"You're disgusting!" Riley stepped forward, and Seth grabbed her around the waist. "Screw that guy. Let me go!" She stabbed a finger in the red-haired man's direction. "You expect us to believe you're her sperm-donor? Like that makes a difference! She doesn't know you! What gives you any claim to her?"

Blaire shook her head. "What kind of father abandons a baby like that?"

"Oh, come now. You children don't understand." He frowned as if sad.

Charlotte knew he wasn't. The man had no feelings. How could he be her father? It made her stomach sour.

"I went to Ireland on an assignment and met your mother. It was a whirlwind love, and you were conceived in only a few months. I was granted an extension on my visa to stay with her, and once you were born and she passed, I gave you to the orphanage."

"I don't care! Why are you here now?" Her eyes burned. She wanted answers for so long, but now that the man in front of her was telling her history with clinical detachment, she didn't want to know anymore. If he wasn't her father, he knew enough about her to know her birthplace and about the orphanage where her mothers adopted her from. But anyone could find that information if they dug deep enough.

"Oh, Charlotte, I love you. Don't you see? Now that you know about these monsters, you can come with me, and we can build a bigger empire. You can even bring your Korrena. He can join us." The deranged smile that crossed his face made her stomach knot and sour.

"Fuck that," Aiden said, his hands running over her arms. "You can take your empire and shove it."

"You expect us to believe you run an entire organization with Vasirian at your beck and call?" Dominic crossed his arms. "You're human."

"Well, when you have the kind of money I have to grant someone unfettered access to any vice they desire, people tend to fall in line—Vasirian or human."

"Great. So he's rich," Riley grumbled.

"I still don't see how that matters," Charlotte said. "Aren't all of you rich?"

Dominic shook his head. "Not exactly. Those of us who follow the law and come from families who've been around a while have more assets than most, but rogues typically abandon their families to live a life away from the rest of our kind. They lose access to the things the Blackthorn Clan grant our kind and lose the support of their families." He looked at the red-haired man. "If a human has enough money at his disposal to provide a comfortable life, coupled with access to things they couldn't get easily—like drugs and weapons, it wouldn't be a stretch to believe he could manipulate them to do as he wanted."

"But they could easily overpower him. How the hell?"

Dominic looked at Riley. "If he dies, what happens to his assets? It's not like they have claim to any of it. His longevity benefits them."

"You've gotta be kidding me." Riley threw her arms up. "Idiots."

"Money and vices control even the most powerful men." The red-haired man shrugged. "Think of human government. How many of them are swayed by lucrative donations despite having the power to crush the ones who offer them riches?"

"Anyone else over the monologue?" Riley jutted her hip to the side, crossing her arms. "Blah blah blah, I'm so rich and powerful I manipulate people less fortunate to get what I want. Seriously. Can you be any more obvious? All you need is the thin mustache to twirl in your fingers and you'll have nailed the smarmy villain role."

The man glared at her.

Charlotte looked down at her feet.

This man didn't care about her. He only saw an opportunity to get to Blaire by appealing to a daughter's heart, thinking she would fall into his arms once he made contact. She wasn't an idiot. She knew better than to trust a man who abandoned her without a second thought—*if* he was even the man he claimed to be.

Using his underling's obsession and heartbreak against him to isolate her so when he made himself known she would come, having no one else to trust. That by knowing the supposed truth, she would trust him and help him get his hands on Blaire.

It sickened her to consider any additional reasons he had for his behavior. Why was he involved with the Vasirian if he was a human? What made him use his fortune to manipulate them? What did he gain from that?

What he didn't count on, though, was the trust she had of the people gathered around her. They accepted her and let her in. She was no longer alone. No longer the outcast. They were her family. Her mothers were her true parents.

"Come now. We can break that bond of yours if he's unwilling to join us." He didn't know they hadn't sealed their bond yet.

Aiden moved her behind him and stepped forward. "Father or not, I will kill you before I let you touch her."

The rogues at the man's side stepped forward, and he held up his hand. "Do not interfere. We have other things to deal with first." His gaze moved to Noah, who stood next to Lukas.

"As for you, traitor, you will die for your insubordination."

Noah narrowed his eyes. "Fuck you, James."

"Recognize my voice, do you? No matter. You'll be dead soon

enough."

She looked at Noah. So the man claiming to be her father was James. The one who kept tormenting her after Brent died. The one who orchestrated everything might be her father. The idea of sharing DNA with someone so vile disgusted her.

"Leave him alone," she said. "Why are you doing this? This is my family. Leave them alone."

James sneered at her, dropping all pretenses of a loving father. "Oh, sweetie. You are as stupid as your mother was, it appears." Her eyes rounded. "Do you think these monsters care about you? That they would care about a species beneath them who isn't good for anything more than being a glorified blood bag for them to feast upon? You poor delusional girl."

The sudden one-eighty he took, belittling her and trying to put a rift between her and the people she loved, made her furious. They weren't monsters. They were more of a family to her than he ever had been. Her lower lip trembled as she held back the words she wanted to scream at him. Her nails dug into her thighs.

"I'm done with this family reunion. Take care of them," he said, turning to the rogues at his side. "Keep the blonde alive. Someone has a vested interest in her." He disappeared into the shadows of the trees piled in the center of the clearing again, returning to whatever hole he crawled out of, evidently done with trying to sway her to his cause.

When the rogues advanced, Seth, Lukas, and Aiden met them in the middle. The rogues outnumbered them. She looked around. Another rogue held Noah on the ground with gloved hands around his throat, snarling at him with fangs bared.

To her left, Riley clung to the back of another rogue like a monkey, tearing into their shoulder with her fangs. Maybe she was more intimidating than Charlotte thought.

Blaire screamed when a rogue lunged at her, and Dominic intercepted them, tackling the man to the ground in a flurry of fists and fangs as they bit and punched at each other.

Charlotte ran in her direction. "What do we do?"

"We can't run. There are still rogues on campus with security. If they catch us in the forest, we're dead. Watch out!"

She screamed when she turned around and a rogue came at her with a bar held above his head. Before the bar connected with her head, Noah crashed into him and tackled him to the ground, snapping his neck.

When he staggered to his feet, he caught Aiden's eye. They froze, staring at one another, both panting from their fights. Aiden nodded and turned back to the battle as Noah moved to join him; the shared moment of acceptance was over.

Riley screamed, grabbing Charlotte's and Blaire's attention. They looked in the direction she did.

A rogue slammed a baseball bat into Seth's stomach while another tackled him to the ground and grabbed his face, attempting to get his hands around Seth's throat to snap his neck.

Riley cleared the distance to Seth, flinging herself at the rogue's back, sending them both over Seth's body. They rolled, and the rogue ended up on top of her. She shrieked, her eyes blazing a glacial blue as she clawed the guy's face until he recoiled, giving her the opportunity to throw his weight off her and mount him. She bent and sank her teeth into his throat, ripping out his jugular.

"Holy crap," Charlotte said in awe.

"Riley adores Seth," Blaire said, watching Riley get up and rush to Seth, who looked worse for wear, fussing over him while Dominic dispatched the rogue with the bat. "If I could, I would do the same for Lukas."

Charlotte remembered Blaire had the power to turn her love into a weapon. Not with teeth, but with a blade. She took on a rogue for killing Aiden, leaving little doubt she would do the same for Lukas.

When an arm banded over her shoulders, and a hand grabbed her arm, Charlotte screamed. Someone had ambushed them from behind.

Blaire turned. "Charlotte, no!"

Aiden and Noah turned at the sound of her name.

She felt the cold press of the barrel of a gun at her temple and her blood froze in her veins. Her eyes flew to Aiden's, worried about what the sight did to him. He stood stock still, eyes wide and trained on the gun.

This couldn't be happening.

Noah came toward them, and the rogue holding her from behind shouted at him.

"Stay the fuck back!" said the man with the ponytail. She recognized his voice. "Now, you!" He pointed the gun at Blaire. "Come with me or she dies." The barrel pressed against her head again.

Aiden snarled, and she looked over at him. His eyes glowed, reminding her of a green pit viper. He pushed past Noah and ran toward them, teeth bared, fangs descended. Another rogue intercepted him, and they hurtled toward the ground, colliding with Charlotte and the man holding her.

Quickly righting himself, ponytail-man snatched her from the ground. His eyes darted all around, but he couldn't find his gun. "Oh well, we'll get better acquainted this way, then." He opened his mouth, and she watched in horror as his canines lengthened.

Blaire called out her name and ran at them, crashing into her and dragging both her and the rogue to the ground again.

Blinking away the dazed feeling after her head smacked against a log, Charlotte focused on the body hovering over her, straddling her lap. It felt too light to be the rogue. She squeezed her eyes shut and reopened them to find a blurry veil of unmistakable blonde hair hanging over her.

"You'll always be my sister," Blaire said, panting, shielding Charlotte with shaking arms braced on each side of her head.

Before Charlotte could get her wits about her to respond, the rogue with the ponytail ripped Blaire away from her.

Her focus returned in time to scream as the rogue sank his fangs into Blaire's throat.

42

Wounds

Aiden snapped the neck of the rogue beneath him and then rose to his feet, chest heaving from the exertion.

He needed to get to Charlotte.

Shame weighed down his heart. Seeing the gun against her temple had paralyzed him with fear. He thought his freeze reaction to the gun pulled on them in the courtyard earlier was a one-off, but no.

When faced with the same scenario he went through, but from a different point of view, he choked, unable to do anything to save the woman he loved, while Noah tried to reach her instead.

Noah.

Aiden had to acknowledge the guy's resilience. Faced with everyone's mistrust and threats of death, Noah still threw himself into the fray to help, protecting Aiden's Korrena instead of allowing the rogues to harm her. In his eyes, that alone made Noah worthy of a second chance.

Charlotte's screams ripped him from his thoughts.

She lay on the ground, face twisted with agony and fear. He followed her gaze to find the asshole with the ponytail sinking his fangs into Blaire's throat.

"Blaire!" Lukas roared, shoving away from the rogue he'd been fighting. He ran for Blaire as Aiden cleared the distance to get to them.

When Aiden reached them, he tore the man away from her, allowing Lukas to catch Blaire when she collapsed.

Dominic closed in to assist Lukas.

Aiden and the rogue tumbled to the ground. The rogue snarled beneath him, sweeping his hands over the ground to reach the gun they landed near. Aiden's hands wrapped around the man's throat, but the rogue wedged the gun between them and pointed it at Aiden's chest, forcing him to rise.

He wouldn't let the fear of an inanimate object stop him. Not this time.

They grappled for control of the gun, snarling and grunting in their efforts until a crack shattered the air. His ears rang and buzzed as the surrounding sounds became muffled and dull.

The rogue beneath him stopped fighting, and the gun slipped from their hands, landing on the grass beside them. Aiden lifted his hands, and the fresh blood coating his skin shook him. His vision blackened around the edges, his breaths came in harsh pants, and his head swam as the buzzing continued.

He didn't feel pain.

Patting his torso, he searched for the wound. The ringing in his ears disoriented him, making it hard to concentrate on the world around him and the task at hand.

His gaze dropped to the rogue beneath him, who had stopped fighting. Vacant eyes stared up at him.

He scrambled off the dead rogue and vomited onto the ground, his fingers digging into the grass as he continued to dry heave long after his stomach emptied.

His mind ping-ponged back and forth between visions that had haunted him for months and the present, the two events blurring together until he could only cling to the sounds of crying and the feel of Blaire's healing magic in his memories.

Bloodied hands clutched the sides of his head and he wailed into the surrounding nothingness. Tears like acid scorched the skin of his face as they broke free after months of confinement.

"—den!"

His body bent forward, and he tucked his head, fighting against the demons in his mind that threatened to consume him as sounds filtered through the fading ringing in his ears.

"Aiden!"

Pressure met his lips; the strong taste of salt met his tongue when he parted his lips in surprise. In reflex, his lips moved against the softness caressing them.

The scent of buttery brown sugar and pineapples stole him from the nightmare he couldn't escape on his own. He blinked as the moonlight of the world around him came into focus for the first time since the gunshot.

Charlotte pressed her hands on top of his on the sides of his head, kneeling in front of him. Her kisses were tender and coaxing, urging him to come back to her. Her desperate longing for him bloomed in his chest, stealing his breath.

His hands lowered with hers, and she broke the kiss to look into his eyes.

Tears tracked down her face, trailing through the blood on her cheeks from where she kissed him. "Don't leave me," she whispered.

Aiden surged forward, yanking her into his arms, clinging to her as he sobbed against her neck.

For months, he'd kept the emotions over what happened to him trapped inside. He thought his only problem came from having nightmares because he felt nothing in the waking world, but he had suppressed the trauma. When he first told Charlotte about what happened, and a tear slipped, he thought nothing of it. But it marked the first crack in a fissure that formed and splintered at the worst moment. In the middle of combat with his Korrena in danger.

He released her and took her face in his hands.

He yearned to tell her how much he loved her, but now wasn't the time. With his defenses shaken, would she believe him? Instead, he brushed his lips over hers once, trying to convey everything he felt without words in the tender move.

She was the first stitch in the wound of his psyche.

He shook his head and exhaled a breathy laugh when they parted after his emotions were under control. "I can't believe you kissed me after I threw up." His amusement dispersed when he took in her grim expression.

"Aiden, it's Blaire," she whispered.

He squeezed his eyes shut as the events of the last hour filtered back into his consciousness. The fight. Charlotte's supposed father. Blaire. The bite.

He pulled Charlotte to her feet and turned, taking in the sight of Lukas kneeling on the ground, cradling Blaire in his arms. Dominic had joined Noah in fighting rogues who tried to get to Blaire, while farther away, Riley and Seth struggled against their own opponents.

Both Charlotte and Aiden rushed over and lowered next to Lukas and Blaire.

"Is she alive?" Charlotte asked, her voice breaking.

Lukas held his hand against Blaire's cheek. "She's fine. I think she passed out from the shock of it all." He turned her head to allow them to see her neck.

Two obvious, but shallow, puncture wounds branded her neck, along with a tear in the skin where Aiden had pulled the rogue away from her before he inflicted fatal damage. She didn't show any signs of pain, and her breathing remained calm and stable.

Lukas met Aiden's eyes. "You saved her life."

Aiden fell back from his crouched position onto his backside, burying his face in his hands.

Charlotte leaned against him, her small hands clutching his bicep. "She saved mine." She sniffed and swiped her cheeks. "Blaire?"

He lowered his hands as Blaire's eyelids fluttered open.

"Thank fuck," Lukas murmured before pulling her against his chest. "I love you so much. Don't do that to me."

Blaire groaned and put her hand on her neck. "Shit, that stings. I forgot how much it hurts when it's not you."

Lukas growled. "You shouldn't know what it feels like from another to begin with."

"I'm okay." She touched his face. "It probably looks worse than it feels. He didn't drink anything. Aiden pulled him off me too fast." She looked up at Aiden. "I guess we're even?"

Her laugh sounded weak, but he understood it as an attempt to lighten the mood. Lukas seemed tense. She needed to defuse the situation so they could help the others.

Sounds at the edge of the forest stole their attention. They looked up as Blackthorn Security, decked out in black tactical clothing, filed out of the trees with weapons drawn.

One man made hand signals and barked orders so fast Aiden couldn't understand. Bodies fanned around them, converging on the few remaining rogues and the reinforcements that arrived from the other side of the clearing.

Had security arrived later, their small group wouldn't have survived the battle. Before, only a few outnumbered them, and it already proved difficult to hold the rogues off because students weren't trained in combat, but their reinforcements tripled those numbers.

Where had James disappeared to?

A man crouched next to them, eyes scanning the surroundings as he spoke. "Is she okay? Do you need medical?"

"Yes," Lukas said at the same time Blaire said, "No."

The security guard looked between them.

"I'm fine. I got bit, but I'm good."

The security guard waved over another man who carried a bag. "To be on the safe side, since you're human, let him look you over." He looked at Aiden and Charlotte, his eyes focusing on Aiden, nodding to the blood that saturated his shirt, coating his hands, arms, and face. "You injured?"

"No, this is his," Aiden said, motioning to the rogue on the ground.

He lay on his back with his leather jacket open and a huge red stain coating the chest of his white T-shirt. If he hadn't recovered by now, the likelihood of the shot penetrating his heart or lung was high.

"Once you're cleared with the medic, I want you all to get to the administration building. We'll meet on the ground floor for a debriefing." With those last words, the man stood and moved to join the rest of security, who were rounding up the rogues who hadn't fled at the sight of them.

"I need a medic!" Riley called out.

Aiden turned toward his sister, several yards away. He rushed toward her as she struggled to walk with Seth, who appeared on the brink of collapse. When he reached them, Riley collapsed to her knees, letting Seth fall into Aiden's arms.

"What the hell happened?"

Riley looked up from her place on the ground as Charlotte came up to her side, kneeling as well. "He'd already taken a beating. A bat to his stomach and ribs. But this asshole tried to snap his neck, and when I got them separated, two more jumped on him while I was occupied. They bit him and tore into him and, and…" Riley started sobbing. "One of them had a knife!"

"What the fuck? Did he get stabbed?" He looked down at Seth, who hadn't opened his eyes or said anything. Determining his injuries proved difficult because of the numerous tattoos adorning his arms and the blood soaking his torn T-shirt.

"Yes!" Riley screamed at him. She scrambled forward on her knees, jerking up Seth's shirt. Next to his Korrena mark along his Adonis belt, a stab wound poured blood down over his jeans.

Charlotte gasped.

Aiden quickly moved Seth to the ground, putting pressure on the wound. They only needed to stabilize him until his preternatural healing took over.

The area wasn't near a vital organ, but he didn't know for sure. He wasn't a medical major. He'd already changed majors twice. Considering what kept happening with his friends, maybe medicine would be worth switching to.

Lukas and Blaire approached with the medic from before and another woman who carried a similar bag.

"He's been stabbed," he told them. Riley couldn't provide the information they needed fast enough. "Several bite wounds. He's also taken several hits with a bat to his torso."

Charlotte struggled to pull Riley away from Seth's body, so Aiden helped pull his sister away as she fought against them, weeping and cursing.

"Wake up, Seth! You have to wake up! You can't leave me!"

Blaire made a strangled noise, and Lukas pulled her into his arms as they moved away from the medics surrounding Seth.

Riley trembled in Aiden's arms as he kept them tight around her, stroking the back of her head.

This year hadn't been fair to her.

She not only had to watch her brother die, but now she had to watch her Korrena—the man she loved since before she even knew the meaning of the word—lay broken and battered, life hinging on how quickly his healing abilities could compete against the natural progression of death.

They stood there for so long the security teams had time to clear the field, leaving them standing around the medics working on Seth. Dominic went with them, likely to inform the headmistress and the Blackthorn Clan of what happened. Two additional medics joined them to help tend to Seth's injuries.

With his shirt cut from his body, and the blood wiped away, they could see the bruises marring his skin. His ribs had to be broken; the entire area was black and purple. His abdomen sported mottled splotches of purple, blue, and yellow. Bite marks from where the rogues had tried to tear chunks out of him branded his arms and upper body. Two nasty gashes on his collarbone displayed how they tried to rip his throat out, but Seth must have moved too fast for them to make their mark.

Aiden's eyes burned.

The locations and nature of the markings and wounds left no doubt in his mind that Seth had narrowly escaped death several times during the fight. He fought like hell, and he deserved to live for that alone.

He needed to live. Not only for himself, but because he couldn't leave Riley. He'd never forgive himself if he died, leaving her behind. Whatever waited for them after death beyond that space of floating purgatory Aiden found himself in, Seth wouldn't enjoy it. Not knowing he left Riley behind like this.

Noah joined them, and Aiden nodded at him.

The area brightened. Dew glittered under the rays of the morning sun as it rose in the east. Light blue and purple ivyleaf morning glories littered the field, their trumpet-shaped blooms opening wide, gracing the world with their beauty even as blood stained the ground around them.

As the first direct rays of the sun broke over the forest surrounding the clearing, Seth groaned.

"Two hours and fourteen minutes," one medic said.

"What does that mean?" Charlotte asked Blaire.

The female medic closest to them turned. "We attempted to keep him stabilized without moving him until his body's healing capabilities kicked in. It took him that long. We record things like this for future emergencies."

Aiden hoped there wouldn't be a need for that information, but if something this severe happened to Seth again, if more than the recorded time passed, it could mean he wouldn't recover.

Riley broke from Aiden's hold and tried to push through the medics, but they held her back.

"He's still injured. His body has to recover or you risk opening his wounds and refracturing what we suspect are several broken ribs."

"Firecracker," Seth croaked.

Riley sobbed; her body slumped in the arms of the medic. "You asshole!"

Seth's laughter turned into a cough as he clutched his side.

"You all need to get to the administration building now that he's stable," the woman said, passing Riley to Aiden when he stepped forward, meeting Seth's eyes. "We will take him to the medical wing for a thorough examination now that he is no longer in danger if we move him."

He nodded, still looking at the man he considered his brother.

Seth's eyes were glistening, but he said nothing. He didn't have to. Aiden knew enough about Seth to know he recognized he'd almost died. Seth swallowed and blinked, the tears gathered in his eyes spilling over his temples. "I love you, Firecracker," he said, voice rough as Aiden led her away to join the others.

43

Red Carnation

Breakfast was a somber affair. They avoided the cafeteria, taking their breakfast on the ground floor of the administration building after security set them up with egg, sausage, and cheese biscuits with mini bowls of fruit. They also brought coffee, tea, and bottles of orange juice and water. An open cooler containing blood packets occupied the middle of the circle they formed on the marble floor.

Charlotte's head buzzed with questions about the events of the night, but the one that stood out the most made her speak up. "Why did it take Seth so long to start healing? Don't you heal right away? I thought that's what you said."

She found it difficult to shake the image of blood pouring from the stab wound from her mind.

Aiden shook his head, swallowing the bite of biscuit in his mouth. "We do to an extent, but it takes a while for the healing to make a real difference depending on the severity of the injury. In his case,"—he looked at Riley—"the injuries were so severe and numerous, his body ran the risk of not being strong enough to heal in time."

"It's why they refused to move him to the medical department until he became stable," Dominic said, taking a seat next to them.

Riley sniffed, drinking from her blood packet in silence. She'd remained silent the entire time security recorded their statements. Charlotte didn't know if it was the shock of the fight or seeing Seth near death, but it had been eerie for her not to talk.

The heavy doors of the foyer of the administration building opened, letting sunlight in that blinded them. When the doors slammed closed, echoing in the cavernous space, Seth approached them in a clean outfit. His neck and face appeared bruised, but nothing as severe as earlier. The swelling had disappeared.

Riley sat with her back to him, head down.

He stared at her without moving, and Charlotte watched as his eyes became glassy.

"Firecracker," he said, voice rough.

Her head snapped up, and she twisted to see him. Dropping her blood packet, she scrambled up from the floor and barreled into him, clinging to his waist as he winced, but didn't push her away. She buried her face against his chest and wailed like a child.

He buried his face in her pink hair, whispering words Charlotte couldn't make out. He moved his hands to the side of Riley's head, tilting her face to look her in the eye before kissing her deeply.

Charlotte looked away, catching Aiden's eye.

"He'll be okay," he said, motioning for her to eat. She'd barely touched her biscuit.

Seth led Riley over to sit with everyone and lowered himself cautiously to the floor. His movements weren't natural, and he favored his left side.

"Are you still in pain?" Charlotte asked.

"Sore, but my ribs aren't broken anymore. I'm still bruised, but that should be fine soon enough."

"What about the bites and the stab wound?"

Seth lifted the edge of his shirt, showing the dip near his abdomen next to the V at the edge of his jeans. A faint raised pink scar marred his skin, with minor discoloration in various spots where bruising had faded.

An intricate tattoo of a horizontal S edged with lines and spikes bordered the scar. She'd seen a similar tattoo on Riley when she changed her clothes the other night when Charlotte was in the room.

That must be their Korrena mark.

"That's incredible," she said.

"What?"

"How you're able to heal like that."

"Oh. Yeah. The surface wounds heal faster, but there's still some muscle damage that needs to repair itself. It's not like the bites. Most of them are gone except the ones near my neck, but those will be gone in the next couple of hours."

It amazed her how their species worked. What she wouldn't give to recover from ailments and injuries at the rate they did.

Her gaze traveled to Blaire, who sat talking with Lukas, Noah, and the headmistress. She worried how the bite from earlier would affect Blaire. She never healed properly. Bruising that would only last a few days for one person would last weeks on her skin. Doctors never discovered the reason why.

Blaire noticed Charlotte's gaze on her, and she smiled, getting up and moving over to where they sat. "How are you feeling?"

"I'm alright. This has been a lot, but I'm not hurt or anything."

Blaire nodded in understanding. "It overwhelmed me at first. I didn't expect to join a university where I'd be pulled into fights and crazy rituals, that's for sure."

Seth snorted, putting his arms around Riley when she crawled into his lap. It was clear to everyone how shaken his brush with death left her. She still looked frazzled.

"How's your neck?" Aiden asked.

Blaire touched the bandaged side of her neck. "It feels fine. I mean, it isn't comfortable, but it'll heal."

Charlotte placed her biscuit on the wrapper in front of her. "Are you going to be okay, though? Like, with the bruising."

"Oh, let me tell you." Blaire laughed, her eyes lighting up with joy. "So, remember how I told you about when I almost died to that ritual down in the temple below us?"

Charlotte nodded.

"You did die," Lukas said, joining them. His lips brushed her temple before he looked at Charlotte. "One of the worst days of my life."

Blaire had told her all about how after the Order discovered her blood carried magical affinities, they experimented on her until taking her to an abandoned temple beneath the academy not seen in centuries. They tried to sacrifice her to an ancient deity they'd read about in an old tome. *What a joke.* Lukas had to make the choice of turning her into a Vasirian or letting her die, but he didn't do it, not wanting to steal her freedom of choice. Her own magic brought her back.

"Fine. I died, but I'm fine now," she said, waving Lukas off with a kiss on his cheek. "The strange thing about it is something happened to me after that. When the magic brought me back, it healed all my old scars, too. Not only that, but I don't bruise as severely as I did before, nor do they last as long."

Lukas muttered, "Now you don't look like I beat you up every time we have sex anymore."

Charlotte's face flushed, and Aiden and Seth started laughing.

"He's not rough," Blaire said, mistaking Charlotte's flushed face and wide eyes as worry. "He doesn't hurt me."

"Oh, no… I…" She looked at Aiden and he smirked, raising an eyebrow in challenge. "Nothing wrong with a little roughness," she mumbled.

"Wait. What?" Blaire said, leaning over. "Did you say what I think you just…" Her gaze moved to Aiden. He didn't even try to hide the smug grin on his face. "I do *not* need to know more."

Riley threw her hands over her ears, snapping out of her funk. "Nope!"

Aiden laughed and leaned down to whisper in Charlotte's ear, "You know you enjoy every bit of it, Kitten."

She rolled her lips in to avoid whimpering at the husky timbre of his voice.

Headmistress Velastra joined them, her hands coming together in a sharp clap that drew their attention. Charlotte was thankful for her clapping for once.

"As much as it pains me to share this news, your alleged father was not one of the rogues captured and taken to the dungeons below."

"What? Where is he?" Aiden asked.

"I suspect he fled when you all were occupied with defending yourselves."

Dominic sat forward, grabbing a blood packet from the cooler. "I've already contacted the clan about James. They will send word to their contacts throughout the US so there's pressure to find him."

"What if he leaves the country?" she asked.

"I doubt he'll do that. If he's in the position he claims to be in, he's not going to abandon it when he can use those at his disposal to hide him. He'll likely either remain in the area or return to Florida. We still need to determine if he's your father or not."

"That we do have the answer to." A short woman wearing tactical gear with her blonde hair in a tight bun high on her head stepped forward. She held up papers, passing them to the headmistress. "We ran samples of the blood on the wall to determine that it is, in fact, human. While we didn't have James's blood to run against the samples, we did get a hit from a hospital in Florida. He had a car accident several years ago and needed a blood transfusion."

"How did you know to check the hospital?"

The security guard looked down at Blaire. "One of the rogues we captured alive gave us his surname, and we ran it until we got a hit in Florida. Seeing the crash report, we took a chance on checking the hospital. Not sure why they kept his pre-transfusion samples after the first week, but..." She motioned to the papers the headmistress frowned at. "His DNA is a match for the blood on the wall."

The headmistress sighed long and hard. "It would seem he is your father."

Charlotte's head jerked up at that. "How do you know?"

"The alleged father cannot be excluded as the biological father of the tested child. Based on the analysis of DNA loci listed above, the probability of paternity is 99.999-and so forth percent." The headmistress looked up from the paper. "I know you may not wish to hear this, but James Robertson is your father."

Charlotte slumped. She couldn't help but wonder what drove her father to abandon his humanity to run with the worst of the worst in the Vasirian world. Why did he do it? Something had to have driven him to do the things he did. If he had the kind of money he claimed, what did he gain from aligning himself with gangs—human or not?

"Sometimes people are just bad," Noah said, making her realize she must have said a part of her thoughts out loud. "James isn't a good man."

Dominic nodded. "Stressing yourself over the reasons he chose the path he did will get you nowhere. Sometimes people make choices because of some profound reason or trauma, but sometimes, sometimes people are just evil. I know it's not what you want to hear because you've just learned he's your father, but it's not on you. His shortcomings aren't your burden to bear."

Aiden took her hand in his. "You're not a product of your father. He might be your blood, but you obviously didn't take after him."

If she'd grown up with him, maybe her life would be different, and she wouldn't be the person she grew up to be. Instead, she could thank her mothers for the life they gave her. They ensured she became someone not influenced by evil.

"We have to find him, though," Dominic said. "To have a human roaming free like this with our secrets, with a hoard of rogues under his control, is unheard of. Money or not. I'm also concerned about his motives. Why is he involving himself in our world so deeply?"

"I think it has to do with the person who is supporting him," Noah said.

"What do you mean?"

Noah looked at the headmistress. "He's scared of that person, but I think their influence allows him to stay in power. I think it's an ego thing. Anytime any of the guys questioned him, he spoke of the Red Carnation."

"Red carnation?" Riley's nose wrinkled. "What does a flower have to do with anything?"

"It's not a flower. It's what James called the person over him. I guess it's a code name or something. I told the security team about it."

"Code name?" Seth's brows rose.

"I've not read over those documents yet," the headmistress said. "I intended to do that today until this happened."

"This Red Carnation is dangerous," Dominic said. "If they have enough influence to make the rogues fall in line behind a human…"

Lukas sat forward, resting his forearm on his knee. "Shouldn't the Blackthorn Clan say something about them too? Not just Charlotte's dad?"

"Sperm-donors don't deserve that title," Riley snarked.

"Huh?"

"Dad is a dad. A real parent. A father is the dude who contributed his chromosomes to create life. Biology. James doesn't deserve to be called anyone's dad."

Lukas held up his hands in surrender. Riley obviously held strong feelings he wouldn't contest.

The headmistress shook her head. "So far, the Red Carnation isn't making themselves known. Putting a spotlight on them, making them aware we know who they are, might drive them into greater action."

"Until we ensure Blaire's safety, or she makes the change, we have to play defense," Dominic said. "We don't know enough to know what this person will do."

"There's no telling how they'll respond to this failure as it is."

Aiden's words were met with several nods of agreement. Until they knew more, they were nothing more than sitting ducks waiting on the hunter to find them.

44

Fractured Fate

Days passed with no information on Charlotte's father, and the lack made her restless. She tried to distract herself with Aiden's collection of video games and even joined some random online groups to interact with people other than those around her. She needed some sense of normalcy. Something human.

It helped until it didn't.

With classes starting in a little over a week, she finally met with the student liaison and settled on Business Administration so she could delve into several facets of her mothers' businesses and potentially be able to create her own in the future. She didn't know why she never considered a broad degree like that before.

In need of a change of scenery, she entered the main building, heading up the stairs to the canteen to find herself a snack.

Aiden insisted on joining her.

He still didn't enjoy letting her roam the campus alone, concerned for her safety. She didn't blame him, considering rogues had infiltrated the academy grounds and nearly killed Seth. She would never have survived that. She didn't have the perks that came from being a Vasirian.

After they grabbed a few canned drinks, candy, chips, and a blood packet for Aiden, they made their way down the hall until a flash of burgundy and sparkling rubies on silver chains rounding the corner caught her eye.

She took off in a sprint down the hall.

"What the—Charlotte!" Aiden ran after her.

They skirted the corner in time to see the Oracle disappear up the stairs to the third floor. When she entered the library, they followed.

Charlotte's gaze moved around the room. A few students sat at the tables near the windows, preparing for their upcoming classes; but otherwise, the space seemed as abandoned as the day Noah arrived.

"There," Aiden said, pointing to a side hallway. "I know where she's going."

He led Charlotte through a pointed archway and down a narrow hallway lined with painted portraits until they reached a small room at the end. Stepping inside, they found the Oracle standing at the back of the room on the other side of a long table surrounded by several chairs like a boardroom, but fancier. Carts filled with spare books lined the walls.

"You have questions," the Oracle said with a soft smile, turning to look at Charlotte.

"What?" She blinked and looked up at Aiden. Was she talking to him?

"There's something you've considered recently but haven't shared with your friends," the Oracle said, moving to the side of the table. "Or with your Korrena pair." She paced back to her original position.

"The Celestial Conclave spoke of your disturbed sense of mind surrounding your question. I'm here to ease the burden."

Aiden looked at Charlotte.

Charlotte worried her lip. The thing that stood out to her most was something she tried to avoid thinking about, but it kept coming to the forefront of her mind with recent events. The thought bothered her when she tried to sleep at night, when she considered the future with Aiden.

"That, child. Whatever you are dwelling on at this moment is why I am here to give you the answers you seek."

"How do you know what I'm thinking?"

"The Celestial Conclave speaks to me. With the magic suppressing my mind increasingly unlocked as Blaire's powers awaken, my connection to them grows. Now, tell me, child. What do you want to know?"

"I…" She looked up at Aiden.

The space between his eyebrows dipped with his pinched expression. If she didn't know better, she would think him mad, but his confusion often looked like anger.

"Go ahead. Ask her," he encouraged, a soft smile highlighting his full lips.

She turned back to the Oracle. "I've been wondering if it's possible for me to become a Vasirian."

Aiden made a choking noise, and she pivoted to look up at him. Was he angry she'd asked? His face went slack, and his eyes appeared shiny. "I need a minute," he mumbled, lowering himself into a chair, setting the bag of their goodies between his feet.

Charlotte twisted the toes of her sandals on the hardwood floor, clasping her hands tightly in front of her. Had asking been a mistake? She really wanted to know if it was possible. If Aiden wanted her to be with him for a long time, that seemed the logical next step.

Nothing about her life felt settled. Change sent her into depression and made her hate existing. The only change that hadn't done that to her was coming to Blackthorn Academy. It felt like she belonged—at least once she sorted out her issues and spoke with her friends about her insecurities.

Existing in the human world, doing the mundane day to day, felt more like a chore than anything with a purpose. The only thing that mattered to her outside Aiden's world was her mothers, but even then, they weren't like other people's parents. The things they enjoyed weren't typical. Things Charlotte grew to love. What the human world deemed normal never fit with her.

She wouldn't go so far as being cliché and say she wasn't like other girls, because she loved things other girls loved. Clothes, pretty accessories, getting her nails done… But she knew in her heart she needed more than what the world she grew up in could give her.

"You never belonged in the human world," the Oracle started, interrupting her thoughts. "Had we never experienced a fracture in the balance between our kind and yours, you would still have found stability in this world. Your fate was always to be a part of the Vasirian world."

"What do you mean?"

"While you are not a direct descendant like your friend, your blood still resonates with the power of a witch."

"So can I be like the rest of you?"

Aiden's head snapped up to look at the Oracle as if he wanted to know the answer too. Charlotte couldn't tell what he felt because her own intense emotions of hope and longing overpowered everything.

When the Oracle's eyes softened, and her mouth turned down, a look of pity crossing her face, Charlotte knew the answer before she said it.

"The magic that brought about your early awakening isn't strong enough to allow the transition. The magic that stirred within to awaken your bond held only the power to call to your fated one and vice versa. If you were to try now, you would most certainly meet your demise. Until Blaire transitions, you cannot cross from your world to ours. Your own magic is required to transcend the boundaries between species safely."

Aiden cursed.

"I know it is not the answer either of you wishes to hear, but soon it will be safe for Blaire to take the step she has expressed she is ready for. After that, you can do what is necessary to find your true place."

It bothered Charlotte that Blaire hadn't become a Vasirian yet.

At first, she felt anger toward Blaire for not going through with it if it would save an entire species. It seemed selfish. But then she learned everything Blaire had gone through, and that she wanted to be a Vasirian but couldn't for valid reasons. The knowledge changed her perception. There had been a lot more to the story than she realized. It made her feel guilty for harboring such negative feelings about her best friend. All she could do now was support Blaire until the time was right, and that's what she intended to do.

"Never forget, you belong in this world, child. The events unfolding are the way they should be. Your destiny has always been linked to his." The Oracle extended her hand toward Aiden. "Even the initial months of your existence set you on the path to lead you here."

"What does that mean?" Aiden asked, finding his voice. It wavered, but she didn't know what that meant.

"Her father's absence and her mother's death. Had those two events not occurred, Sara and Elizabeth Walsh would have never adopted a baby girl from Ireland. Charlotte would have grown up in Ireland and never found her way to this part of the country, never crossing paths with Blaire, nor you."

Aiden put his elbow on his thigh, rubbing at his forehead with his thumb and first two fingers.

"Sara Walsh knew to go to Ireland."

Charlotte's eyes turned into saucers. "What do you mean Mom knew to go there? I thought the adoption agency contacted them about me first."

"They did. They provided your adoptive mothers with a list of various countries." The Oracle smiled. "There is more to Sara Walsh than meets the eye, child."

"Okay, at the risk of sounding like a broken record…" Charlotte threw her hands out at her sides. "What does that *mean*?"

The Oracle's laugh sounded melodic and sweet. Not something Charlotte would expect from such an old woman. "The voices."

"Voices?"

"Does she not speak of the voices?"

"Yeeeah," she said, hesitation heavy in her tone.

For as long as Charlotte could remember, her mom had shared things the "spirits" would tell her. Many years ago, she opened up to friends about it, but they thought she had schizophrenia—or some other mental health disorder. She lost people whom she thought cared about her. To shield herself and her family, she stopped speaking of it outside of their home. Charlotte's ma always said it was her mom's intuition talking to her, but she never outright said the voices weren't real or that her mom had mental illness.

"I am not the only one the Celestial Conclave whispers to."

Charlotte lowered herself slowly into the chair to her right as the weight of this new revelation settled over her.

"Like you, she is another human with dormant magic lingering in her blood. It has guided her in all facets of her life, even if she is unable to harness it to its full potential. Had our worlds never split apart, she would have the same capabilities as I have. A seer and prophetess for the Celestial Conclave, but as a human."

She leaned back, her hands lifting to cover her mouth.

Aiden interlaced his fingers, sitting forward in his chair, both elbows on his thighs. "Does that mean when Blaire becomes Vasirian, Sara will awaken, too?"

"That's correct, but not much will change for her. The Celestial Conclave has always reached her through the barriers put in place during the Blood War. The only difference will be awareness. She will learn of this world and the reasons behind why her mind leads her in the right direction. Why the voices guide her as they do."

"Will she find a Korrena if she's magical like me?"

That her mom might discover a mate in the Vasirian world when the balance righted itself turned Charlotte's stomach. What would her ma do? She didn't want to imagine the heartbreak.

"No, child. Not every human with magical affinities will be destined to pair-bond with one of our kind, but there will be many who will. Sara is not one of those humans."

She blew out a breath, the relief chasing away the acid churning in her stomach.

Aiden asked, "Do they know about our kind? Her mothers, I mean."

The Oracle tilted her head as she studied Aiden, a genial smile crossing her face. "They know what they need and share what they must."

He snorted, shaking his head.

It seemed as if her mothers knew a lot more than they ever let on, but this time Charlotte was thankful for the Oracle's cryptic words.

If word spread that her mothers even suspected the existence of the Vasirian, they faced consequences Charlotte could never stand by and allow without a fight.

45

Unexpected Desires

Aiden stepped ahead of Charlotte and looked around their dorm room, entering the bathroom next to check for intruders—his new routine of the past few days. When Blackthorn Security gave them the "all clear" to return to their dorms after their meeting in the administration building days ago, he wondered how she would respond to entering the dorm again after James had violated the space. He'd charged in ahead of her to ensure they were alone and felt a flare of gratitude through their bond, showing she appreciated the protective move.

Her father was still missing, but Headmistress Velastra had assigned increased security on the grounds and the dorms, so no one got in or out without security seeing them. A guard stood posted at the entrance of each dormitory building. Still, he always double-checked. How something so small as her release of a held breath filtered through their unsealed bond, he didn't know, but he'd take it.

Charlotte crossed the space to go to the bathroom, but he couldn't wait today. After the meeting with the Oracle, he needed to hear a direct answer to the question burning through his nerves like an inferno.

He grabbed her arm before she could get too far into the room and spun her around.

She looked up at him.

He narrowed his eyes, and his jaw clenched as he worked the muscles. It took every ounce of his willpower not to throw her over his shoulder and take her to his bed.

The hope and longing he felt when he sat in the room with the Oracle mirrored his own so strongly that he didn't know where Charlotte's emotions ended and his began. She wanted it, but he needed to hear her words again. He needed to hear her say it to him, not to someone else.

He tried to sound calm, but his voice came out coarse and low. "You want to be a Vasirian?"

"I do."

The way she answered with such firm resolve made him groan.

The bag of goodies they picked up at the canteen crashed to the floor as his arms came around her. His hand threaded the back of her hair and gripped the back of her head as he slammed his mouth onto hers.

When she gasped, he shoved his tongue into her mouth, kissing her roughly, walking her backward until she bumped the wall beside the ensuite.

She moaned, squirming against him but not able to move with the way his hard body pressed her to the wall. He held her hair in a tight grip.

"I can't believe you want that," he said against her lips, voice like gravel.

She looked up into his glowing eyes that reflected in her own. "Of course I do," she whispered. "I love you. Why wouldn't I want to spend as long as I can with you?"

His knees almost buckled at the words she had never used before. He questioned it once. There was a time when they were in her bed that he felt something he was sure was her love, but she said nothing. Hearing her say she loved him out loud made his heart soar.

"You have no idea how much I love you," he whispered reverently against her lips before stealing a deep kiss, pouring all of his heart into it.

His hands came down to grab hold of her thighs and lift her. She immediately wrapped her legs around his waist, never breaking the kiss.

He walked her over to his bed and crawled onto it, holding her against him the entire way until he lowered her to her back. His body cloaked hers as he dragged open-mouthed kisses across her cheek to her neck, where he sucked the sweet tasting skin there into his mouth.

She arched her neck, giving him better access. He increased the suction, coaxing out a gasping breath.

"Aiden?"

He nipped her bruised skin. "Yeah, Kitten?"

"Can we do the thing?"

"What thing?"

He trailed his tongue over to the other side of her neck, where he gave the skin there the same treatment. If she'd let him, he'd leave a necklace of his marks on her so everyone would see she belonged to him.

"The seal," she said on a moan as he worried her skin with his teeth, angling her hips to grind against his hardness.

He paused, lifting his head to look down into her eyes. "You're ready?"

"I might not be able to become a Vasirian yet, but I want to be as connected to you as we possibly can."

"Fucking hell." Aiden dropped his head forward. "You're perfect. Absolutely perfect." His lips captured hers again as he rolled his hips against her center.

He sat back on his heels and worked her shirt up her body. She sat up so that he could pull it over her head, but it caught at her nose, reminding him of when he used her shirt before to both blindfold her and restrain her arms.

As much as he enjoyed the adventurous things they tried, this wasn't the time for that. He wanted to cherish her tonight. He wanted to give her the world.

The mistakes of the past might put kinks in the path leading where they were meant to be, but Charlotte belonged in his world. The Oracle may have acknowledged her fate, but he was claiming it. No matter what it took, he would keep her in his world.

Charlotte helped him free her head and arms from the shirt, tossing it to the floor. Her hands slid over his abs while he removed his shirt.

She leaned forward to run her tongue from above his navel to the center of his chest. He shuddered. When her lips hovered over his pec above his nipple, her hot breath fanned over the skin. He looked down at her.

As soon as their eyes met, she swirled her tongue over his skin and then pulled the flesh into her mouth. He groaned and dropped his head back. She was marking him. Not with her nails in response to his roughness, but she marked him with intent.

It was the hottest thing he'd ever experienced.

"That's so good, Kitten."

She hummed at his praise, swiping her tongue over the bruise she left. It wouldn't last long, but until it disappeared, he would cherish it.

Maneuvering herself onto her knees in front of him, she slid her hands over his chest, admiring her work.

His hands settled on her lower back and pulled her flush to him, kissing and nibbling at her neck, inhaling her intoxicating scent. He slid his hands up to her bra and flicked open the back clasp. She pulled back, letting the lacy lavender fabric fall between them.

Her fair skin flushed pink from her cheeks to the tops of her breasts when he ran his tongue over his lips.

"I love these perfect tits of yours," he said, lifting his hands to caress them, weighing them in his hands.

Last night, he had the pleasure of seeing her try on the uniform she would wear in a little over a week to ensure it fit.

Never before had he thought anything other than the uniforms were an inconvenience when they were adults with their own clothes, but seeing her full hips in the little skirt and the button-down hugging her ample breasts made him want to bow down and thank whoever came up with the idea of wearing uniforms.

He hadn't been able to resist taking her against the wall beside the closet while still in uniform.

Her plaid skirt made it easy for him to pull her panties aside and bury his cock deep into the heat of her body. He shuddered as fantasies of taking her all over campus crossed his mind.

But now her breasts were proudly on display for his viewing and tasting pleasure.

He bent, taking a hardened nipple into his mouth, teasing it with his tongue.

Her head dropped back, her beautiful curls cascading down her back. He loved her hair but couldn't wait to see it pinned up again with his mark proudly displayed at the base of her neck. He would need to buy her an entire collection of pins and clips, and wide-neck or backless shirts to show off his claim to her. Maybe he would go around shirtless.

When his mouth released her breast with a pop, she lifted her head. "I want to taste you," she said, dropping her eyes down to where his jeans felt too snug at the zipper.

Who was he to deny her what she wanted?

He stood from the bed and made quick work of discarding his jeans and boxer briefs, while she did the same with her shorts and panties.

Crawling to the edge of the bed, she placed a hand on his hip, using the other to wrap around the base of his shaft. She squeezed, making it twitch in her hand, and his eyes dropped to half-mast, already drunk on the sight of her bent over about to take his cock into her warm mouth. Looking up into his eyes, she lapped over his cockhead, gathering the beaded moisture there like a kitten tasting cream.

He smirked. She really was like a kitten when she wanted to be.

Tightening her grip on his hip, she opened her mouth and sank down his length, making his mind go blank. His hand moved into the curls at the back of her head, holding her but not controlling her movements, basking in the feel of her soft lips and wet mouth. Taking him deeper into her mouth, she bobbed her head at a steady pace, going deeper with each slide down his shaft.

"That's so good, Kitten."

She whimpered around him.

"You're doing so good."

He never realized someone could blossom so much with a little bit of praise, but she came alive every time he spoke words of approval. It wasn't only her that loved it though. He adored how she responded to him. How she wanted him to be happy with her and praise her. That she wanted to please him and be rewarded for it gave him a high like no other.

He felt that familiar tingle and stepped back, his cock slipping free from her mouth. She looked up at him in question, hands braced on the edge of the bed.

"I don't want to come yet."

His eyes fell to her breasts, heavy and full and oh-so-tempting.

She looked down at herself and then smiled, rising up to her knees and changing position to lay on her back. When she ran her hands over the bottom of her breasts and across her nipples, watching him, he groaned. But when she rested her hands on the tops of her breasts, pushing them together with her arms bent on the outside of each one, he nearly came hands-free. He squeezed the base of his shaft to calm himself.

He wasn't about to decline an invitation like this.

Climbing onto the bed to straddle her torso, he spit into his palm, slicking up his shaft before sliding between the heat of her breasts.

Heaven.

He finally knew where it existed.

His hands came up to move her arms away, taking their place as he slowly slid his leaking shaft through the valley of her breasts. She moaned when he tightened his grip, his fingers sinking into the soft flesh that wrapped his cock in a greedy embrace.

His thrusts grew harder, his balls dragging across her skin, increasing the pleasure of the moment.

Her hands closed over his, pressing down, encouraging him not to be gentle. He growled. He loved that she liked it as untamed as he did. His grip tightened and she arched her neck, moaning and dropping her hands to squeeze the covers.

Before he reached a point he couldn't stop, he slowed his thrusts and pulled away, climbing off her.

Her fingers trailed over her breasts and through the trail of stickiness he left behind. He cursed when she slid three fingers into her mouth, eyes locked on his as she tasted his natural lubricant.

It made him almost regret not fucking her breasts to completion—almost.

He wanted his cum inside her.

He wanted to fill her and mark her with his seed in a way no man ever had.

He understood the risks associated with having sex without a condom, even if she took birth control. It wasn't one hundred percent, and he didn't care. The idea of creating a life that was part of both of them made him feel things he never thought he could.

Fuck, I want that.

But not now.

As much as he would love it, he wanted her to achieve her dreams first. But as soon as she was ready, their home would be filled with children's laughter.

"Aiden?"

He blinked away his thoughts and looked at her. She bit at her lip and looked at him in confusion.

"Sorry. I was thinking about the future." He crawled over her, kissing over her belly until he reached her lips, laying a soft kiss there.

"What about it?"

"About what it would be like to have an army of kids with you."

He laughed when her eyes went comically wide.

"Not now," he said, kissing her nose. "One day." Rising up on his knees, he settled between her legs. "Are you ready for this? There's no turning back. No reversing it once it's done."

As confident as he sounded and acted when he took her to bed, he couldn't deny the sliver of insecurity and doubt that crept in. If she rejected him now, he didn't know what he would do.

"I told you; I love you. I'm ready for this. Ready for more than I can even have right now. Trust me."

Without another word, not allowing further doubt to slip in, he braced one hand on the pillow beside her head, lined up his cock with her entrance, and slid home on the first push.

"You're so wet," he said, voice rough with need. "So wet and so tight. I don't know if I'm going to last long this time."

The teasing never made it this difficult before, but she'd never said she loved him before either. It tested his resolve. Hearing her say she loved him while experiencing her feelings through their bond, knowing what sensations were connected to that word that he would always recognize now when he felt it from her, heightened every bit of pleasure this entire act brought him.

Knowing they were about to seal their bond had his balls drawing up until he wanted to combust.

He bent, pressing his forehead against hers as he slowly pulled out of her before sliding back into the warm heat of her body.

"I love you, Aiden," she whispered against his lips.

Squeezing his eyes shut, he panted over her lips until he couldn't take it anymore. He rose and took hold of her hips, gripping her in a punishing hold as he started to slam into her, rocking her body with each slap of his pelvis against her. She whined and mewled, broken moans between every gasping sound he forced out of her.

"I love you," he grunted. "You're mine, do you hear me?" He thrust hard, jolting her body up the bed, her bouncing breasts hypnotic. "Do you?"

"Yes!"

"What are you?" he demanded.

She sobbed and moaned, thrashing her head as he pounded into her. "I'm yours!"

He fell forward, caging her body as he slowed his movements.

Her eyes fluttered open, staring up at him. The half-lidded gaze didn't hide the tears forming. It wasn't from pain or sadness—her love and need for him flowed through their bond.

His sweaty forehead met hers.

"I'm going to bite myself so my blood is available to you, and then I'm going to bite you. When I do, I want you to take a little. You don't have to take a lot. Just a little when I take yours, and then you can stop." He didn't know if she would respond badly, but he wanted her to know what it would take to seal the bond. "Understand, Charlotte?"

Her breath hitched at the use of her name, not the pet name he called her when they normally were in bed together.

Time and a place.

This was something beyond play. A joining that was written in the literal stars. Destined by their creators from their birth.

He lifted up and bit into the side of his wrist. Her mouth parted in surprise as blood ran freely down his arm and dripped onto her pale skin. He needed to bite deep to ensure the wound stayed open long enough to complete the ritual without healing.

Cloaking her with his body, he rocked into her again, slowly and sensually, rotating his hips every time he slid all the way inside her. His lips trailed across her neck and down her sternum to her breasts. He kissed the spot he always marked on the inner top of her right breast. This was where he'd do it. He always knew it would be there.

When her walls tightened around his shaft, he looked up at her while sinking his fangs into the softest part of her breast. He began to drink, lifting his arm up to her face, and she took his hand in one hand and held his forearm with the other as she licked his wrist before latching on.

Groaning, his eyes rolled back in his head. He expected her to take only what was needed, but she started drinking from him like she was starving for it. He detached from her and shuddered as he felt the pull of his blood from the wound.

Moaning, he lowered his head and bit into another spot on her breast, probably deeper than he should have. Blood poured from the wound, and he lapped it up. He fed from her in deep, gluttonous gulps that bordered on too much. He wanted to be careful. Tender. Cherish the moment. But he couldn't stop. He popped off her breast, lifting enough to brace himself with his other hand on the pillow as he drove into her like a man possessed.

Charlotte's eyes were closed, and her hands tightened on his arm as she pulled his blood into her mouth.

He'd taken more than he normally would.

Her breasts were smeared with blood but didn't continue to bleed because of his saliva. The path where he dragged his tongue through the blood that spilled down her breasts and over her ribs painted her pale skin in strokes of deep crimson. His own blood from where he bit himself mingled with hers as it dripped from her smooth skin onto the bed at her sides. Leftover blood ran from his mouth, down his chin, and over his chest and abs.

He bathed in her blood, a baptism that exorcised his former life without her.

They'd done enough to seal the bond, but it didn't seem like Charlotte wanted to stop. It wouldn't hurt him, and he knew she wasn't taking a lot like he did. He understood the desire to continue to drink. His Korrena's blood made him feel alive. Made him ravenous.

He trailed his fingers of his free hand through the blood across her belly and sucked the digits into his mouth, claiming another taste of her.

When she finally broke free, he leaned back, his hands gripping her hips as he railed into her. She cried out, and the sight of his blood on her lips, staining her teeth and tongue, became his undoing.

His thrusts stuttered and he slammed home, pressing as flush to her as possible as he coated her insides, marking her in all the ways he possibly could.

The way her walls fluttered and clutched at him made him jerk and shudder, his breath stalling at the overwhelming sensation on his sensitive shaft. When the last of the aftershocks faded, he slipped out of her, watching as his cum leaked from her body.

Scooping up what slid out, he pushed it back inside, working his fingers gently in and out of her now tender hole until he was satisfied his essence would stay deep inside of her.

He collapsed onto his side next to her and pulled her back flush to his chest, spooning her.

"That was incredible," she said, breathless and spent. "I can't believe how good that tasted."

"What?"

"Your blood," she said, twisting her neck to look over her shoulder. "I thought it would be gross, but it tasted like sweet candy."

He smiled. Her blood had a similar taste. Intoxicating like a drug, sweet like candy. Perfection.

"So we're bonded now, right? Like, officially sealed?"

Lifting her hair from her neck revealed the mark he'd seen before in a deep black like a fresh tattoo. He growled in satisfaction. "Sealed and done. You're mine and I'm yours."

"You have the same thing, right?"

Turning as she sat up, he waited for her judgment.

"It's beautiful," she said in awe, tracing her fingertips over the mark that mirrored hers at the base of his neck. "And mine looks the same?"

"That's how it works."

She squealed, and he laughed, pulling her into his arms and planting a soft, lingering kiss against her lips. They were covered in each other's blood, and hers was all over his face; but she didn't seem to mind, so he kissed her again.

"You really like being mine?"

"I love you, Aiden. Of course I do."

His chest hurt with the overwhelming happiness he felt. Never in his wildest dreams did he think he would have this—have her.

And to know as soon as her magic awakened, allowing her to survive the transition, she'd join him and they could spend hundreds of years together without his worrying about losing her to the ailments of humankind, it made everything he'd endured over the last year worth every second.

"I will always love you, Charlotte."

46

BELONGING

Sitting on the couch in her mothers' living room with Aiden and Riley felt strange after recent events. Charlotte didn't know how to act. After all, she met her father and took part in a fight resulting in the deaths of several men and women.

Even if they weren't good people, many of them still had families. While she sat next to the man she loved as he talked with her mothers and his sister without a care in the world, Charlotte wondered if others were grieving the loss of their family.

"What has you looking so gloomy, sweetheart?"

"What?"

Her mom sat forward and placed her can of Diet Coke on the coffee table, her silver bangles catching the sunlight filtering through the large bay window in their living room. "You look like something's troubling you."

Aiden's hand tightened around Charlotte's.

"My father," she started, and both of her mothers stiffened.

Riley stopped playing with Molly, lowering the stick with a toy mouse dangling from it, looking in Charlotte's direction.

"What about him?" her ma asked, her chin turned up as she tilted her head back, eyes shuttering.

"I wanted to know if you know anything about him. Like, who he is. Where he lives. What does he do for a living?"

Her mothers shared a look before her mom got up and came to sit on Charlotte's other side, opposite Aiden. "Your father is American," she said, taking Charlotte's hand. "We never told you anything about him because you never asked."

"I know. I was afraid to know because I thought if I asked about him or my birth mom, you'd think I didn't want to be with you anymore and send me away."

"Yeah, that will never happen," her ma said.

Riley's phone clattered to the floor when Molly jumped into her lap, knocking the phone from her hand, demanding her attention. "Okay, then. I guess Seth can wait."

Aiden chuckled. "He can talk to you when we get back."

Her mom placed her other hand over Charlotte's, sandwiching her hand. "Liz is right. You're our daughter, and you were always meant to be our daughter."

Knowing the things she did, Charlotte wondered if there was a deeper meaning to those words than a mother's love.

"As I said, your father is American. His name is James Robertson, and he has lived in Florida from the time he left after your mother passed away." Her mom tightened her grip. "He…" She sighed. "Your father is not a good man."

Her ma and Riley snorted at the same time.

"Understatement of the century," her ma said. When her mom leveled her ma a withering look, she held up her hands. "What? I know we shouldn't badmouth her biological parent, but what decent person abandons their baby? I'm sorry, Sara, but I don't care how old she gets, I'm going to always hate that man."

Her mom huffed. "I'm sorry if it upset you to hear that. Liz gets heated about your father, and I don't blame her."

"I'm fine. I don't have good feelings about him either."

Riley stroked her hand over Molly's back as the cat loafed in her lap, purring like a motorboat.

"Is there anything else?"

Her mothers shared a look again, and she suspected they knew a lot more about him than they let on, but was it something that revealed more than they were supposed to know? If so, Charlotte wouldn't force them. Instead of risking it, she changed direction.

"Actually, no. It's not worth dwelling on."

Aiden ran his thumb over the top of her hand in soothing circles.

Taking the out offered to them, her ma asked, "So are you ready for classes? It starts this week, right?"

"Next."

She'd told them about her plans to take Business Administration, and they were both ecstatic about the opportunity to find her own path. After training with them in their business, she could open her own doing something she loved instead of sticking with fashion or animal care. Once she found out what she wanted.

"Does this mean you're going to stop taking your medication?"

She looked at her mom. "Maybe eventually. I need to talk to my doctor. Even if things are better for me, that doesn't mean I won't have depression. I mean, if it's clinical. I need to talk to them and find out what they think."

Starting and stopping her medication whenever her moods wavered from one extreme to the other didn't sound like the best idea. One of the biggest reasons she became depressed was a loss of stability. She didn't want to trigger the dark feelings anytime something shifted in her life—especially now that she was part of a world full of unpredictability. At least the medication gave her a fighting chance. Love did great things, but it wasn't a magical cure-all if something was wrong on a chemical level and not environmental. Time and meeting with her doctor regularly instead of once a year would provide the answers she needed.

"That's smart of you," her ma said. "Whatever you need, no matter what the doc says, we'll support you."

Aiden squeezed her hand.

She wondered if when her magic surfaced after Blaire became a Vasirian she wouldn't need medicine anymore. She didn't think transitioning would cure her of her depression—it wasn't like cancer or a virus, but she did wonder if the combination of becoming Vasirian and having living magic in her blood would alter the chemical state of her brain. The possibility was yet another reason she looked forward to transitioning.

She hated that she couldn't do it now, but the Oracle said without her own magic, she wouldn't survive. She didn't have Blaire's magic—or any for that matter. The magic that sparked her bond with Aiden lived inside him and was only enough for that purpose. She couldn't wait to have her own magic.

"Life at Blackthorn is going to keep you busy," her mom said, shifting the subject, keeping her eyes on Aiden. "I expect to see you, but if we have to wait a while before that can happen, we both understand. Given the path you've chosen, there may be a time when coming home won't be an option for a while. Just know we'll be here when you're balanced and ready to come home."

Riley's forehead lined as she stared at Charlotte's mom. The way she'd worded that must have sounded strange to Riley, too.

Charlotte had told her what the Oracle said about her mothers. They'd talked with the others in their small circle, but they all knew to keep the information close to the chest or they risked her mothers' minds.

She looked at Aiden, and his grip tightened. "I'll always come back," she whispered.

"Good!" Her mom gave her hand one last squeeze before standing. "Who wants tilapia for dinner?"

"Why don't we go out?" her ma said. "That way, you don't have to cook for everyone."

"We can go home," Riley said, sitting up, causing Molly to jump off her lap with an irritated tail swish.

"Nope," her ma said. "You're not going anywhere. We haven't seen you kids in a while, and you're about to be monopolizing my girl's time for a long while to come."

Riley pursed her lips and nodded. "Yes, ma'am."

Charlotte laughed. It amused her to see her boisterous friend turn sheepish in the face of her ma's assertive ways.

"Fine." Her mom tugged the hem of her peasant blouse. "If we're going out, I still want seafood. Let me get my purse."

"That woman could eat your body weight in clam strips if you let her," her ma said to Aiden.

He chuckled and put an arm around Charlotte. She settled into his embrace, content to enjoy the moment.

While she couldn't openly discuss what it meant to be at Blackthorn Academy, she felt settled in the knowledge that her mothers likely understood things weren't as they seemed to the outside world. It eased the burden on her mind to know she didn't have to lie to them, because they wouldn't put her in the position to do so or they would risk not only themselves, but her.

Birdsong rang out around where they sat at the center of the hedge maze.

It was the first time Charlotte had entered the sprawling labyrinth of greenery filled with statues of winged creatures in black marble, ivy leaves clinging to their bodies. She avoided it because a part of her questioned if she entered, would she end up stepping into a weird world like that old movie her mom was obsessed with from the eighties about a goblin king who kidnapped a teenage girl's baby brother because of his obsession with her.

Considering all the other peculiar things she discovered about this new world, and that yet another world existed that she knew nothing about, that Blaire only knew from her dreams, she didn't want to take any chances.

Turned out, the hedge maze was nothing more than a simple maze made of hedges. Nothing more, nothing less. *Imagine that.*

A bubbling fountain sat at the heart of the hedge maze, much smaller than the one in the courtyard, surrounded by marble benches and small tables.

She stretched out on the blanket Riley brought out for them all to sit on next to Aiden. Her belly felt as full as her heart.

Few could see them here; their only view was of the upper floors of the dorms and the school buildings. The entire area provided a sense of peace and privacy, the noise beyond deadened by the layers of hedges between them and the rest of the campus.

Riley sat perched in Seth's lap between his crossed legs, babbling to Layla about a new pair of boots she saw when she looked online last night. Blaire sat with her back to the fountain base, shoveling forkfuls of pasta salad into her mouth while Lukas spoke to her about something his parents asked about his study program.

Charlotte wouldn't mind having other students around, but it was nice to get away from the stares and background chatter surrounding her bonding with Aiden.

Piper and Lindsay volleyed questions at her after they heard the news, wanting to know what it felt like to have a sealed Korrena bond, how the emotional tug-of-war felt, and other questions that even bordered on too much. They spoke to her like she belonged in their world—like she was one of them. Alex still cut her dirty looks when they passed each other in the cafeteria or courtyard, but they never engaged in conversation, so she took it as a win.

She gazed at the fluffy white clouds overhead.

Whenever they went to the cafeteria in the days following the seal of their bond, at least one brave student approached with questions for her, Aiden, or even Blaire and Lukas. Aiden said with another human on campus, curiosity won out, and students took the chance to ask questions. Lukas said they never got approached before.

Even after classes started, they would continue being a hot topic of conversation, but things would settle down eventually. There were only so many questions someone could ask.

Not everyone embraced the idea of two humans on campus. It didn't escape her notice that some students gave them a wide berth, while others talked in hushed tones as they passed—wary, if not downright hostile in the things she overheard. Most of it came from fear of another rogue attack on campus.

She sighed. She couldn't blame them for being afraid. Still, she hoped one day those who hesitated to accept her and Blaire would eventually find peace with their presence.

At least no one tried to bully them.

Charlotte looked up as Dominic rounded the corner of a hedge. Sunlight from the midday sun dappled across his face where it streamed through the bits of foliage hanging over a particularly beautiful statue next to him of a creature she didn't recognize.

"I have news," he said, taking a seat on the edge of the blanket and grabbing the only unopened container of grilled chicken and pasta salad remaining. His eyebrow piercing caught the light, stealing her attention. She wondered if it had hurt.

Everyone stopped talking and focused on him.

"They've found your father," he said, looking at her. "Like we suspected, he returned to Florida to recoup his losses and formulate another plan."

"Where is he now?"

Dominic looked at Aiden. "After his capture two nights ago, they transported him directly to Cresbel Asylum—"

"What the hell?" Seth said. "He's human."

"You're right. They didn't move him there to imprison him."

"So what'd they do?"

Dominic looked at Riley. "They wiped his memories before transporting him back to the States."

"Wait. Back to the States? Where is Cresbel Asylum?"

"That's..." Dominic lowered the container and sucked a breath through his teeth. "The exact location isn't information privy to the masses. Only members of the Blackthorn Clan, like me, know the exact location."

"I thought it was in Eurasia, somewhere in Russia," Layla said, her lashes fluttering as she blinked in confusion.

"Well, yes. That's well-known amongst our kind, but that's a lot of land to cover. It's not in a convenient location for a reason."

"Why?"

He smiled. "So the humans don't find it." He winked, and she dropped her gaze, flushing. "And so rogues don't try to infiltrate the walls."

Riley shifted on Seth's lap. "So her father's not there anymore?"

He shook his head negatively, meeting Charlotte's eyes next. "He's back in Florida; but in wiping his memories of everything to do with the Vasirian, they had to eliminate his memories of you."

"What? Why?" Blaire said, her hand covering her mouth.

"We don't know how far back the memory of our kind goes, but he knew of us before Charlotte's birth."

"Wait a minute," Charlotte said, sitting upright. "You're able to see inside his head? That's insane. I never thought about how you wiped memories. How can you get in someone's head? What else can you do? Did you find out anything else?"

Dominic laughed at her rapid-fire questions and set down the container of food.

"The way compulsion works allows some of us to not only paralyze the body, but also influence someone to our will. Not all of us have the ability, but it's never used for harm—unless rogues use it. Beyond that, there exists an even smaller number of Vasirian who possess both the power of compulsion and the ability to manipulate memories. They can't see every thought and memory a person has, rather they single in on a subject—in this case, Vasirian—and purge every piece of information associated with that subject."

"That sounds dangerous. What about everything around it? Like, if you took away my memory of Blaire, how would I fill in the gaps around things we did and things I did while knowing her?"

"You wouldn't. In some cases, the mind is able to piece together enough information to smooth over the loss of a person or subject matter and it doesn't influence much. But in other cases, where the subject is a dominant part of the person's mind, it acts as a reset."

"Reset?" Layla asked. "I don't know a lot about compulsion. No one in my family can do it. What does a reset do?"

Charlotte didn't like the sound of it. By definition alone, it unnerved her.

"Most who have a memory wipe after learning of the Vasirian have seen them once, and only need that moment in time eliminated. It doesn't affect their lives in any way. With your father, he's known about us for years. There will be gaps in his memory, but he is stable. His mind was strong enough to recover, and he seems forgetful at worst. If he delved too deeply into it, the doctors would likely conclude a case of amnesia—but he would never recover from it."

"Okay, but how did you know you needed to get rid of his memory of Charlotte?"

Dominic looked at Riley, who looked seconds away from springing out of Seth's lap and going on a tirade around the central garden.

"After such a deep wipe, the authorities at Cresbel ask questions and run a human through a series of tests to assess the possible damage and how far back their memories of our kind go. They do this by bringing up events and people related to the person throughout the years." Dominic looked down at the ground, his lips thinning. He didn't look happy about what he had to say. "When asked about you, he didn't know anything about you. We didn't explain who you were, only asked if he knew you. We didn't want to disrupt his psyche by informing him of a daughter he couldn't remember."

Arms slipped around Charlotte's waist, dragging her into a lap. The scent of vanilla and orange surrounded her.

The news hit harder than she wanted to admit out loud. Even if her father was an evil man who chose the wrong path in life, it still hurt to know he wouldn't know her if they met on the street.

Though mere days ago she wouldn't have known him either. Was it so different?

"If it helps," Dominic said, and she looked up. "He doesn't remember anything of the things that turned him into the man you met. His mannerisms became docile and polite. With this, he'll get a chance to start over and build a new life for himself. Whatever darkened his heart and made him seek power over our kind became lost."

Riley crossed her arms. "Hopefully this time he chooses the path of not being a jackass who abandons his children and tries to run a syndicate filled with a species more powerful than him, like some glorified mafia boss."

Charlotte toyed with the edge of her mint-painted fingernail.

As much as it saddened her to know he would never know her, if the loss gave him the chance to be a better person and grow a life where he could become the man he was meant to be without the influence of the rogues and whoever was above them, she would accept it. Not that she had a choice if it happened or not, but she could choose to be angry, throw a fit, and act irrational about it, or she could accept it with grace and see it for the positive it was.

Sometimes a loss was necessary to grow something greater.

Aiden moved her hair away from the side of her neck, placing a gentle kiss against her skin. His arms hugged her closer, and she sank into him, accepting his warmth and soothing love.

"I still wonder who is pulling the strings behind all this," Lukas said, elbow resting on the edge of the fountain, thumb pressed against his mouth.

"Whoever Red Carnation is," Aiden said. "Do the other members of the Blackthorn Clan know anything about it? Did they recognize the name?"

Dominic shook his head. "For now, only Adrian knows. He fears it getting out into the public if the other members of the royal family or the extended clan hold open discussion about it."

Seth raised his brow. "He doesn't trust them?"

"Why wouldn't the king trust his own family?" Layla asked. Once things settled the other day, they had filled her in on everything that happened.

Charlotte noticed she didn't know as much as the others, but Blaire told her that Layla had joined their circle after Lukas helped her with a bully problem. She was there for him while Blaire went through the Order's experiments, and he was suffering. While Layla kept away from the danger, she made a good friend, so they never hesitated to keep her informed of what happened when she wasn't around.

"Nothing like that," Dominic said, glancing at Layla. "Adrian knows there's a leak somewhere, whether it's a bug or an inside plant in the staff. If they hold open court, the information will spread. It's happened once already. Until they have more information on whoever this is, the king wants a lid kept on it."

"It isn't the first time the rogues brought up someone above them. Until we can find out who it is, Blaire will continue to be a target," Lukas said, eyes narrowing. He glanced at Charlotte. "I suspect you will be, too. Being human, they might try to use you to get to her again."

"Especially knowing that Blaire will risk herself for you," Seth said.

Lukas nodded. "They all saw the way Blaire tried to save you."

She looked down at her lap. "I didn't mean to make it harder for you."

Blaire pushed off the ground and moved over to plop down beside

Charlotte. "Hey."

She looked up at Blaire.

"I told you. You're my sister. You haven't made anything harder for me. I don't want to do this without you. I'm glad you're going to be here when I go through the transition."

Charlotte's smile turned watery, and she sniffed. "Really?"

"Of course. We've been together for years. You think a few fangs and psychos are going to change that?"

Aiden kissed her neck again as she laughed.

"I'll be right behind you," she whispered.

"Huh? What do you mean?"

She looked over her shoulder at Aiden, and he nodded.

"After you do it, I want to transition too. I asked the Oracle already if I could do it, but she said it wasn't possible until you do. The magic that woke up our Korrena bond isn't strong enough for me to survive, or I'd already have done it."

Riley jumped to her feet. "Seriously?"

Blaire covered her mouth.

Charlotte nodded.

"Holy shit, yes!" Riley looked seconds away from bursting into dance.

Blaire leaned over and wrapped her arms around Charlotte, hugging her. She sniffled. "I'm so glad I won't go through this alone."

"You have Lukas," Layla said.

"I'm already a Vasirian. I think it's different for them." Lukas stroked Blaire's back as she held onto Charlotte, who started to cry.

Riley rushed over, dogpiling into their hug, all three of them crowding Aiden. He fell back on his hands, laughing.

While Charlotte didn't completely understand her place in their world, she wouldn't run away. She belonged in their world. Belonged with them. She didn't need a mystical oracle to tell her that. Her heart and their actions told her.

Her friends needed her as much as Aiden did. Her heart belonged to him.

While the future remained uncertain, she held hope.

Even though she couldn't become a Vasirian until Blaire took the first steps, it didn't matter anymore. The most important thing for Charlotte was staying with her family. Nothing meant more to her than family.

As they broke from their hug, she looked around at the faces surrounding her. She now had seven additional members of her family she would do anything to keep.

No longer on the outside looking in, she finally found a place where she could keep her family and secure the future that mattered most to her.

Final Note from the Author

Thank you for picking up (or downloading) my book and completing it. I hope you loved it as much as I loved creating it. I appreciate every one of you.

If you enjoyed this book, and the others, please consider leaving a written review. Indie authors rely heavily on the reviews of their readers to make it in the self publishing world, and sites like Amazon, use those reviews to determine visibility.

Stay in Touch

Join Stephanie over on Facebook in Stephanie Denne's Murder Mates Facebook Group! It's a place to discuss current works, future works, and interact directly with Stephanie.

https://www.facebook.com/groups/743979797516659

Social Media

TikTok: https://www.tiktok.com/@stephaniedenneauthor

Facebook: https://www.facebook.com/stephaniedenneauthor

Instagram: https://www.instagram.com/stephaniedenneauthor/

Twitter/X: https://x.com/sdenneauthor

Patreon

Become a member of the Patreon Murder Mates for exclusive content. Bonus scenes, alternate universe content, WIPs, snippets, covers and news before it's public. Guaranteed ARC spots, and more!

https://patreon.com/stephaniedenne

Newsletter

Sign up for Stephanie's Newsletter to keep up to date on the latest news around the Blackthorn world and future series, and get special sneak peeks at the writing process and chapter previews for future books.

http://eepurl.com/h_N5uP

About the Author

Stephanie Denne is an author of Paranormal Romance and Dark Fantasy for new adults and adults with a focus on mental health and trauma healing. Her debut new adult novel Mark of the Vasirian released in January 2023.

Inspired by art and music, she felt the need to give life to character's that had been rolling around in her mind for 12 years. Never having written anything before, when she sat down and started drafting, she discovered that she had a passion for the craft and the story naturally grew into something much bigger than she could fit into one book—much less five, or even one series!

Born in the United States of America in the Southeast, Stephanie has now called Ontario, Canada her home since 2011. When not writing, she can be found reading her favorite stories, playing video games with her husband, painting with watercolor, or cuddling with her Golden Retrievers. But not the cat—the cat has her own agenda.

Acknowledgments

To everyone who supported me through the creation of Fractured Fate, I want to extend a huge thank you. Your dedication to the Blackthorn Saga has meant the world to me, and I can't wait to finish the journey with you!

As always, thank you to my wonderful editor Kelly for being such an amazing editor, going above and beyond in guiding me not to make stupid decisions, while still helping me maintain my voice and goal for the series. For teaching me new things with every book to help be become a better writer. I couldn't have asked for a better editor for this series, and its spinoffs.

A huge thank you to my ARC team in helping me establish a footing for this book and give me advanced feedback. I take your words to heart and love seeing your reactions!

[illegible] to extend a big thank you to Lieutenant Norris of the Athens-Clark County Police Department. I was so nervous to call and ask my questions for reference in my book, but I wanted to do it right. Too often, authors and movie directors take huge creative liberties and don't portray how local law enforcement would handle a situation. Lieutenant Norris listened to my questions, the timeline of events I intended to happy around Charlotte's stalker, and reassured me that he had no problem giving me that information so that I could build a stronger story. Though, given the strange nature of the Vasirian (and a few Vasirian officers sprinkled in) we did have to suspend reality a little, so everything that happens may not be a play-by-play of how the local law enforcement in Athens, Georgia handles these sorts of cases, especially knowing every case is different. In the end, this is a fantasy world. A story of fiction. No real officers are depicted, and any similarities are strictly coincidental.

As a final thank you, I want to thank a very sweet person from TikTok, allistermarie, for giving me feedback on emergency phone operator procedures when I was stuck. I appreciate you taking the time to let me know how it works!